D0437205

HALF-BLOWN ROSE

Also by Leesa Cross-Smith

Every Kiss a War

Whiskey & Ribbons

So We Can Glow

This Close to Okay

Cross-Smith, Leesa, 1978-author.
Half-blown rose : a novel

2022
33305250541244
ca 05/27/22

HALF-BLOWN ROSE

A NOVEL

LEESA CROSS-SMITH

GRAND CENTRAL PUBLISHING

NEW YORK BOSTON

This book is a work of fiction. Names, characters, places, and incidents are the product of the author's imagination or are used fictitiously. Any resemblance to actual events, locales, or persons, living or dead, is coincidental.

Copyright © 2022 by Leesa Cross-Smith

Cover design by Laywan Kwan. Cover art © Chester Collections/Bridgeman Images.
Cover copyright © 2022 by Hachette Book Group, Inc.

Hachette Book Group supports the right to free expression and the value of copyright. The purpose of copyright is to encourage writers and artists to produce the creative works that enrich our culture.

The scanning, uploading, and distribution of this book without permission is a theft of the author's intellectual property. If you would like permission to use material from the book (other than for review purposes), please contact permissions@hbgusa.com. Thank you for your support of the author's rights.

Grand Central Publishing
Hachette Book Group
1290 Avenue of the Americas, New York, NY 10104
grandcentralpublishing.com
twitter.com/grandcentralpub

First Edition: May 2022

Grand Central Publishing is a division of Hachette Book Group, Inc. The Grand Central Publishing name and logo is a trademark of Hachette Book Group, Inc.

The publisher is not responsible for websites (or their content) that are not owned by the publisher.

The Hachette Speakers Bureau provides a wide range of authors for speaking events. To find out more, go to www.hachettespeakersbureau.com or call (866) 376-6591.

Library of Congress Cataloging-in-Publication Data has been applied for.

ISBNs: 978-1-5387-5516-7 (hardcover); 978-1-5387-4039-2 (Barnes & Noble edition); 978-1-5387-5517-4 (ebook)

Printed in the United States of America

LSC-H

Printing 1, 2022

For me, for you, pour Paris.

Part One

VINCENT & CILLIAN

1

INT. MODERN ART MUSEUM - LATE AFTERNOON

It is autumn in Paris, City of Light. Vincent's in her scarf – the one she always wears – wrapped twice like death.

NARRATOR (V.O.)

Loup takes his time gathering his things: the pale wooden pencil upon the table, the black sketchpad and well-squeezed paints with bright, flat caps. Vincent watches him, keeps watching him, until he notices her and she looks away. Her friend Baptiste, who teaches modern art history and a course in color down the hall, stands so close she can feel his breath.

"*Café?*" he asks, and Vincent nods. She wants to know if Loup is still looking at her, but she can't bring herself to check. What if he isn't? She'll die on the spot in the almost-empty classroom. "*On y va,*" Baptiste says, stepping in front of her, knowing she'll follow. She wants to turn and look at Loup again. Is that what she'll do? Only to be crushed? No. The room blurs and she walks straight out, staring at the back of Baptiste's head.

When he stops, she runs right smack into him.

"Sorry. I'm sorry," she says.

"Loup-dog, you coming?" Baptiste says, turning. Vincent continues staring ahead, at the back of Baptiste's blazer this time—velvet, the rich shade of the Bolognese she's simmered all day in the slow cooker in her apartment. Vincent *feels* Loup behind her, smells his pencils.

"Yes, I'm coming," Loup says by her ear, and she files it away somewhere hot and dark.

They are both next to her now. She doesn't look at Loup as they walk down the hallway, out the door, across the busy street to the café. In her periphery, Baptiste is adjusting the bag on his shoulder, laughing easily with his friend. They know each other well, but Vincent always forgets exactly how. She listens to the two of them speak in quick clips of French and English.

"Quiet little mouse," Baptiste says to her, frowning in his funny way.

When they find a small table out front and put their things down, Vincent watches Loup walk inside, disappearing into the bathroom corridor.

"You know I don't want him here! Why did you invite him?" she growls, lighting her cigarette as soon as she's in the chair.

"Oh, pshh, why do you do this? You *like* Loup."

"You know I don't want him here," Vincent says again. She and Baptiste go to the café together all the time; Loup never comes along. "*Bonjour. Deux cafés et un café au lait, s'il vous plaît. Merci*," she orders quickly from the radiant, blushed waitress. Is every woman in Paris so effortlessly beautiful she'll never die? Only blink, then flicker to haunting? Every time Vincent visits the city, for at least a few days after arriving she has to stop herself from staring at the women she encounters. Young and old, they all somehow look like an entirely different species. She forgets this when she's in the United States but remembers quickly upon returning.

This time she's been in Paris for three months.

"Please. You think he's *delicious*. You want to eat him up like he's a cake," Baptiste says, pulling out his phone and texting. Tippity-tappity quick-quick.

"I'm forty-four," she says.

Baptiste looks at her, saying nothing.

"He's twenty-four," she says.

Nothing.

"I'm literally *twenty* years older than he is," she says.

Baptiste begins texting again, silent.

"He's a child," Vincent says. "*Un bébé!* I could be his mother."

Nothing from Baptiste.

"*Va te faire foutre!*" She smokes. "Who are you texting?" She mocks his face, his annoying fingers, his precious phone.

"Mina!" he says, smiling slyly. His wife.

"*Va te faire foutre*," she says again. Baptiste *tsks* at her, kisses the air. This is how she and Baptiste always talk to each other. They share a birthday—same date and year—and they were friends from the moment they met three months ago.

Born to Ghanaian French parents, Baptiste grew up in Paris and is fluent in Twi, French, and English. He is six foot three, skinny and strong, royally handsome, fantastically nerdy, and stylish in a casual way. With his velvet blazer, he is wearing a pair of slim black pants that stop right at his ankles, no socks, and a pair of clean white Stan Smiths with navy-blue heel tabs. Sometimes people actually stop him on the street to take his photo for their sartorial Instagram accounts and blogs. What he and Vincent participate in is friend-flirting and nothing more. He loves his wife ferociously and what Vincent feels for him matches up almost exactly with what she feels for her brother—a sugary adoration that smooths out any flaws.

* * *

Loup returns not half a moment before the waitress with their coffees. Vincent goes to snub out her cigarette, but Loup extends his arm for it. She passes it across the table and looks into his twenty-four-year-old eyes. He smiles sweetly, as if she hasn't been ignoring him at all.

"*Voilà!* There you are! Hello, Vincent," he says with her lipstick stain in his mouth. She feels as if she has rocketed into space.

They smoke and drink their coffees, and it isn't long until Baptiste says he has to go meet Mina and leave the two of them to fend for themselves. But yes! He will finish his coffee first.

"I love their coffee," Baptiste says, *mmm*-ing to Loup and Loup only. Vincent drinks hers. The coffee is hot, the wind cool, and she loves her thick, warm scarf—the wasabi-colored one her brother brought with him on the train from Amsterdam last month.

"Thank you for the cigarette," Loup says to her.

"You're welcome," she says.

Baptiste leans over and kisses her cheeks; Loup stands as he leaves.

"Right, sure. *Au revoir*, Baptiste," Vincent says dramatically and waves as he walks away, like she won't be seeing him again at the art museum in the morning.

"A woman called Vincent," Loup says like a sigh once they are alone. Loup, who smells like summer and dark green, reminding her of Kentucky forests back home. But how? Is there some sort of tree oil he's mixed with lemon water, spritzed and walked through? Do twenty-something-year-old guys *spritz*? Maybe he rubbed it under his arms, into the bushes of hair he has there; she saw flashes of it—dark and thickish—during the ungodly heat wave. And she doesn't want to, but she also remembers his white pocket T-shirt and short shorts, the plain gold chain he sometimes wears around his neck. His summer shoes, Nike Killshot 2s with midnight-navy swoops. The cream-colored knots of ankle above them. How she feels like an electric wet rope when Loup leans back in his chair in class and crosses his legs, puts his sketchpad on his knee.

* * *

"I can't stay long... I'm having people over for dinner. I'm making pasta," Vincent says. So far, ninety percent of the time, Loup only gets this snippy interpretation of who she is. Bah. Nothing to be done.

"Is Baptiste coming? Mina?"

"No... they have a thing."

"I don't have a thing and I love pasta," Loup says.

"It's not special. Everyone loves pasta."

"Can I have pasta with you for dinner tonight?" he asks easily, like those words alone will jiggle her doorknob loose. His hair is wild and romantic, hanging past his earlobes; he tucks some curly strands behind one of them. His jacket is unzipped and Vincent glances at the loose collar of his shirt—in the oranged almost-evening sun, his necklace twinkles like it's electric too.

"Loup—"

"I still can't believe Vincent is your real name," he says.

A clatter from inside the café: the crown of a waitress's head as she bends and stands, bends and stands. Vincent watches her through the window, digging the fingernails of her right hand into the palm of her left under the table.

"You keep telling me this. Call me Ms. Wilde instead."

"What kind of pasta, Ms. Wilde?"

Vincent finishes her coffee. The waitress asks if she'd like another and she says *non, merci*. Loup says *oui, merci* to the refill, even though his cup is half-full.

"I considered puttanesca at first... and now well, it's a bastardized version," she answers him, the sauce already on her mind. Baptiste's blazer was Bolognese, her scarf wasabi. She looks at Loup, sharply ravenous.

"Ah, prostitute spaghetti" is his reply. "Who are you having over for dinner?"

"You're asking a lot of questions," she says after pausing too long.

"That's a problem, Ms. Wilde?"

"And that's another question."

Cigarette and coffee—Vincent lights another; her cup sits empty.

"I have to go," she says, not moving.

"You have a husband? I asked Baptiste and his answer was vague. You don't wear a wedding ring," Loup says.

"So not only do you ask *me* a lot of questions, you ask Baptiste a lot of questions too."

"I do about you... sometimes."

Vincent looks at him and mouths the word *wow*. "You like prostitute spaghetti?" she asks.

"I like prostitutes."

"I like prostitutes too," Vincent says, defensively.

"Your husband will be at your dinner party tonight? It's his place also?"

"Why do you assume I have a husband, even when I don't wear a wedding ring?"

"Well, you do wear this ring," he says, tapping the big cloudy moonstone on her index finger.

"Right. *A* ring. It's clearly not a wedding ring."

"But it is a ring."

"Wow, insightful. Yeah, I really have to go," Vincent says.

"Too rude for me to invite myself along? I'd like to come."

"Loup—"

"*J'ai faim!* Feed me, please. I'll help. I'll earn my keep!" he says from the other side of the table, taking a posture of prayer.

The apartment is her parents'. In the past, she and her siblings have popped in, using it whenever they're in the city, whenever it isn't already occupied by renters. Now Vincent is the "renter," although her parents would never let her pay for it. Her parents don't need the money; they live on the wind, making their home wherever they find themselves. Right now, it's Rome.

* * *

Vincent's guests aren't expected for another hour. Loup does most of the talking on the walk to her place, and he and his brown Chelsea boots bound up the stairs next to her, like an excited puppy about to pee itself. She imagines telling her sister about him, how much they'd snort when they laughed about this puppy-boy. One of their favorite things to do together? Laugh at men. They love to laugh at Cillian when he is being ridiculous. Vincent is thinking of Cillian as she opens her door—he and Loup have the same damn Chelsea boots. So does Prince Harry. Prince Harry's and Loup's are the color of peanut butter; Cillian's are chocolate. Apparently she's reached the stage of hunger where she can *only* think about food.

"I'm only letting you be here because I don't want you to starve. It's my duty to feed another human being. It's in the Bible... look it up," she says, hanging her bag, coat, and scarf on the hook next to the door. The Bolognese is ready and perfect, she can tell from the smell that met them in the hallway.

"You're a good Christian, Ms. Wilde," he says. He takes his jacket off and folds it neatly over the arm of the couch.

"Ugh. Drop the *Ms. Wilde*. Too weird. Go back to Vincent," she says, walking into the kitchen, feeling like she's sprung a leak. She will get her period a whole week early, all because of Loup's rangy, dark tenderness in her apartment, behind her, filling the spaces between.

She takes the lid off the slow cooker and stirs the sauce with a wooden spoon. Tastes it. *So good*, she thinks angrily, *nothing else matters—past, present or future—except this sauce*, and blames it on PMS brain.

Loup is in her apartment; they are alone. How did it happen? She seriously considers the idea that she has reeled through time. Zapped from the United States to France over the summer, then zipped to another dimension where she lets twenty-something-year-olds come back to her place in their slouchy striped shirts to hurt her feelings with their violent youth and attractiveness and deeply chaotic sexual energy. Loup has sequences of moments when he's *always* moving around everywhere, like a wasp invasion. So much! He never stops. Can he do a backflip? Run a six-minute mile? Ride a horse? Do those complicated dyno rock climbing moves Cillian had been all too eager to show off once he'd mastered them?

Instead of dwelling on Cillian, she imagines Loup's body doing those things.

Vincent hears the floor creak beneath him in the living room. He seems to be everywhere at once out there until he pops into the kitchen with her scarf around his neck, holding the amber glass skull he's taken from the window ledge.

"Memento mori," he says, clinking it softly on the countertop. "Right on. It smells so good in here, Vincent."

He emphasizes her name, always making a big deal out of it. First day of journaling class in the summer, she'd introduced herself and given her students their assignment.

Make a list of words you love. This can be very simple. For example, I love the word brush. Brush *is not a fancy word, but to me, it's beautiful. Keep writing words for as long as you can, in whatever language you'd like. And if there's a special reason you love the word... if there's a special memory attached, include that. If the word reminds you of a song or a color or a movie or a specific person or moment, include those things too. We will paint them later.*

Remember, it's a museum class. Stay or leave. Talk or don't. You've paid your money. What you do or don't want is up to you. We're all adults here. Enjoy!

When she was finished, Loup had raised his hand. She acknowledged him and he said her name like it was a question.

"Correct."

"Like . . . Van Gogh."

"Yep. Exactly like Van Gogh."

"You teach art and your name is Vincent, after Van Gogh."

"Correct."

"Vincent . . . that's one word I like," he said.

"All right. Thank you," she said, her face warming.

"Are your parents artists?"

"Yes. Both of them."

"They are successful artists?"

"Yes. Very, actually."

"What are their names?" he asked. Several students continued listening; others were already sketching and writing.

"Um, their names are Aurora Thompson and Solomon Court . . . Soloco is what my dad uses for work."

"I've heard of them. Your mum planted herself in a greenhouse for the winter and your dad did all of that graffiti and neon album art for those funkadelic bands . . . I forget some of the names . . . but I recognized your parents' names easily. Isn't that funny?" he said.

"It is. It is funny," Vincent said with an atomic thrill.

Another student mentioned having heard of Soloco as well, saying he was "a lot like Basquiat."

Not only did her dad do the neon album art for those bands, he was also a songwriter who'd penned a batch of killer spacey funk hits in the midseventies and early eighties. Those songs were still used in commercials, movies, and TV shows, and a huge chunk of her parents' fortune was owed to that fact.

"Yes. And boom, now I've heard of you too . . . their lovely daughter," he said. His comment was followed by a low *ooh* from one of his classmates.

"That's plenty," she said. "And since we're doing names, what's yours?"

"Loup. As in *wolf*."

"Wolf," she translated herself.

"Wolf," he repeated, and shoved his tongue between his teeth.

"That's my scarf," she says to him in her kitchen.

"It smells like you. You don't mind if I wear it?"

"I don't want you to get sauce on it."

"You don't like me as much as I like you—"

"Look at that guy! Turn around and look." Vincent points over his shoulder out the window at the man she can see in the next building, two floors up. He is naked again, blasting his tribal music, beating his stomach. "He does this at least once a week."

Loup turns to look and swivels back to laugh. He slaps the counter, rattling her dishes.

"Ugh, I like you just fine, but I don't want you to get sauce on my scarf! My brother gave it to me."

"How many brothers do you have?" Loup asks, watching the naked man drum and drum. The first time Vincent had seen him do it, she was so sure he was pleasuring himself that she'd squealed and crouched, scared to look again. She must've stayed like that for a full five minutes before daring to peek and seeing both of his hands clearly smacking his chest and stomach, moving down no farther. Vincent stands next to Loup now, watching too.

"Wow, I'm starving," she says, her mouth watering for the sauce. Loup, still watching the naked man, reaches into the bowl on the counter and starts peeling a clementine.

"*Une faim de loup*," he says. "Hungry like a wolf."

He's right. She is. Hungry *like*, hungry *for*.

"I have one older brother, one younger sister," she says. When Loup finishes peeling, he sticks his thumb in, pulls it out, hands the fruit to Vincent. She eats without saying thank you.

"What are their names?"

"What's it matter?"

"I only want to know because I like you."

"Give it a rest. You're twenty-four."

"I know how old I am. Nice of you to keep track, though. *Merci*."

"Their names are Theo and Monet."

"Your parents love a theme."

"That they do."

"Are your brother and sister artists too?"

"Isn't everyone . . . somehow?"

"I have a little sister," he says. "And you like the clementine. Good! I made it for you."

"Please. You only peeled it for me," Vincent fusses, like he was serious.

"Oh, shh, I'll make you a clementine anytime you want me to, Saint Vincent van Gogh. Then I'll paint a still life of the peels for you, frame the canvas, and even come over here and hang it on your wall," he says, scooping the curling rinds from the counter and pocketing them.

"You're stealing those?"

"No. You gave them to me," he says.

Vincent is eating, watching the naked man through the window.

"Do you think he's handsome?" Loup asks.

"Not really," she says.

"Kind of?"

"Maybe . . . kind of . . . if I got close," she says, shrugging. "Doesn't he get cold, totally naked with the window open like that?"

"You're attracted to men?"

"Sure I am," she says, the currents of her heart screeching.

"Is Drum Guy one of your guests? One of your mates?" Loup nods toward the window.

"Oh, right. Of course. He's my *best* friend. Any second he'll get dressed and be at my door. We go way back, mm-hmm."

"Yeah? What time are he and the rest of your guests arriving?"

"Forty-five minutes," she guesses, not looking at the clock.

Loup reaches into the cup of Vincent's hand and takes a clementine segment, eats it. He goes into the bowl, grabs an apple, and bites. When he gives it to Vincent, she bites too—once, twice—and hands it back to him.

"Thirty minutes," she says.

Loup peels the banana and breaks off the top. He hands it to her and slowly slides what is left of the bottom between his lips.

"Fifteen minutes," she says.

Loup twists the stem off a fig and bites the skin; Vincent snatches it from him and eats.

"Five minutes," she says.

Vincent gets a handful of sunset-glowy grapes and Loup plucks two.

"Right now. They're probably coming up the stairs," she says with a half-full mouth.

"We need to boil water for the pasta. We should get started," he says, chewing, both of them staring at the naked man through the window.

Vincent knows the man can't see them because he always keeps his eyes closed, sometimes thrashes his head back and forth like he is under a spell, shakes his hair like a tree shedding leaves. The frenetic drumming is thunder echoing across the air, slipping up and storming those rooftops Vincent can't unlove; on lucky nights she dreams she is a French cat, hopping them in lambent light. Paris is all rooftops. No matter where she looks, there's so much history and something new and unrelentingly beautiful to discover.

"Yeah . . . I know," Vincent says, holding still in sweet pain, probably bleeding. She watches Loup get three pomegranates from the bowl and juggle them. He stops to let one roll his palm—sticky fingertips to flicking wrist.

2

Vincent's October Dinner in Paris Playlist

The Reminder by Feist
"La vie en rose" by Louis Armstrong
"You Send Me" by Sam Cooke
"Afternoon in Paris" by John Lewis and Sacha Distel
"Circus" by Mélanie Laurent
"Tightrope (feat. Big Boi)" by Janelle Monáe
"Cloudbusting" by Kate Bush
"Losing You" by Solange
"Hunger" by Florence + the Machine
"Vossi Bop" by Stormzy
"Nikes" by Frank Ocean

Vincent is one glass of red wine deep when her guests show up. All day she'd forgotten they'd pushed dinner back an hour so everyone could make it. She and Loup were alone for much longer than she originally intended, but she put him to work. After all that fruit, she's not the least bit hungry. In fact, she's so full her stomach is sloshing like an overflowing bathtub.

She'd left Loup standing in the kitchen and gone to her bedroom and changed before anyone else got there. Now she is barefoot in a black long-sleeved cashmere romper and picking at the caprese salad she made that morning and left to marinate in the fridge. She laughs and drinks and talks with her guests at the table; there is a bouquet of dark purple Japanese anemones in the middle of it.

The anemones are from Cillian. He has a bouquet of flowers delivered to her every Saturday afternoon. *Les pivoines, les coquelicots, les lys, les marguerites, les orchidées, les jonquilles*—the apartment always has fresh flowers. When her downstairs neighbors and her friends visit, they show up with them too.

The candles flicker; Feist plays softly. Everyone pours wine and praises the food. Some sit on the cushy living room chairs and others are together on the couch, eating with their plates carefully balanced in their laps. Her guests return to the kitchen for cake and coffee. The ones who haven't been to her place in a while comment again on the huge windows and the gorgeous view; even the Parisians don't tire of talking about the zinc rooftops. They joke that the plants may take over the apartment soon; Aurora's fiddle-leaf fig tree is over six feet tall and Vincent was raised in the kind of house where sometimes, the kids call their parents by their first names.

Every other Wednesday, Vincent's new circle of friends and *des connaissances* have a big dinner together. It's a casual, rotating cast of characters, and their meals last however long they need to, depending on the conversation. *Très* laid-back, *très* Paris. Whenever it's warm, they eat outside. Last month they'd picnicked in the grass of Luxembourg Garden. Now there are thirteen people in her apartment—Loup the unlucky thirteenth. After dinner, he buzzes around, talking to the people she knows like he knows them too. He pops next to Vincent occasionally to tell her how much he likes her friends, to tell her how good the sauce was again. Loup had been the one to check the pasta for al dente–ness. She reminds him of that.

"Wait. You're *complimenting* me? Saying *I* had something to do with this magic?" he says, leaning close.

Vincent doesn't know much about what Loup does when he's not at the art museum. Since the summer he's been taking both her journaling and her creativity classes. A few weeks in, Baptiste had told her that Loup "liked" her and Vincent asked Baptiste what he meant by that. Baptiste smiled and said, "Stop pretending you don't know exactly what I mean when I say he likes you." Vincent asked how old Loup was, and when Baptiste told her, she ended the conversation.

Wednesdays, Thursdays, and Fridays, Loup's there in front of her. And he and Baptiste go back further than the museum. Something about Loup's uncle or brother and Baptiste's cousin or wife or sister-in-law. On purpose, Vincent forgets specifics about Loup's life. She is terrified of having feelings for him. Terrified to get into bed or a relationship with such a young man. She only knows his name is Loup Henry and he's involved in making some sort of electronic music. Maybe it's solo, maybe it's a band. *Quelquefois*, he skateboards to the museum, and after class, when the timing works out, she sees him skateboard away. And sometimes he dresses like a soccer player in exhaustingly short shorts, but she's not sure if he actually plays. He might've mentioned it, but if so, she would've mentally swatted the information away like it was a gnat. She just knows that when Loup wears his track jacket, he zips it all the way up to his chin, and she believes it makes a man one hundred percent more attractive when he does this. It's how Cillian wears his; it's how he's always worn his, back when they were in college and even now.

If she lets herself, she misses Cillian—and she knows this is true because the fruit has soaked up the alcohol in the wine; she's thinking clearly.

Her downstairs neighbors, the Laurents, are drinking beers from green glass bottles and smoking on her balcony, their little orange lights dull and bright, dull and bright. The Laurents are outspoken, funny, and cerebral, and they know her parents well. She always invites them when it's her turn to host. She likes the Laurents. They are white and radical, both in their seventies, politically and socially aware. They met marching toward the Sorbonne during the May 1968 protests when Mr. Laurent dropped his glasses and Mrs. Laurent picked them up so they wouldn't get stepped on by the massive crowd. They like to say they fell in love building barricades together, something Victor Hugo would've written about. Even now, most times when there's a demonstration in Paris, the Laurents put on their yellow vests and join in with handmade signs, chants, and flags. Whenever Vincent goes downstairs to have tea with them, a casual conversation can quickly morph into a more serious one about the history of Paris or Charles de Gaulle. Maoism, Marxism, the bourgeoisie. Once, she met them in the lobby on their way to a protest and Mr. Laurent tried to get Vincent to come with them and to sing along as he belted "Do You Hear the People Sing?" from *Les Misérables*. He told her that she may be an American, but now she's here, so *vive la France*! He held her hand as she happily echoed him.

The apartment is in the 1st arrondissement, near the Louvre, where Mr. Laurent works. He is the one whose connections helped Vincent get a speedy long-term work visa and the job at the modern art museum.

In addition to the journaling and creativity classes, Vincent teaches another that focuses on jewelry making. She's wearing a pair of earrings she made—terra-cotta, moon phase. So light she sometimes forgets she's wearing them until someone compliments her and asks where she got them. She has business cards at the ready in her bag, always.

GO WILDE! BOLD HANDMADE JEWELRY BY A WOMAN CALLED VINCENT.

"Well, you like taking credit for things," she says to Loup now. "It's not a *compliment*. Just stating a fact, really. You literally boiled the water. And...by the way, my parents gave me a really frilly middle name to counter Vincent, in case you were wondering. You're probably not... but you do talk about it a lot, though... my name," she says.

"I bet your middle name is beautiful too," Loup says.

"You're right. It is," she agrees. She simultaneously wants Loup to leave and to spend the night with her. She likes how he always blows right past her attitude and goes straight for intimacy. Not in a forceful, creepy way, but in an open way, like a kind family member or a therapist. Much like how a mother can ignore the fussiness of her child because she knows it's only temporary and just part of being a mom.

Vincent has never seen her mood affect Loup's; he is more stone than sponge.

"Vincent, beauty, you've moved your recycling?" her friend Agathe asks, holding up an empty wine bottle and shaking it slowly like she's ringing a bell.

Agathe works as a curator at the Louvre with Mr. Laurent but is always visiting the modern art museum for one thing or another. She's also a sculptress and touches everything a lot, *seeing with her hands*. She is different from any other girlfriend Vincent has ever had, but it's more of a vibe and hard for her to pinpoint exactly how. One element is aggression. With Vincent's closest girlfriends back home, the friendships had happened slowly and more organically—the roots and blooms growing after they'd gotten to know each other and realized they had things in common. She and her best friend, Ramona, had known each other for years in college and working art shows side by side before they'd fallen into their close friendship. But Agathe had come on to Vincent so strongly, it was like Vincent didn't have a say in whether or not they'd become friends because Agathe had already decided for them. As if the north and south poles of their heart magnets lined up and smacked together, simple as that, and now they were stuck. "Soon, we will be close friends," Agathe said deliberately after their first coffee date.

Agathe is baroque and sexually fluid. The only vibrator Vincent has ever owned came from her after they stumbled into a conversation about them. The vibrator is expensive and modern and so oddly shaped, Vincent hadn't known what it was when she first opened the soft, dark box. She thought it was an abstract art sculpture or some sort of new electronic gadget that hadn't made its way to the States yet.

Vincent adores Agathe but it takes her around five years to get to know someone half-well; for *absolutely* well, it is probably more like ten, and she has known Agathe for only three months. And even then, as she's learned via Cillian, whom she's known for more than twenty-five years, people can still surprise her, in both good and bad ways.

For as long as they've known each other, Cillian has loved praising Vincent for her warmth and openheartedness, but when he's frustrated with her, he complains about her reticence, saying she's an *emotional tease*. That she can shut off and disappear her feelings behind a trapdoor when she feels too exposed. He says that sometimes even when she seems open, she's still unapproachable and gives off mixed signals. Once when she wore a silky lace camisole beneath a wool cardigan, Cillian said she was telling him that yes, he could touch her, *if* he could deal with the prickliness.

In the kitchen, Agathe is wearing a long velvet skirt, much like the one she gifted Vincent a month prior. Baptiste's blazer, Agathe's skirt—it's a velvety sort of night in Paris. The skirt is a purple so dedicated to its depth that it's almost black, reminding Vincent of outer space. Agathe is also wearing a pair of earrings that Vincent made for her—huge red circles hanging from smaller ones, like planets and their moons. The mix of otherworldiness suits her well. In general, Agathe has a ribald manner, but even when she's well behaved, Vincent finds her a little dangerous. Like a controlled fire.

Vincent opens the cabinet door beneath the sink, *voilà*-ing Agathe the recycling box.

"Thank you. Did you have some cake? Did you, Loup?" Agathe asks. Tonight, she's brought a white cake with burgundy buttercream maple leaves on top. She taps his shoulder with friendly aggression, as if she's starting a game of tag. Loup doesn't seem to mind one bit; he taps her shoulder and squeezes it.

"On it," he says, and smiles, grabbing a fork and holding it up.

"Me too, in just a sec. It looks lovely. Thanks again for bringing it, girlfriend," Vincent says to Agathe, smiling, and excuses herself to the bathroom.

Not bleeding yet. It is the second time Vincent has checked this evening. While she is peeing, she opens Cillian's latest texts, from three nights ago. The ones she hasn't responded to.

I miss you, Vin.

Please call me.

I fking hate this and will do anything in
my power to make it stop.

After she washes and dries her hands, she turns off the light and stands there in the dark. Once the first rapid-fire round of emotions exhausts itself inside of her, she lets the phone illuminate her face as she reads his texts again and makes an impulsive decision to call her husband back for the first time in two weeks. She counts the hours, calculating what time it is in Kentucky; she's been in Paris for months and still has to do this. Cillian should be in his office between classes. She calls him and it rings and rings and rings. He finally picks up.

"Vin?"

"Right. It's dinner party night, Cillian. I'm hiding in the bathroom in my own apartment, calling my estranged husband in the dark," she says, annoyed, as if he'd called and interrupted her.

"Estranged . . . I hate it. Thanks," he says in his slight Irish lilt. She's missed that. His family left Dublin for California when he was a teenager and his tongue is forever a mix of Irish and American English. *Irglish* is what they decided to call it long ago. His *t*'s are softer, his *r*'s are harder, still and always. It's all very pleasing to Vincent's ears, even when she's annoyed with him.

"It's the correct word. It means we are no longer close. We've certainly lost our closeness, agreed? On several levels. You're there and I'm here. But . . . as far as words go, you'd know more than me . . . You're the writer, yeah?" Vincent says. She can hear her guests clinking on the other side of the door. Loup laughs and she wonders what made that happen. She wishes she'd brought a glass of wine with her to the bathroom—the entire bottle, had she known she was going to call Cillian.

"Okay, well, you're faffing about and I'm being serious."

"I'm being serious too. You're the famous writer! I saw a whole stack of your books in Shakespeare and Company last week. How's that going, by the way? Movie deal still on?" Vincent asks, not raising her voice. Her ability to feign calm in intense situations is something that drives Cillian mad and he knows she knows that.

Cillian sighs. "Vin—"

"Have you talked to Colm?" she asks after their son. She puts the phone on speaker and, by its flashlight, she pokes her index finger in and out of the plant pots, checking to see if they need water. When she discovers some dry ones, she takes her toothbrush out of the glass and sets it on the counter, fills the cup with tap and begins watering the plants.

"I did. This morning."

"Have you talked to Olive?" she asks with the phone close to her mouth before moving it away and watering the Chinese evergreen.

"Yes. Few days ago, over text. She's stressing about finals already, a full two months early, so right on track for her, actually," he says.

Vincent talks to both of their children at least every other day, which is a lot, she thinks, considering how grown they are. Olive is twenty-one, brainy and focused on her premed studies at Vincent and Cillian's alma mater in Tennessee. Colm is twenty-four and a filmmaker, having gone to film school in New York and still hanging out in the city, ready to marry his fiancée in the summer. Colm's wedding is the next time she plans on seeing Cillian in the flesh, exactly what she'd told him when she said she needed a break and left for Paris.

"Is the movie deal still on?" Vincent asks again, checking both sansevierias. The snaky plants are easily her favorites. They're not dramatic or needy; the light from the small bathroom window is plenty for them and they only require watering every two weeks or so. She gives them what's left of the water in the cup since it's been about that long and refills it for the ferns.

"Where did Vincent run off to? *Salut!* Is she on the balcony?" Someone behind the door is looking for her: a kind but sometimes overstimulating woman from the art museum who likes to switch from English to French in the middle of sentences.

Vincent finds that the French she knows sticks easily when she's in Paris but gets lost as soon as she lands in the States again because she doesn't use it enough there. She immerses herself in it as much as she can when she's here. Her phone language is in French and even when she watches movies or TV shows in English, she turns on French subtitles. She is continually surprised by how many different languages she can hear on her walks—more than just French or English. There are always bits of German and Spanish. Asian languages and Arabic, too. Vincent likes the stretches of time when she can walk and zone out and not recognize what anyone is saying. Her brain doesn't have to do any work and she finds the secret sounds calming.

The woman from the art museum says something about *les meubles*: the furniture. Vincent is a little embarrassed by how much guests always gush over the apartment. It's not hers and she didn't design it or buy any of the things in it. The apartment is all Aurora. The compliments aren't Vincent's to take. Feels like stealing. What they mean is *Congratulations on having a cool, stylish mother!*

"Yes. The movie deal is still on," Cillian says as if it pains him. "Can I talk to you about it? You can have a say in how some things are portrayed—"

"Why? It's *your* book."

"I never meant to hurt you. All this happened because I was actively trying *not* to."

His words are so meaningless, Vincent can't think of an immediate response.

"But you did, Cillian. And we've been over that. And now, we're *estranged*," she says slowly after a moment, giving the last of the water to the ferns and tapping the speaker and flashlight off, returning the phone to her ear. She puts her toothbrush back in the cup.

"Vincent, are you in there? I'm leaving, but thanks again for having me. Your place is astoundingly lovely," the woman from the art museum says from the other side of the door. She tags some French on at the end.

"Hang on. I'm coming out," Vincent says to her and flips on the light switch. She squeezes her eyes shut at the brightness, like if she opens them, she'll see something terrifying. "Cillian, I'll call you back later."

"Sure. When? You say that, but then...you don't do it."

"Tomorrow. I'll call you tomorrow."

"Promise?"

"Really, Cillian?"

"I just wanna talk to ya. Maybe video chat?"

"Yeah. Okay. Maybe. I'll call you. I will," Vincent says, tapping the *End* button without a goodbye.

When she opens the bathroom door, the woman kisses her cheeks and thanks her again for dinner. They don't know each other well and Vincent likes that. None of the people in her apartment know what sent her to Paris or that she keeps her wedding ring in the little zipped pocket of her bag. She can be whomever she wants to be. And when she talks to the Laurents or Baptiste or Agathe about Cillian, she uses the word *ex* because it feels closer to the truth.

Vincent sees Loup over the woman's shoulder. He is on the balcony drinking a beer, talking to the Laurents. They are nodding and smiling. Loup is handsome and very European-looking in Vincent's scarf again. Through the window, he flickers gold in the candle glow.

Outside of ephemeral high school romances and a couple of college flings, Vincent has never seriously dated an American man—or any man besides her husband. She and Cillian have been together since she was eighteen; all she's ever really known is an Irishman in her bed. And Loup, this *wolf* inviting himself over and prowling her apartment with a cigarette tucked behind his ear, this *wolf* she is trying her best to fight off, is the same age as their marriage. He is the same age as their son.

3

Cillian's fourth book is called *Half-Blown Rose*. He'd revealed the title to Vincent after it was already sold. She's had this phrase tattooed in small cursive strapping over her right shoulder since she was twenty-one. She read it in *Jane Eyre* when she was in high school and knew it would be her first and only tattoo. Jane says of Rochester: "He gathered a half-blown rose, the first on the bush, and offered it to me." Sometimes the sentence runs through Vincent's head like a prayer—a yearning. Charlotte Brontë wrote the line, but once Vincent read those words, they belonged to her too.

Unlike his previous books, Cillian wrote *Half-Blown Rose* in secret. When Vincent would ask him what this book was about, he would tell her he hadn't figured it out yet, only that he was "experimenting with form" and it would probably end up being about "both everything and nothing." Even after he sold it, he said he was superstitious about showing her. That it would maybe curse the book, bring bad luck. Who wanted to risk that?

Cillian had always been open about sharing his work in the past; this sudden change was jarring to Vincent. The whole process was kept so tightly under wraps that even when she sneakily scoured the Internet for clues, there wasn't much to be discovered, as if the mystery was part of the book's promotion. Vincent found snippets of people saying things like "As is the case with a lot of great art, it's a bit undefinable" and "You just have to read it for yourself."

A month before its release, Cillian got a box of finished hardcovers on their doorstep and promptly put them in the garage. And on publication day, Vincent went to the indie bookstore across the bridge, where the booksellers wouldn't immediately recognize her as Cillian Wilde's wife, and bought a copy. She was going to read it in secret and, if he wanted her to, she'd pretend like she hadn't, at least around him. No way could she or would she tell her friends, their children, or her family that she hadn't read her own husband's new book, the one he'd finally nabbed seven figures for.

Cillian left early for work and later, at the indie bookstore closest to their house, there'd be a release party. Vincent reluctantly made cookies with half-blown roses on them, annoyed that he was stealing one of her favorite things but trying her best to be a supportive wife too, because Cillian was an extraordinary writer. She'd loved his writing long before he'd gotten his first book deal and she'd loved his previous books, the ones he hadn't been weird about.

The cover was a gray so pale it was practically white, with a collage of red half-blown roses filling the space at the bottom. The font masculine and minimalist. Both the front and the back of the book were covered in glowing praise from writers Cillian had long respected and admired.

"Explosive! A firecracker of a book! Cillian Wilde is here to stay."

"If you aren't reading Wilde's writing,
you're wasting precious time."

"Half-Blown Rose *is one of the best, most intimate books I've ever read. And I mean it."*

"Thrilling, engrossing, unique, amazing! I felt everything and hated turning the last page. Give us more, Cillian. Please!"

*"Call it fiction or autofiction... who f*cking cares? Cillian Wilde deftly tackles the literary world again with freshness and charm."*

"It should be no coincidence Cillian Wilde shares a surname with one of Dublin's greatest writers. This is a book of which even Oscar (and Joyce) would be proud."

Vincent sat in the car, turning the book over and over in her hands, patiently reading the blurbs first. She would've been overwhelmed with joy for Cillian if he hadn't acted so damn bizarre about the whole thing. And it was only when she stopped to google *autofiction* on her phone that she got a sick pit in her stomach. *Fictionalized autobiography*. Vincent's eyes ran over names like Rachel Cusk and Karl Ove Knausgård, but she'd never read them and she'd never once heard the word *autofiction* come out of Cillian's mouth.

The pit in Vincent's stomach sank even deeper when she opened to the back and saw his author photo on the jacket flap, a picture of him she'd never seen. She didn't even know who'd taken it, didn't recognize the name next to the photo credit. At first she thought Cillian was wearing someone else's sweater—her brain already anticipating another shock—before remembering it was the cable-knit toggle cardigan she'd bought for both him and Colm for Christmas two years ago. Heathered oatmeal, thick and expensive. Cillian was wearing it open over a plain white T-shirt and dark jeans.

In the picture, he had his elbows on his office desk at the university. He was turned to the side, leaning his head against his folded fingers, smiling slightly at the camera. It was a good picture of him. His hair was short on the sides but shaggy on top, like the photo was taken a week after a great haircut. His beard was neat, streaked with gray dashes the color of rain. His glasses sat on a stack of papers and next to them, some hardback books and the cream-colored Swedish lamp his mother had gifted him when he got tenure years ago. His mother had been on "a waiting list and everything" for that lamp, she'd bragged.

Cillian looked exceedingly handsome in the picture, but he always looked handsome to Vincent. One time when she was wine drunk in college, in a rare instance of insecurity that she never repeated, Vincent had voiced her sneaking suspicion that some people thought he was more handsome than she was pretty. She would never forget the look on his face as he made his eyes wide and laughed, saying in one of the thickest Irish accents she ever heard spill from his mouth, "Are you crazy right now? That's the dumbest thing I've ever heard. You sound like a complete maniac, do you know that?" He'd then taken her face in his hands and kissed all over it, telling her how beautiful she was. His beard softly scratched her cheeks, his kisses smacking. "Look at you, Vin. Crazy as everything and out-of-this-world beautiful," he said.

In Half-Blown Rose, *Cillian Wilde takes us from the posh suburbs of Dublin through California and Tennessee, until at last we reach the verdant hills of Kentucky. This is the story of an Irish teenager named Cian Woods who comes to America, writes his way through college, and marries a young black woman named Pica(sso) when he gets her pregnant, derailing his plans for the future.*

All the while, Cian keeps his biggest secret:

There was a brokenhearted young girl in Ireland who'd claimed to be pregnant with his child once too. It was one of the reasons his family left Dublin.

Written closely, with a confessional-like hand employing dreamy fragments and mixed media, Cillian Wilde tackles youth, marriage, lust, racism, manhood, fatherhood, and forgiveness in this book closely mirroring his own life. The New York Times *dubs* Half-Blown Rose *"a new voice in what some call autofiction," "a sneaky masterpiece, a printed jewel."*

Vincent's heart fluttered and rocked like a small nest of birds. Hands shaking, she turned to the dedication page.

For my wife and children. For forgiveness and love. Let's hold one another together forever, yeah?

She flew through the first fifty pages in her car in the bookstore parking lot, her ears roaring until her phone chimed with a text from Cillian.

JACKPOT. Scored the cover of the NYTBR next week. ☺

Vincent turned her phone off without responding. She tore through the entire book in a few hours, her body full of enough red-boiling rage, she thought she'd explode into a million fucking pieces. Halfway through, she took a break and drove to a coffee shop to puke and use the bathroom. She held a dripping paper towel to the back of her neck until someone knocked on the door asking if anyone was in there. She got an ice water; she couldn't eat a thing. She texted Cillian to let him know she'd see him at the bookstore later that evening. She went for a long drive, crying in her car. She went home and packed up the cookies for the release party.

At the bookstore that night, Vincent played the role of loving, supportive wife in the audience while Cillian read sections of his novel. Mostly about his childhood friends and growing up in Dublin. The reading was suspiciously anodyne, and it wasn't until they returned home that

Vincent even told him she'd read the entire thing already. She was baffled that he *still* hadn't said anything to her about what he'd written in the book. Who was this man?

When they talked about it, she angry-cried until her throat was swollen. She asked Cillian if there were any other bombshells he'd decided to leave out. He said no. She asked him if he'd ever cheated on her and he responded, "God, no! I was worried you would think that." And she said, "You were actually *worried* I would think something? Because it doesn't seem like you worried about anything when you were writing it."

There was too much to fight about. She couldn't remember it all.

She asked him what he'd thought was going to happen when she read it, and he didn't have anything to say.

His tears were of shame and remorse, and he admitted which parts were and weren't fiction, including everything he knew about the girl in Ireland. In the book, Cian considers contacting her but decides not to. Cillian told her that part was true. He hadn't reached out to her and still didn't know for sure if he had another child. Vincent asked him why not. Why hadn't he made a point of finding out if he had another fucking kid out there somewhere? Cillian said he was working up to it...slowly. He told her the girl was Nigerian and she'd been adopted by white parents.

When Cillian reluctantly revealed he'd sold the movie rights to *Half-Blown Rose* too, Vincent finally stopped him without asking any more questions. She couldn't bear to hear another word.

Cillian slept on the couch.

The next morning he left for the first leg of his book tour and Vincent called her parents to make sure their apartment in Paris was available.

Vincent's Travel Playlist | Airplane | Louisville to Paris

"I Need a Forest Fire" by James Blake (feat. Bon Iver)
"Only Love" by Ben Howard
"C'est si bon" by Eartha Kitt
"Heaven's My Home" by Sam & Ruby
"I Say a Little Prayer" by Aretha Franklin
"Feathered Indians" by Tyler Childers
"Living in Twilight" by the Weepies
"Keep It Loose, Keep It Tight" by Amos Lee
"Higher Love (Steve Winwood Cover)" by James Vincent McMorrow
"White Lies" by Paolo Nutini
"Moon River" by Frank Ocean
"Like a Star" by Corinne Bailey Rae
"Little Sparrow" by Leyla McCalla
"Am I Wrong" by Nico & Vinz
"Beacon Hill" by Damien Jurado
"Lion's Mane" by Iron & Wine
"Cranes in the Sky" by Solange
"Greetings in Braille" by the Elected
"Heartbeats" by José González
"Re: Stacks" by Bon Iver

Two weeks later, alone on the plane to France, Vincent attempted to sleep and read. She tried to listen to music and the French podcasts she'd downloaded. She started and stopped three different movies and two different TV shows, sticking with *Chewing Gum* for the longest because she found the lead's face so soothing. The pilot's voice was soothing too. The soft click of the announcement system and his collective *we*, the wishes for them to relax and enjoy the flight. She had a habit of developing crushes on the pilots' voices whenever she flew. She liked how comforting they were, how the pilots stayed up there isolated from everyone else, taking care of things, making sure the passengers felt safe. There was nothing for her to do, nothing for her to take care of. Her only job was to sit in her seat and let someone else do all the work. She tried her best to hold on to that idea of letting go as her brain soaked in a cloudy jar of grief and anger.

There was a small, weird glimmer of guilt as she replayed everything.

Yes, this was unexpected and disorienting, but it was also exciting. Maybe it was because she was headed to her favorite place on earth, but.

It had been so easy to leave.

Vincent's guests have hugged and kissed her and left. The moon is high. She is on her balcony looking up at it. Loup is a little drunk in the chair next to her, his long legs stretched out, ankles crossed. It is autumn-night cool and Vincent is wrapped in a blanket. Loup is still wearing her scarf, and his jacket is pulled closed but unzipped.

"You never told me your middle name," he says.

"Raphaela."

"Oh wow, I love it."

She agrees with him. And after she asks, he tells her his middle name is Michel. She says she likes it and doesn't swat it away. She wants to remember it, possibly forever.

"Looks like your mate didn't end up making it," Loup says, nodding toward the naked drummer man's window.

"Yeah... well, he was busy. He'll show up next time, I'm sure," Vincent says, and finds herself laughing. She knows it's more dumb than funny. She hasn't eaten anything else, not even Agathe's cake, and she's drinking another glass of wine. She can feel it shaking hands with the others.

Loup goes into his pocket to show her the clementine peels he put in there earlier. He shoves them back in, telling her they're his souvenirs from tonight. In French, the word *souvenir* means *memory*. Vincent finds all of this painfully romantic and rolls her eyes at him, which only makes him smile more and it's awful, his smile. How is that smile allowed on that face? She feels powerless now and it's Too Much.

"*La lune est si belle ce soir*," he says slowly.

"It really is," Vincent says. "It's full tomorrow. I have a cute app on my phone that sends me a notification when the moon is full or new. I didn't get it today, so it must be tomorrow."

"How much French do you know?"

"Are you worried about that? Is that why you speak it slowly to me? Don't fret. I know enough. Well, enough and *not* enough, really. But I learn more every day. Most of the people at the museum and my students too, they speak English, and honestly that makes me feel guilty," Vincent says, intentionally letting him in. The wine helps loosen the lid on her feelings, even the ones she has for Loup. She's liked him since the first moment she saw him—black T-shirt and *those* shorts, that *smile*, those *eyes*, that *nose*, that *hair*—but also? It doesn't have to mean anything. People meet people they like all the time.

On the flight to Paris she promised herself she'd try her best to keep it loose and let her emotions stretch out, go wherever they wanted. Not fight against them as much. When she wants a croissant or *pain au chocolat*, that's what she eats. When she's tired, she sleeps. When something's dumb or funny, she laughs. Anytime she has the sudden urge to leave her apartment to go watch the Eiffel Tower glitter in the black, she does that and doesn't have to tell anyone about it. There is no one else to take care of or look after here. Being in Paris and being simply *Vincent*, not Vincent the wife or Vincent the mom or Vincent the daughter or Vincent the sister, allows her to strip down to a base level.

* * *

"I do sometimes speak French slowly for you. And that's bad for me because I like the look on your face when you don't understand. Your little celestial nose... it scrunches up," he says, pointing at hers. "But tell me why it makes you feel guilty if someone can speak English."

She watches the wonder of his eyelashes as he blows a smoke ring at the moon. "Never mind," she says.

"No, please, really. I'd like to know."

It's not that someone can speak English, it's that they're choosing not to speak French to me. It makes me feel lazy or like I don't belong here. Like I haven't earned it yet. I should know... more. Vincent weighs the possibility of being honest with him. There are so many conversations with Cillian she wishes she could take back. Not because of the emotions she felt during them, but because they simply weren't worth it. In the long run, they'd made no difference. She could've powered a nation with all that wasted energy.

She's shared enough tonight.

"Forget it. That's not what I meant. It's hard to explain. Honestly, never mind," she says. "So... you're from Paris? You were born here? Grew up here?"

Vincent has no clue what time it is. She asks him that too and he tells her it's almost one. She holds her hand out for what's left of his cigarette and he gives it to her. It's from her pack anyway; he's only returning what is rightfully hers.

"Born in London and grew up there. Paris, too, yes. Both. We traveled a lot to Spain... Italy... the States. Everywhere, really. My mum is an opera singer. My dad is a pianist. I have dual citizenship, here and in England. My mum is from Paris, my dad London. I come from a family of hippies-sometimes-vagabonds. Bobos, right? You come from a family of artists, so you must understand," he says, and now that Loup's told her he grew up in London, she realizes she's always heard it in his mouth too.

Vincent imagines how pretty Loup's opera-singer *mère* must be. Loup is pretty in a feminine way that doesn't detract from his masculinity, as if his face has been sculpted by a lover who missed him so much, they overromanticized him when they did it.

"I do understand. We stayed in Kentucky and Tennessee for a while growing up," she says, remembering how Loup said *Kentucky Fried Chicken* in his faux American accent the first time they'd discussed where she was from. It's what everyone says to her about Kentucky, and it's also true there is a KFC not half a block from the apartment. "But my parents have always lived like hippie vagabonds. They're definitely bobos. It's how they raised me. And you say I'm from a family of artists, but you're an artist too," she says.

Loup is one of the people in class who stares off a lot, daydreaming, thinking, seemingly not in a rush to get to work. But whenever Vincent wanders through the room, taking peeks at what everyone is doing, she sees that his pages are full of color and depth. Even his early pencil sketches look like they could jump right off the page and come to life. In that way, Loup reminds her of her dad and brother because they make hard work look easy.

"I only signed up for the classes because of Baptiste. I keep taking them because of you."

"Tell me exactly what that means," Vincent commands, looking right at him, the night pleasantly pressing down. There is a candle dimming on the table between them. She puts out the cigarette and finishes her wine. She is content on her balcony in Paris now, drunksy and treading the waters of intimacy with the son of vagabonds. *Let's see how honest you really are.*

"Tonight, it means... I'm kind of drunk. Do you mind if I sleep on your couch?"

Half a point. He definitely gets half a point for honesty.

Loup has fallen asleep on the couch in his clothes with one of Aurora's hand-knit scrap blankets draped over him. After changing into a T-shirt and soft shorts, brushing her teeth and washing her face, Vincent goes to her bedroom and texts Olive, picturing her out to dinner with friends or maybe sitting at a coffee shop with a pumpkin-flavored drink and a dog-eared book.

~~Oh hey yeah there's a guy in the apartment pretty close to your age. You two would probably be friends! Maybe even date!~~

Your dad said he talked to you a few days ago. Good.

How are you feeling about that?

Cillian hadn't written an unkind word about either of their children in his book, although his protagonist was concerned about society's potential mistreatment of them because they're biracial. Colm had been upset and frustrated upon reading the book and hearing Cillian's explanations, but Colm is an inquisitive person and approaches everything like a problem to be solved. He demanded to know which parts were true or fiction and wanted to hear *everylittledetail*. He started texting and calling his dad more than ever, hoping to fill in the blanks. There were all sorts of conversations between them that Vincent wasn't privy to, and she preferred it that way. Both Cillian and Colm gave her the edited versions, allowing the puzzle of their discussions to fuzz together for her from different angles. Cillian and Colm were equally aggressively intelligent, and being in a room with them while they argued could drain Vincent enough to make her want to sleep for a week. She was grateful to her son for digging in and defending her and their family when she was far too exhausted to do it.

But Olive had reacted differently and more harshly to the book and Cillian's secrets. She was in Tennessee and refused to answer her dad's calls or texts for almost a month afterward. She felt like she didn't know him anymore and told him that. It made Vincent feel good, knowing that in their own ways, both of their children were on "her side" about this. Cillian didn't stand a chance. And although it broke a part of Vincent's heart, she appreciated both Olive's staunchness and her reasons for refusing to talk to her dad. Their daughter firmly believed Cillian needed to sit with the scope of what he'd done, and it was okay if that meant he didn't get to FaceTime with her while she walked to class, or that if he wanted to chat about the latest Bon Iver album or episode of *Dateline*, he'd have to wait until she was ready.

Cillian and Olive had been so close before this, it had made Vincent a little jealous, which she felt weird and bad about. Olive's borderline coquettishness with her dad wasn't unlike Vincent's with her own. She had observed that most dad/daughter relationships were complicated, and the bonds seemed to be either intense or nonexistent, with no real in between. Cillian and Olive's had definitely fallen into the intense category, but Vincent certainly hadn't *enjoyed* feeling a bit smug upon seeing Olive's relationship with her dad fractured by his secrets. She recognized and *felt* it, but! She hadn't enjoyed it! She really was relieved when Cillian said he talked to Olive recently.

Olive writes back.

It's fine. I've been so busy, it doesn't matter right now.

I mean... it takes a lot of energy to be angry with someone.

Vincent hears herself in Olive's words, *It takes a lot of energy to be angry with someone*. Vincent had said the same thing to Cillian when he'd asked if she was still angry with him. They talked about being mad versus being angry. Being mad didn't pain her as much as being angry. She could be mad at him and carry on. But she told him anger wasn't a state she could choose to stay in for very long; she let it in and felt it, and as soon as possible, she allowed it to pass through her body. Like a ghost walking through a wall.

Vincent gets up from her bed to go look at Loup again in the salt lamplight. He's supine on her couch, one arm up over his head. His other hand is flat on his stomach. She wonders what this means for them now. Have they unlocked something? Will it be wildly awkward in the morning? What if she wakes him up and asks him to kiss her? Invites him into her bed? Would he be equally energetic in there or would she see a slow change in him creep up like color in a mood ring? Is she really that eager to know what Bed Loup is like?

Her *yes* and *no* feelings tangle like necklaces.

Before today she hadn't had coffee with Loup in a café and he'd never been to her apartment, and now he was sleeping on her couch, the one her parents had gotten at the boutique on the Seine years ago. It was the first piece of real furniture they bought for the apartment; Aurora sent her a smiling selfie with it.

Vincent is remembering the photo tearily for no discernible reason and wishing the almost-full moon would just go ahead and pull her uterine lining to shed so she can reclaim her brain.

She goes to her bedroom and texts Olive again.

It's true. You're very good with your energy, RADIANT CHILD OF MINE.

I love you madly.

Heading to bed. Talk soon. x

She texts Colm.

I love you! Tell me things soon, sweet boy. x

When Vincent wakes in the bright white morning, she gets her wish—blood everywhere. Sticky and red, between her legs and on the sheets. She takes off her underwear, strips the bed, and wraps her clothes in the sheets for the laundry. There is blood dripping down her leg. One big drop makes a neat plop on the floor and she stands dizzy and dissociating, looking at it, thinking about what it means to be a woman, how it feels to bleed and bleed and bleed and cramp and suffer in accordance with God's will. She remembers Cillian touching her once, neither of them knowing she'd started her period. How red the tip of his finger was when he pulled it away. How he smiled and said, "Wow, you women are quite impressive... You can do that at will, can you?"

When she looks up, Loup is walking down the hallway, rubbing his face.

Loup.

She left the bedroom door open and Loup is in her apartment. Loup is in her apartment because he slept on the couch.

"Loup!"

"Oh shit, Vincent, I'm sorry! Wait... you're okay? You're bleeding?" he says as he slaps a hand across his eyes.

4

It was an unseasonably cold fall when Cian saw Pica for the first time. The coffee shop inside the main library on campus was brand-new that semester. Cian had begun working there as soon as it opened. He also had a running gig in the Writing Center, tutoring and helping his fellow students edit their term papers.

He knew how daffy and dramatic it was to think that he'd fallen in love with Pica at first glimpse, but that's what it felt like. She was saying her name for the third time and spelling it out for the librarian attempting to get into her account.

"It's Picasso. Like the artist. P-I-C-A-S-S-O. Then... it's Taylor-Cline. T-A-Y-L-O-R-C-L-I-N-E," she said so patiently, Cian wanted to applaud. He had been standing on the other side of the espresso machine, but moved and wiped down the condiment counter to get a closer look at her—this girl named Picasso he was fascinated by already. He hadn't even gotten a proper look at her face.

The librarian was spelling her name back to her very slowly as she typed, and Pica stood smiling. When she noticed Cian, she smiled at him too. Her yonic lavender earrings swung with the swift turn of her head. Without thinking it through, Cian waved at her, feeling like an idiot a split second before doing it. As if he'd left his body to fend for itself and he was above it somehow, like, "See ya... you're on your own, buddy." And now he'd seen her pulchritudinous face in all its glory.

At least she'd remember him—the complete dork behind the counter who waved at her without moving his hand. He held it there frozen for way too long.

Once Pica settled her business with the librarian, she came over to the coffee shop and waited in line. When it was her turn and he asked for the name to write on her cup, she said Pica and spelled it for him.

When he finished making her drink, he said her name aloud. After handing her the cup, he told her that his name was Cian, but she hadn't asked. And why would she have asked? Why had he suddenly forgotten how to be a person?

"Hi, Cian," she said.

Wait. Did she remind him of Shalene? The way Pica had said his name definitely reminded him of her.

Once Pica was gone, he went to the bathroom and put his forehead against the back of the cool door, thinking of Shalene and what she looked like now, what she was doing. Was she okay? Did she ever think about him? Cian stayed in that bathroom stall for too long, spiraling through memories of Dublin and all he'd run away from when his family left for California.

And Pica, he was thinking about her too.

Q: How long would it be until he would see her again?

A: Two hours.

Cian's shift was over and as he was walking out of the library on his way to poetry class, Pica was walking in.

"That was a really good mocha, by the way. I need another, but definitely decaf this time," she said. And without knowing exactly how, Cian found that they'd stepped aside, out of the foot traffic flow. It only took one sentence of conversation and they both subconsciously decided that they wanted to be alone to continue talking to each other. Had she fallen in love with him at first glimpse too? His brain was telling him ridiculous things and Cian didn't want to seem too eager, but maybe? Maybe she sensed something in him, something he hadn't known he'd been giving off? A silent alarm that only Pica could hear. The door next to them kept opening and closing, letting in the sharp, cold wind, but underneath his hat and scarf and coat, Cian was beginning to sweat.

"Excellent. I'm glad you liked it," he managed to say. The sweating, the cold, the dizziness from how much Pica reminded him of Shalene, though she was different enough not to remind him of Shalene at all—the paradox prickled like a panic attack.

"You're Irish," Pica said.

"Your full name is Picasso," he said. "I overheard... at the counter."

"I love that we're standing here telling each other facts. Just the plain truth, right? No bullshit."

"No bullshit. None at all."

"Promise? Let's never bullshit each other," Pica said, laughing. She said it like they'd known each other intimately for a long time in a way that no one else could understand, somewhere in a secret heart of their own that they'd created—a new, third heart beating between them.

That new heart beat so strongly, so loudly and confidently, Cian asked her if she wanted to meet him after his poetry class so he could make her a decaf mocha and she said yes.

Not even a month after Vincent had arrived in Paris, Cillian texted her, asking if she would video chat. She asked him what for. She'd been limiting contact with him to once a week at that point, and that contact had mostly been texting, only one regular phone call. Video chat was quite a leap.

Because I want to talk to you about something. I want to tell you something.

Something you don't want to text?

Right.

Why not?

Because I want you to see my face.

Not because you want to see my face, but because you want ME to see YOUR face?

Both, Vin. It's both. Please?

Ok...hang on.

She put on her flowy peony robe, went to the bathroom to check her face and fluff her hair. Pressed her index finger into the little pot of cherry lip gloss on the counter and applied it. Why shouldn't she look ravishing and red-lipped when Cillian saw her for the first time since she left him?

She lit candles, poured a glass of wine, and cozied up on the couch with her laptop.

When Cillian got on, she could tell he'd been crying. It would've been startling to see his face regardless, but seeing that he'd been crying was a heavy weight that attached itself to every emotion she was already feeling. Vincent resented him for putting her in this position. She'd come to Paris to deliberately get away from him, to get away from having to take care of everyone else. She'd been happily alone. *Libre.* Swimming in the morning, wandering the city in the afternoon, making dinners with the windows open in the evening. Faking calm until she found it. She didn't want to regress; she didn't want to manage Cillian's guilt. She wasn't going to let him pass it over to her like a cold. No.

"I'm here," she said. She took a sip of wine and put her glass on the floor. She wouldn't mention the crying; he would have to be the one to bring it up.

"Hi, Vin. I'm glad to see ya," he said. Seeing his face and hearing his voice... it was like she had a wind chime hidden deep inside of her and a slight breeze was in there with it.

"Hi, Cillian. You wanted to talk about something?" Vincent asked him calmly.

Cillian was wearing a sweater she'd bought for him, the color of a muddy carrot. He was wearing his glasses too.

"It's not steaming hot? Why are you wearing a wool sweater?" she asked.

"It was cold in here."

"What have you got the thermostat set on? Turn the A/C down."

"You usually do that."

"Right. But I'm not there. I'm here," she said. They were quiet, just staring at each other until Cillian cleared his throat.

"I wanted to tell you that Siobhán emailed me. The girl from high school. Shalene... from the book," he said, as if Vincent could ever forget her pretty name and who she was to him. He took his glasses off and rubbed both eyes at the same time with one hand. He kept doing it.

"Okay. And? You really did get her pregnant when you were a teenager?"

"I did," he confessed, still rubbing his eyes.

"And... did she have a fucking *baby* or not, Cillian?" Vincent asked. At this point she was more angry than annoyed. She was more angry than sad. She was more angry than anxious. She saw the whole story unspooling before he could tell it, like she had some sort of lazy prescient powers that finally decided to kick in. "She had the baby and they're out there somewhere and you never told me about it. You wrote a book about it instead. A whole-ass *book*," Vincent said. She took two big gulps of wine. She got her box of cigarettes off the rug and lit one. She never smoked inside, only on the balcony, but she'd just found out for sure that her husband of twenty-four years had a secret love child. The situation called for smoking at *least* one cigarette indoors. It was fine. The windows were open.

"Vin, I was fifteen. She was fifteen. She had the baby... a boy named Tully. He'll be thirty-one next week. He wants to meet me... in Ireland when I'm there next month. I... I'm so fucking sorry, Vin. I fucked this up completely. All of it... them... you... us. It's my fault," he said, putting his glasses back on but taking them off again immediately.

He was crying and Cillian wasn't a big crier. Vincent wished there were some way she could be a proper friend to him, split herself in two so one of her could be who he needed. There was a chunk of her heart that hurt for him. His father had ripped him from his home when he was a teenager and Vincent hated thinking of Sad, Lonely, Teenage Cillian. She'd always wished they could've known each other back then and been friends.

And even now, Friend Vincent could comfort him, stay up all night listening and talking, tell him to carry his laptop to bed with her face serene and soothing through the blue light of the screen. But the Estranged Wife Vincent he was getting on the other side of the computer couldn't offer much in the way of sweetness or forgiveness. She hadn't even *begun* to process everything yet. The book had only been out for a month! It was still as if she'd just stepped dizzy off an amusement park ride and everything was spinning around her as she stood there dumbstruck.

"You have a thirty-year-old son in Ireland. His name is Tully. Did you talk to him?" Vincent asked robotically, as if she were being fed the questions by someone off-camera. She smoked; she loved smoking in Paris.

"You're smoking," Cillian observed softly, and sniffed.

"Did you talk to him, Cillian?"

"Not yet. She sent me pictures."

"Send them to me. Yes, I'm smoking and yes, send me pictures of your secret son."

"There was so much I didn't—"

"Are you sending them to me?" she interrupted, checking her phone already.

"Yes, I'm sending them to you," Cillian said, and nodded. He was looking down at his phone; Vincent stared at the top of his head.

In silence, she looked at the photos that arrived on her phone screen. Cillian's son Tully, no DNA test required. Four photos total: two baby pictures, one when he was a teenager, and one in his late twenties. It was like seeing an old photo of Cillian. Vincent started crying and taking deep breaths.

"He's got your smile. He looks just like you. He looks like Colm," she said when she could. Cillian, Colm, and Tully had the same bright eyes and nose. If Vincent had somehow bumped into Tully as a stranger on the street, she would've thought he looked like her son, like her husband. She would've wanted to ask if he was a Wilde, that's how strong the resemblance was. "You have another son who looks just like you. Now he's a grown man," Vincent said, as if saying it aloud was helping her figure it out somehow. Her brain couldn't focus on a single emotion. Instead, a storm of them hurricane-swirled inside her. She put her cigarette out and stood to go over to the window and push it open farther. She stuck her head out a little and held it there, drinking the air like water.

"Vin. Vin, where did you go?" Cillian's voice said from her laptop speakers. "Are you in the room, at least?"

"Yes," she said, crying with her head out the window. She focused on a woman walking on the sidewalk below, holding her phone close to her mouth and speaking French loudly in a fussy tone, having a little relationship crisis of her own, maybe.

"I'm going to meet up with him when I'm in Dublin," he said.

"Her too?" Vincent asked into the room.

"I don't know. Would that bother you?"

"I don't see why that matters."

"It matters."

"I don't care...but I do care that you're doing the right thing here. That's not a compliment. I don't really feel like *complimenting* you at the moment, but it's the right thing...meeting him. A bit late, but you have to do this. He's your son," she said once she was back on the couch. She shrugged at her husband and shook her head, wiped her eyes.

A stretch of silence.

"I've just dug a deeper hole for us," Cillian said. He wasn't crying anymore; he looked spent and handsome. Vincent tried to get out of her own way so she could feel tenderness toward him because it was what he needed. It was what she needed too, though. Was he aware of that?

"I've fucked everything up and I promise I'm trying to fix it," he said.

"What's his last name? Tully's."

"Hawke."

"That's Siobhán's last name too?"

"Right," Cillian said.

Vincent mined him for more information. Cillian told her Siobhán got married when Tully was small and both she and Tully had taken the man's last name. She was still married to him now and they had a daughter; Siobhán had told Cillian that her husband was Tully's father and always would be.

"You only fell in love with me because I reminded you of her," Vincent said. She'd never seen a picture of Siobhán, but he basically said as much in the book. Vincent and Cillian had been together for so long, she knew it was more complicated than that, but it still made her feel unoriginal and disturbed.

"That's not true," Cillian said, shaking his head.

"*You* put it in the book... not me."

"But you know it's not what I meant. Obviously not everything in the book is one hundred percent true, ya know that."

"I don't know anything, Cillian."

"I love you because you're *you*. Period."

"Does she hate you? I would," Vincent said. An ambulance whined in the distance and Vincent crossed herself like she always did when she heard or saw emergency vehicles. She also did it when she saw a hearse. It was an Aurora thing that had been passed down the line of women in her family. Vincent had been raised by a half Catholic and a casual Baptist.

"There's a siren? I can't hear it," Cillian asked, knowing what it meant when she made the sign of the cross like that. Vincent nodded. Cillian knew her so well it was annoying. Like most couples who've been together for a long time, sometimes he knew what she was thinking and could guess how she would react to things. That's why it hurt her so much that he'd kept his book a secret, that he'd kept *all* of this a secret. Because he knew *exactly* how much it would hurt her. He didn't even have the excuse of ignorance. "Siobhán said she'd forgiven me a long time ago. Tully knows everything. That we were young and clueless and that my parents made me leave. She said he looked me up plenty of times but never contacted me. I promise. I haven't kept that from you," he said, like he was proud there was at least *one* thing he'd done right.

"You owe her a lot of money," Vincent said.

Cillian kept talking, saying Siobhán told him that his parents had sent her and Tully money when she was a teenager. That Cillian's dad had worked something out with Siobhán's parents secretly, paying Siobhán and her family off to keep it all from Cillian. Cillian asked his mom about it as soon as he got off the phone with Siobhán and his mom finally confessed everything. Told him they'd sent Siobhán and Tully money until Tully had turned eighteen. The layers and layers of lies and secrets were labyrinthine.

Knowing Cillian's parents had kept his son a secret from him and knowing that if his dad hadn't died before she could meet him, he probably would've wanted Vincent to go away too made her feel dim inside. No light, no echoes. She absorbed what she could.

"What if some guy had done this to Olive? You have a daughter too, Cillian," Vincent said.

"I'm aware. I don't have anything to say besides the fact that I'd obviously be devastated and ya know that."

"A huge part of your life is a lie," she said, bleary from crying. She had a class to teach in the morning, and she could barely keep her eyes open.

"Vin, I'm sorry about everything. I want to fight hard for this. I *will* fight for our family," Cillian said, looking at her and putting a hand on his chest.

"We'll talk next week. You need to tell the kids this yourself. Colm and Olive have a half brother they never even knew about," she said, just in case he needed to have the heft of this explained to him again. "What kind of man are you? What kind of man does something like this?"

She didn't give him a chance to answer. Just closed her laptop, got in bed, and cried so hard she fell into a deep, easy sleep.

First thing in the morning, before heading off to the museum, Vincent googled *Siobhán Hawke* after texting her siblings and parents in their group chat, giving them the short version and promising to tell them more later. She scrolled through Siobhán's Facebook page for an hour, looking at photos of her, her husband, and Tully. Siobhán had kind eyes; she and Vincent did resemble each other slightly, even more if she squinted. Probably another reason why Tully and Colm looked so much alike—their mothers could have been sisters or cousins. Looking over her page, Vincent couldn't help but like Siobhán, her interests and posts. They had a lot of the same tastes in book-to-movie adaptations and creamy chicken recipes. She clicked through her friends and family. Scrolled around on the hospital website where Siobhán was pictured and listed as a pediatric nurse.

She then googled *Tully Hawke* and found his YouTube channel. He was a singer/songwriter who updated about once a week. Vincent watched the latest video, wildly disoriented from how much he sounded and looked like Cillian and Colm. She listened to one of his songs on repeat while she got ready for work. It was really good. Slow and quiet, called "Come Back to Me." Vincent thought about leaving a comment but couldn't bring herself to do it. Instead, she clicked the thumbs-up button and had the song stuck in her head for the rest of the day.

"Can I do something? Can I help you... do something?" Loup asks from the hallway with his hand still covering his eyes.

"I'm feeling a little dizzy. It's my period... I didn't eat enough last night. You fed me all that... fruit," she says, holding her bloody sheets in front of her body, only half-concerned she is standing in front of him naked from the waist down, bleeding onto her floor. She gets into her drawer for new underwear and pulls a pair on, almost falling down. She grabs another to take with her to the bathroom. Shouldn't she be more embarrassed by this? Isn't this mortifying? Has Cillian worked every last bit of embarrassment out of her and she's running on empty now? Her family and friends found out Cillian's secret at the same time she did. How much more embarrassed could she have possibly been? Maybe she'll never be embarrassed again, like that emotion is now extinct and she won't be able to feel it, no matter what happens.

Will it be replaced by something else?

All she feels is hunger, cramping, and the urge to pee.

"I'm going to put this in the laundry, but first I really have to go to the bathroom," she says, wrapping the bloody linens around her so both her front and back are covered. She takes teeny tiny steps out of her bedroom because it's all the sheets will allow.

After going to the bathroom to clean herself up and stick a pad to her underwear, she wraps herself in the sheets again and meets Loup in the hallway. She doesn't know she's fuzzing out and falling until she feels Loup's hands catching her, warm through the cool of the cotton.

He is saying her name and touching her face. He is helping her over to the couch. He's unwinding the bloody mess of fabric from her body and putting Aurora's blanket on top of her. Loup disappears down the hall and returns after how long? Vincent has fallen asleep for a moment and woken up. Loup is standing over her now. The electric kettle roars in the kitchen.

"Hot water bottle and tea? Toast too? Helps my sister. She has endometriosis," Loup says.

"I'm sorry. I'm very lucky I don't have that. It's only this bad for the first day. I don't normally pass out...if that's even what I did. I don't know what happened," she says.

"I totally saved your life. Told you I'd earn my keep," Loup says, smiling at her.

"Oh, wow, you're truly delusional...and thank you. That's what I mean. Thank you," she says.

"What would you do without me?"

"Hmm, don't you have somewhere to be this morning?" she asks, half joking. But. She doesn't know where he lives; maybe he doesn't have anywhere to go.

"You're calling in? Rescheduling the class?"

"I have to. Obviously," she says.

Without asking, Loup goes back to her bedroom and retrieves her phone, hands it to her. "Then no. I don't have anywhere to be this morning. What kind of tea would you like, Vincent?" he asks while she texts the woman at the museum and then Baptiste, letting them know she won't be there today.

"Cinnamon," she says as a sharp cramp rips across her middle. She says yes to Loup's toast and asks him to bring her three ibuprofen as well, telling him where they are in her bathroom closet, getting more and more specific until she hears him rattle the bottle in confirmation. He gives them to her with a glass of water and when everything is ready, he brings her the hot water bottle along with a teapot and toast. The woman from the museum texts back that she hopes Vincent feels better. They will double up her classes on Friday to make up for the missed day.

Loup sits on the floor in front of her, eating toast too. He's made four slices and filled their teacups.

"Have I ever told you I'm in a band? Just for fun, really. *L'art pour l'art*. We donate all the money we make from our gigs and merch.

We don't have any albums or anything but it's um, electronic music, borderline trip-hop... lo-fi techno. Sometimes there are vocals. We go back and forth about that. There's one girl in the band..." He trails off, with seemingly zero concern for finishing the sentence.

"Where do you donate the money?"

"Most of the time it goes to organizations that help the homeless... feed the hungry."

"Wow, I love that. That's... that's amazing, actually. What do you call yourselves?"

"Anchois," he says.

"Anchovy?" Vincent translates. Loup nods. "You play an instrument? Or do you sing?"

"Sometimes I sing, but most of the time I make music with drum machines and synthesizers. Electronic boxes of sound." He uses his hands to show her how small they can be; he stretches his arms to show her how big they can be too. "It's me and my friends Apollos and Noémie. Sometimes Emiliano and Sam too. Apollos is my roommate."

Vincent relaxes. He actually does live somewhere, with someone.

"Sounds like you have a lot of friends," she says, deadpan. She swallows the toast and drinks her tea.

"I liked meeting *your* mates last night," he says, and tells her she should bring some of them to hear Anchois play next Friday at this club in Le Marais, near his apartment on rue des Arquebusiers, in the 3rd arrondissement.

Parisians love their *quartiers*, and Vincent loves strolling to Le Marais for falafel and something cold to drink, wandering around, taking her time walking back. Walking in Paris is one of her favorite things to do. She's walked down Loup's street many times, never knowing he could have been up there somewhere, buzzing and talking and painting and eating and reading and sleeping.

Baptiste texts.

Hope you feel better soon!

Oh and have you confessed your love
to Loup yet?

Or maybe he's confessed his to you?
You are LOVEsick...that's it?

Don't leave me in suspense, Veedubs!

Vincent Wilde to V.W. to Veedubs; she respects how strongly Baptiste sticks to his nickname game.

"Just a sec. Sorry. It's your best mate Baptiste, harassing me," Vincent says to Loup as she texts back.

Wow would you like me to stop
speaking to you entirely?

Conversation bubbles on the screen immediately.

Never ever. Let me know if you need
anything?

I will. Merci.

Coffee after class tomorrow, ça te dit?

Baptiste had taught her *Ça te dit?* for *Do you want to?* the first day they met.

Oh oui, mon pote. x

Loup is looking at his own phone and waits patiently until she is finished.

"Do you know he's my cousin? Well, actually, Mina is... on my dad's side," Loup says. "Our grandmothers were sisters," he adds, widening the branches of their family tree. Vincent is almost positive Baptiste has told her that twice, but it's one of the things she keeps forgetting on purpose.

Her brain is blurry with cramps and overall period pain. When she's less dizzy, she'll take a shower, since that usually helps. For now, she just makes an intense sound of discomfort and Loup asks if she is okay.

"I'm fine. Tell me more about your anchovy band if you expect me to come see y'all," she says.

Loup laughs as he repeats her *y'all*, adding a cowboy twang. Vincent laughs as much as she can. He tells her more as they finish their toast. They talk and drink more tea. She says she'll try to make it to the Anchois show, maybe bring Agathe along. She gets him to write down exactly when and where it is. She's already thinking of what she will wear—black lace under mossy-green wool.

When Vincent asks if he has a job, he says he occasionally DJs and bartends for a catering service owned by his roommate's family—fancy corporate events, weddings, birthday parties too, but it's only part-time.

"I inherited money from my grandparents that I could've used for university, but instead... I use it for freedom," he says, lifting an eyebrow. He smiles all rascally and wild, baring his teeth.

Around lunchtime, Vincent is surprised at the mild disappointment she feels when Loup says he's leaving. He says, "I'll get out of your hair," and tucks a slip of his own hair behind his ear. It is an accidental joke and she would normally make a note of it, but she's too tired. She wants to sleep. She lies down on the couch, curled around the hot water bottle and its fuzzy cover.

"I wiped up your bedroom floor and the sheets are in the dryer. And when I was in the bathroom I ordered both chicken and shrimp fried rice for you from Lili. Some egg rolls too. I remembered you had stuff from there in class once. It'll be here in about five minutes. I thought maybe you wouldn't want red meat so soon after the Bolognese last night... that's why I went with the chicken and shrimp. I don't know why, I just figured," he says as she's drifting off. "I'll wait and get the food from the guy, then I'll see you in class tomorrow? It's the least I can do... you fed me, and you let me stay the night—" he says.

"Well, you saw my period blood *and* my *vagin*, so we're even..." Vincent fills in, half-asleep. "I'm kidding," she says, although she isn't. "*Merci. Merci beaucoup, jeune homme*," and she lets herself go.

Dipping in and out of dreamy mists, she hears Loup talking to the deliveryman, hears the smiles in their *merci* and *merci beaucoup*. The rustle of paper and plastic, the hush of it quieted on the kitchen counter. She feels Loup's gentle touch on the top of her head. His whispered "*Au revoir, Vincent Raphaela*." The soft click of the apartment door closing.

5

After sleeping and showering, Vincent gets back on the couch with her hot water bottle and the box of shrimp fried rice. She calls Cillian like she promised she would. He answers immediately, thanks her for calling (it's so excessive, she stops him), and tells her that he misses her. She ignores him. Instead, they talk about the kids. Vincent mentions a few innocuous things about her classes and the weather. Cillian goes on about shake-ups at the university for approximately two minutes. Vincent is lying with her head upon the armrest, listening intently with her eyes closed. Even through her annoyance, focusing on Cillian's deep, pleasant voice is better than focusing on her body throbbing with pain.

"Gah, I miss you madly, Vincent. I mean it... I'm going *mad* without ya," he says.

"Good," she says softly.

"I don't know how to respond... that you think it's good. I can't get anywhere near your heart again? You've settled on that?"

"Consider what you're asking me, Cillian."

"I have been considering it... It's all I consider."

"You're asking me if you can get anywhere near my heart. But if you weren't near my heart... if you weren't *in* my heart, I wouldn't be upset, would I? I would've divorced you already or I'd be sleeping with someone. I would've... found someone," Vincent says with her eyes closed tight. Loup's annoyingly handsome face flickers in the staticky black. *Really?* She doesn't have Loup's phone number and even if she did, what would she do, text him? And say what? The mere thought of it is a mess. Vincent pinches the bridge of her nose.

"You're not seeing someone? No one at all? We should have this out in the open."

"Should we? Should we have things out in the open, Cillian? Because I agree that we should have things out in the open. I've always thought this! Has it *just* occurred to you?"

"Vin... I'm sorry," Cillian says.

Vincent wishes she had been keeping track of Cillian's apologies. There would be pages and pages of tally marks in her journal.

"I am not seeing anyone, I am not sleeping with anyone," she says.

Loup's chain necklace twinkles in the light of her mind. So do his short heat-wave shorts—pale peach with some sort of reflective stripe, a flash of alien glare right there up high on his thigh. She remembers looking at the bright bait of it like a hypnotized fish.

"I love you. I love our children. You are all in my heart. And Cillian, please remember what we said about you not surprising me in Paris—showing up here. I need this space," she finishes.

Cillian says he remembers and he understands. He apologizes again. (Really. She should've been counting. It's at least two hundred at this point.) They chat a bit more, and he tells her he loves her before they hang up.

Pica?

He liked her.

He liked her a lot.

It took him a wicked long time to tell her this.

She came in for coffees and they'd talk and flirt. Sometimes Cian would see her with a group of friends—skateboarders in hoodies and girls with pink hair from the art building, guys with fat black rings in their ears. Once he saw her in the evening chalking FRIENDS DON'T LET FRIENDS JOIN FRATS *in front of the humanities building with some girls Cian recognized from his creative writing classes.*

"Cian, join us!" Pica had hollered, waving him over. He liked how easily she discerned his propinquity through the darkness. He and his roommate both went over and joined Pica's group. "This is my friend Cian the Irishman. And he said I could call him that, so no worries," Pica said, smiling as he waved to everyone. The girls lifted their small chalky hands at him.

Afterward, Cian asked her out for a drink and she told him she wasn't twenty-one yet, so he and his fake ID went and bought the beers and all of them went back to his apartment, climbed out his window onto the roof, and drank them under the moon.

It was like that.

Pica popping up on campus, Pica waving him over, Pica introducing him to loads of people who got cooler and cooler as the months went by. She was always warm and bonhomous and he knew she liked him, but he didn't know if it was romantic or not. She had the kind of personality that made it seem like she was flirting with people even when she didn't mean to. Intense eye contact, listening, asking the right questions, laughing a lot. She would open up, then open up some more. That was Pica—a rose in full bloom. Being in her hot light felt good. And everyone around her loved it and seemed to flirt back, even the girls. Maybe she had a secret heart with other people too. Cian hadn't dated a girl in ages. He'd been working and writing instead, finishing one short story collection and starting another.

In the beginning of Cian and Pica's relationship, from that unseasonably cold fall until the first warmth of the spring, when they were just friends, when it was all so easy, he let her do most of the talking. She told him about her family, her siblings. But she didn't tell him that her parents were famous artists until the day they were walking together and heard a song blasting from the speakers in the quad. They were leaving campus, heading to their separate parking lots, separate cars.

"I love this song. Never gets old," Cian said, looking over at her. She was wearing a long orange flowered skirt that day, her thin white shirt tied in a knot at her navel. Swingy earrings, like always—she'd told him she made them.

One of the university organizations was having an end-of-semester party in the sunshine. It was a little early; there were two full weeks of classes left in the spring semester and one week of finals. The Tennessee campus was a mix of woodsy and urban, earthy green and space gray. The sky was cruel that day—so brutal and beautiful it made Cian a little anxious, as if maybe it would be his last day alive. He'd heard them called "bluebird days" when the sky was cloudless and blisteringly blue, usually after snow. It was officially spring and hadn't snowed in almost two months, but it still felt like a bluebird day, and bluebird days were perfect and any too-perfect thing felt like an apogee.

"Yeah... my dad actually wrote the hook to this song... with his friends... He wrote a ton of these. It's weird, I know. I'm not lying. You can look it up if you want. His name is Franklin Cline. He goes by Incline. He did the art for the album too... Both of my parents are artists," she said.

"Your dad wrote the hook to this song?!" Cian stopped. The fun and surprise of what she'd said had snapped him back to hope.

"Yep. A whole bunch of them. No bullshit. None at all," Pica said. She was wearing sunglasses. Cian wanted to see her eyes and he told her that. She pushed the frames atop her head and they stood there, the music loud and pulsing against the trees. That savage sky, the afternoon. Her eyes were bright brown and warm, like gingerbread.

"That's like... one of the most amazing things I've ever heard. Uh... this may get awkward, but I think I worship your dad," he said, putting his hand to his heart. What he didn't say: And Picasso, I think I worship YOU. You see, you've gone and left me no choice in the matter.

"Oh, I'll tell him, trust me. He'll love that," she said, shaking her head and pushing her curls out of her face. She seemed a dab shy, talking about her dad. Maybe it was the money. Cian wondered how rich her parents were.

Pica could be argumentative, but she was so wildly intelligent and attractive, Cian didn't mind. She was smarter and more observant than he was, but he wasn't the kind of man who could ever let her know that. She loved discussing politics and injustice and art and poetry and religion, and she could fit in with anyone, anywhere. Whether they were on his roof or in the library, on a walk or at a restaurant, Pica was comfortable, forever magnetic.

After getting to know her better, he'd somewhat unglued her from Shalene. Maybe she didn't remind him of her anymore anyway. His family had left Dublin and all that behind to start brand-new. Maybe it had all been a phantasm.

It felt like one.

Didn't it?

Vincent looks at her text messages after getting off the phone with Cillian.

One from Ramona, saying hi with hearts. Vincent sends hearts in return and they reconfirm their video chat date for Saturday.

One from Colm telling her not much was up—he and his fiancée, Nicole, are going apple picking Saturday morning. Vincent sends him apple emojis, tells him to call soon and to tell Nicole she says hi.

One from an unknown number.

You like the rice? You're feeling better?

It doesn't bother or surprise Vincent at all that Baptiste has given Loup her number. No more fighting it. Now things are beginning to feel inevitable, like she's swallowed a sleeping pill and here it comes . . . she's getting tired . . . letting go.

I haven't taken one bite yet. Just about to. Feeling ok. Thank you.

Your place is amazing

I know, right?

Do you care that Baptiste gave me your number?

I probably should, shouldn't I? Violation of privacy and all.

I just figured since I've slept on your couch...

You mean... since you've seen my vagin...

I didn't actually see your vagin! (I'd like to say "unfortunately"... but am not sure how inappropriate that would be. I can't see your face, so I don't know.)

Loup, I'm... pretty sure you saw my vagin. DON'T LIE.

Ah, unfortunately... I did not. C'est la vérité.

Vincent starts feeling dizzy again, from the conversation. She puts the phone down and eats some rice—big overflowing bites of it out of the little deep spoon she loves the most.

OK then. No worries. And by the way, the rice is delicious. Merci.

Good. I hope you keep feeling better and I'm really looking forward to seeing you tomorrow.

Are you now?

Absolutely.

À demain, Loup.

À demain, Vincent. x

She opens her contacts list and types WOLF next to *Name*. Puts the wolf emoji there and the big red X. She turns on the TV but doesn't look at it. Instead, she lets *ah, unfortunately... I did not* rattle her brain before it zooms down and races through the rest of her body like it could shoot her right out through the tempered glass windows onto the leafy pavement.

Vincent doesn't mind being alone. She can miss her children and Ramona, her siblings, her parents, and even Cillian sometimes, but she's not lonely. At the museum, she is constantly surrounded by people and her phone pings regularly with messages from the ones she loves.

It's not loneliness that compels her to put her laptop on her thighs and finally compose an email to Cillian's son, Tully. Instead, it's an undefinable emotion she doesn't attempt to fully decode. The feeling is heavy, bright, and not unpleasant.

According to Cillian, he and Tully speak about once a week, whether it's over text or email. Occasionally on the phone. They've only met the one time when Cillian was on book tour in Dublin, but they've both been floating the idea of meeting up again soon. Tully's contact information is on his website next to a beachy black-and-white photo of him with his guitar.

To: TullyHawke@gmail.com

From: VincentRaphaelaWilde@gmail.com

Subject: Hi Tully. My name is Vincent and I'm married to Cillian Wilde.

Dear Tully,

I'm Vincent Wilde. I married your biological dad back in the late nineties, but only recently heard about your mom and you.

I want to start by saying two things:

1. I am so sorry for how you and your mom have been ignored by Cillian all these years.

2. I've been listening to your music every day since I found your website a few months ago.

I guess I should get out one more thing too:

I am nervous about writing this email! You don't owe me anything! Cillian owes you and your mom a lot!

None of this is our fault, but here we are.

I'm sure Cillian has already told you how much you favor our son, Colm. Maybe he's even shown you pictures.

The song of yours I've listened to most often is "Come Back to Me." It's so good. It reminds me of Elliott Smith and I love Elliott Smith. The song feels like a heartbeat...necessary...like *not* having it or not listening to it could lead to disaster. My dad is a songwriter/musician...I seem to always find myself surrounded by musicians. Congratulations on your music and for what appears to be a really great life. ☺

Cillian and I are estranged right now. He hates when I call it that, but there's nothing else to call it!

Now I am living in Paris alone. My reason for coming isn't particularly great but being here is quite lovely. I teach jewelry making and creativity classes at the modern art museum.

I am on my soft couch typing this; there is a half-eaten box of shrimp fried rice on the table in front of me. It's late-October cool and I have the window open a little. I've just made a fresh pot of cinnamon tea.

I realize this is overly chatty and maybe that's weird, but IF you want to, I'd love to hear more about you! Completely understood if you don't want to share too much with a stranger, but you can even just tell me about your music or what's out your window! You can talk about Dublin or anywhere else you've traveled! Cillian and I took a trip to Ireland not long after we got married. I'd love to visit again someday. Sometimes I find myself wanting to go everywhere all at once. It's like that quote that talks about putting *everywhere* on your list. Exactly my feelings.

Tully, my heart goes out to you and your mom. I mean that. Do you think she would mind me reaching out to her via email? I thought it'd be best for me to ask you first since Cillian told me the two of you talk regularly.

As ever,
Vincent Wilde

PS: I'm a woman! I realized I didn't say that at the beginning. I am a woman called Vincent, after Van Gogh. Cillian calls me Vin. You can call me whatever you'd like.

By the next morning, Vincent is feeling a little better, but she still loads up with ibuprofen and hot tea before walking over to the museum. The cloudy sky is flat-brush-streaked with gray and ecru. She sits on the bench outside the entrance and tucks her chin into her scarf as she checks her email. There is one from Tully. Vincent gets goose bumps upon seeing his name.

To: VincentRaphaelaWilde@gmail.com
From: TullyHawke@gmail.com
Subject: RE: Hi Tully. My name is Vincent and I'm married to Cillian Wilde.

Hi Vincent,

Honestly, your PS: "I'm a woman!" was a bright spot of joy in an otherwise dreary day. And by dreary, I mean literally dreary... as in the weather here... not dreary in my soul. It's cold and rainy out of my window this morning in Dublin.

I love Paris in the fall. I love Paris anytime. That's how the Cole Porter song goes, right? ☺ My mam used to listen to Ella Fitzgerald singing it all the time when I was growing up. She loves Ella. I'm confident everyone on earth loves Ella or honestly, I'd have a hard time sleeping at night.

Wild(e) to see your name in my inbox, but a lot of wild things have happened to me in the past few months.

Same for you, I know... from what both Cillian and Mam have told me.

Thank you for saying such nice things about my music. "Come Back to Me" is the second song I ever wrote. The Elliott Smith comparison is a HIGH compliment. He's one of my favourites. When it came out three years ago, it got decent airplay around here. The YouTube stuff helps, and the streaming sites... but I have another job too. I own a little guitar shop with my sister and my cousin.

I told Cillian this because it's true: I didn't grow up thinking my life was lacking anything. I thought my stepdad was my biological father until I was like seven and even after I found out he wasn't, nothing changed. He'd legally adopted me when I was four and raised me as his own. I've always considered/called him my father... maybe Cillian told you all this already? You said estranged, but that can mean a couple different things... depending.

Thanks again for writing and for listening to my music. And do tell me more about your dad's songwriting/music if you'd like.

I want to meet Colm one day and Olive too. You. Everyone... if it could happen ? Wild(e) times, indeed.

I asked Mam and she said she'd be fine with you reaching out via email. She said to tell you thanks for asking first. Her email is SiobhanSunshineHawke@gmail.com. She's aces, as you will soon see.

Be well,

Tully

PS: By the way, I'm totally a man. Just so we're absolutely clear on that. ☺

6

Make a list of colors you observed this morning both at home and on your way to the museum. Which colors repeated most often? How did they make you feel?

This time there are eleven women in the class, four men. The ages range from early twenties to midseventies. The oldest woman told Vincent her age on the first day. "*J'ai soixante-quinze ans*," she'd said as she put one hand on the back of Vincent's and the other in her palm. Her name is Alma, after the small river that flows into the blue mouth of the Black Sea.

The creativity class focuses mostly on color and observations, the journaling class on memory and ontology. Some of the students will read their thoughts on color aloud while the others nod and smile and say things like *oh, I love that* and *wow* and *sounds so pretty*. The classes are always calm, soothing islands in Vincent's day, no matter what else is happening. She can't even imagine what she would've done if the vibes had been off. Hopped on the first plane to anywhere else? Started crying and never stopped? Back in the summer, her mental state had a sort of supernatural fortification she felt like she couldn't take all the credit for, but that didn't mean she couldn't have been broken at any moment by the slightest thing. The transition from Kentucky to Paris had been preternaturally smooth and she was grateful for it.

She feels the ibuprofen and tea working slowly inside her, making her pain easier to bear. Most of the people in the classroom have their heads down, busily writing, sometimes stopping to look up and think, then return to the page. Vincent is watching Loup chew on the end of his pen and stare at the wall. He turns to look at her—two shared secret smiles.

It felt as if she'd been holding her breath until he walked into the classroom with his skateboard at the last minute. He winked at her. Winked! And she'd missed him (??) although it hadn't even been twenty-four hours since the last time they'd seen each other. She thought of him standing in her hallway. Of her in her bedroom, naked from the waist down. How he touched the top of her head and called her *Vincent Raphaela* in what has now become her favorite accent—*Loupish*.

Gray and ecru: the sky

Gray: pavement

Orange: a little boy's puffy jacket

Yellow: lemons on the kitchen counter

White and blue: Loup's Nikes

Black: Loup's jeans

Black: Loup's track jacket

Brown/black: Loup's hair

Green: Loup's skateboard deck

Cream: Loup's skateboard wheels

White: my phone

Black: the text of Tully's email reply

Red: the blood between my legs (also the blood Loup saw running down my legs yesterday)

Vincent is behind her small desk and when it's time, she asks if anyone wants to share their colors and observations. One middle-aged gentleman observes that his wife has worn white pajama pants and a blue shirt three days in a row, and this morning—she was wearing a white shirt with blue pajama pants. Vincent likes the man. He is white, an American, and his name is Jonathan; three months ago, he and his wife were living in Kyoto. A girl who rarely shares speaks up about the purple plums in the bowl by her kitchen sink and holds up a little clementine from her bag, proof of orange. Her name is Bunmi and she was born in Paris. Vincent adores her. She always wears winged eyeliner and either overalls or embroidered skirts. Once she wore a pair of yellow cowboy boots to class. Another woman mentions waking in *l'heure bleue*, the blue hour.

The assignment for the next class is for everyone to come back with a new list of observations, this time focusing on only one color: green.

As everyone is leaving, Loup stops at Vincent's desk. Ridiculous, her feelings. Dazing, this dual desire and disdain for his attention.

"Bonjour, Vincent," he says as Baptiste steps into the classroom. She *bonjours* Loup quickly and looks at Baptiste.

"Loup-dog, Veedubs," Baptiste says, smiling at them.

"Bap-muthafuckin-*tiste*" is Loup's response. The two of them do a complicated handshake that Vincent has seen only once before. Most often, the men turn into teenagers around each other.

"You heading out?" Baptiste says to him.

"*Ouais*," Loup says, lifting his chin.

He's holding his skateboard. His backpack slouches over his shoulder. Vincent wonders what else he has in there besides paints and brushes, pens and pencils, a sketchpad. He'd been quiet as the class discussed their colors. The Breton stripes of her shirt, *la marinière*? Blue as berries. Her jeans, a storm at sea. Her lipstick makes her mouth look like she's just eaten a cherry popsicle. Did those observations make it into his journal?

"All right, then. *À bientôt*," Baptiste says.

"*À bientôt*," Loup says back to him, and taps his shoulder.

Loup looks into Vincent's eyes. "Have a great weekend, Vincent. You look lovely, by the way. I'm glad you're feeling better," he says to her, and lifts his hand. Walks out.

"Thank you," Vincent says, but she doesn't know if he hears her.

She and Baptiste go across the street to the café in between classes. They talk politics and the Black Lives Matter march scheduled for Sunday evening. The Laurents already mentioned it to her. She pictures them putting on their vests after church.

"I'll go. Are you going? Is Agathe?" Vincent asks, and takes a big bite of her *pain au chocolat*.

His long legs are crossed and he is drinking his coffee. The soft light from the stubborn sun scatters through the clouds. Baptiste nods and tells her both Mina and Agathe are going too. He lets Vincent know where to meet them on Sunday and reminds her to bring her water bottle because last time she forgot.

"And yeah...Loup told me he slept on your couch," Baptiste says, putting his cup down and barely leaning forward.

"Wow. You've shown great restraint in waiting fifteen whole minutes before bringing *that* up."

"*Merci*," he says, laughing.

"When'd he tell you that?" Vincent asks, picking at her bread.

"Yesterday."

"Why didn't you invite him to the café with us today?" she asks, wondering where Loup is now, what he's doing. Soccer? A music thing? Probably something stylish, laughing and pushing his hair out of his face.

There's a gentle motor whirring between her thighs.

Baptiste sits back and takes his coffee cup with him. The café is crowded, the street too. Everyone walking past seems very busy and determined while the café patrons sit in the coolness, barely moving.

"Wednesday you were 'mad at me' for inviting him," Baptiste says, hooking his fingers for the quotes as best he can with his cup in his hand, "and now you're 'mad at me' for *not* inviting him," he finishes, finger-quoting again.

"He's got some... thing?" Vincent asks. *He's probably seen my* vagin, she doesn't say.

"He's helping Noémie move something. Have you met Noémie?"

"She's the girl in the band? Did you ever tell me he was in a band? Did you ever tell me he was Mina's cousin? I thought maybe he was *your* cousin." Vincent eats more of her bread, drinks more of her coffee. Baptiste pulls the pack of cigarettes from his pocket and offers her one that he lights before his own.

"I'm pretty sure I told you he was Mina's cousin. But you're... you're dreamy... I say things and you stare off while I'm talking... then later, you catch what I've said. You remember it somewhere back there," Baptiste says, tapping the back of his head. He's wearing his velvet blazer again and everything he just said is one hundred percent true.

Are some parts of her that easy to know?

"Yes, he slept on my couch. And he made me tea, so to you, we're practically married," Vincent says.

"You'll like Noémie. She's *interesting*," he says, smoking and looking over at a man walking past. Baptiste holds his hand up at him and the man waves back.

They finish their coffees and cigarettes and walk back to the museum together. Baptiste is talking but Vincent is being dreamy again, thinking about whether Baptiste knows her as well as he thinks he does. She's also wondering how *interesting* Loup thinks Noémie is, Tully's song still stuck in her head.

To: SiobhanSunshineHawke@gmail.com

From: VincentRaphaelaWilde@gmail.com

Subject: Dearest Siobhán

Hi. I'm Vincent. Thanks so much for telling Tully it was okay for me to write you. It would be completely understood if you didn't want to hear from me! This is all beyond bizarre and there's no easy way to start this! I'm going to dive right in.

When I heard about you, I left Cillian. I don't know what the future looks like for us. I'm sure Tully has told you everything. You and Tully did and do deserve so much more.

I was telling Tully how much he looks like my son, Colm. And well...you've read in the book about how much Cillian thinks you and I resemble each other. For what it's worth, I think you're beautiful. I mean, obviously!

From what I can find out on my own, you have a great, happy life!

I can't even say exactly why I'm compelled to reach out...you certainly don't owe me a response...but part of me would feel remiss for not doing what I can to mend a fracture.

And there's a fair bit of connection between the both of us being black women married to and having had children with white Irish men, although I'm American...I'm willing to bet we have a lot in common. It feels like it already and we've never even spoken.

I told Tully I'd love if we could all meet someday and I mean that. I love his music! I've been listening to it every day. So quiet and pretty.

I'm glad you reached out to Cillian when you read the book. I can't imagine that was an easy thing for you to do and I know he's glad too.

Please know I'm sending you nothing but love, from Paris.

As ever,
Vincent

To: TullyHawke@gmail.com
From: VincentRaphaelaWilde@gmail.com
Subject: Green

Tully,

Thank you for sending over your mom's email. I wrote her! Our families are forever connected... regardless of what we decide to do about it. Please do tell me your sister's name the next time you write! And please do tell me about the guitar shop! Sounds so cozy... a little guitar shop in Dublin. I like picturing Dublin on a rainy day... all the gray and green.

I made *green* the subject of this email because in the creativity class I teach, green is the color for the week. Each week we study one color. And by study I mean... observe. We discuss the green things we encounter, the green things from our memories. My journaling class focuses specifically on memory and, in a way, categorizing those memories. One of my favorite assignments is asking everyone to set a timer for ten minutes to write down every memory that comes to mind. The memories can be minuscule or hugely important. The goal is to simply write and write, not censoring or editing... and to consider everything. Nothing is off-limits. It can be very emotional for some people.

For my own side of the green memories assignment this time around, I wrote about the faded green T-shirt Cillian wore the one time we went to Dublin together. (So bizarre and sad to think we were ALL there in the same city, at the same time!) And the green of the pub sign that we walked under when we went out for fish-and-chips. Also, I have a green sweater I love... my best friend knitted it for me a couple Christmases ago.

Tell me about the green you see! I'll deffo keep you posted on what other colors we do, if you want to play along. I never really get tired or bored of hearing everyone's answers. They're all so varied and interesting. It's a lovely way to get to know someone, really... by listening to their color connections and memories.

My dad is Solomon Court. Soloco. He's an artist and he wrote a ton of songs in the late seventies, early eighties. A lot of trippy funk. I'll paste some links at the end of this!

I met a friend here in Paris who is a musician too. Electronic music.

I've listened to all three of your albums, by the way! Bought them instead of streaming! I've been letting them play while I make earrings. That's another job I have.

You're signed with an indie label? Are you working on a new album right now?

Glad we've started talking. Glad I was able to write your mom. Glad I know you're a man, so there's no confusion there, either! ☺

As ever,
Vincent

A week later, Vincent—in her wool and lace—and Agathe are walking to Le Marais for the Anchois show. Vincent hasn't seen Agathe since the Black Lives Matter march and she hasn't seen Loup outside of the museum. She's been busy baking clay and making jewelry while listening to Tully's songs and Tracy Chapman and Paul Simon and letting her ears nip away at a twenty-hour audiobook on the history of Paris. She's been curling up with Colette's novels, endless teapots. She's been slow-roasting tomatoes and cooking small dinners while listening to breathy, trumpet-heavy French music. She's been reading Susan Sontag's journals, underlining and highlighting the things that make her think. She's been letting French movies play quietly in her bedroom while she's sleeping, convinced it's helping her soak up more of the language. She's responded to all three of Cillian's texts and talked to both of their children. She's avoided looking directly at her naked drumming neighbor when she's heard him begin his routine.

Also, she's been emailing with Tully, which is something she hasn't mentioned to Cillian. She and Tully talk about music and Paris. They talk about music and Ireland. Tully was stoked and starstruck to find out that Soloco is her dad. Vincent talks about Colm and Olive. Tully doesn't ask many questions about Cillian, but he talks about his stepdad, Felix, and his mom. His sister's name is Blathnaid. He has a girlfriend named

Eimear, and he talks about her too. He sent Vincent a photo of them from last summer when they were in Vienna. Vincent congratulates herself again on how she'd been right about Tully when she thought he'd be as kind and funny and openhearted as Colm.

Agathe is stunning in a very French way—equal parts goddess-confident and laid-back. She reminds Vincent of Gustav Klimt's *Judith and the Head of Holofernes*. Agathe, just as dark-haired and defiant. Vincent thinks the fact that Agathe is always dating at least two people at the same time is fascinating. Freeing. There is a part (a big part) of Vincent that is *very* married and there is a part (a big part) of her heart locked inside that cage. But there is also a part (a small part) of her that has rattled loose. That part of her pulses on their walk to Le Marais and whishes through the curls of her hair. The whishing causes Vincent to stumble in her ankle boots. She accidentally knocks into Agathe and they both laugh.

"Are your legs wobbly from the Gideon 7000?" Agathe asks, touching Vincent's shoulder to stabilize her.

"What? Girl, no! I haven't even used it," Vincent says. The vibrator Agathe gifted her is still snug in its velvet box in the back corner of Vincent's top drawer.

"Well, what's the point in me gifting you a highly rated, expensive, *very* lovely vibrator if you're not going to use it to give yourself wobbly legs?" Agathe says, adding a bit in French. Vincent catches only some of it.

"You're *what* with me?"

"Disgusted," Agathe says. She takes her red-nailed finger and points to the right. They turn that way. "You wouldn't be so horny for Loup Henry if you'd let the Gideon 7000 do its proper job," she says. They step aside to let some faster-walking people get by. She touches Vincent's earring—a black buttercup the size of a bottle cap. She tucks some of Vincent's hair behind her ear.

"Horny for Loup Henry," Vincent says, a little annoyed but loving how it feels in her mouth, how it sounds melting against the bracing breezes of the Paris night. The day after the dinner party, she'd made the "mistake" of telling Agathe she was confused about her feelings for Loup, and every time they've talked since then, Agathe has brought him up.

"He's going to love this whole thing you have going on tonight. You look *so* pretty," Agathe says quickly, like she can't help it.

"*You* do." They tell each other this often.

Agathe points across the street to where they're headed. "Nighttime fun for everyone!" she says, taking Vincent's hand.

Earlier in the evening, Loup texted her for the first time since the day after he'd slept on her couch.

Are you coming?

Yes.

C'est bon bon bon.

She closed her eyes like she was spinning.

The club is packed, but Vincent spots Baptiste easily in the swooping lights, a head above the crowd. Earlier in the day they'd eaten their lunches together in the art museum courtyard, laughing and talking. She waves and he smiles at them, starts walking over. His wife, Mina, is next to him, drinking something clear—a lime bobs with the ice.

Mina is an ecotheologian, something Vincent had never heard of until she'd met Mina for the first time and heard her say it. "It means she loves God and nature and hates capitalism . . . and that we're not having children," Baptiste had said, with Mina nodding her head in agreement.

She works at the Jardin des Plantes and has a PhD in botany. Like Baptiste, Mina is erudite and unshy about it. She can be closed-lipped at times but cannot stay quiet once someone says something she doesn't like or agree with; then she will talk for ten minutes without letting anyone get a word in.

Vincent is convinced Mina doesn't like her very much, but thinks if their situations were swapped, Vincent wouldn't like Mina very much either. She's probably concerned with how much time Vincent and Baptiste spend together at the museum, their coffee and cigarette dates afterward. Vincent makes a point of telling Baptiste to invite Mina along to everything, but he says that while Mina isn't antisocial, she can't seem to make herself *care* about socializing. Vincent understands this and, because of that understanding, feels perfectly neutral about Mina most of the time. However, since Vincent is so aware of Mina's posh mien, she sees her name like that in her head: *Mien-a*. Or when Mina is being particularly stubborn about a point she wants to make, it's *Mean-a.*

Standing in a foursome clump by the bar, Baptiste and Agathe *salut* each other and ease into a short conversation, then Agathe pulls away from the group to order two drinks. Mina's wearing a satin bomber jacket over her stretchy green dress. When Vincent pays special attention to a color, it shows up everywhere. Mina wears a lot of green. The dress is pretty and Vincent tells her so.

"Thank you. It's the same green as your sweater, innit?" Mina says in her rounded British accent. Several years back, she and Baptiste lived in Highgate village in London, where Mina is from. Mina steps closer to Vincent. She smells softly of expensive floral and sandalwood perfume. She holds the flash of green fabric at her wrists against Vincent's sweater.

"It is," Vincent agrees, smiling at her.

"Have you been here before?" Mina asks. Baptiste is turned around, talking to someone Vincent can't see.

"No, but I walk over to Le Marais a lot for falafel. And Loup says he lives around here too?" Vincent says, adding a question mark as if she doesn't already know the answer.

"He does. Have you heard his band before?"

Mina rarely shows this much continued interest in her. Vincent considers Mina Harker from *Dracula* and wonders if Baptiste's Mina has telepathic powers like her namesake. Can Mina read her mind about Loup? Vincent diverts her thoughts for a moment, just in case.

"I haven't, but I'm ready for whatever awaits," Vincent says, picturing Colm and Olive there with her, the two of them giggling at their mother making awkward small talk in a hip Parisian club. Besides their group, everyone else in the club seems to be in their twenties, early thirties at most.

Agathe is back quick with the drinks and hands Vincent her gin and tonic. Mina gives Agathe a small, tight smile as the lights flash faster.

Vincent looks at her phone and sees a text from Cillian.

> It's nighttime there already. Good night
> Vin. x

She puts her phone away. The music pulsing, the strobes pleasantly disorienting—Vincent would like to get a little drunk and zone out.

"You will mike Loup first," Baptiste says, leaning down to Vincent's ear.

"What did you say?" She raises her voice over the noise.

"You will like Loup's shirt," he says more clearly.

Baptiste is drinking an Irish beer from a brown bottle and Vincent's life with Cillian feels every bit of the four thousand miles away. She watches Baptiste pick at the label. He's more reserved when Mina is around. He's nothing but lovely to Vincent and they still tease each other, but he's not as obvious about it. Instead, she gets a Lo-fi Baptiste, the same way Loup gets Chaotic-Energy Vincent most of the time.

"Why will I like his shirt? Do you know that sometimes you only talk to me about Loup? Nothing else. What do you get out of it?" Vincent says to him and takes a drink.

"You only hear what you want to hear," Baptiste says so earnestly, Vincent wonders if it's true. He's nodding aggressively at her. She laughs.

"Like *whose* shirt?" Agathe asks, popping her face between them.

"You'll see," Baptiste says, pointing his beer at the small stage in front of them.

A black guy and a white guy walk up the side steps one after the other and Vincent wonders which is Loup's roommate, Apollos, and which is Sam. Another black guy takes the stage and Vincent remembers Loup mentioning someone named Emiliano too, and she can't match any of them to their names until a girl with a thick bleach-blond braid over her shoulder follows them—Noémie. She is wearing a strip of lights around her head. Maybe that's what Baptiste meant when he said Noémie was interesting.

Next. Loup, smiling, walks onto the stage and looks out at the crowd. He raises both arms, crosses them, uncrosses them. When he's under the lights, Vincent can see he's wearing a loose, pale yellow T-shirt with Van Gogh's *Sunflowers* on it. Baptiste bends to say *ouais* in Vincent's ear and she feels like she's jumped from something high up and is still falling.

7

Cian never called Jack racist to his face until they were settled into their new home in California. At the dinner table, when his dad was talking about Dublin, the words came out before Cian could stop them.

"It wasn't the job or the Troubles... you only wanted us to leave Ireland because of Shalene... because she's black... because you're racist. You wouldn't have done it like this if she was white," Cian had said, putting his fork down. He was tired and lonely and homesick for Dublin. His mam, Aoife, left the roast simmering in the slow cooker all day along with carrots, onions, and potatoes. She made it because it was Cian's favorite meal and she wanted him to feel loved and comforted so far from home, but he had no appetite.

He'd grown up hearing his dad talk with disgust about white people and black people dating, marrying, and having children. None of that mattered when Cian looked at Shalene. What he saw was a really pretty girl who made him laugh. The girl he secretly kissed for the first time against the wet, white brick wall after school that rainy Thursday in September. They laughed after they bumped noses.

Cian wrote Shalene effusive letters and stories. Fairy tales he'd make up about the two of them fighting dragons together and living in Scottish castles with a menagerie of magical animals and secret gardens. They hung out after school at their houses when their parents weren't home. Most of the time they were careful, but sometimes they were as sloppy and reckless as Cian felt in his heart. All he thought about was Shalene, Shalene's mouth, Shalene's tongue, Shalene's ass, her breasts, the sweetness between her legs. He could barely be around her without wanting to be inside of her. And she was just as crazy for him.

One afternoon, everything happened so fast and neither of them did anything to stop it. He'd rolled off of her, bare and sticking to his thigh. Afterward, they kissed for ten minutes without stopping. They were wet with sweat in her bedroom with the window cracked open, too hot and steamed up to notice the October chill.

Once, Cian had asked his dad what he'd do if Cian wanted to bring a black girl home and his dad had told him never to ask him that again. Soon after, his dad found a picture of Shalene under Cian's pillow. Then, Shalene's parents told Jack they knew Shalene and Cian were sleeping together after her dad had come home from work early one day and caught them home alone. After that, their relationship got fuzzier and more complicated, so they took a break because they didn't know what else to do. And once her parents made her switch schools, the froth of Cian and Shalene's feelings for each other shook and settled, with no confident hearts to call home.

It wasn't until Cian was in California, eight thousand kilometers away from Dublin, that he'd learned Shalene was pregnant with his baby. Cian's dad had broken the California news the week after he ran into a visibly pregnant Shalene with her parents at the chipper across town. Seeing her was the final push for Jack to move his family away, but Jack didn't tell Cian about seeing Shalene and her parents until they were already in San Francisco.

"Your father—" his mam said quickly at the dinner table. Jack put his hand up, stopping her.

"You don't get to decide what I am or am not in this family," Jack said.

"I'm going to write her and let her know—" Cian started.

Jack, now red-faced, slammed his fist on the table. Aoife steadied the glass in front of her.

"You will not contact her or her family. You'll do as you're told. That's the

end of the discussion. Don't be ungrateful. I won't let you disrespect me in my own house," his dad warned.

Cian had grown up terrified of his dad's outbursts, the quickness with which he turned violent. After asking to be excused from the table, Cian went upstairs and wrote a letter to Shalene.

Shalene,

Hi. I miss you, I do. I don't know what happened with us. It was stupid how we both pulled away. Now I'm in California and you probably don't ever want to see or talk to me again. But I do think I love you and I've never been in love before. We're young, I know. And everything got all fucked up.

Why didn't you tell me what was going on? Why didn't I come find you?

If it's my baby, please write me back. PLEASE. It's something I want to know. I need to know. IF YOU LOVE ME TOO, PLEASE WRITE ME BACK. I didn't want to leave Ireland. I would've stayed if I could've.

Love,
Cian

Later that night he put it in their mailbox, leaving the flag down, knowing that the mailperson would see it and get it to Dublin anyway.

Cian was asleep when Jack came into his bedroom and stood over him.

"If you wanted to have sex with a black girl, that was your business. If you're dumb enough to get her pregnant, it becomes mine," his dad said quietly. Cian's eyes were half-open and he could hear the ceiling fan spinning in the dark, but the air remained still. Jack's face was shadow. Cian—awash in a blurry surfeit of discomfiting emotions—thought maybe he was dreaming.

* * *

The only thing his dad said about the small hole Cian punched in the wall was that it was Cian's job to patch it up.

Shalene never wrote back. Cian worried she was ashamed he was the father, that she didn't want anything to do with him. It was overcomplicated and too embarrassing for his fifteen-year-old brain to process, so Cian simply stopped trying.

It wasn't until his dad had passed away that his mam told him she'd checked the mailbox before the mailperson got it. That she tore up the letter and chucked it in the bin.

Vincent gets buzzed off one gin and tonic since she skipped dinner. She and Agathe step away from the stage and share a cup of green olives to recover, watching Anchois play another song. The people around them are dancing, some wildly jumping with their arms up. Agathe is telling Vincent some complicated art museum gossip loudly in her ear, taking breaks to pull back and look at her. Vincent watches Agathe's expressive, catlike face; she isn't much of a gossiper, so it must be important. Vincent listens but finds it hard to follow since she can only hear half of it anyway. Also, because she's hyperfocused on Loup.

His hair falls in his face and he lets it stay there as he nods behind the keyboard and the blinking electronic boxes he told Vincent about. The music is a mix of bells and beeps and deep bass—like sex on a spaceship and heavy things dropped into water. Vincent likes it because it's not anything she would typically listen to. It makes her feel even farther away from home and the parts of her life she wants to forget. Like how she has no real idea how she will feel from one day to the next, so knowing how she'll feel upon seeing Cillian in person in New York for Colm's summer wedding is impossible.

She misses her husband, but the husband she misses is the one from before, and Before Cillian doesn't exist. She's always having to re-realize it's *him*—that phantom of a man—she is grieving as their marriage melts like a popsicle.

Moving up to the front with Agathe, Vincent can feel the bass in her mouth, the backs of her ears. Baptiste is standing off to the side because he's so tall. Mina is in front of Vincent and Agathe, letting her head slowly bop from left to right. When Colm and Olive were small, Vincent bought them a little yellow plastic toy flower that did the same thing whenever you put it in the sun. When Mina turns around to smile at Vincent, she smiles back.

The song ends and everyone claps and whoops. Loup crouches to adjust a pedal underneath his setup. Vincent gets on her tiptoes and sees he's wearing his Nikes. She pictures them kicked off on the floor next to her door. She's tried to put the sunflower shirt out of her mind for fear it will send her spiraling, but there it is, glowing under the spotlight. Loup straightens and one of the guys says "*Un, deux, trois, quatre*," and a new song starts.

Mina turns around. "I love this one. Noémie's going to sing. She has a *really* pretty voice," she says.

"Oh yeah? That's awesome. Cool. *Chouette*," Vincent says, regretting the fact that she sounds like a stoned fourteen-year-old boy.

This new song is softer and sleepy. After a few minutes of only instruments, Noémie begins singing into the microphone. Vincent can't make out every word, but Noémie's voice is pleasant and light. French lyrics. Something about *l'oiseau bleu*, "blue bird." The song is a dulcet mix of her vocals over the ethereal mysteriousness of the music. Now the strip of light around Noémie's head is flashing in rhythm with the music. Vincent thinks that maybe Olive and Noémie could be friends; they look around the same age. Something that feels like both tenderness and melancholia peeks from behind a cloud in Vincent's heart when she thinks about the fact that everyone on that stage is young enough to be her child.

The people surrounding them dance lazily, close together in the dark. Mina sways to the music. When the song ends, Baptiste comes over. Both Vincent and Agathe have stopped drinking and when Agathe steps away to take a phone call, Vincent is left alone with Baptiste and Mina. It's fine, although Vincent certainly prefers not being their third wheel. For something to do, she pulls her phone out of her bag and looks at Cillian's text again.

She writes him back.

Good night, Cillian.

It would make him feel better, but Vincent can't bring herself to add a heart emoji. She puts her phone away and looks up at Loup, knowing he cannot see her. The stage lights are too bright. As she is thinking this, he holds up his hand to shield his eyes. He scans the audience, and next to her, Baptiste raises two fingers in a peace sign. Loup smiles at him and does a peace sign too, then somehow in the darkness he finds Vincent's eyes and looks into them, or she thinks he does. Either way, he smiles. A new song starts. Loup hasn't sung or put his mouth to the microphone, but now he adjusts it and begins humming while one of the other guys plays a keyboard. Noémie, behind a keyboard of her own, plays a kazoo.

It takes an entire song for Agathe to reappear and after that, Anchois plays one more before they say *merci* and leave the stage.

After the show they all stand outside by the back door, waiting for Loup. The sign above the exit glows red, washing them in a grenadine, heart-beaty light. The others are discussing American politics and Vincent doesn't join in because she's in Paris and doesn't want to talk about American politics. It's nice, this distance. And Mina—the only one with the performative air of asceticism—is also the only one of them who is *actually* drunk, not buzzed. Her voice has gotten louder and when she takes a break from talking, she touches Baptiste's shoulder twice in the same spot and squeezes. Baptiste laughs and excitedly begins relating something Mina said to either fauvism or fascism when Loup pushes the door open. His hair falls in his face and the wind blows it back almost in slow motion, like they're in a movie. Like THE DREAMBOAT will slide across the bottom of the screen in capital letters as "Killing Me Softly with His Song" whispers through the air.

Upon seeing Vincent, he puts his arms around her and hugs tight. It took three months, but this is their first hug. Vincent, rhapsodic, blinks back a small start of tears.

"So glad you're here. *C'est bon bon bon*," he says, nodding into her hair.

When he pulls away he does his complicated handshake with Baptiste and kisses Mina's cheeks, Agathe's too. He thanks them for coming. Baptiste says something in French that Vincent doesn't understand; Loup responds in English. It's endearing and intimate how most often, they speak a lot of Franglais to each other when they're around her, how they let her in. Vincent catches the French words for *recording* and *brand-new*. The sound of one of the words reminds her of Loup's shirt and the French for sunflower: *le tournesol*. Turned sun.

"I really enjoyed it. I loved the songs... your little electronic boxes and the vocals," Vincent says, looking at him. Noémie is standing over Loup's shoulder, talking and laughing with the boys in the band. Vincent could only see Noémie in profile when she was on the stage. Vincent would like to see her face full-on to gauge how she thinks Loup feels about Noémie, but she doesn't turn around.

"*Merci*," he says, bowing his head. "And! Dig the shirt," he says, holding the hem of it out to make sure she can see it clearly.

The deep red light of the sign makes the shirt and sunflowers look more orange than yellow, and the wind ripples the fabric. Loup is wearing a pair of faded black jeans with it and his chain necklace. Now that he's shown Vincent his shirt, he zips his black track jacket all the way up, just how she likes it. He gets an elastic band from his pocket, knots his hair back in a little loose twist. Vincent has never seen it like that, never seen his naked face without the frame of his hair. Rarely seen the unabashed gloriousness of his little mountain of a nose with no curls of distraction ready to fall across it.

EXT. LE MARAIS – NIGHT

Vincent is quite transfixed with Loup. She can't take her eyes off him.

NARRATOR (V.O.)

In that moment, Vincent's body is filled with warm, melting starlight.

"I like it," she says, mostly about his shirt, but also about everything that is happening.

"Oh! Vincent van Gogh . . . I get it. You wore it because you knew she was coming. That's sweet," Mina says, pointing at her cousin, sliding her finger in the air from his collarbone to where the now hidden shirt stops under his jacket.

"It *is* sweet, *very*," Baptiste teases. He lets them know he and Mina are leaving.

"But it's so early," Agathe says, looking up at Baptiste.

Mina glances at her phone to check the time. "It's not early," she says without emotion.

"Well . . . it's relative, I guess," Agathe says. She and Mina shrug in synchronicity, though they do not agree.

"Are you leaving too?" Loup asks Vincent.

"I—" she begins, looking at Agathe.

"I've got options tonight. There's another thing . . . with other people . . . listen, you're good. Enjoy! *C'est une nuit magnifique*," Agathe says. She tells them specifics about the other hot spot she's heading to, claiming the night is still young.

Vincent thinks of the French word for young. *Jeune*. How she used to get it mixed up with the Spanish, *joven*. How long will she feel young? *Jeune. Joven*.

Agathe hugs Vincent and they kiss goodbye. Baptiste and Mina say their goodbyes to everyone too.

"Would you like to go for a walk?" Loup asks her. *Très jeune*. She nods. One of the guys from the band and another new guy are loading up a fat, bumper-stickered orange van with keyboards, wires, and equipment. "I usually help, but I won a bet. Emiliano lost," he says close to her ear.

"What was the bet?" Vincent asks, turning to him. She notes that the shorter white guy is Emiliano, leaving the black guys as Apollos and Sam.

"Ah... I'll tell you later. Let's get out of here," Loup says.

He lets his band members know he's leaving but doesn't introduce any of them to Vincent, and she doesn't know how she feels about that. But she knows how she feels when they're walking away, when Loup puts his hand on the small of her back as they turn the corner. Under autumn stars and Nabokov's arabesques of light, she feels *sauvage*.

They saunter slowly toward the Seine.

8

Luster of yellow-white lights on water. Vincent and Loup sit and smoke and talk, letting their feet dangle. Their knees are almost touching, but Vincent is making a deliberate effort to keep space between them. The air is soft and cool; Vincent left her scarf at home.

"It really doesn't bother you that I'm old enough to be your mother?" she asks.

"Pfff. When I first saw you, I thought you were maybe ten years older, tops. You look very young...you know that. You have mirrors. Also, you're the only one thinking that way. I'm certainly not thinking about it," he says, smirking.

She has some gray hair but not a lot, and she actually likes it. When she wears her hair down, it's mostly hidden; only a bit of silver flicks through the black. She doesn't bother with dyeing it anymore and loves thinking about it all going white one day.

"If you say *black don't crack* I'll put this cigarette out on your forehead."

"*Comment?* What does that mean...*black don't crack*?" Loup asks, shaking his head at her and sounding *so* French it makes her smile.

"Oh, right... Yeah, never mind... it's stupid. What time is it? I never know what time it is when I'm with you," she says, pulling her phone out of her bag. She feels floaty and free, like a teenager again. It's late and everything surrounding them is painfully pretty. How do Parisians get anything done? How are they not all just wandering around, mouths agape in wide-eyed wonder?

"Good. You're complimenting me again. And again, I'll take it," Loup says. "It's Friday night. Who cares what time it is? Not me."

"It's actually Saturday now." She holds her phone so he can see the time, so close to his face he squints in the light.

"Brilliant. Even better," he says.

Vincent's phone vibrates with the screen turned toward him—a little earthquake in her hand.

"Looks like you've got a text from someone called Cillian," Loup says before she can turn it around. Vincent, dizzied, looks at the message.

I love you, Vin. Talk soon?

"Oh . . . it's—"

"Hey, it's not my business. I mean, unless you have some jealous husband who would be interested in killing me for keeping his wife out so late?" Loup says, smiling the sort of smile that usually leads into a full-blown laugh, but he pauses it there and finishes his cigarette. He pats her thigh and puts his hand flat on the concrete.

"I don't . . . have one of *those*, no," Vincent says.

It's dinnertime in Kentucky. She wonders what Cillian is doing for it back home. He hates to cook. He's probably been getting takeout every night or eating cheese toasties and frozen pizzas.

"But I do have . . . well . . . we're separated. And he's in Kentucky and I'm sitting here smoking on the Seine with a twenty-four-year-old," she says, putting her cigarette out as easily as her teenage-dream feelings were extinguished by Cillian's text.

Loup is the first Paris person she's told that she and Cillian are *separated* instead of using the word *ex*. She lets her knee rest against Loup's for the first time and it feels as important as the moon landing.

"Separated," he echoes, looking out at the water. A passel of young men walks behind them talking and laughing. A Bateau-Mouche bobs on the other side of the river. The Eiffel Tower, in the distance, shimmers and stabs the night.

"Cillian and I have been together for like, twenty-five years. Since around when you were born, actually," Vincent says, putting her head on his shoulder. It feels as important as discovering the double helix.

"Wow. Well, that's a looong time. I'm quite old, you see," he says.

"Agreed. It is a long time." She gently pushes herself against him. "And it's weird because I don't feel the way I thought I'd feel here, and up until this point in my life, I've had a fairly strong grasp of who I am and how I respond to things. I would've guessed that I'd feel lost or depressed being in Paris on my own, but I don't. I feel good. I learned something new about myself because I didn't know I could feel like this . . . so far away from everything else in my life. Surprise!"

"Ah. Well, I love all of that and I'm glad to hear it. I'm *very* glad you're here. It's relaxing, listening to you explain things. Also, your hair smells good. Definitely not *une surprise*, though. I could've guessed it," Loup says.

"Merci beaucoup."

Some quiet.

"You're more than welcome at my place. Do you need to get back home now?" he asks.

Vincent nods. The fabric of his track jacket is worn and warm, even in the chill, catching her tears of relief. To be in Paris. To be on her own.

"Can I walk you?"

Vincent closes her eyes and nods again.

On the way to her apartment, Loup points out his favorite spots—the waxed curbs and stone of the fountain where he and his friends skateboard, the place he got his favorite vintage Casio synthesizer. And as they pass one bakery and discuss the French bread law, he takes her on a detour up place Sainte-Opportune to show her the boulangerie where his sister works.

"What's her name?"

"Lisette. She's twenty-one," he says.

Twentytwentytwenty. Vincent knows nothing about numerology, but the world *has* been shouting twenties lately. *Twenty-five. Twenty-four. Twenty-one.* Loup and Lisette are the same ages as Colm and Olive and, like Colm, Loup was born first. Vincent thinks of Loup's mother out on a romantic nighttime walk with Colm and feels an oblique, softened version of jealousy. Like it's set under a pillow or drowned out by noise.

"Loup and Lisette... that's lovely. So pleasing to hear and say," she says. "Do you get along?"

"Pretty much. She never fails to call me out on my shit, though," Loup says with a voice full of *ha*.

A hand-holding couple is walking down the sidewalk and Vincent and Loup decide to split, letting them pass between. In a move she finds endearingly eager and laddish, Loup lifts himself onto a low ledge and exuberantly hops back down, landing next to her. She wants to squeal, but instead she locks arms with him and they stay that way until they're in front of her place.

"This is when you go home and I go inside," Vincent says, thumbing toward her building.

"Understood. But first I have a question," he says. When she stays quiet, he continues, "Do you want to see something?"

"Sure," she says, adjusting her bag and knotting the belt of her trench coat.

Loup leans over and does a handstand, walking away from Vincent and back toward her, jingling. His jacket and shirt slip up, revealing his tummy and the dark downy line disappearing into his jeans. He pushes at the ground and puts his feet down again.

Vincent claps and tells him that with the fruit juggling and the handstands, he's certainly missed his circus calling.

"I can't kiss you or come in... so it feels like I have to do *something* with this energy or I'll explode," he says.

"Oh, please," she says, but what she means is *FUCK*. Not knowing what else to do, she hugs him. When she pulls away, while they are still close, she puts her hand on the side of his face. "So... you're a bottle rocket?" she asks. *I'm a bottle rocket too, just watch. Just wait.*

"If you say so."

"Is that the same energy you had when you said *unfortunately* you didn't see my *vagin*?"

"Absolutely. It was one of the most unfortunate moments of my life," Loup says, nodding. "You were holding blankets. I hated those blankets!"

"You'll tell me more about your bet with Emiliano later?" she asks him when they finish laughing.

"Yes. And you'll tell me more about Cillian later... maybe, only if you want to?"

Cillian.

Not Cillian.

Loup.

Loup, I can't kiss you.

But, can't I kiss you?

Can't you kiss me?

Can't we do whatever the hell we want?

"You really want to kiss me? Even though we have a lot to sort out?" she asks, with his earlobe between her finger and thumb, looking into his eyes like she can climb inside.

Loup whispers something in French and ends with "*Bonne nuit*, Vincent." He pulls her close and hugs her again. Takes her hand and holds it out for a second before letting go.

"*Bonne nuit*," she says. He turns.

She watches him walk away from her. Waits for him to turn around. He does. Then he takes off across the street in a slow jog, slipping between two people walking opposite directions—hieroglyphics in the dark.

In the rosy-gold warmth and half-light of her apartment, Vincent hangs her coat by the door and enters his whispered words into Google Translate just to see them, even though she's absolutely sure she heard them right.

My only desire.

Junior year of high school, Cian started a literary journal and called it FOCAL, *the Irish word for* word. *The school had a literary journal years before, but they'd ditched it. Cian was energized for the revamp and got along well with the teachers. The same teachers whose classrooms and supplies he needed to use. He spent long hours working on it after school.*

Cian's father stayed busy; Cian would go days without laying eyes on him. And his mam was preoccupied as well—church and neighborhood association meetings and his dad's work events.

Without knowing exactly how, most days, if he stayed distracted enough, Cian was able to put Shalene out of his mind. He'd written her and she'd never responded. He was too embarrassed to try to call her. Plus, she was probably all wrapped up with the baby. Her baby. Their baby. Maybe. His mind reeled thinking that maybe something awful had happened to Shalene or the baby. Maybe one of them had died. How would he know? His friends from Dublin, the ones he still talked to, they didn't know Shalene. He couldn't ask them. Even if they happened to hear about something awful befalling a girl their age, they wouldn't be able to make the connection.

Cian envisioned himself going back to Dublin after graduating high school and trying to find her. Maybe he'd see her walking along with a toddler on her hip. A boy with his hair. Or a girl with his eyes. Often, when he couldn't sleep, he'd lie in his bedroom in that big glass cliff house on the water and think about it.

Jack made good money at the tech company. Cian didn't want for anything and it was easy to make friends because of it. The Woodses' home became a proper hangout after school and on weekends, especially when his parents were busy or out of town. One weekend over Christmas break, with his parents gone for four days, Cian and his friends threw a rager. Girls he didn't know were doing lines of coke off the side of his mam's bathtub upstairs; guys he'd only met in passing pushed into keg stands on the deck.

There were loads of people in the kitchen, some he recognized, some he didn't.

One girl, Emma, the daughter of his English teacher, stood in the refrigerator light.

"Hey, Cian. Do you care if I make a grilled cheese? I'm not drinking. I

promised them I'd be their designated driver," she said, pointing at the girls in flannel across the kitchen. "And I really want a grilled cheese."

"You can stay, if ya want. Most people are staying over. And yes, absolutely you can have a grilled cheese. My mam has a whole drawer of expensive cheese down there. Use whatever you'd like," Cian said.

He liked Emma; she was pretty and nice. She wore oversize sweaters and ripped jeans, a pair of floral Dr. Martens. They had one class together: Photography. The first day they met, their teacher paired them up to interview each other and Emma told him about her favorite band, Nirvana. She pulled a cassette of Bleach *out of her backpack, said she'd make a copy for him, and gave it to him the next day.*

"Oh, thanks, but it's fine. We won't crash here. You're off the hook. This place is amazing, though... you literally *live in a glass house," she said. "Aha, found it!" She held up a new block of Cheddar and closed the fridge.*

Cian opened it back up to retrieve the butter and went into the pantry for the bread. Together, they made a path to the counter. Someone had turned up "Poison" by Bell Biv DeVoe in the living room and the kitchen cleared out a bit.

"What's that?" Emma pointed at the toastie machine.

"Americans have a lot to learn about toasties," Cian said, assembling her sandwich. He explained what it was and how he liked making grilled cheese in a toastie machine more than he did in a pan. He said it was basically the only thing he could make on his own as he wiped the edge of the butter knife against the foil wrapper.

"Your accent... do people always want to talk to you about it? I love it. Say my name," Emma said.

"Your name is Emma. Emma Sharp," Cian said, smiling over at her.

"I love it. I could listen to you talk all day. My dad says you're a really good writer. You're one of his favorites."

"He's one of my favorites too."

"Can I read some of your stuff sometime?"

"That's embarrassing, right?" Cian said, laughing. He put her sandwich in the toastie machine and turned around to look at her.

"It doesn't have to be," Emma said, shrugging. "Soon enough I'll be able to read it in FOCAL *anyway."*

The first issue was set to publish after the new year. Emma's dad was the main teacher involved; it was his classroom that Cian stayed in most often after school. Mr. Sharp was hip and cool, so unlike the nebbishy English teacher he'd had the year before.

"I'm actually not going to have a piece in the first issue... I thought that'd be weird since I'm the editor," Cian said.

He leaned against the counter the toastie machine sat on and could feel the heat pressing at his back.

"Oh... well, the next one, right? But you should give me a sneak peek."

"Show me more of your pictures so I can use some of them for the literary magazine and I'll show you what I'm working on," Cian said. In class, he'd seen her with a thick journal filled with black-and-white photographs. "That, plus this cheese toastie, equals a deal."

"Deal," Emma said, holding out her hand for him to shake, and he did.

When she asked to see his bedroom, he took her up there. He'd never forget how "It Must Have Been Love" by Roxette was playing from the stereo underneath them in the living room. How he could hear the swelling strings and thumping bass as he watched Emma eat the toastie he'd made for her and wander around his bedroom touching things. She talked and wiped her mouth and looked at the pictures on his wall, getting close. He lay back on his bed, not knowing why the whole thing made him so emotional.

Later that night, in the dark hallway corner outside his bedroom, they kissed for the first time to a rowdy choir of partygoers downstairs scream-singing the chorus to "Africa" by Toto. And it was really fucked up that he thought about how much his dad would like her.

Emma was white; Emma wasn't Shalene.

How big would Emma's eyes get if he told her that he had a kid in Ireland? That he didn't even know if it was a boy or a girl?

When Pica asked about his first girlfriend, he didn't tell her about Shalene. He told her about Emma Sharp.

9

Saturday morning, Vincent is in her white nightgown and fuzzy cardigan, drinking hot chocolate and eating blackberries from a teacup. She texts Agathe:

WOULD YOU BE PLEASED TO KNOW I NOW HAVE WOBBLY LEGS???

Agathe writes back.

THIS IS THE GREATEST TEXT I'VE EVER GOTTEN FROM YOU.

I should probably be offended. I always write v good texts!!

Agreed, but this particular one is AMAZING. If you spent the night with Gideon 7000, I'm assuming you went home... alone?

Basically. Did you have fun?

I did! Got home at a decent hour too.
And what of our Loup, pray tell?

Disappeared into the night.

Although I am admittedly jealous, he's VERY cute. Reminds me of that actor all the little girls like.

Who?

Timothée... Something.

Timothée Chalamet. Right. Same-ish hair and dreaminess, sure.

And like you could forget they look around the same age! Totally different nose though. Also, Loup's ass is phenomenal. Bite it for me once you get the chance, promise?

Wow, I'm a Nose Person and Loup's nose is a problem because I'm OBSESSED with it.
Also... COMPLETELY IGNORING THAT ASS-BITING COMMENT FOR NOW BUT...?? Wait, you're jealous of what?

Of how much you like him! Your demeanor changes completely whenever he's around.

It does?

Oui! You get testy, but also . . . you have this sexually frustrated glow. It's annoying!!!

I've never heard of a sexually frustrated glow, thank you Agathe! :P

You're not as mystérieuse as you think you are! :P What are you doing today?

You tell me, since I'm not mysterious!

I'd guess you're probably filling jewelry orders? Maybe later you'll go for a walk?

Exactly what I'm doing. Are you some sort of witch??

I wish. I just know you, that's all. I'm at the museum for the rest of the day, so talk to me later. Stay wobbly!!! x

Bless your heart, I love you. xo

I love you too.

Vincent finishes her breakfast and gets texts from Loup with a link to a song: "Pour un flirt avec toi" by Jane Birkin and Christophe Miossec. *For a flirt with you.*

Good morning, Vincent. Listen to this.
Tell me what you think?

The electronic stutters
especially...can express what the
words cannot.

I dare you to send me a song you think
I should listen to.

Football in the park now. Putting my
phone away for a bit but let me know
what you're up to later?

Vincent tells herself she'll listen to the song once she is ready, once she can't stand waiting a moment longer. She puts on her black linen overalls and goes into the studio, uses the crystal knobs to push the windows open. A light drizzle vamps the glass.

For a flirt with you.

She'd opened her online shop ten years ago. She only brought the bare minimum of her art supplies with her when she moved to Paris; Aurora had so much already. There is a shelf of rainbow-painted tin cans on the wall above the table where the clay oven sits, all of them neatly filled with brushes and tools—wire cutters, pins, jump rings, earring hooks, scissors. Not long after arriving in Paris, Vincent went shopping and loaded up on boxes of polymer and terra-cotta clay, glazes, more acrylic and oil paints. A pasta maker for smoothing clay. Parchment paper, a rolling pin. She ordered the same molds and cookie and clay cutters online that she uses back home.

For a flirt with you.

* * *

Vincent's Saturday mornings are reserved for filling orders. Today she has around fifty to ship out. Then she needs to sand and buff a few pieces and get a batch of terra-cotta beads and pendants in the clay oven.

For a flirt with you.

While those are baking, she prints out the labels for the envelopes and clicks the little corresponding boxes on her online shop interface, so the customers will know their packages are on the way. They will be, when afternoon rolls around and Vincent takes them over to the post office by the Louvre like she does every Saturday. They've come to expect her swooping in wearing her overalls, her hair piled messily atop her head. "*Going Wilde again*," one of the older gentlemen occasionally says to her after *bonjours*, which never fails to brighten her day.

For a flirt with you.

Vincent in the Studio: Playlist #1

"Brave" by Sara Bareilles
"Countdown" by Beyoncé
"Burn" by Ellie Goulding
"Cherry Bomb" by the Runaways
"Video" by India.Arie
"Give Me One Reason" by Tracy Chapman
"Wonder" by Natalie Merchant
"Seether" by Veruca Salt
"Savage" by Megan Thee Stallion
"Blank Space" by Taylor Swift
"L.E.S. Artistes" by Santigold
"Cobrastyle" by Robyn
"Just Like a Pill" by P!nk
"Hold On, Hold On" by Neko Case
"I Try" by Macy Gray
"Believe" by Cher
"Does Your Mother Know?" by ABBA

"Criminal" by Fiona Apple
"What Kind of Man" by Florence + the Machine
"Running up That Hill" by Kate Bush

Vincent hasn't turned any music on yet. It's usually the first thing she does. The only sounds are coming through the window. A hush of catchy cars and voices. Flitting ribbons of birdsong. The *plung* of a church bell and a ball—*boingboingboing*.

For a flirt with you. For a flirt with you.

Although it's nearly impossible to concentrate, Vincent digs in and gets twenty-five pairs of earrings ready to ship. Half of her orders. The Jane Birkin song she's never heard is haunting her and she wonders if her life is about to change.

She can't stand it any longer.

She lies on her back, turns on the song. Puts her phone on her stomach, closes her eyes. She imagines Loup in his short shorts playing soccer in slow motion—his coltish body, lustrous with cool mist.

Vincent in the Studio: Playlist #2 (Version Loup)

"Pour un flirt avec toi" by Jane Birkin and Christophe Miossec
"Pour un flirt avec toi" by Jane Birkin and Christophe Miossec
"Pour un flirt avec toi" by Jane Birkin and Christophe Miossec
"Pour un flirt avec toi" by Jane Birkin and Christophe Miossec
"Pour un flirt avec toi" by Jane Birkin and Christophe Miossec
"Pour un flirt avec toi" by Jane Birkin and Christophe Miossec

"Pour un flirt avec toi" by Jane Birkin and Christophe Miossec
"Pour un flirt avec toi" by Jane Birkin and Christophe Miossec
"Pour un flirt avec toi" by Jane Birkin and Christophe Miossec
"Pour un flirt avec toi" by Jane Birkin and Christophe Miossec

When Vincent can get up off the floor, she dizzily texts Loup, knowing it will be a while until he sees it.

I love the song. Thank you for sending it.
What I think: I listened to it ten times in a row, unable to get off the floor.
Later, I am making creamy farfalle and peas and going for a walk. Will you be hungry?
Here is one for you. X

She sends him "Flower" by Liz Phair, thinking of the despair Cillian would feel if he knew she was sending a twenty-four-year-old a song they used to listen to together, but it was the first song Vincent thought of that expresses *exactly* how she's feeling. She pressed *Send* before she could be embarrassed by the lasciviousness of it all. It's something she'd never do unprompted and it's something she'd never do stateside, but Loup. And this is Paris and the sun has peeked out from behind the gray. Is that a rainbow? And yes, in "Flower," Liz Phair crudely sings about wanting to fuck a guy and yes, Vincent (crudely) wants to (crudely) fuck Loup. Her brain and heart can attempt to jump around it, but that's where it (her *vagin*) always lands.

LOUPLOUPLOUPLOUPLOUPLOUPLOUPLOUPLOUPLOUP.

Cillian had his secrets and kept them and kept them and kept them even though Vincent worked hard never to keep anything from him; things that revealed even the parts of her she didn't particularly like or want to admit, she told him, and sure, maybe he told her things too, they've been married for twenty-four years, but he hadn't told her the absolutely biggest most important thing that he should've told her and no he hadn't cheated on her but there are things besides adultery that can rip a marriage apart and she hasn't been touched by a man she's wanted to touch her in months and last night she pulled the Gideon 7000 out of its box and used it, thinking of Loup, thinking only of Loup, thinking only of Loup and feeling guilty in a way that made her want to do it again and again because it made her feel *alive* and not like she was wasting her life just waiting for someone else to tell her their secrets because she was forty-four and could keep her own secrets and make her life whatever she wanted it to be instead of waiting and waiting and waiting and waiting and waiting and waiting and waiting and waiting and waiting and waiting and right now? right now she wants Loup Henry to listen to "Flower" by Liz Phair and she wants him to get so horny listening to it, thinking of her, thinking of her thinking of him, she wants him to get so horny listening to it that he worries he may come before he can peel those drippy peach short shorts off.

Vincent finishes filling the rest of the orders and walks to the post office with a full bag of packages. When she gets back to the apartment, there is a bouquet of purple irises from Cillian and a letter from him too—paper-bag brown envelope, wine-dark wax seal. Postmarked ten days ago. She opens it once she's inside.

My dearest Vincent,

Letters worked for Mr. Darcy and Captain Wentworth, among many others, so who am I not to try? I become downright frowsy in the evenings without you, walking our hallway in these pajama pants you gave me last Christmas and the Barack Obama T-shirt we got from donating to his campaign back in 2008. During the day, I can pull myself together a bit, but that's only for show... for work. This big, empty house? Apocalyptic, being here without you. And it feels like death, knowing this is all my fault.

To tell you that I don't know what came over me would do no good, I realize, but it's true.

I knew I had a hit. I knew my agent could sell this book for a lot of money if I wrote it. And I knew that by writing it, I would tear our family apart. It felt a little too "deal with the devil"-ish and still sounds that way.

At the very least, I should've told you to your face beforehand, even if I'd decided to carry on.

I'm not saying anything new here and I fear as a real man, I've strayed impossibly away from the gallant, fictional gentlemen I mentioned in the first line of this letter.

I just want you to know that I think of you constantly. I send you flowers every Saturday as I imagine you in Paris with the wind in your hair. I imagine you there with the sea-green stone turtles in the fountain. I think about the time we went to the Jardin Marco Polo together when the kids were little and sat under the trees reading and eating cheese and strawberries. How radiant you were in the dappled sunlight... a bright star, like a Keats poem... how the grass made a crisscross pattern on your upper thighs... how you were wearing that thin white dress I love so much. That dress I loved to take off you. I imagine you in that gauzy white dress in that green-green grass in that lush garden and I can only just pray that one day, somehow you can find your way back home to me.

I really am half agony, half hope.
Vin, please?
I've loved you for so long. I love you. I will always love you.

x
Your Cillian

She pictures him out for a run or grading papers in his office at home and texts him.

I just got your letter. Thank you for it and the irises. They're purple as moonlight.

We can set a time to talk again in a weekish. Ok?

He responds quickly.

Grand. Holding my breath until then, love.

Even after what he's done, Cillian's written words find a way to her heart. She feels swoony when he calls her *love*. He's always called her that. Him calling her that feels unfair. Like a cheat code trigger to all the positive emotions she has about him, casting the negative ones into the darkness, if only for a moment. And maybe she'd like to spend some more time sorting out how she feels about it, but wow, there are also new texts from Loup.

I am speechless and . . . unabashedly begging at this point.

Putting away my phone again to finish
the match, but I can come over soon?
Walk with you tonight?

I am considering heading to your door
on my hands, Vincent.

Vincent's tears don't surprise her. She knows her complicated feelings are oil and water, but this is Paris, which allows them the magic of mixing.

An emotional hangover from Cillian's letter? Yes.

Unhinged with lust for Loup? Absolutely.

She puts more terra-cotta in the oven and goes to her bedroom to lie down. What else can be done?

Months after the Christmas break party, Cian and Emma were high school happy together as a couple and Cian was right: His dad loved her. His mam loved her too. Emma's dad, Mr. Sharp, seemed okay with their relationship most of the time. Cian was Emma's first boyfriend, and he half worried that Mr. Sharp was having a hard time knowing Cian touched tongues with his daughter.

Emma joined the FOCAL *staff and Cian talked her into doing the photography for it. They spent several days a week after school in her dad's classroom, reading submissions and formatting the literary magazine. Sometimes her dad would order pizza and two liters of neon-colored caffeinated soda for them. And on the days there weren't* FOCAL *things to do, Cian and Emma would go back to either one of their parentless homes and kiss until they were tuckered out.*

Cian's mam, Aoife, seemed a different person when his dad wasn't around. With Jack, she was sometimes submissive and quiet. When it was just her and Cian, she was much more open and cheerful. Cian knew she swapped her personality because she thought it was what his dad wanted—a milder, ersatz version of herself to temper his bristliness.

One day after school, when Emma had come over for a few hours and left, Cian and Aoife were in the kitchen making dinner together. She got him to chop tomatoes for the salad while she fried steaks in a cast-iron skillet.

"Cian, I'm going to ask you a question that may embarrass you, but I'm asking it anyway," Aoife said, turning and taking a sip of dark wine. Her oenophilia, appeased.

"Mam—"

"Are you being careful with Emma? Not only sex, but with her heart? With Shalene, I know it was different..."

"We haven't had sex," Cian said.

It was the truth. He and Emma fooled around, sure, sometimes a lot. But the thought of putting himself in a position where he could potentially get a girl pregnant wasn't something he was interested in. There were nights when he dreamed about having sex with Emma and as soon as he rolled off, she was nine months pregnant. Times when he dreamed Shalene was in the room with them, rocking a baby and watching him move inside of Emma. Shalene would alternately smile and frown the whole time, shaking her head.

"When your dad isn't around, we can talk about whatever you want. He's... not as willing to discuss things as I am. And I want you to know I always liked Shalene. She seemed like a sweet little girl. Very pretty. I'm sure boys were falling all over her. She's so unique... and I'm not saying that just because she's black. I know you think your dad and I are horrible Catholics and virulent racists," Aoife said.

The steaks sizzled loudly; smoke poured up into the range hood. Cian couldn't tell if his mam was crying, but it sounded like it as she turned away from him and sniffed, using the spatula to poke at the skillet.

"Who said anything about Catholics? Dad is the virulent racist. I don't think you are. Shalene was—" Cian stopped when his mam cleared her throat, but she didn't say anything. "Emma and I are fine. We're okay. You don't have

to worry about it, but… thanks," he finished, chopping the last tomato and tossing it into the salad bowl.

Like they did on most nights, he and Aoife ate quietly in front of the television. This time they watched Dead Poets Society *on cable. Aoife loved Robin Williams and he never failed to make her smile. Cian stared at the screen, feeling almost guilty for how glad he was that his dad was working late again.*

Cian's mind eased around the topic of Shalene. Even when he thought of her and the baby it felt like he was thinking of a literal past life, like he'd been reincarnated as another New Cian fresh off the conveyor belt. Very similar to but not quite the Original Cian, and constantly in need of new batteries.

New Cian and Emma went to see Nirvana open for Dinosaur Jr at the Warfield in June. Nirvana played his favorite song that night: "Lithium."

New Cian climbed with his friends a few times a week at the rock-climbing gym not far from his house. Sometimes he and Emma would get snow cones and go for walks along the pier. Sometimes they'd take her golden retriever along.

Emma worked at that snow cone shack a few days a week. Cian's parents didn't want him having a job, preferring he focus on school and writing instead. So he wrote short stories.

After devouring "The Body" by Stephen King, Cian wrote a short story about his group of lads in Dublin. How they played football in the park and how Finn's little sister had a crush on Cian. How the boys got blutered on Guinness and showed up to Bobby's great-nanny's funeral barely able to hold it together without laughing, claiming his great-nanny would've loved it since she lived to be 101 and Guinness was her favorite.

Cian and the lads did a decent job of staying in touch. He liked to call them from his dad's office, mooching off the free long-distance.

When Cian showed the short story to Mr. Sharp, Mr. Sharp told him it wasn't just good… it was really *good. He let Cian know about a contest he should enter; Cian did it and won a thousand dollars.*

"So, you're like this child prodigy?" Pica asked him when he told her about winning first place in a national writing contest when he was a teenager.

They were at her apartment, in her kitchen. She said her parents paid for it so she wouldn't need a roommate. It was a spacious loft with lots of windows and a verdurous view of campus in the spring.

Her bracelets clinked softly as she dipped their tea bags in and out of the mugs.

"Well, I was omnilegent and also dating my English teacher's daughter," Cian said.

"Omnilegent. I don't think I've ever heard anyone actually use that word in a sentence before... clearly it's true."

"I mean, not to brag. I like the attention, though. Keep it coming, please."

Pica laughed with her mouth wide open when he looked at her.

"Oh, right, definitely not to brag, attention whore!"

"Keep it coming... I can take it," Cian said. He moved his arms in a bring it on *motion and Pica shook her head.*

"Were you in love with her?" she asked him easily.

They'd promised "no bullshit" the first day they met and sometimes it was like she was in a never-ending game of truth-or-dare with him. Nothing was off-limits. He never thought she was holding back from him, which made him feel even worse, knowing he was keeping something huge from her. They hadn't kissed or even gone on an official date yet, but there was an intimacy that went well beyond casual friendship—an intimacy mostly forged by Pica and her openheartedness.

And a part of him felt like Pica was just the type of woman who would understand... if he told her about Shalene and the baby. But a voice inside him repeated on a regular basis that it was a bad idea to tell her and he didn't want to do anything to lose her or what they had... what they were moving toward. He was occasionally zapped frozen with the fear of making a big sudden movement that would scare her off. She was his butterfly.

"I was... I mean, I was young, but I think *I was in love with her... It's hard to know, looking back, right?" he said as Pica put their mugs on the table*

and sat across from him. "Have you ever been in love?" he asked, conflicted about what he wanted her answer to be.

"I've been in very, very serious like," she said, smiling and palming her mug with both hands.

"Yeah... maybe that's what it was with me and Emma... very, very serious like."

"I mean, I'm assuming you were sleeping together? I'm not being a pervert! I just think it makes a difference... sometimes," Pica said.

Cian put his hot mug to his lips. He didn't like tea; that was her thing. And his blood was rushing harder now that the conversation had turned sexual. Pica looked perfectly perfect sitting there glowing in the sunset light—her full lips and the tenderness in her eyes. He was wild about her and it felt like love already, but they hadn't even kissed.

Why hadn't they kissed?

He nodded and put the mug back on the kitchen table. "Yeah, we slept together, but it was high school... and then senior year we broke up... mostly because we were going to different colleges and all that."

"Classic, right? Always happens. It's kind of what happened to me and my high school boyfriend. He was the only person I had sex with in high school."

"Very, very serious like, right?"

"Exactly," she said. "And you don't think I'm a pervert? We're clear on that?"

"Pretty damn clear, yes. So can I kiss you?" he asked.

Had he been possessed? He didn't remember making the decision to ask; his mouth had made it for him.

"I was actually going to be mad at you if you didn't try to kiss me tonight," she said, sitting back. She laughed. Cian laughed too.

He stood and went over to her side. She got up from her chair and sat on the kitchen table. He put himself between her legs and kissed her for the first time.

"Say omnilegent *again," she said with their mouths touching. He obeyed.*

That quick, they were tangled and knotted like those invisible, similar strings that bound Edward Rochester to Jane Eyre. Those strings were already wrapped around him and Pica and they'd twisted, squeezing tight, never to be loosened.

10

Vincent has regrets. She sits up in bed after her nap, trying to think of a way not to undo but to soften her brazenness in sending Loup *that* song. Her feelings haven't changed! But the timing of Cillian's letter has certainly cooled them. *Cillian cock-blocks me from Kentucky* is so stupid and silly, she actually laughs thinking it.

Your Cillian, she hears on a loop, not to be confused with *Loup*, which is actually pronounced *Lou*, but she still has *Loup* on a loop in her head too. She hadn't meant to fall asleep but hadn't minded it either. It was the only thing that made proper sense while she tried to navigate her feelings.

Note: The navigation failed and her emotions have ended up on the curb and crashed to the ground and smashed into whatever craggy rocks line the shore of the wild, raging hell of water she's floating her heart boat on.

She gets up and puts a pot of water on the stove. While it's boiling for the farfalle, she writes Loup back.

Yes! Come over. Anytime is fine, but I'm making dinner right now. We can eat?

And talk?

And later, walk?

And while I do love your handstands, I will be using my feet! ;)

Flirty, but not *too* flirty. She doesn't want Loup showing up thinking that tonight is The Night because tonight is decidedly *not* The Night. Even if he does show up all Romeo Montague and *direct my sail! On, lusty gentlemen!* All dark eyes and handstands. That fucking hair. That phenomenal, bitable ass.

Shall I bring anything? he writes.

Yourself, she responds.

Vincent texts her children, reminding them that they have a video call planned for tomorrow morning, their time in the U.S. She texts her sister, Monet, to ask for a life update. She texts her mom to tell her again how much she loves the studio, the apartment in general, and asks her to send a selfie of them in Rome because she misses her parents' faces. She sends a photo of herself to the family group chat that includes her brother as well as her parents and sister. A photo of her with her hand raised in a wave to the camera, a thought bubble in a cloud above her head that reads LOVE YOU, MISS YOU.

She takes a shower and puts on her long velvet skirt and an off-the-shoulder sweater, a pair of big terra-cotta arch earrings. Everyone in her family has talked back and she saves a photo of her parents they sent. Monet calls her instead of texting, and Vincent puts her on speaker and leaves the phone on the counter while she finishes dinner. Monet talks about work and the on-thin-ice relationship she has with her current boyfriend. She asks Vincent how she's feeling about Cillian and Vincent tells her about the letter. That she had to take a nap afterward. Monet finds this hilarious and they laugh about it. Her brother, Theo, texts asking when she's coming to Amsterdam, and she tells him hopefully soon. He lets her know her nieces will be there for Christmas—his twenty-year-old twins.

Dinner is ready. Loup shows up freshly showered in his zipped-up track jacket with his wet hair behind his ear on one side. He is holding a bag with a bouquet of blooming alstroemerias peeking out from one corner. He kicks his sneakers off, and Vincent looks at them by her door, the same way she's imagined them. She wants to paint them and name the still life: *Loup Is Here*. He's wearing a pair of navy-blue socks with gray squiggles all over them. Barefoot, she taps her big toe on his.

"*Coucou*. And you're not very good at following instructions," she says, taking the bag from him.

"*Coucou. Je suis désolé*," he says. "I'm sorry."

"You didn't have to translate that for me. I know what *je suis désolé* means."

Loup launches into a soft, slow paragraph of French that Vincent doesn't understand. She stands there looking at him, watching his mouth and breathing him in—white soap and October.

"Also, you look like an autumn leaf. You always look so good," he ends.

"*Merci beaucoup*, asshole." She gives him a nose scrunch and a smile. Her legs are already Loup-wobbly.

Vincent puts the flowers in a vase of fresh water on the counter and unpacks the rest of his bag. Two pomegranates, a humid bottle of Champagne. Bread, a triangle of Pont-l'Évêque, a jar of black fig jam. A hard pack of Gauloises too. The contents are a Sylvia Plath–esque journal list of Paris, poetry, and romance.

"Just to be sure...you're the same Vincent Wilde who sent me

'Flower,' correct?" Loup asks. He looks at her and picks up the jam glass, inspecting it.

"This dish has pancetta in it. It's, um, a Jamie Oliver recipe I've been making like once a week for forever. And apparently you and I only eat pasta and fruit in this apartment together," Vincent says with a hot face and an adrenaline-spiked heart. She turns away from him to look at the plates on the counter.

"So shy again! I'm sorry, but I don't know how else to be around you. After you sent me that song it was hard to concentrate on the rest of the match, honestly. We lost, by the way. Totally your fault," he says.

Vincent hears him put the jam jar down. There is music coming from her phone—a dreampop mix Colm had made for her after she'd asked. She hears an ambulance in the distance and crosses herself as she turns back to Loup.

"Noémie does that. Crosses herself when she hears a siren. I've always thought it was cool," Loup says, pointing at her heart.

"Parmesan?" Vincent asks, holding up the cheese grater.

Loup taps his fingers on the counter.

"Vincent, can I kiss you? Because I honestly don't think I can eat until I kiss you. But if you say no, it's okay…I just won't eat. I'm a wreck, can't you tell?" he asks.

"I want to talk about something first," Vincent says, getting her phone from the counter and stopping the music. "Yes. I'm the same Vincent who sent you 'Flower,' which was…looking back…a smidge over-the-top, I suppose…but I had a feeling and leaped after it instead of waiting and thinking because I'm trying to do more *actual* living instead of *waiting* to live, which is why I'm here in Paris and why I got this tattoo when I was like, practically your age," she says, pulling her sweater off her shoulder and showing him. "It says 'half-blown rose' because I read it in *Jane Eyre* and there's also a poem called 'Look, Delia, how w' esteem the half-blown rose' by Samuel Daniel…and Shakespeare talks about it in a thing too…but it reminds me of being in a state of, I don't know…constant blooming and *becoming*…never giving up…do you understand what I mean?" she asks.

Loup is taller than she is. He's leaning against the counter, just looking down at her, listening. He puts his arm around her waist and pulls her closer. Honeyed, she melts there.

"I understand. And I love it," he says, touching her shoulder and kissing the script. Every light inside of her is burning.

"But that's not even what I want to tell you. I want to tell you that I have two children, and my son... he's your age. He's twenty-four. My daughter is twenty-one. Baptiste knows about them. He hasn't told you this?" she says, only moving so she can hold her phone up and show him a photo of her children from the previous summer. She and Cillian had met Colm and Olive at the North Carolina beach house they'd rented often while the kids were growing up. Colm was in a T-shirt and his swim shorts, Olive in an orange sundress. They were both sun-soaked and happy, actually smiling at the camera after Vincent had begged them for at least one decent photo.

Vincent points to Colm and Olive and tells Loup their names and where they are in the world. She tells him about Colm's wedding in the summer and how it's the next time she's supposed to see Cillian again, leaving out everything pertaining to *Half-Blown Rose* the book.

Keeping one arm around Vincent's waist, Loup takes the phone from her and inspects the photo. He smiles at it.

"Baptiste is a vault when he wants to be, you should know that. So no, he didn't tell me, no," Loup says, shaking his head. "That's a good-looking family you got there, Vincent Raphaela van Gogh," he says, handing the phone back to her.

"I wanted you to know, in case it was going to weird you out or whatever... the age difference... the fact that you could be my kid. I've been thinking about it ever since Baptiste told me you liked me," Vincent says.

"I asked him to tell you. And in case you need a reminder, I'm not your *actual* son." Loup laughs. "You're making connections here when you don't really have to. It's a choice."

"If you're fine with it and you still want to kiss me, if it's still your only desire, you can kiss me," Vincent says. She puts her phone down and the world screeches to a halt.

If this were a film, it would be a split screen. On one side—Cillian, alone, waiting for her call. On the other—Vincent with the phone in her hand, preparing to confess that she kissed Loup in her kitchen. That she wasn't drunk or confused. That she was doing exactly what she wanted and she wasn't waiting around. And yes, maybe it is wrong because she's married, but she doesn't know what Cillian is doing with his free time or even if anything he's told her in the past is true. His book provided a new filter she has to put over everything she knows about him and their life together.

INT. VINCENT'S KITCHEN – EVENING

Vincent and Loup, kissing. Vincent gets on her tiptoes.

NARRATOR (V.O.)
Cillian lied to her for a long time and this kiss with Loup may go nowhere. Maybe she'll only regret it. Doesn't matter. It's happening. Finally.

The Vincent/Loup kiss slowly fades into a flash-back of Vincent and Cillian kissing.

NARRATOR (V.O.)
Cillian is an excellent kisser; Vincent wouldn't have allowed herself to marry a man who wasn't.

The room swirls with wind, flowers, and a page torn from Half-Blown Rose that reads: "Cian and

Pica were tethered from their first kiss that spring day in her kitchen."

Loup is an excellent kisser too. Their kiss doesn't feel like a first kiss at all. Loup kisses like he is already familiar with her mouth, takes his time moving his tongue against hers. He is holding her face and his handstand energy is slowed. Beguiling. They've *Freaky Friday*–ed and now she's the one buzzing. They're making soft, baby-animal noises of relief with their mouths together like that. Breathing hard, she has to force herself to push back from him a little.

"And what about the fact that technically I'm still married? Is that okay?" Vincent asks.

"If this is okay for you, it's more than okay for me," Loup says, gently pressing his hand on the small of her back, and they are kissing again like they're slowed by water. He tastes like mint warmed by the sun.

Mouths and tongues and their upright bodies smashed together until she stops and steadies herself against the counter, lets her thumb push at her bottom lip.

"All right, all right. Yeah...you should be able to eat now. I think we should eat. That's what we should do. Let's eat," she says, turning to the stovetop and grabbing the pasta fork.

They've kissed now. That's Something. An inevitable force beyond her control, like a tornado or an earthquake.

Or more like the *puh-powee* of a mushroom sprouting after a warm, wet night.

Loup says something quickly in French that she doesn't catch.

"That's your new thing now? Saying things I can't understand?" She scrunches her nose up at him again. He laughs lightly.

"Yes, Vincent. I can eat a little," Loup says. He makes a show of taking a deep breath in and rubbing the back of his neck. Smiles at her as he unzips his jacket, revealing the slouchy striped shirt she loves so much.

"Seen your mate lately?" Loup asks.

Vincent is cross-legged on the couch, holding her plate. Loup is doing the same on the rug in front of her. One of the windows is slightly open. It's almost too cool for it, but she loves the windows too much to leave them closed. Leaving them open means she can hear the constant, lovely whisper of *I'm in Paris, I'm in Paris* like a heartbeat on the wind.

"Who?" she asks.

"Naked drumming buddy," Vincent says, using his elbow to motion toward the window.

"Ah. Just say *best friend* from here on out. Makes it easier. And yeah. He was up there the other day. He's one of my constants," she says. At this point, Vincent guesses she'd feel mildly bummed if naked drumming guy never did his routine again. It's part of her Paris life now. "Speaking of best friends... what was your bet with Emiliano?"

Loup takes a bite and Vincent thinks about his mouth on hers; there's a hot flash down her back and it rests between her legs.

"It's dumb, but he bet me you wouldn't come to our show... but you did."

"So, he had to put your stuff up last night?"

Loup nods. "And he had to give me a hundred euro."

"That's half my money, when you think about it."

"I'll gladly give it to you. You could ask me for anything and I'd give it to you," he says.

Vincent is pleased she left the window open because now she's hot all over.

"Did you think maybe I wouldn't come?" she says.

"I had full confidence in you, and you didn't let me down."

He asks her how often she talks to Cillian.

"Whenever, really. I got a letter from him today. He sent it ten days ago," Vincent finds herself saying, though she doesn't intend to tell Loup *too* much about anything. Just, enough.

"Was it a nice letter?" Loup asks, putting his empty plate on the floor and leaning back.

"It was fine. I don't know where he and I will end up and I'm being honest with you when I say that. I still love him... but our relationship is *extremely* complicated and I'm not just being dramatic," Vincent says, shaking her head. She takes a drink of water and puts her empty plate on the floor next to Loup's.

"Understood. I mean, of course you still love him."

"Are you currently in love with anyone?"

"What if I say I'm in love with *you*?" He raises an eyebrow.

"Shh."

"What? *For a flirt with you!* It's what I do!"

Vincent stands, definitely wanting to kiss him again. But instead, she bends to pick both plates off the floor. Takes them to the kitchen and places them in the sink.

"Put your jacket on, Loup. We're going for a walk."

They make their way across Pont Neuf and pass the gothic glory of Sainte-Chapelle in the dark. Vincent thinks of the gray copies of *Half-Blown Rose* inside Shakespeare and Company as they walk by. They turn up place du Petit Pont, heading toward the Notre-Dame.

Vincent loves making this loop.

She also loves people-watching in the Parvis de Notre-Dame and wandering through the flower market on quai de la Corse. The eerie peace of strolling through the Cimetière du Père Lachaise and seeing the final resting places of Chopin, Comte, Richard Wright, and Jim Morrison. Pissarro and Proust. Édith Piaf and Oscar Wilde. So many artists and writers and thinkers she loves and obsesses over. Over a million people are buried there and it's too overwhelming for Vincent's head to hold, but she walks through time and time again, trying. She also loves walking from the apartment to Luxembourg Garden and the

Sorbonne, the Latin Quarter. All the narrow streets, cafés, and bookshops along the way. After she'd arrived in Paris and settled in, she spent days atop the double-decker tour buses, listening and learning, making notes in her journal. She'd re-created some of those journeys on foot, alone, with her bag strapped to the front of her chest to properly beware of the pickpockets her parents had warned her about.

Vincent looks over at Loup and asks what he's doing for Halloween. She doesn't know what Halloween looks like in Paris. Maybe they don't do anything at all.

"I'm not doing anything. Couple years ago, Apollos and Sam threw a big party. Sam is American. Americans love Halloween," Loup says.

"We do. When my kids were little, we always did the same thing. Made chili and watched *Clue*, had a bunch of kids over... took them all to every house in our neighborhood. It's a cozy night back home," she says, remembering those nights so fondly it hurts. Nostalgia is a knife.

"*Des bonbons ou un sort*," Loup says in a singsongy voice. *Trick or treat.*

As they walk, Loup is running his fingers along the walls of the buildings they pass, reaching out to touch the lampposts as they wait for the crosswalk lights to change. She takes his hand and holds it. "It's not weird for me to talk about these things?" she asks.

"Look. Green light of the pharmacy. I'm still keeping track of green," Loup says, pointing with his free hand. "And no. Why would it be weird for you to talk about your family? Thinking it's weird is the only thing that's weird. Right?"

"I guess," Vincent says as they walk along the Seine.

Seine again. Sin again. Sin from my lips? O trespass sweetly urged! Give me thy Seine again.

Remembering Loup's tongue in her mouth, Vincent doesn't want to talk about her family anymore.

"By the way, I really loved kissing you. Ah, today is all about me making confessions," she says.

Loup stops and gently tugs at the hand of hers he's holding, pulling her down the stone steps of the Crypte archéologique de l'île de la Cité and kisses her. Stops to tell her he loves kissing her, then kisses her again. Tells her he could kiss her all night if she'd let him. Says he wanted to kiss her the first moment he saw her in class.

"I remember you were wearing a red dress with little white flowers on it that buttoned down the front and I wanted to undo those buttons. You were also wearing huge half-moon earrings. See? I am making confessions too," he says, with his mouth close to hers. He kisses her throat, the lobe of her ear, that part of her neck right underneath it. She wants to make a sound but doesn't; she imagines the echoes.

I wanted to undo those buttons.

He remembers her dress.

But in between kisses she tells him he can't spend the night. Yes, she sent him the song but...not yet. She's not ready for whatever would happen if she let him sleep in her bed. They'll have to wait.

How long? She doesn't know.

And although there continue to be occasional threads of the snippiness she used to cast over him like a wet net, she finds herself more relaxed and sleepier around him too. It's the same feeling she got nursing her babies—her body releasing the calming oxytocin and prolactin hormones, softening her sharp edges, even when she didn't want them softened.

No more lace under wool. When she's with Loup it's lace under slick satin, slipping away.

"*C'est moi qui décide*," she says softly. *It's me who decides*.

"Absolutely," he says, kissing her mouth again and letting his leg rest between hers, which immediately makes her want to change her mind. She looks up at the skinny clouds like smoke as he kisses her other ear, catching it softly between his teeth. *Sous le ciel de Paris*. She thinks of Cillian and whether she's already gone too far to turn back now.

"Let's walk. Let's walk," she says, breathless, and slinks under the arm Loup has pressed against the stone. She adjusts the belt of her trench coat and walks up the steps to stand in the lamplight. Looks over her shoulder at him, hooks her finger so he will follow.

They stop and sit, watching the river, the lights rippling on the water. The night as electric and blissful and lovely as it was twenty-four hours ago. She points and tells him about the tango lessons she considered taking over the summer when she saw that the classes were taught right next to the water. She'd sat and watched them in the sunset light, the happy couples, young and old. *Maybe next year*. Vincent lets her head rest on Loup's shoulder again as he tells her about how he was a little shit when he was in primary school, one time getting sent to the headmaster for catching a frog during break time and putting it in a cup on his teacher's desk. She tells him if he killed the frog and added chocolate, it would sound just like a Roald Dahl story.

"And this was in London?" she asks.

"*Ouais*. Primrose Hill," he says.

"So, you've always been a bit of a bad boy... got it."

"Don't beat yourself up about it. All women love a bad boy," he says, and she playfully scratches at his arm. He rubs the spot, faking that she's hurt him. He calls her *une tigresse* and takes her hand, holding it warm between his.

After some quiet he asks her to tell him more about Colm and Olive and she does, trying her best not to make connections where there shouldn't be any. Yes, Loup and Colm are the same age and around the same height, but so what?

Colm and Theo's visits to Paris in September had overlapped for a few days around her birthday and when the boys were standing next to each other, she could've sworn Colm had gotten taller, even though he told her he's been the same height since he was fourteen.

They snake their way back to the 1st arrondissement and are in front of her apartment building again. Loup kisses her by the door. On the sidewalk, he bends over and does a quick handstand.

"*Au revoir*. Thank you for kisses, thank you for dinner," he says, upright again and breathing harder. He puts both hands on his heart as he's walking backward. "You're going to destroy me and I will allow it."

"I—" she begins with a now unbottled sadness she hadn't quite expected.

It's the word *destroy*. Her brain resets, and she thinks of how she felt reading Cillian's book for the first time. Sometimes when she processes it all over again, the entire cycle of her emotions flicks through her at high speed. *Destroyed. Destroy*. She thinks of Aurora's hot pink copy of *The Woman Destroyed* by Simone de Beauvoir on the bookshelf in her bedroom.

The French word for *destroy* is a cognate, making it easier for Vincent to remember—*détruire*.

The French word for *destruction* is *destruction*.

Besides *loup*, a few of her favorite French words are *quelquefois* (sometimes), *pamplemousse* (grapefruit), and *bisou* (kiss).

Now she has a least favorite: *détruire*.

She's frozen speechless and sleepy, watching Loup walk away.

"Nothing to be said and nothing to be done about it. Believe me, it's a good thing. A *very* good thing. *Une très bonne chose!*" Loup says, hopping and raising his voice with the French.

11

It was Cian's mam who told him his dad had cancer.

"Pancreatic and spreading," she'd said, lighting a cigarette and looking at the ocean. She was sitting at the glass table on the deck and Cian could tell she'd been crying, though she tried to hide it.

On Cian's first day home after junior year, he'd known something was off as soon as he walked into the house. Everything was too neat, too perfect. The air was too still. His dad's car was in the driveway, but Jack was nowhere to be found. Cian wandered through the house calling for his parents without getting a response. He found his mam outside and watched her drinking tea and rubbing her eyes.

"He didn't want me to tell you while you were away at school and get you all worked up. And besides, there's nothing to be done, really, since he refuses to have any more treatments," his mam said, and sniffed. She pushed the pack of cigarettes toward Cian and he sat, took one and lit it. He and his mam had never smoked together; Cian only smoked at parties when he was having a drink. That's what he needed: something to drink, something to do. Without saying anything, he stood from the table and grabbed a bottle of caffeinated soda from the cold core of the refrigerator. The certificate from his short story award was stuck to the fridge with a shamrock magnet. He touched it and stepped outside again, sliding the glass closed.

"He's in the hospital?" Cian asked after sitting. He smoked and popped the top of his drink, took a small sip.

"No, he's golfing with Marty. Marty and a whole gang of guys just came over here to pick him up not even an hour ago. They don't know what's going on. He doesn't want them to," Aoife said.

Cian had one living grandmother in Dublin—Aoife's mother. She always came to stay with them for a few weeks when spring rolled around. He also had a load of aunts and uncles and tons of cousins, but hadn't seen any of them since he'd left Ireland. Cian sometimes felt a misplaced guilt, as if by getting Shalene pregnant, he'd been the one to purposely rip their entire family apart.

He wished they'd stayed. He started to cry at the table with his mam, not about his dad dying, but about leaving Dublin.

"I'm sorry to upset you as soon as you got here, but I'd put it off for so long," his mam said, standing up enough to reach across the table and rub his shoulder. "Bridie's coming tomorrow to stay for a while and help out with a few things. Maybe you and her can help me talk some sense into him."

Bridie was Cian's favorite aunt, his mam's younger sister, who'd recently gotten married to a man in the Irish Republican Army and moved to Belfast. Cian was glad he and Bridie were going to be in San Francisco at the same time, even though the reason was shitty.

He wiped his eyes and asked his mam the questions he needed answers to. How long had his dad known about his cancer? Why did he always have to be so fucking stubborn?

His mam filled him in on everything and added, "I'm already tired of talking about it... I'm tired of thinking about it. Talk to me about something else." She told him to hold on a second and went inside to refresh her tea, then returned and lit another cigarette.

"I have a girlfriend. Her real name is Picasso, but she goes by Pica. She's an artist... her parents are artists... they're rich. She's black and I'll never tell Dad that because I love her. I'm mad *about her. I want to marry her someday," Cian spilled out. He pulled his wallet from his back pocket and flipped to the picture of her that he kept there—Pica in a white sundress with her wild, curly*

hair pulled back from her face. She was wearing a crown of white clover, and big marigold earrings, laughing in the sun.

"Picasso," Aoife said softly, as if the name alone had already won her over. She took the wallet from Cian and examined the picture closely while she smoked. "She's beautiful. And I know you think about Shalene and the baby in Dublin. You and Pica will make beautiful babies too," she said, petting the plastic film and letting herself cry some more.

As we continue mining and organizing our memories, let's center our focus on only good memories for now. No matter how small. Don't censor yourself. No neutral memories and no bad memories. We're categorizing only the good ones. You can write, draw, or paint them. Paragraphs or lists. A mix. It's up to you. Let's freewrite for twenty minutes and then whoever would like to share is welcome. This exercise is meant to be enjoyed. If you're not enjoying it, take some time to try to figure out why.

Vincent sits behind the desk and squeezes a smudge of dark blue paint onto her paper, mixes it with a dab of white to create an ocean hue. Her memory: The beach house in June. Sitting outside and reading for hours next to the sighing ocean, just their little family and no one else.

It's Wednesday and Baptiste and Mina are hosting the dinner party this time around. Baptiste has informed Vincent that Loup is coming, although Loup had already told her this when he'd texted the night before. This is the first time she's seen Loup since the Saturday-night kissing. She looks at him scribbling away in his brown Moleskine. She hasn't said a word to Baptiste about the kissing and knows Loup hasn't either because Baptiste would've definitely teased her about it. She and Baptiste had gone to the café after her jewelry-making class yesterday and not a peep.

Loup sent her a good-morning text on Sunday, reiterating how much he'd enjoyed kissing her, how he couldn't wait to kiss her again. He also sent her links to AnchoisMusic.com and the @AnchoisMusic Instagram.

The last photo they uploaded was of Loup doing a handstand in front of a poster for their next show, the following Saturday night in Le Marais again. He asked if she wanted to come. She told him she'd be there and spent too much time poking around the pages, as well as Noémie's Instagram and the other guys' in the band. Loup told her he didn't have an Instagram account and Vincent felt a blip of relief. Not having one made him seem a little older and therefore made her seem slightly less *cougarish*, even though she hated that word and hated thinking of herself that way.

She scrolled through photo after photo, taking screenshots of the ones she wanted to save—several of Loup onstage, one of him drinking a beer in the park with Apollos, and another of him skateboarding with Sam, now that she knew who was who. On the About section of their website, there was a photo of all of them, with Loup front and center in his black track jacket and jeans, bent over and laughing. On Noémie's page there was a recent photo of her and Loup sitting cross-legged in front of a television, playing a video game together.

He sent her another song: "Kiss" by Prince. She sent him "I'm Kissing You" by Des'ree.

C'est toi qui décide, he texted at the end of their conversation. *It's you who decides*.

Vincent's Gideon 7000 had never seen more action and she told Agathe that. In return, Agathe texted her about five hundred exclamation points. But Vincent didn't tell her about the kissing.

She hadn't told anyone about the kissing.

It was her turn to keep a secret, and having it felt like a smooth rock in her pocket that she could rub to remember.

The class paints and writes quietly until Vincent stands and asks if anyone would like to share. A tall young woman with hair like fire stands and talks about her dad teaching her how to ride a bike. An older gentleman talks about the day his grandson was born. Loup holds up a piece of paper. He's colored half of it blue and the other half is covered in swirling black text. He tells a story about cliff diving into the Mediterranean Sea. He makes eye contact with Vincent, smiles at her. She holds up her paper and shows the class that she's also painted her paper the blue of the ocean. She tells them about spending two weeks in North Carolina with her children on the water, fudging the guidelines only a little by leaving Cillian out of it completely.

They take Métro Line 1 to Baptiste and Mina's. Line 6 is Vincent's favorite because it goes over the Pont de Bir-Hakeim crossing the Seine and allows her the prettiest view of the Eiffel Tower. For the most part, she prefers walking over taking the Métro, but Baptiste and Mina live *just* far enough away and it's *just* chilly enough.

She and Loup sit next to each other across from Baptiste on the train. Baptiste and Loup laugh and laugh about something that Vincent doesn't entirely understand, but they try their best to include her. She doesn't need anything else from them; she quite enjoys their ridiculousness.

Baptiste and Mina's place—a darkly elegant apartment filled with art and jewel tones—is in the 8th arrondissement near the avenue des Champs-Élysées. Mina had asked Vincent to bring a bottle of red and a bottle of white. After greeting everyone in the kitchen, Vincent takes the wine from her bag and puts the red on the counter, the white in the fridge. Mina—in a turtleneck dress and tights—thanks her and steps over to Loup, fussing at him for not bringing the tea light candles like she asked.

"This is the first time I've actually invited you to one of these things! The host makes the dinner and everyone else brings something. That's how it works," Mina says in a whiny voice. Vincent can't tell if she's kidding or not with that voice. Maybe it's a cousin thing? Vincent doesn't know how close they are. She imagines Mina babysitting Loup and shoving a bottle of milk in his mouth until it disturbs her so much that she stops.

Loup takes both hands and puts them on the sides of Mina's face.

"*Forgive me,* Hermina," Loup says, revealing her full name for the first time to Vincent. "I'll make it up to you," he says, kissing both of her cheeks. Mina swats his arm and sits down to chop an onion. Vincent loves that people in foreign countries sit down to chop. Americans do everything standing up.

Baptiste stands across from Vincent, looking down at her. He smiles and touches her shoulder.

"You all right, Veedubs? Your energy seems a little...scattered," he says.

"Does it? Maybe it's just you," she says, smirking up at him.

"You're not getting lonely on me, are you? Your daughter...she's coming to visit for Christmas?" he asks, bending his body down a little to get closer to her face. It makes her laugh.

"Right. And my best friend, Ramona. They're flying in together from Tennessee. I'm not lonely. This is the first time I've lived on my own since I was in college and I'm enjoying it much more than I thought possible, actually," she says.

"Are you marking this down? This conversation we're having that isn't revolving around Loup?" he asks quietly.

"Well, you've ruined it...Now it is."

"It's not." Baptiste shakes his head. "Am I going to meet Ramona and Olive? Will you allow it? I know you like to keep things very separate, don't you?"

"You're always acting like some sort of fortune-teller. Do you know how to be normal?"

"Not really, no," Baptiste says, laughing.

"Of course you can meet them if you want. I'll warn them about you," she says.

When there's a light knock at the door, Baptiste opens it to reveal Agathe with a box of cookies and two people—a man and a woman she casually introduces by saying that sometimes they're a *throuple*, even though no one asked. The man is as tall as Baptiste and looks to be around thirty. Vincent doesn't catch his name but she hears the woman's: Gigi. She's pretty in an alienish way and looks like she's barely twenty-five, if even. Baptiste shakes hands with the man and tells him Agathe is nothing if not full of surprises and the man opens his mouth to let out a deep, unexpected giggle that makes Vincent like him immediately.

Vincent is sitting on the couch with a glass of wine, chatting with a woman from the modern art museum. Vincent has lost Loup but swears she can *feel* him somewhere behind her. Probably on the balcony smoking with someone he's just met, talking to them like they're suddenly reunited friends.

The woman from the museum is talking about her family. Her son lives in Spain and her daughter-in-law is pregnant, due at Christmas. The woman is going to Barcelona to spend December with them and planning on staying even longer, depending on when the baby comes. Vincent listens and nods, lets her talk, asks questions. The woman is funny and interesting. She takes out her phone and shows Vincent pictures of her son, their house, the progression of her daughter-in-law's pregnant belly. The baby is a girl and they'll name her Lucía. When the woman opens her mouth to say more, Mina announces that dinner is ready and, in unnecessary, excruciating detail, explains that there's enough room at the table for everyone to sit properly; they don't have to eat in the living room.

Vincent feels a hand on her shoulder and turns to see Loup, fresh from the balcony. They get food and sit next to each other at the table across from Agathe, who is appropriately flanked by the other two members of her throuple. Agathe smiles at her and touches her earring—a *thanks for being my friend* gift from Vincent.

"I love them. I've been wearing them every day lately. Have I told you that?" Agathe says. She's wearing the pair that Vincent calls *Agathe* because Agathe was the first person she gave them to after finalizing the big ginkgo-leaf design.

Agathe turns to Gigi. "Vincent made these. She makes outrageous jewelry. I'll get her to give you a card so you can check out her shop. Gigi works at the little contemporary art gallery in the seventh, Citron Clair. They should be selling some of your stuff. You've probably walked past it a million times." Agathe does a funny dismissive wave Vincent's way. "She walks everywhere. She's such a *flâneuse*," Agathe says to Gigi about Vincent, then says something else in French that Vincent can't translate. Agathe apologizes to her immediately afterward. "Gigi's English isn't as good as mine. I just said the same thing to her, but in French. I don't want you thinking I was being nasty." She takes a bite of her food.

"I don't think you're being nasty and you're right, I do love to walk. Anywhere, really, but especially here. You know I love it when you call me a *flâneuse*, Agathe. *J'adore me promener dans Paris*," Vincent says to both of them. She is picturing Agathe and Gigi naked in bed with the man, whose name she's forgotten even though Agathe said it again right before they sat down to eat.

If she's honest with herself, it definitely doesn't *not* turn her on a little, imagining Agathe, Gigi, and this guy together, but the practical logistics of a threesome have never appealed to Vincent. How do they decide what goes where and when? Does someone keep track of when it's time to change positions? If two of them decide to have sex while the other is busy, does the third get jealous? Are there a lot of rules or none at all? Vincent thinks the only way she could ever be okay with having a threesome would be if she could guarantee she'd never see the other people again. Ever.

She considers asking Agathe these questions the next time they're having wine together. She thinks of how delighted Agathe would be to spill every detail. She looks at Agathe's idiomatically French neck and profile across the table as she's talking to Gigi and thinks of how Agathe will lap her questions up like a mango, juice dripping through her fingers, sucking on the pit.

Vincent doesn't realize she's gotten hypnotized by her own thoughts until she feels Loup's hand on her leg. He gently squeezes her thigh and she looks at him. He smiles, digs into his food. She puts her hand under the table and Loup takes it, lacing his fingers with hers. Her stomach swoops so deeply, she has to stifle a gasp. It's the warmth and the secrecy. The sexiness of his fingers, the slipping of skin on skin.

The food is delicious and Vincent's aroused senses are overstimulating. She takes her hand from Loup's and puts it on the table, slowly flattens it and stares at it. She looks up to see Agathe looking at it too; Agathe meets her eyes and smiles slyly. The man next to Agathe asks Loup about Anchois, tells him that Agathe was talking about seeing them play in Le Marais. Loup puts his fork down and gives a quick *ha* and starts filling the guy in. He lets his leg rest against Vincent's while he's talking, moves it up and down slowly.

Vincent takes a deep breath and turns her attention to Mina, tells her how good the food is, then wraps a leaf of spinach around a small cube of feta dripping with vinaigrette. Eats it carefully with her fingers.

"Isn't it, though?" is Mina's reply. Agathe voices her agreement. Mina half smiles at her and asks Baptiste to fetch a bottle of wine from the fridge.

Mina's invited a friend who isn't part of the usual dinner group. She'd introduced her as a well-respected member of the French intelligentsia and a genius botanist, an instructor at the Jardin des Plantes botanical school. "There's a menagerie too. We have a binturong that's just given birth to bearcats we've named Françoise and Poivre. Oh, you *have* to come visit the menagerie. It's been there since 1794. Don't you love how old everything is here? Americans are fascinated by old things!" Mina had rambled out as she poured Vincent a glass of wine.

Mina had been chatty at the Anchois show and she'd chatted Vincent up in the kitchen tonight too. It hasn't been like this before, but maybe this is how it is now. And although it's hard for Vincent to imagine being friends-friends with Mina because they are just So Different, Vincent does find herself letting Mina do most of the talking and—even if only sometimes, even if only subconsciously—trying to say things she thinks Mina may find interesting. Maybe it's finally working; Mina has warmed up to her since the summer. Vincent doesn't allow herself to think about how Mina's feelings would shift if she knew how badly Vincent wants to sleep with Loup.

Loup.

He says her name softly from behind as Vincent heads toward the bathroom after dinner. She turns to find him eating one of Agathe's pumpkin cream cookies, tossing the last bite in his mouth and wiping his hands together to shake off the crumbs.

"*Coucou!* Fancy meeting you here," he says.

"We're reduced to playing handsie and legsie under the table now, are we?" she asks. One of Baptiste's abstract paintings hangs on the wall next to her—big splotches of orange and swaths of pale blue against a cream background. Someone has dimmed the lights and turned up "Beast of Burden" in the other room; the orchidarium in Mina's office at the end of the hallway emits a cosmic, humming glow. The air in the apartment has shifted from dinner party to after hours. Baptiste's laughter floats out of the kitchen with Agathe's quickly joining in harmony.

"Come here," Loup says with his arm around Vincent's waist, pulling her into the bathroom. He turns on the light, closes and locks the door behind them.

The mosaic walls are busy and dramatic—amethyst and gold, with a small sun above the towel rack. Skinny tiled lines of sunlight wrap from one end to another.

Vincent reaches over to flick the light off and they kiss; he tastes like pumpkin sugar. They keep kissing like it's the end of the world and their mouths, their tongues are all they have left. She moves him against the counter and turns her back to him, directing his hand down her skirt, between her legs.

"Are you sure this is okay?" he asks with his breath hot in her ear. She nods.

As he starts, she swirls her hips against him slow until she can't stand it and has to go faster.

"You're so warm," he says.

"You're so wet," he says.

"You feel so good," he says.

"You smell so good," he says.

"You taste so good," he says after putting his finger in his mouth.

She comes quietly, holding on to his wrist. She pushes off and stands behind him now.

"Would you like to do this yourself or let me help?" she asks with her body loose and flickering hot, her finger and thumb pulling at the cool button of his jeans.

"*C'est toi qui décide*," he says with his head down, breathing hard. She unzips him and touches him for the first time in the dark.

When he finishes in her hand, he whispers her name.

As they clean up, she wonders if Cillian can forgive her *la petite mort* in a little bathroom. She wonders if she even wants him to. There's a satisfying soreness between her legs that makes her feel dirty in a good way, as if she and Loup were at it for hours and not just a few quick minutes.

"I didn't think this was going to happen tonight. I didn't plan this," Vincent says. She'd mapped the bathroom when the light was on and finds her way to the toilet, pulling down her skirt and underwear, sitting. "I can't pee right after I've... finished, but I need to go," she says. She lets herself laugh about it.

"I'm not apologizing for anything," Loup says softly, moving through the black.

"Last month I was avoiding you and now here we are," she says, still trying to pee to no avail.

"Well, I have to be honest with you... I like being here *much* better," Loup says. Vincent can hear his smile. "You were killing me!"

"*Killing*? Really, Loup . . . you're—"

"Yes, *killing*. Absolutely. I chose my words with care. You would've been responsible for my death," he says, laughing and barely raising his voice.

"Stop it. Shh!" she says, laughing too, which makes Loup laugh more.

Realizing she won't be able to go for at least five minutes, she wipes and stands up from the toilet. As she is adjusting her clothes properly, there is a knock followed by Mina's voice.

"Is someone in there?" she asks.

"Yes," Vincent says at the same time Loup says "Uh."

"Should I . . ." he says so quietly it takes Vincent a moment to realize it.

"Just turn on the light," she says. Both of their hands go to the switch and flick. Both of their hands go to the knob.

Mina starts talking before the door is open. "Oh, I didn't know—" She stops when she sees them. "The, um, lock can be tricky sometimes."

"Yes! It's fine. Thank you, Mina. We're fine. This bathroom is gorgeous. The entire apartment is, really . . . I tell you that every time I'm over here, don't I?" Vincent says, looking down. She steps around Loup and walks into the hallway without meeting Mina's eyes.

Vincent turns to catch a glimpse of a smiling but clearly flustered *Wolf*, who smells like her now, desperately trying to listen to his cousin. She watches him lean against the doorway, his dark, wild curls falling across his face.

12

From: SiobhanSunshineHawke@gmail.com
To: VincentRaphaelaWilde@gmail.com
Subject: Re: Dearest Siobhán

Hi Vincent,

It is very kind of you to write me. Tully has lovely things to say about you and I wish we could've met under better circumstances. I'm sorry to hear you've left Cillian, but I hope you won't judge me for saying it's understood. I'm not quite sure how he was able to detach himself so fully from Dublin and all he left behind.

I don't remember why we broke up. He doesn't either. And I didn't talk to Cillian after he left. Looking back, I can only imagine it was because we were both ashamed and confused and scared. Both feeling the exact same way, which wouldn't have helped us at all. It wouldn't have been a comfort for me to look into his eyes and see the same fear. It wouldn't have made us feel more connected, it would've just made us angry that neither of us had a clue what we should do or how it would all turn out in the end.

When I found out that he and his family had moved away, I waited (and waited) for a letter from him... for anything, really. I couldn't process the fact that he'd left me alone to deal with everything without so much as a word. I hadn't thought Cillian capable of that level of cruelty. And I'd just resigned myself to the fact that he was out of my life completely until I saw his book at the shop here in Dublin and picked it up. When I read that he thought of me so often... of the baby so often... that he'd written me a letter and just assumed I'd gotten it and not replied... I didn't know what else to do but reach out and tell him about Tully and the money his parents sent us all those years ago.

I'm rambling, I know... but I've held everything in for so long! And the loneliness of being abandoned almost crushed me at times. I didn't know how strong I was... or could be... and my story is a story not only of survival but of grace and mercy. I've always trusted God to provide and all of this is proof. This would be an entirely different email if I'd written it some years ago, but now is now. We've all moved on in our own ways.

I didn't see Cillian when he came to Dublin to meet Tully over the summer. I'm not sure what Cillian has told you? Tully talks about Colm and Olive and I've seen pictures. Olive is a stunner and Tully and Colm do look so much alike! Handsome, young half-black Irishmen, they are.

For the record, I do think you and I resemble each other somewhat. I think you're beautiful and I think this is all very strange. I think we are doing the best we know how.

In a way... we are family and always will be.

I hope you continue to enjoy Paris, and thank you again for emailing.

Be well,
Siobhán

Jack Woods knew he was dying, and he tried to take advantage of the desperate time to make (what he could) right with his family. He confessed to two dalliances in his younger years and Aoife told him she'd known all along, had just been waiting for him to be man enough to own up to them. She was glad he finally told the truth and said she'd already forgiven him. The confession made

Cian so sick he flew back to Tennessee and stayed for two weeks, completely out of touch, knowing that if his dad died while he was gone, that would have been the last time he saw him.

It was now the fall of Cian's senior year at university and he would graduate in the spring. He'd loaded up on summer classes the years before and felt comfortable taking a lighter schedule that semester so he could travel between Tennessee and California when he needed to, while his dad was sick.

He and Pica were still completely smitten with each other. Most nights when he was in town, he stayed over at her place. Their relationship was passionate and easy; sex with Pica was different. He didn't know why or how, it just was. And the thought of never sleeping with anyone else wasn't just okay, it was preferred.

He'd found her, his Person.

Although she hadn't met his parents, he'd met hers. They were exactly how Pica had described them—artsy and free. Rich too. Cian was let down when he felt like her dad was a bit gauche, always making a big deal out of footing the bill for dinner or talking about how his children would never want for anything because of how much money he'd made with his art and songwriting. But her mother was kind and interesting, warm to everyone. It was easy to see where Pica had gotten it from. Cian liked Pica's brother and sister too.

He really did want to marry her someday.

And he told her almost everything about everything, just like the "no bullshit" they promised each other the day they met.

But he never told her about Shalene.

—ɯ—

Over Christmas break, Jack brought up Shalene, and Cian's ears perked up because Jack hadn't mentioned or even mildly alluded to her since the night when Cian was in high school and had called him a racist to his face.

"I want you to know that I'm sorry for the way I handled the situation with Shalene Byrne. Snatching you away like that. I never thought it was right... I knew it was wrong... but it's what I had to do in order for you to have the life you deserve," Jack stuttered and slurred through a fog of heavy painkillers. Cian was reading Updike in the chair next to the bed and had thought his dad was sleeping.

"The life I deserve? What's that mean?" Cian asked, setting the book in his lap.

"You're destined for great things, your mam and I have always known. We didn't want you sidetracked by one stupid mistake," Jack said, turning away from his son and letting out his breath. The curtains were closed. Night had come quickly on the shortest day of the year.

"I don't know what to do about it. I want to reach out to her. I want to talk to her and I can... I can make my own choices now, but I'm paralyzed. I want my kid to know me. I want to know them. It's not like I've forgotten—"

"You've already started over. Don't stop now. And in spite of what you think, I've always loved you. You're my only son," Jack said before falling asleep.

You wanted everyone to live life your way and we're all suffering for it *stuck thick and unsaid in Cian's throat as Aoife came into the bedroom with a tray of tea and warm butter cookies.*

—⁂—

> John "Jack" Woods, 65, originally of Dublin, Ireland, died peacefully at his San Francisco home on December 23, after a long, valiant battle with pancreatic cancer. He was CEO of Oceanwide Tech and a member of Ocean Gate Country Club and the Ocean Gate Golf Team. He leaves behind his wife, Aoife Woods, neé O'Reilly, and one son, Cian Woods, alongside two brothers, three sisters, a host of aunts and uncles, and far too many cousins to count.

HALF-BLOWN ROSE

"We're not considering abortion, correct? Just so I'm clear?" Cian had said to Pica not long after she told him. He thought they'd done everything right, but there might've been a broken condom the previous month. Those stupid flavored ones they passed out in front of the student health center. Did he have the most potent fucking sperm on earth?

"I—"

"It's fine, I understand. And I said... considering. There's just a lot more I need to do first and we haven't discussed it. You're a feminist and pro-choice—"

"I tell you I'm pregnant... and the first thing you want to talk about is abortion?"

Her eyes were practically neon pink from all the crying—so much crying her face looked unfamiliar to him. A Kafkaesque moment he knew would be with him forever.

"I'm sorry, Pica. And it wasn't the first *thing. You never said you hadn't thought about it."*

"I figured it was obvious, Cian. Just because I'm pro-choice..." she started, putting both hands on her stomach. He went to her and held her tight. "If it was someone else's and not yours... maybe I'd make a different decision, but it's yours. It's mine. It's ours*," she said.*

He put his hands on hers and shushed her, thinking of what his dad had said about biracial children... how they struggle with knowing who they are and where they belong. Bullshit. Cian didn't believe that, did he? And if he did, was it only because he'd heard it so many times?

And why did Pica say "if it was someone else's"? He trusted her. They were in a monogamous relationship. He wasn't sleeping with anyone else and neither was she.

Right?

He hated himself for the flick of relief he felt, imagining the baby as someone else's.

Would he ever be able to stand up and take responsibility for anything?

He couldn't when he was fifteen, but now... now he could. Couldn't he?

"Yes, of course. I'm so sorry. I'm sorry, Pica. Of course. I'm just in shock, that's all. It's ours, love. It's our baby."

—~~—

Dear Reader,

Memories... pages ripped (sometimes violently) from the books of our lives. Memories... feathers falling (oh so softly) all around us. In real time as they're happening, as mere flashes, as wishes or nightmares. They carry us, they haunt us, they anchor us. We cannot escape them.

Close your eyes. Do you see them? Can you feel them? They are yours.

They are blips. They are of much importance.

These are mine.

Yours,

Cian Woods

—~~—

You are invited to the graduation of Cian Woods, who has completed his Bachelor of Arts in English, with a focus on Creative Writing. The ceremony will take place on May 1 at Vine Leaf University in Nashville, Tennessee.

—~~—

You are invited to the wedding of Picasso Taylor-Cline and Cian Woods! May 15 at Hearthill Farm at six o'clock in the evening.

—~—

He's here! Cian and Picasso joyfully announce the birth of their son, Cowan Paul! Born on October 13, he weighed seven pounds, seven ounces, and was twenty-one inches long.

—~—

You are invited to the graduation of Cian Woods, who has completed his Master of Fine Arts. The ceremony will take place on May 1 at the University of Louisville in Louisville, Kentucky.

—~—

Cian Woods was awarded the F. Scott Fitzgerald Short Story Award, which includes publication of his first collection and $25,000.

—~—

Cian Woods was named one of *Titus* magazine's 25 under 25.

—~—

She's here! Cian and Picasso joyfully announce the birth of their daughter, Oona Roisin! Born on January 15, she weighed seven pounds, one ounce, and was twenty inches long. She joins big brother Cowan, who is over the moon with love for his new baby sister!

—ꝏ—

Cian Woods was awarded the First Fiction Award, which includes publication of his first novel and $50,000.

—ꝏ—

Cian Woods's second novel, RAINBOW WEATHER, was sold after auction, to James & Sons, in a major deal, with a third novel to follow.

—ꝏ—

Cian Woods was awarded the Kentucky Goldenrod Grant for creative writing.

—ꝏ—

Cian Woods was named one of *Catchword* magazine's 30 under 30.

—ꝏ—

Cian Woods was named one of *Fetching* magazine's 35 under 35.

—ꟺ—

Cian Woods was named one of *Bliss & Burn* magazine's 40 under 40.

—ꟺ—

Cian Woods the Pusillanimous cannot tell his wife and children the truth about why his family left Dublin, because it's both a blessing and a curse to be so fucking good at making up stories.

—ꟺ—

Look, Delia, how w' esteem the half-blown rose

Of Nature's gifts thou mayst with lilies boast,
And with the half-blown rose. But Fortune, O,

—ꟺ—

Half-Blown Rose because Cian's wife has one tattoo.
Half-Blown Rose because his life in Ireland was unfinished.
Half-Blown Rose because the three syllables are like heartbeats, repeating repeating repeating.
Half-Blown Rose. Half-Blown Rose. Half-Blown Rose.

—ꟺ—

Half-Blown Rose.
Borne Half Lows.
Born Flows Heal.

To: VincentRaphaelaWilde@gmail.com
From: TullyHawke@gmail.com
Subject: Re: It's Blue Now

Vincent, I've been noticing a lot of blue this week. The sky on Friday, Eimear's navy coat, the gum in a gumball machine at the pub. This new guitar we just got in the shop...it's a very calming blue. Like Bob Marley singing "Three Little Birds" blue. I think you're turning me into a synaesthete!

I've been working on a song, but couldn't think of a name for it, and decided to call it "It's Blue Now" after the subject of this email. I'm uploading it to YouTube as I write this. If you give it a listen, tell me what you think? I've come to trust your opinion. Artists have to stick together.

I still can't believe Soloco is your dad! Please tell him that I think he's cracker.

Be well,
Tully

PS: Let me know what next week's colour is so I can play along? I look forward to them.

To: TullyHawke@gmail.com
From: VincentRaphaelaWilde@gmail.com
Subject: The new color is yellow

And wow, Tully, I LOVE this song. (!!) Especially the bridge. Your bridges knock me out! I get the bridge of your song "Christchurch Place" in my head a lot. I'll deffo tell my dad you think he's cracker and send him the links to your music. I know he'll love it all. He listens to everything as long as it's good, and good you are. Truly.

Am off to walk around Paris and listen to "It's Blue Now" and get to know it more, as I'm looking for yellow! Since yellow and blue make green, I'll keep my eye out for that magic too. More soon!

As ever,
V

PS: Your mom is absolutely aces, correct. Her email warmed my heart.

After Mina caught Vincent and Loup practically in flagrante delicto, Vincent cleared Baptiste up on some things.

Yes, she and Loup kissed, dot dot dot.

But no, she and Loup hadn't had sex.

Yes, she was embarrassed Mina assumed something else happened in their bathroom.

No, Vincent didn't regret anything.

Non, je ne regrette rien.

Not yet.

November passes in a flurry, with Vincent making a point of connecting with her children often, teaching, making jewelry, taking photos of the new pieces, updating the Go Wilde! website, and filling orders. Every other day, she goes to the Franprix on the corner for bread, fresh fruit, and vegetables.

Loup comes home with her after classes several times a week, the two of them making chickpea stew or *bœuf bourgignon* or *oeufs cocotte* or some other comforting, bubbly dish and watching Jean-Luc Godard movies together.

They watch *Une femme est une femme* more than once. Vincent tells Loup how much she loves the scenes when the couple is having an argument and have stopped speaking. Instead, they take turns walking around their place with a lamp, looking for books with titles that sum up their feelings.

Vincent and Loup make a habit of kissing on the couch until she forces them to go for a walk. Sometimes she's inspired to put on winged eyeliner and stripes, always in her trench coat, always with a red lip. Once, a pair of red tights like Anna Karina in *Une femme est une femme*.

When Loup handstands down the sidewalk and back, she files every last drop of coordination, focus, and strength it takes for him to do that in a tight, kindled corner of her mind, saving it for when she's back home alone with her Gideon 7000, or as Agathe likes to call it, her new best friend.

I'm a bit jealous of both Loup and the Gideon 7000 now actually! MDR, Agathe texts, abbreviating the French *mort de rire* (dying laughing) in place of the American *LOL*. Vincent responds with an *mdr* of her own.

Vincent still hasn't seen it, but she's given Loup three more hand jobs at this point. They are always in the dark, always in her bathroom, as if anywhere else in the apartment will make it *too* real. And she feels it four other times—while they are both mostly clothed—thick and stiff between her legs on the soft couch as he holds her rocking hips on top of him. Once, he gently licks and sucks her nipples until she comes—his own climax surprising him, the wet blooming dark. *Voilà!* That is the vision she has in mind when she talks to Cillian and he asks what she's been doing. She almost whimpers remembering it and is so glad they aren't video chatting, or he would've seen a suffering mess of both guilt and desire pour across her face.

Loup sends her "Everybody Here Wants You" by Jeff Buckley.

Vincent sends him "Tessellate" by alt-J and "Furnaces" by Ed Harcourt.

He sends her "Can't Feel My Face" by The Weeknd.

He sends "I'm Your Man" by Leonard Cohen and "Power over Me" by Dermot Kennedy.

It is frustratingly intense, thinking of Loup picking out those songs and applying them to her. So much that she has to lie down; she considers investing in a fainting couch.

She sends him "Because the Night" by the Patti Smith Group.

He sends her "Angel" by Massive Attack and "Can't Get You Off My Mind" by Lenny Kravitz.

She sends him "Partition" by Beyoncé and "Justify My Love" by Madonna.

He sends her "Talk" by Hozier and "The Sweetest Taboo" by Sade.

After receiving those two, she takes to her bed yet again.

She sends him "Lovesick" by Banks and "Two Weeks" by FKA twigs.

He sends her "Rue Saint-Vincent" by Yves Montand after they walk there together through the cool, fizzling night so he can point to the sign that reads her name.

They send each other "Je t'aime... moi non plus" by Jane Birkin and Serge Gainsbourg back and forth every morning for a week.

Vincent puts the songs together in a playlist—names it *Lust in Conversation*—and listens to it on her walks, pretending she's in *un film français.*

Loup had been too much of a bad boy in school to properly read *Jane Eyre*, so she buys him a copy. He texts her a row of exclamation points when the fortune-teller is revealed to be Rochester and when he finally tells Jane the truth about Bertha. Loup takes a picture of the phrase "half-blown rose" circled in pen and sends it to her too.

On what is Thanksgiving in the States, when Loup thinks she might be feeling a little low spending it away from her family, he comes over and gives her the still life he's been working on. The clementine peels he pocketed that first dinner party night he was in her apartment, painted on a table next to a vase holding a lust-red half-blown rose. A tiny tiger paws behind the glass, distorted by the trick of water.

For Vincent. Ma clémentine. Ma rose. Ma tigresse.

He hangs it just like he said he would, in a frame over her bed.

It is December now; the days have gone cold, the darkness stretches. Last week, Vincent took a day off from teaching because her period was so bad again. Loup came over and made her tea and toast. Tomorrow, Olive and Ramona will arrive to spend Christmas week with her.

Tonight, she is walking to an Anchois show alone because both Agathe and Baptiste have plans, although they said they may try to meet her there later.

Like all evenings, the sidewalks and streets are busy enough to allow Vincent to feel comfortable walking alone. She wanders toward Le Marais, taking her time, trying a new route. She loves getting lost in Paris; there's nowhere else she'd rather lose her way.

She gets catcalled turning down rue du Temple and again walking up rue de Braque, because it looks like she's wearing nothing but shimmery black tights underneath her trench coat. Her dress—diaphanous and red—is not quite to her knees. Her lips match the fabric and Vincent is sure it will be easily recognizable as the dress of a woman going *through* it. A revenge dress. She'd seen it in a shop window on her walk through the mall and went in to try it on, telling herself she'd keep it only if it fit perfectly, and it did. She's wearing it with black velvet wedges, smoking and strolling through the snappy, starry night.

When she gets to the club door, her phone vibrates in her bag and she sees that it's Cillian. She steps aside and answers.

"*Salut*," she says.

"Vincent, love. How are you? Olive is due to arrive tomorrow, right?"

Ah, how she loves his voice, his accent. Fucking annoying. Even after all this?

"She is. She and Ramona are on the same flight," Vincent says.

She was always comforted by the fact that Ramona lived in Nashville too, near Olive, but she's even more comforted by it now that she's in Paris. Ramona, happily childfree, has been like a second mom to Olive, and knowing that her best friend is nearby if her daughter needs anything makes Vincent feel a lot better and less guilty about being so far away.

Their family made the decision over the summer that Olive would spend Christmas with her, and Colm would spend Christmas with his dad in Kentucky. The boys have plans to go skiing in Indiana and finish the James Bond marathon they started last Christmas.

"When's Colm getting in town, tonight or tomorrow?" she asks Cillian.

"He changed it to the day after tomorrow because of the film they're workin' on. Some sort of complicated scheduling with one of the actors," Cillian says with a bright lift in his accent that Vincent quickly recognizes. He's buzzed or maybe even drunk. She does the math to figure out what time it is in Kentucky, six hours back. Three o'clock in the afternoon.

"And speaking of days...lovely to hear you're day-drinking. Enjoying yourself, are you?" Vincent says. "Now that you're on break, you've really let loose." She leans against the building, watching a stream of people trickle through the club's doors. She tucks her scarf around her neck some more; her legs are freezing.

There's rustling on Cillian's side of the phone line and then a woman's voice.

"Vincent, the long-lost wife! Vincent, you have to come home. Your husband is a mess without you. We're playing darts and he just made me do two shots of tequila in broad daylight!" the woman says, practically screaming the last part.

"Vin, I'm sorry. Sorry for that. It was Hannah from work. You've met her. It's an impromptu thing, we're not alone. Jamal is here too. You remember Jamal, don't you? I'm sorry I had to call and disturb you, I just miss you so much. My life...my life isn't the same without you in it. Is your life the same without me in it? What the fu—" Cillian interrupts himself. It's quieter on his side now. He's stepped away from the people and noise. "Vin, what are we *doin'*?"

Vincent's heart is beating hard and she's embarrassed at the absurdity of feeling jealous about Cillian day-drinking with a woman when she's standing in *that* dress outside of a club where she's going to see a young man she's *thisclose* to sleeping with.

She imagines Cillian with his hands all over Hannah, their hot holiday breath mingling sweet. The two of them panting and touching next to a Christmas tree; Cillian plucking fir needles from Hannah's hair afterward. Vincent wonders if he's at the same bar near campus that sells mead. The cozy, dark-wood one where he likes to have his special evening classes as they study *Beowulf*.

"My life isn't the same without you in it, no. And I don't know what we're doing. I'm not thinking about that... I don't know what I'm thinking about. I'm just looking forward to Olive and Ramona right now. That's enough," she says.

"Have you stopped loving me?" he asks.

"I wish."

"I don't! Please don't stop. I'm beggin' you."

"I can't... even if I want to," she says with boredom coolly surfing her voice like a wave.

"I love you, Vincent," he says.

"I know you do."

"Cillian, it's your turn again. Come back!" Hannah's voice perks through the speaker. She laughs. Cillian laughs too, then stops, realizing it's a bad move.

"Yeah. You better go. Don't want to miss your turn. I'll talk to you... later," Vincent says, ending the call.

Vincent orders a gin and tonic and drinks it, leaning against the pole off the side of the stage. Loup knows she's there, but she's sure he can't find her. The lights on him are too bright, the lights on her are flashing. She likes these sorts of situations, where she doesn't know anyone and they don't know her. She doesn't feel lonely. She hasn't been lonely once since she's been in Paris, which feels like a lie she would tell herself even if it weren't true.

She's felt a lot of things, but never lonely.

Lonely is a negative word. *Alone* is neutral. She likes feeling *alone.*

I am alone, she thinks, and the word *alone* is positive.

After several fast songs, a slow one. Noémie starts singing. No band of lights around her head this time. Her hair is in two space buns and she's wearing a pair of thick-framed glasses. Vincent got a better look at her face snooping through her Instagram account, finding her attractive in a frosty way—like she's from a dark and icy country. Like she had to snowshoe her way to school with hot chocolate every morning and grew up breeding blue-eyed huskies. Noémie sings *where are you going* over and over again in French. It reminds Vincent of one of her favorite ABBA songs, "Voulez-Vous," and right as she's thinking it, Noémie, like magic, starts singing "Voulez-Vous." Vincent's weak prescient powers are clearly back at it again. A couple of minutes of "Voulez-Vous," and the music shifts to "Gimme! Gimme! Gimme! (A Man after Midnight)." Noémie starts singing the chorus. The crowd does too. Vincent drinks and sings along. Everyone is hyped, dancing. A woman next to her is jumping up and down in a sequined dress that blinks in the lights.

Vincent is barely buzzed, but so happy because she loves this song so much and she's laughing because *Gimme! Gimme! Gimme! (A man after midnight)* is exactly what she's beaming to Loup with her mind as she watches him play the keyboard and push buttons on the beeping electronic boxes in front of him. He has a big pair of headphones around his neck and sometimes he holds one side up to his ear and his hair is pulled back in a little twist again.

His shirt is white. He is glowing. He looks like an angel.

She can't wait to be alone with him, to kiss him, to touch him, to smell him, to be enraptured with and ravished by him. She can't stop thinking about it as she looks around at the people dancing and watching the band.

When she turns to her right she sees Baptiste and next to him, Agathe. Vincent waves her arm at them, but they don't see her. Baptiste is bending down and saying something in Agathe's ear. Agathe nods and laughs, puts her arms around his waist. Kisses his mouth. They're surrounded by people, swallowed in the crowd. Vincent gets on her toes and looks until she finds them again. She keeps watching them kiss, wanting to make sure her eyes aren't deceiving her.

Vincent looks away, refixing her vision on Loup.

Baptiste and Agathe? Agathe and Baptiste? They're never flirty with each other. But then again, most of the time when Vincent sees them together, Mina is there too.

Mina being coldish to Agathe at times suddenly makes sense.

Vincent can't sort out her jealousy. It's surprising and completely irrational. Of what? Of Baptiste? Of Agathe? Of the two of them having a secret and not letting her in on it? She's only been friends with them since the summer; Baptiste and Agathe have known each other for years.

Baptiste is married, but Vincent's married too. How can she judge him? There's so much she doesn't know about them. There's so much they don't know about her.

Everyone, everywhere does whatever they want all the time. Keeps their secrets.

Her heart steps on the gas watching Loup up on that stage. She thinks, *I'm finally going to fuck you tonight*, and it feels as easy and quotidian as thinking, *I'm going to sleep in a bed tonight*. And she is, hopefully with Loup beside her. This is her choice. *C'est moi qui décide*.

Baptiste finds Vincent when Anchois takes a break. He and Agathe are next to her now, acting completely normal, like they've only just shown up at the same time by chance.

He kisses Vincent's cheeks.

"Made it, Veedubs. And it ain't over till it's over, right?" he says.

"Mina couldn't come?" Vincent asks, feeling nasty for immediately bringing up his wife, but her mind is reeling.

"Nah. She's working late," Baptiste says over the hum of a hundred different conversations.

"*Coucou!* You look beautiful," Agathe says. "This dress! A goddess, you are!" She takes Vincent's face in her hands.

"It's new. I just got it yesterday," Vincent says, feeling suddenly childish and out of place. She tugs at the hem. She's holding her coat and starting to sweat.

"What are you and Loup doing after? Or shouldn't I ask?" Agathe says.

Baptiste asks if they want any drinks. Vincent says no. Agathe orders a wine from him and he heads to the bar.

"You know... sometimes I think... God, if he wasn't married. He could get it regularly, no questions," Agathe says once he's out of earshot.

Vincent doesn't respond, she just smiles at Agathe and looks at the stage. Someone has turned on a smoke machine and Anchois walks out again. Loup waves to the crowd.

"Are you all right?" Agathe asks.

"Yes! I'm good," Vincent says, and tells Agathe she looks beautiful too.

The music starts and Baptiste returns. Vincent's ready to go home.

This time Loup—now in a red beanie pushed back off his forehead—introduces Vincent to everyone as he loads his equipment into the van. Vincent has never seen him wearing the beanie before and any first or new thing for them makes her feel moonstruck. They all exchange *salut*s and Noémie says she's heard a lot about Vincent's art classes from Loup and even checked out the Go Wilde! website. Baptiste and Agathe hang around for a bit and then go their separate ways, as far as Vincent can tell.

"Are you cold? We can go for a walk. Or actually, do you want to come back to my place?" Loup asks Vincent, putting his arm around her. They are already walking toward rue des Arquebusiers, where his apartment is.

She wants to go home but she's never been to his place and Loup's beanie and the gin and the dress and the ABBA and the phone calls and the texts and the secret-keeping have her feeling overly emotional. Her yes is breathy and quick.

They leave their layers on, their shoes by the door. Loup's apartment is nicer than she imagined, even though he'd told her that he inherited money from his grandparents. She's still been picturing milk crates and concrete blocks, maybe a futon, a TV, a gaming system. But no, Loup has curtains and real furniture—a nice couch, an actual coffee table with a small potted neon pothos in the middle of it. Vincent wonders if it was a gift from his mom or Apollos's mom or maybe another woman.

His bedroom has two big rectangular windows and the walls are barely brown, like a tea stain. The air smells faintly of him. Earthy-musk shampoo and unlit cigarettes. There is a large canvas leaning against the wall, covered in what Vincent now recognizes as Loup's paint strokes. There's a short, fat Christmas tree in the corner with lights that blink on when Loup flicks the switch. He closes the door behind them.

His bed is rumpled white sheets and a navy-blue comforter with a Paul Klee postcard and a Basquiat poster tacked to the wall above it. One side of his bedroom is dedicated to his music setup: laptops and a panoply of electronic boxes. There's a desk with two keyboards on it—one big, one little. And a cubby underneath loaded with candy-colored wires, adapters, and microphones. Boxes of records and neatly organized, dated tapes, stacked CDs and MiniDiscs, a small bowl of memory cards on the floor next to those.

"What are all these?" Vincent asks.

"Remember the day I asked if I could record you in class?"

Vincent nods. He'd said something about how he recorded lots of random things. While he was talking, someone dropped something and she'd been distracted by his profile and his hair falling in his face as he turned to look at it on the floor, so she only heard half of what he said.

"This is that day," Loup says, holding up a memory card. She takes it from him. It has a tiny *VW* on it and the summer date. "Well, there's more stuff on it too, but I have all kinds of things recorded. Sometimes I use them for music...other times I have them just because." He touches the tapes, telling her which ones are of his British great-grandfather talking about World War II, his French grandmother reciting a Baudelaire poem she memorized in school. "This is an argument I had with Lisette over me not doing the dishes last Christmas," Loup says, holding up a CD. He explains that he transfers the recordings over to CD and memory card sometimes, depending on how much room he has on his computers. "But now, most of the time I record with my phone."

"This is fascinating. I love it," she says, touching things. "Are you recording us right now?"

"No. I would never record without asking you. I always ask first."

"Is your roommate coming home tonight?"

"No. He's not."

"Can we lock the door anyway?" Vincent asks, pointing. Loup locks it. She undoes the belt of her coat, revealing that red dress to him for the first time. "We match," she says, motioning to his beanie. He snatches it off, drops it. Takes his jacket off too.

"You're gorgeous. This dress is so sexy it's criminal," he says, touching it, pulling up at the hem. "*You're* so sexy it's criminal."

"Get it off me, then. *C'est moi qui décide*," she says, turning to let him unzip it. She holds her hair up. "But I have questions before we do this."

Loup kisses the back of her neck as her dress falls to the floor.

"You've been tested for things? Are you sleeping with anyone else? I'm not sleeping with anyone else."

"Yes, I've been tested for things. Nice and clean. Would you like to see the paperwork? I really do have it in here somewhere," he says. "And no, I'm not sleeping with anyone else."

"Okay, good. What are your parents' names?"

"Juliette and Daniel. Juliette being my mum, Daniel being my dad, in case you want extra clarification," he says.

"Merci."

He pulls one bra strap aside and kisses her shoulder. Kiss, kiss.

"How old is your mom? Is she older than me? Please say she's older than me."

"She's fifty-five. Now can we stop talking about my mum, please?"

Vincent is tickled by his answer and his mouth on her.

"Who did you go cliff diving into the Mediterranean Sea with? When was that?"

"Five years ago . . . my cousins Étienne and James. I have a picture. Do you want to see it?"

"Yes."

"Right now?" He pauses.

"No."

He pulls the other bra strap aside and slowly cups her breasts from behind; she presses herself to him.

"Who was the last person you had sex with? I'll tell you mine. It's my husband, Cillian, the only person I've been sleeping with for the past twenty-five years . . . longer than you've been *alive*," she says as Loup's hand makes its way down the front of her tights.

"You're obsessed with our ages. No one gives a shit about stuff like that," he says with slightly beery, minty breath next to her face. She loves how it smells. "And it was this girl in London . . . Dominique, back in September, but it's over now and I don't see her anymore. Now do you understand why I've been doing fucking handstands?" he says, laughing against her neck.

"When's your birthday? See? Shouldn't I know this?"

"How would you know this? You read minds? It's April twelfth," Loup says.

He will be twenty-five in April and his finger is inside of her.

"I told you mine was in September," Vincent says, letting out a ragged, low sound against her will.

"Right. The fifteenth. I remembered," he says, turning her to face him.

"One time you said you loved prostitutes. Does that mean you—"

"No, Vincent. I meant I love them because they're people... people like you and me."

"Good! That's what I meant too! And can we not tell anyone else about this until later? Even your best friend Baptiste. He'd get too much *I told you so* pleasure out of it. Let him wonder."

"You like keeping me a secret?"

"Not a secret! People are already assuming. Your cousin basically caught us!" Vincent says. Loup takes his shirt off with one hand.

She removes her tights, her underwear. Now she's naked in his bedroom. It's finally happening. She touches his hair.

"I don't care about anything at all right now except you," he says, like he's in disbelief. "Let me be your secret."

"Will you still do handstands for me after this? I like when you do them."

"*Ouais... tout le temps.*" He is hungrily kissing her neck.

"Thank you for playing ABBA tonight. I love ABBA," she says.

"Good. I know. That was for you."

"You have condoms?" she asks with her mouth against his bare shoulder. Softly, she bites him and wonders what Cillian and Hannah are doing in Kentucky at this very moment, six hours back in time. If Cillian could ever imagine that she's doing what she's doing in Paris at this very moment, six hours ahead.

"I do."

She thought it would happen in her bed, but instead it's in his. Feeling histrionic, she takes her time appreciating how fucking beautiful he is naked, strobing in and out of the shadows and slips of gossamer light. This body of a young soldier, strong and spare. And there it is—uncircumcised like Cillian's. Vincent relishes the sight of it; she doesn't have to try to imagine anymore. She watches it disappear as Loup slinks between her legs. He is patient and focused, licking and kissing before he's inside of her.

She has a trio of little deaths in Loup's bedroom, the last one slow and warm after three in the morning with him telling her over and over again how good she feels. Saying it with his mouth against her ear and his hand behind her head, gently tugging her hair.

Tomorrow when she leaves his bed she will let him know they'll have to cool it while Olive and Ramona are in Paris.

Keeping him like a secret.

She will wake up early, go home. Shower and change clothes. They will arrive on her doorstep. They'll make hot chocolate and decorate the Christmas tree and put on matching pajamas. Olive and Ramona will do their best to adjust their jet-lagged body clocks.

And while they are sleeping, Vincent will be wide awake, pleasantly aching.

Cette tigresse, le loup a gagné.

This tigress, the wolf has won.

Part Two

VINCENT ET LOUP

1

MONTAGE: THE STREETS OF PARIS, VINCENT'S APARTMENT – DAYTIME, NIGHTTIME

Time-lapse footage of Christmas: twinkle lights, presents, food, and wine. Vincent, Olive, and Ramona. Eating, drinking, and laughing. Calendar pages flipping.

NARRATOR (V.O.)

"Are these from Daddy?" Olive asked upon seeing the bouquet of fluffy mimosas from Cillian on the kitchen counter.

Vincent, Olive, and Ramona wandered and walked in the bright December cold. To Saint-Germain-des-Prés to shop. To the 7th arrondissement to drop off more Go Wilde! earrings at Citron Clair after the first batch sold out. To Les Deux Magots to have coffee and bread with butter and honey like James Baldwin and Picasso. Through the 2nd and 9th arrondissements to the Sacré-Cœur to light candles and pray. To the Louvre for a backstage tour courtesy of Mr. Laurent and to the modern art museum for the same thing, led by Baptiste himself, who was stoked to meet people from "Vincent's real life," he said. And while they were there, Vincent did a pretty good job of pretending like she hadn't seen Baptiste and Agathe kissing.

She did the same thing when Agathe came over for dinner on Christmas Eve eve. Vincent made her mom's Christmas cranberry meatballs and mashed potatoes. Agathe showed up with mille-feuilles and *chouquettes* she'd bought and a figgy, spiced Christmas cake she'd made. She knew Vincent's favorite boulangeries and patisseries in every arrondissement. Agathe scooped up *religieuses* and the *pain au chocolat* she loved from the one on rue Yves Toudic in the 10th. When Vincent stressed about there being an overload of French pastries in her apartment, Agathe, annoyed, forced her to confess that there were certainly worse problems to have.

It was so lovely being in Agathe's presence, Vincent found herself forgetting she was miffed at her. When Olive was around, Agathe toned down her bawdiness a bit and asked Olive genuine questions about school and her life. And Ramona and Agathe got along well too, even staying up late and drinking wine long after Vincent and Olive had gotten in bed together, the two of them falling asleep quickly to the soft laughter on the other side of the door.

In a bold move, Vincent hadn't even asked Agathe not to mention anything about Loup to Olive or Ramona, simply trusting that she wouldn't.

Agathe had passed the test.

Mrs. Laurent hadn't.

Before Olive and Ramona left town, they had her over for tea and cookies. Luckily, when Mrs. Laurent had said something about the "charming young man" who frequently visited the apartment, Olive had been out of earshot in the kitchen, refilling her mug. Vincent considered telling Ramona everything, knowing she could trust her, but Ramona's husband adores Cillian. Asking Ramona to keep her secret and not tell Peter would've been asking too much of her. Vincent explained the "charming young man" away easily by telling them he was a student, an almost-apprentice who helped her bake clay and ship orders sometimes. She told them he was very friendly and talented, wrapping up the conversation before Olive rejoined them.

EXT./INT. VINCENT'S APARTMENT – DAYTIME

NARRATOR (V.O.)

Vincent wouldn't see Olive and Ramona again until Colm's wedding in July. They'd all blubbered as they said their goodbyes. When they were gone, Vincent went back inside and cried herself to sleep in the middle of the afternoon.

Loup was in London with his dad's side of the

family. After she woke up, she made herself a pot of tea and texted him.

When you're back in Paris, can we spend the entire weekend in bed watching movies and eating takeout?

Hmm. Depends. Who is this?!

Her brain went dumb, her blood icy. There were quick gray bubbles on the screen.

Before you get mad, I'm kidding, Vincent Raphaela!!!

Say no more. Luckily, I'll be there tomorrow.

She laughed and sent him a photo of herself in her warm pajamas, giving him the middle finger. She typed out *va te faire foutre* for good measure.

He wrote I love pillow talk from my lover and it was the first time either of them used the word *lover* like that.

Oh, lover, she wrote back, because Vincent loves having a lover. She pictured Cillian telling someone his wife has a lover.

I have a young French lover.

I've taken a lover, her thoughts repeated, powering her up.

I didn't take him; he gave himself to me.

I've been gifted a lover.

"I'm thinking of traveling as much as I can for about a month, eventually ending up in Amsterdam to visit my brother and his family. Want to come with me?" Vincent asks Loup one night in the middle of March. Posing the question while he's still inside of her isn't the worst idea. Their simultaneous orgasms still flickering and glowing hot.

Even in the bleak midwinter, Paris had been lovely. She went for her walks and kept the windows open when she could. But lately Vincent has imagined herself on trains through the rain and sun of the French countryside, rushing toward spring. She's always wanted to travel wherever the wind takes her, like her parents, but has never done it. She didn't take a gap year; she went to college in Tennessee instead. She studied abroad in Italy for a few weeks before she and Cillian got serious, and after that, she got pregnant and married. She doesn't regret those things! She just wants to take full-blown-rose advantage of the time and space she's been given now.

Vincent lays out her plan. She'll put Go Wilde! on vacation for a month and get someone to cover her classes at the museum. Mrs. Laurent will come up to the apartment a couple of days a week to water the plants. They can go to London and hang out, rent a car when they leave. She's never been to the Brontë Parsonage so maybe they can drive up there. She's looked up several adorable little inns they could stay in, ones with gardens and chickens and big rooms for rent with lots of windows. What if they came back to Paris and rented a little Citroën and drove to the Côte d'Azur? It's where *La piscine* takes place and Vincent loves that movie. It's one of the films she lets play in the background while she makes jewelry. And as a heart-eyed Francophile, she wants to see more of France.

Afterward, they can catch the train up to Amsterdam. Her brother lives near Museumkwartier and he's a good secret keeper. Loup will love Theo and Theo will love Loup. They can go to the Van Gogh Museum, the Stedelijk, and the Rijksmuseum. Vincent loves the canals and flowers so much, she's a bit delirious and overstimulated talking about it with Loup.

"So... what are your plans for the next few weeks?" she asks him. His hair is tickling her nose and she tucks some of it behind an ear for him. He moves off and lies next to her, looking up at the ceiling.

"There's this club in London... Emiliano knows the guy who owns it and he's always trying to get us to come up for a gig. Would you mind if I had an Anchois show one night?" Loup asks.

"So... yes? You're coming with?" Vincent says.

Loup turns to her, letting his head rest on his hand.

"Sometimes it's like we live in two completely different worlds. You live in this world where you think things matter... that really don't... like our age difference," he says.

"Please! I haven't said anything about that in like, forever." She pouts.

"And you live in this world where you think I wouldn't go *anywhere* with you if you asked, which is also ridiculous."

"But why should I assume you don't have plans? Or that you can take a month off from your life?" she asks.

"I can do whatever I want. I have money even if I don't work. You were raised rich, so why do you act like you don't understand?" Loup asks, covering his face. There's light, muffled mirth bubbling behind his hands.

"I never want to assume anything. Not anymore."

"What do you mean, not anymore?"

There have been nights when their pillow talk has crept dangerously close to Vincent revealing more about Cillian or their marriage, but talking about any of that right now would be like popping a balloon with a machine gun.

"I just mean... everyone is full of surprises and I try my best not to assume anything. I wouldn't just *assume* that you're able to run away with me," she says.

Loup kisses her and puts his hand on her bare hip.

"I'm picturing hopping on trains and walking everywhere, wandering wherever we want to go... like *Before Sunrise*. That's my inspiration here," she says.

"I haven't seen it."

"Okay, well we're watching it tomorrow."

"All right. But I don't really need inspiration, Vincent. Honestly, I don't even care if we come back at all," he says, laughing and pulling her on top of him. Grabbing her ass. Smacking it so hard it stings.

They spend the next day in bed with takeout Chinese and wine, watching the entire *Before Sunrise* trilogy. In the movies, Jesse and Céline walk and talk. Vienna, Paris, Greece. The sexual tension is painful. They stop to eat and drink. They argue. They kiss and make love, powerless under the cumbersome weight of their desire. They're Vincent and Loup. Vincent feels like Céline's personality is more like hers than any other character she's ever seen in a movie and tells Loup this.

"I noticed. Sexy, smart, independent. And! She worships both Paris and a good argument, which is *exactly* like you and exactly like a lot of French women. You definitely act like one," he says. "So yes, Saint Vincent, I agree." He rubs behind her ears like she's a kitten.

Loup has a request.

That Vincent make an audio recording of one of her orgasms so he can use it for a new song he's working on. He tells her she can record it alone or he can record it for her. When she asks him if he's ever done this he says yes, one other time, with his first real girlfriend. He doesn't use the clip of her anymore, that's why he needs a new one.

When they're alone at his place, he shows Vincent the sampler and how he can record a sound into it and play it back. How he can distort it as much as he wants. He records himself saying "*Salut*, Vincent Raphaela van Gogh" and speeds it up so it sounds like a chipmunk. Slows it down until it's a ghost. He layers it over itself and they get at least five different looping versions of "*Salut*, Vincent Raphaela van Gogh."

Happily high up and floating on ardor, Vincent agrees to do it and tells him he can record it himself, but he can't assist in the orgasm. He gets on the floor, she gets on the bed. She lies back and, after undoing them, puts her hand down the front of her jeans.

Pretending she's alone works, but what works even more is opening her eyes to see Loup, watching her. He looks stoned, but he's not, he's just horny. Cillian's horny look is confident and cold; Loup's is hungry, desperate. She can appreciate them both for what they are—the look on a man's face when he's stripped down to his base level, be it hunger or violence or intense *I want you NOW* sexual arousal.

The need under the need.

When it's time, Loup gets on his knees and moves toward her, holding the microphone by her mouth as she hums and moans, racing after what she wants and needs-needs so badly now that they've gotten to this point. In her mind, she hears Loup saying *yes, I'm coming* like he did the day Baptiste invited him to the café with them for the first time and thinks about how badly she wanted him then. She thinks of his thighs and the rhythmic push between them, him saying her name when he's in her mouth, those short peach shorts. Now he's right there holding the microphone so close and she's so close too. She takes the mic from him and holds it to her mouth, letting go loud and lusty, not holding back, not thinking or caring about anything else in the world besides her fingers and Loup hovering over her and wanting to do a good job for him.

He kisses her mouth afterward and thanks her profusely, as if she's saved his life.

For her last creativity class in March, they focus on the color red. Someone mentions hearing "The Lady in Red" by Chris de Burgh and another says they heard someone playing "Redbone" by Childish Gambino while waiting for the Métro. Loup stands and speaks about seeing an alluring woman in a red dress one night before Christmas and says he'll never forget it. Vincent wants to cover her face as it warms, remembering that red dress on his floor and the two of them pretzeled and tussling in his sheets, naked and breathless with the street light pouring in,

In the last journaling class they take a stroll around the museum, then sit in a circle and revisit their happiest memories, reading them aloud to one another. A sharp turn from the preceding week, when some of them had cried remembering their worst. The happy memories light up the room, zooming from face to face like fireflies.

A man talks about going to Venice to meet his online pen pal for the first time. A young woman smiles, remembering the day she got her kitten and the sound the water bowl made on the tile when she put it down, just like the bowl in *Amélie*. Vincent shares how she felt the first time she sold a pair of earrings she'd made. She was eighteen and two days away from meeting Cillian at the coffee shop.

2

On the train to London, the woman across the aisle from them is crying as she talks to the man in front of her. They zoom under the English Channel, through a tunnel of black.

"She keeps staring at us," Vincent whispers as quietly as possible into Loup's ear.

The crying woman is looking out the window now. No, she's back to staring at them. When she glances away again, she focuses on the man in front of her and cries harder.

"I mean, it sucks she's so upset, but why does she keep staring at *us*?" Vincent asks.

The woman is probably wondering what she and Loup are doing together, if she's his mother or if not, how they met each other. Maybe they're a distraction from whatever it is that's making her cry. The woman turns again and watches them like they're her favorite TV show. Vincent smiles at her curtly and puts her head on Loup's shoulder, watching the black through the train window. She's sprung for the plush, marshmallow-like seats, and the ones directly in front of them are empty.

"Probably because you're so pretty," Loup says into her ear after nudging her head up so she can hear him.

"You're full of shit," she says. She puts her head on his shoulder again.

"Wow, you're *really* bad at taking compliments."

"I am not."

"Properly terrible at it," he says, drinking from his green bottle of beer. They're sharing it and he hands it to her. They share everything now—food, cigarettes, drinks. Bodies, toothpaste, beds.

"I've read this book before, by the way... What we're doing... I know how it ends. If a man were writing this story I'd have to die, right? You've read *Anna Karenina... Madame Bovary?*" Vincent asks him. She doesn't know where it's coming from. She feels fine! The Anchois gig is tomorrow night. Emiliano, Sam, Apollos, and Noémie are following in the morning. She's over the moon about traveling with Loup and all the plans they made. Her brother is excited she'll be in Amsterdam soon enough and she's stoked to see Loup's old London haunts, anything he wants to show her. Their hotel is in Kensington and has a private garden out back. She can't wait to get there and see it. Order room service.

She thought maybe it'd be too short notice to reserve rooms at the hotels and inns she wanted, but it wasn't. Probably because it's so early in April and not quite warm yet. In Amsterdam, they'll stay with her brother. She hasn't mentioned a word about her travels to Cillian or her children. As far as they know she's in Paris. But when the trip is over and they're back in the city and months pass and suddenly it's July and Colm's wedding and she sees Cillian in person for the first time in a year, then what? All of this is happening *outside* of her marriage, but what happens when she's *inside* of it again? She hates her brain for attempting to sabotage her freedom and good times already when they haven't even finished crossing the English Channel.

"I haven't read them, but I know what you're getting at. You think this is like that?" Loup asks. He nudges her again so she'll sit up and look at him. The staring woman stares; Vincent stares back at her until she turns away.

"Like what, adultery?" Vincent says quietly. She drinks from the beer bottle once, twice. Hands it to him.

"You're imagining this as a tragic romance, are you? Is it the train? I think it's probably just the train," he says.

"Cillian and I are separated, most likely heading toward divorce. He's probably getting cozy with a woman from work, and I have no immediate plans to reconcile with him. I could if I wanted to...and I haven't," Vincent says.

Yes, Loup, part of it is probably just the train.

A flash of white. They fly out of the tunnel into bright light; Vincent puts on her sunglasses.

"And what about revenge? Do you feel like you're getting him back for whatever he did?"

"Like being with you is revenge for him cheating on me?"

"Wouldn't be the wildest thing, would it? We don't have to talk about it. You don't have to answer," Loup says. The staring woman looks at him and he smiles his wolfish smile at her. She looks right through him and starts talking to the man across from her again, wiping her eyes.

"He didn't cheat on me." Vincent shakes her head.

"Brilliant. Glad to hear it. Would've blown my mind, actually," Loup says, with sugared sincerity.

"But that doesn't mean he didn't *completely* ruin everything either."

"Understood."

Vincent loves the restraint he shows in not pressing her any further. The restraint is just as good as the handstands.

"I'm not using you for revenge. *Pas du tout*. Do you really think that's the kind of person I am?" Vincent asks, turning in her seat to get a better look at him—those deep brown eyes she's grown accustomed to now, flickering in the sunlight as the train rushes north.

"No. I don't. Besides, it was me, not you, who started this whole thing. Thanks for coming along for the ride, though," Loup says, touching her cheek with his knuckles. "And no one's dying," he ends, stretching his optimism into a fine line.

The staring woman has her head turned toward her own window; Vincent watches the man reach out for her hand.

Vincent's Travel Playlist | Train | Paris to London

"April in Paris" by Ella Fitzgerald and Louis Armstrong
"The Book of Love" by the Magnetic Fields
"Theologians" by Wilco
"Love Man" by Otis Redding
"Midnight Train to Georgia" by Gladys Knight & the Pips
"When I Wasn't Watching" by Mandy Moore
"London Boy" by Taylor Swift
"Somewhere Only We Know" by Keane
"Sound & Color" by Alabama Shakes
"Crash into Me" by Dave Matthews Band
"Non, je ne regrette rien" by Édith Piaf
"Africa" by Toto
"Sweet Thing" by Van Morrison
"Tenerife Sea" by Ed Sheeran
"Thinkin Bout You" by Frank Ocean
"Everybody Wants to Rule the World" by Tears for Fears
"Paris 1919" by John Cale
"Dreams" by Fleetwood Mac
"Fill Me In" by Craig David
"Climax" by Usher

Kensington. London. Wednesday, April 11.

It's afternoon and Loup is napping next to me. He's a quiet sleeper. And he smells good when he's sleeping. He smells like what I think a cloud would smell like. A sort of faint sugar . . . mixed with rain. I romanticize everything about him because I don't know what else to do!!!

It's cool outside and I have the windows open. The hotel garden is lovely and apparently Kensington is known for its gardens. We saw loads of flowers on our walk yesterday afternoon.

In the hotel garden:

an ornamental cherry tree...

a magnolia already in bloom

anemones, too...

orange and red tulips.

There were complimentary glass bottles of still and sparkling water in our room... some mints and chocolates. Those shortbread cookies that everyone in England loves so much. I love them too!

I haven't been to England since Colm and Olive were teenagers.

Last night Loup and I walked to the Thames and back to the hotel through lovely misting rain and gray. Such a LONDON afternoon and evening.

Ordered room service: steak and fries for both of us. Hummus and veggies, cold white wine.

Got a little drunksy. I'm so easily buzzed now, it's borderline ridiculous. We took a shower together, had sex (sweetly in the bed, not the shower since I'd prefer not to kill myself), and slept.

For lunch today we got Jollibee and met Emiliano, Sam, Apollos, and Noémie in Hyde Park. Picnicked in a grassy spot near the Princess Diana memorial fountain. So many swans on the Serpentine! It was the first time I'd really hung out with Loup's friends. Apollos is my favorite. He's funny and seems like a good friend to Loup. Sam is from NYC... he's married to a French woman who is five months pregnant with their first little boy... they are naming him Gabriel. Emiliano and Noémie are nice too. They seemed kind of couple-ish there for a moment, but later, Apollos and Noémie were holding hands. Who knows? It's spring and love is clearly in the air!

We all went through the South Flower Walk in Kensington Gardens before we split up and Loup and I came back here to our hotel. His friends are shacking up with some more friends of theirs in Paddington.

In a bit, Loup and I will grab some dinner (probably fish-and-chips from the pub on the corner... Lion's Head or something) and go to the club for the Anchois show after that. I don't even know why I'm recording this as if I won't remember? As if I can ever forget how

Loup's hand feels in mine or how it feels to be staying in a hotel room with a man who isn't Cillian (or Colm) or Theo or my dad for the VERY FIRST TIME IN MY LIFE.

I'm glad I didn't tell many people I left Paris. I haven't even said anything to Monet yet. Sometimes I get so sick of reporting back to everyone. I shouldn't do it as much. I can do what I want! I just want to be as available as I possibly can to Colm and Olive since I'm already so far away physically. It's this guilt... I'll always have it because I'm their mother. Meanwhile, they're off living their lovely lives as they should! They're not sitting around wondering what their mom is up to, that's for sure. And if they knew... they'd want to unknow it as quickly as possible! (I actually laughed here!)

Maybe I'll shred this journal when I get back... make some jewelry or art out of it. Maybe it's art already. Maybe everything is... I don't even need this journal to prove it. Already an artist and always becoming more of one... like a living, breathing Künstlerroman.

Leaving for Paris, leaning into Loup...
my life is performance art...
isn't it?
Cillian writes his books and ~~maybe~~ this is mine.
Le Loup et La Tigresse.

Loup lets his Louis Armstrong, Satchmo T-shirt slip over his head. Vincent recognizes it; Colm has a similar one. Seeing the shirt makes Vincent a little dizzy. She's sitting on the edge of the bed, putting on her ballet flats. She's wearing dark jeans, a black cashmere sweater. A pair of big green arches hang from her ears.

"That shirt... Colm has one like it. He listens to a lot of the same stuff you do," she says, looking down at her feet.

"He sounds dope. I already like him, your son."

He would like you too, she thinks, and looks over to see Loup zipping up his black track jacket. Separate from her relationship with Loup, he and Colm would get along. Colm gets along with everyone, really. He's gregarious and magnetic like his dad, although Cillian is quieter.

Vincent prefers quiet men. She loves how she and Loup can be quiet together. The times when they sit next to each other and read or listen to music without feeling the need to fill every space with words. She doesn't know if Loup is like that with everyone; he and Baptiste never shut up around each other. But with her, it's different.

"Baptiste loves Louis. Baptiste listens to everything," Loup says, like he's seen a Baptiste text bubble over her head.

"I really don't want to be gossipy about this, and please don't say anything to him, but did you know Baptiste and Agathe..." Vincent says, hoping Loup will fill in the rest for her.

"Yeah...he doesn't talk to me about it." Loup leans on the table in front of the mirror.

His reflection: There are two of him now and Vincent imagines two real flesh-and-blood Loups in that hotel room with her. She likes him enough that thinking of two of him makes her heart sparkle and spin. Of all the things that could've happened to her in Paris, Loup is definitely the most surprising, the most fun. Anytime she's ever pictured herself having an affair it's always been with an older gentleman, in his fifties maybe. A brilliant architect who designs modern minimalist homes in Switzerland or a man who was once a danseur and now he paints, wears stylish black glasses and drives one of those expensive James Bond cars.

But Loup is in front of her with his arms crossed and he's stopped shaving, so his face is scruffy. She tries to picture Loup in his forties, twice the age he is now. She would be in her sixties then. *Sixties!* Shit. She pumps the brakes to keep her brain from spiraling too far into the future.

"But they...they're lovers?" Vincent asks, using the word that's only now become so familiar to her. *Paris is for lovers.*

"Agathe won't talk to you about this?"

"I haven't said anything to her."

"Why not? Are you afraid she won't tell you the truth?"

Vincent shrugs. "Does Mina know?"

Loup shrugs too. "But honestly, I think she and Baptiste have something worked out. Baptiste hasn't ever laid it all out for me, but he's alluded to it. And years ago, I know Agathe thought she was pregnant...or *was* pregnant. I overheard Mina talking about it once. I don't know what happened."

"It's making me feel gross, talking about this. Feels too gossipy," Vincent says, standing. She'd considered bringing it up to Loup earlier than this but resisted, content with minding her business. She can only imagine the things people are saying about her back home, how there are surely entire book clubs devoted to *Half-Blown Rose* and dissecting her marriage to Cillian, their family.

You know she moved to Paris? Their daughter didn't come home for Christmas, only their son. Cillian's in that big house all alone now. He doesn't know what to do with himself. He wears wool sweaters in the summer.

She can't fully process how it makes her feel, hearing that Baptiste and Agathe have been lovers for years. Did Agathe get an abortion? Lose the baby? Have it, but put it up for adoption? Is there a little Baptiste/Agathe progeny out there somewhere? A brown baby with her sharp nose and cheekbones, an almost-dimple just like Baptiste's?

They need to leave in five minutes so they can do dinner before the show. Vincent goes to the bathroom to put on lipstick and Loup follows her.

"Baptiste would tell you everything if you asked. He's crazy about you. You could probably get it out of him," Loup says, leaning in the doorway.

"He's been a good friend to me. He was the first real friend I made in Paris," she says, swiping the matte red color across her lips and tapping them together.

She almost wants to cry thinking of that first day meeting Baptiste in the museum. How he offered to give her the "real tour" and took her to see the behind-the-scenes stuff the curator had skipped over. Baptiste pointed out where the *good* coffee was hidden in the downstairs café and took her to the art and office supply room where there were pleasing-to-behold shelves dedicated to rainbows of Post-its, paints, postcards, and pens. He'd been so kind and such a gentleman, never making her feel uncomfortable or like he was trying to creep on her. He introduced her to Agathe that first day too when they met her in the hallway. She'd just popped over from the Louvre to visit a friend.

"You look really pretty," Loup says, meeting Vincent's eyes in the mirror. He takes a cigarette from his pack and tucks it behind his ear. "Do you get tired of me telling you that?"

"*Merci et non*," she says, putting the lipstick in her bag and turning off the light.

After dinner at Lion's Paw Pub in Kensington near their hotel, they take the Tube to Farringdon. On such late notice, Anchois has been slipped in as an opener for some famous DJ apparently everyone has heard of except for Vincent, who admittedly doesn't make an effort to keep up with famous DJs.

Inside the club, Loup asks her three times if she's sure she's okay with him leaving her out there alone. She gently reminds him she's a grown woman and can take care of herself. The place is loud and packed already. They go to the bar and Loup kisses her mouth. Gives her the icy gin and tonic she asked for. They make plans to meet at the back door after the show and Loup reminds her to text if she can't find him. He takes his beer with him and disappears into the crowd, heading backstage.

Vincent checks her phone and sees messages from Cillian. He texts her every few days, even when she doesn't respond.

Vin, love. The Monstera has a new leaf.
That's three since you've been gone.

I'm deffo not over-nurturing her, like you
warned.

I love you.

He's attached a pic of the unfurled leaf of the Monstera in their bedroom. She can see the blue chair behind it, her cable-knit blanket. Where will she go when she gets back to Kentucky? Where will she live? She imagines how she and Cillian will divvy up their things. Maybe he thinks of the Monstera as *his* plant now. She got that plant ten years ago, on her thirty-fourth birthday. If Cillian finds out about Loup, won't he take her plant? Won't he take everything?

It's already dark in the club, but the lights dim even more, making it darker. A new set of lights turn on and flash across the dance floor, which is filled with people swaying in sync with the music. Tech guys move with purpose on the stage, adjusting things.

There's a text from Agathe.

> Happy London! I won't bug you by texting happy whatever city you're in from here on out, but I do hope you have a lovely time. It's good to take a break. I'm only jealous you didn't take me with you. Biz.

And one from Baptiste.

> Veedubs! Your classroom was looking proper puny this evening. Mos def not the same without you. Loup-dog's BIG ANCHOIS SHOW TONIGHT. A+.

Vincent loves their French text slang.

Biz is *kisses.*

A+ is *see you.*

Monet and Theo had texted her too, as if she'd sent out a secret signal that she needed something to do while waiting for the set to start. She texts them all back, saving Cillian for last.

Thank you for taking care of it. I miss my Monstera! I miss a lot of things.

Vincent turns her phone off and puts it into her bag.

She recognizes Anchois songs now. She stands there drinking, wallflower-style behind the crowd while they play a bunch of them. Loup told her they were going to debut the new song tonight. The one she hasn't heard yet because he said he wanted it to be a surprise. The one that uses her breathing and orgasm sounds. He told her he named it "Une tigresse."

When Noémie finishes singing the *oiseau bleu* one, Vincent hears her own faint gasp spilling from the speakers.

The deep bass takes over.

"Une tigresse" is slow and sexy at first, with Loup's and Noémie's voices overlapping in French, then English. When it speeds up, Noémie sings the French, Loup speaks and translates.

> *A tigress loves to hunt. A tigress loves to kill. A tigress has a heart. A tigress has a will. A tigress in my heart. A tigress on her knees. A tigress loves to strike. A tigress, will you please?*

It's truly beautiful and hypnotic. Vincent's now-distorted sounds are repeated, softer and softer until the song melts away. The crowd screams and claps; the smoke machine is puffing. Noémie says *merci* into the mic and Anchois waves from the stage and walks off. Vincent is crying but trying to hide it. She feels a slight sting of panic, afraid she won't be able to stop.

3

<u>Kensington. London. Thursday, April 12.</u>

It's Loup's 25th birthday. He's in the shower. We slept in. Last night was really fun, although I cried through a lot of it. I don't know why I was crying so much. I really wasn't sad. Loup had a hard time believing me when I told him that and... he always believes me. He doesn't really ever question anything I say and in a way it makes sense, because I don't lie to him. (I haven't told him about Cillian's book because I don't want to talk about it, but I haven't lied-lied to him about anything.)

Anchois playing "Une tigresse" for the first time... that's what made me cry. It's really good and sexy and the loop of me breathing and having an orgasm changes throughout the entire song. Sometimes it's louder, sometimes it's quiet. Toward the end it slows down and before the song is over all you hear is my breathing, no vocals or instruments. It was a surreal experience, hearing it for the first time in a big room full of people dancing and talking and drinking. I kept telling Loup how much I love the song. I got him to put it on my phone so I can listen to it whenever I want.

Dominique showed up last night... Loup's ex. ? Whatever they were... I'm not quite sure. She's young and ~~pretty~~ really pretty, with long braids. She looks a lot like this woman who hosts a show on the BBC who's Somali and Swedish. Maybe that's what she is? She touched Loup's stomach playfully last night as they were talking next to me and it felt like I would shatter into a million pieces. I couldn't stop thinking about all they'd done together and wondering why they broke up. I want to ask him (why they broke up) and later, I ~~prob-ably~~ will. And since Dominique was the last girl he had sex with... in September... how much is that going to bug me now that I've met her? She and Noémie are friends... I'm guessing that's how she and Loup hooked up. I don't know how long they dated. Or if they dated. Do I even want to know?

We missed breakfast this morning, but we're going to grab a quick snack and head to the Victoria and Albert Museum. We'll lunch there. Later, we'll do whatever he wants, the birthday boy. Also, cake.

Cillian texted me good night and asked if I wanted to video chat sometime next week. Of course, we'll still be traveling next week. I haven't responded yet.

Some of Loup's friends were hanging out after the show, but we were both tired. I felt a little bad, like I was holding him back from being free and twentysomething, but he said he really was tired and didn't want to stay out any longer.

On the way to the hotel, Loup asked me twice what I was sad about and I told him nothing!

We had quick, quiet sex when we got back here and I wanted to anyway... but on a deeper level I ~~really wanted~~ HAD to after seeing Dominique touch his stomach like that. I just felt so competitive and emotional and irrational and ~~fucking...~~ SOMETHING (!!!) knowing he came back to the hotel with (only) me... because we're Together.

It makes me feel half-gross, but I couldn't wait to ~~claim~~ REclaim (?) him.

I am the one he desires now.

As I was falling asleep, I just kept thinking: he's mine mine mine.

They wander the Victoria and Albert Museum and get veggie wraps and teas at the café, a wedge of mango-and-raspberry cake. It's warm enough to picnic outside in the garden by the water. Vincent is wearing the too-big Anchois T-shirt she bought at the show last night and her black winged eyeliner is hidden behind her sunglasses like a bird in a bush as they nosh in the afternoon brightness.

"No more crying, eh?" Loup asks her. He takes a bite of cake off the fork Vincent is holding out for him.

"Oh, I pretty much cry whenever I feel *any* emotion, it doesn't matter what it is. You'll get used to it," she says, taking a bite herself.

"It's been what...five, almost six months for us? October was the kiss, then Red Dress December...and I'm twenty-five now. A proper old man," he says.

Vincent licks some frosting from her finger and offers it to Loup to do the same. "Happy birthday," she says, and kisses his sugary mouth.

They walk through Hyde Park and Regent's Park to Primrose Hill under a cloudless blue sky. Loup shows her the primary school where he did his froggy business and the tall milk carton of a house he grew up in. He points out where he and his mates played soccer in the park after school. They stop there and share one cigarette. She admires him as he smokes—his fingers, his mouth, how he moves. Her desire is intentional. She's pedal-down and willing it, keeping it steady.

Vincent doesn't want a husband when she's with Loup like this; she only wants a lover.

They walk through a pink petal storm on the way back to Kensington and pop into a pub for dinner. This one's called the Rolling Garden. Flowers follow Vincent everywhere she goes. London is in full bloom.

Loup has his eyes on the TV over her shoulder—a soccer match between red and blue. Vincent doesn't know who's who and finds it all overwhelming, trying to figure out where the ball is and who has it. She turns to give it a good look anyway.

"I'm buying your birthday dinner," she says.

So far they've been splitting bills because Loup's been adamant about wanting to pay. For his birthday, she's ordered an expensive electronic sampler she'd seen him eyeing at one of the shops in Paris and had it delivered to the hotel. They'll pick it up at the front desk when they get back. Vincent realizes how privileged she is to be able to pay for things without thinking about them. She has her own money, her own credit cards. She doesn't have to worry about Cillian knowing too much or tracking her, asking questions.

It's the last full month of school for Cillian before his sabbatical. He'll have so much free time, he won't know what to do with himself. He'll probably write another book, and the thought of Cillian's books makes Vincent need to pee. She goes to the bathroom.

When she returns, there are two pints of beer and a basket of fries on the table. Loup is eating and looking at his phone.

Vincent sits and drinks. He puts his phone away and smiles at her.

"Ordered you a burger and chips. The guy gave me these chips for free. A wrong order or something," Loup says. Vincent wonders what he was doing on his phone. If he was texting someone. She really doesn't want to go down that road, but.

"So, Dominique last night...was that weird for you? I don't know anything about it. Do you want to tell me? She's very pretty," she says.

"Wasn't weird for me. Was it weird for you?"

"She was touching you a lot. Or maybe it was only a little. I was highly emotional last night...I'm not sure what I saw."

Vincent grabs a fry and eats it. The other side of the pub is more crowded than theirs and whenever something important happens in the soccer match, they erupt in little cheer volcanoes.

"You were emotional because of the song, right? That's what you were saying. Or were you emotional because we left Paris? Or maybe it's other things you aren't telling me? Have you set rules for yourself about what you're unwilling to talk about? For me? It's nothing. I'll tell you anything you want to know. I don't see a reason for being any other way in this scenario," Loup says. He takes a sip of his beer and leans forward, laces his fingers.

Now that they've gotten to know each other so well, Vincent can easily recognize the little shifts in Loup's energy. It's happening in the pub. Sometimes he tiptoes around Cillian or the *idea* of Cillian, rarely coming right out and asking her about him. But sometimes, like now, he's intentionally setting her up to serve him information about either her marriage or her husband like he's the savvy general of a little heart-truth army.

"Um. I feel like we've both been really honest with each other about what we're doing. You're an honest person and I love that about you. I hope you feel the same way about me," she says, drinking again. Loup does too.

"I do feel that way about you. And even when it takes you a bit to warm up to things, you always do eventually."

Vincent laughs a little at the joke she could make; Loup smirks at her, knowing.

"I fought off my feelings for you... for a *while*," she says.

"I didn't even attempt to fight off my feelings for you. I knew I couldn't. I didn't waste my time trying. *Ça sert à rien.*"

"*Qu'est-ce que c'est... ça sert à rien?*" Vincent asks.

Part of what makes French so beautiful is that it relies heavily on liaisons and elisions—syllables slurring together like water. It's hard to know where one ends and the next begins. To her American ears, so many of the words sound alike. Vincent remembers hearing *le ver vert va vers le verre vert* for the first time, a joke to those new to French, since all the words in the sentence sound the same. *The green worm goes to the green glass.*

Learning to read French and listening to a native English speaker speak it is one thing. Understanding someone who has been speaking it their whole life is another.

"It means 'it's useless,'" Loup says, pointing at her nose scrunch. "Cute."

"Ah, *merci*. But we were coming from completely different situations, so that makes sense."

Loup sits back in his chair and puts an arm around the one next to him. The sexiest thing about him is how his body moves. It's something he can't fully control, something he's not even aware of, which makes it even sexier.

When the waiter steps up to the table with their burgers, they thank him. He leaves and returns with more napkins and a bottle of ketchup. The other side of the pub whoops and cheers again.

"How long did you and Dominique date?"

Loup takes a bite of his burger and wipes his mouth. Drinks some beer and looks at the screen over her shoulder. She even likes watching him eat. His mouth, chewing. She doesn't necessarily enjoy watching anyone else do that.

"We didn't date, really. We just sometimes would see each other and go home together. Mostly when I was in London . . . when I used to come back here more often."

Vincent eats too, looking over Loup's shoulder to the sidewalk behind the glass. The people passing by.

"Why'd you two stop going home together?" she asks him.

"Because September was the last time I came to London, besides Christmas. And I wasn't out on the prowl then . . . if you remember what happened with us right before Christmas? So no, I didn't see Dominique then."

He and Dominique didn't "break up," they just hadn't seen each other. When he *sees* Dominique, he sleeps with her? Vincent gets a little grumpy hearing Loup say *Dominique* in his accent, since it makes everything sound more important than it is. She's heard him say her name before, but there's something different now since she's laid eyes on

Dominique. Vincent didn't know she'd feel like this until it happened. It's surprising, like being pinched by a ghost. She really wishes they didn't have to do this part—dissect past relationships like this. Maybe there's no possible way to make these things *not* terrible.

She can stop. The conversation can be over.

Why isn't she stopping?

"Oh. When she came out last night, she was probably expecting you to take her home?" Vincent asks. Her stomach does a high kick, but she keeps eating anyway.

"Maybe. I dunno," Loup says, sounding *so* London. Sounding *so* young it hurts her feelings.

"Honestly? I'm jealous. The chemistry between you two almost knocked me down," Vincent says, wondering why in the world she's keeping this conversation going. No way would she have been open with him like this in the winter, when things were just beginning. It must be the spring making her want to spread wide like a flower.

"You know I'm jealous that one day you'll probably decide you've had your fun... and just, *poof*, go back to your husband or someone else, I dunno," Loup says, and thumbs toward the window. "*Tu me détruiras.* You will destroy me. That's what I meant by it. Doesn't matter. I'm still glad we're doing this."

"I will not destroy you. Why would I do that?" Vincent puts her hand on her heart.

"It won't be on purpose. And I'm a willing participant in this. The first time I saw you I thought... *I would let her destroy me.* I'd never thought that about anyone before and that's why I remember it. *Tu me détruiras,*" he says slowly, looking into her eyes.

"*C'est pas vrai.* I will not destroy you. *Je ne te détruirai pas,*" Vincent says. She puts her hand out for him and he takes it. "Will you say that just this once, for me, please?"

"Tu ne me détruiras pas."

"Merci."

The noise rises from the other side of the pub. Someone starts a cheer and there is rhythmic clapping. They both turn to watch. Vincent looks at the screen in order to remember who's playing.

"You're for the red? That's Arsenal?" she asks.

"Right on," he says, chewing and nodding.

They get Loup's birthday present from reception and take it out to the garden so he can open it. The electronic sampler is light blue with black and gray knobs and buttons. Loup smiles at her and nods, thanks her brightly.

"And when I bought it, the color of the week was blue. It's kismet," she says.

"This is too much and you didn't have to do it."

"Of course I did. It's your birthday and you wanted it. Also, you're really fun to shop for."

Loup has a funky, quirky style that leaves room for almost anything. A few weeks ago, she'd found a white short-sleeved button-down with green palm fronds on it and bought it for him on a whim. He wore it often and she'd seen it in his bag too. She also bought him a nice new set of drawing pencils when she stopped in the art supply store for clay.

She ordered him a new pair of steel-gray cotton sheets when he told her he only had one pair, the navy ones. She asked him why every guy in the world only had one pair of navy-blue sheets and he found it so funny, but Vincent swore it was true.

Loup is a thoughtful gift giver, too. He gave her an orchid and a vanilla kush candle in violet glass the first time they saw each other after Christmas. He showed up with an armful of red roses on Valentine's Day, apologizing for the cliché but saying he couldn't see roses without thinking of her. And, unknowingly not to be outdone, Cillian sent her an extra dozen roses on the holiday too, in addition to his regular Saturday flower deliveries.

A couple across the grass argues, not quite loudly, but enough for everyone to hear. When Loup is finished inspecting his birthday present, he thanks Vincent again and leans over to kiss her. He takes the cigarette from behind his ear and lights it, offering it to her. She smokes and listens to the fighting couple.

"I bought your son trainers!" the woman says angrily. Vincent watches her counting on her fingers. "My niece is getting married in the summer and look at us fucking it up!"

The man is wearing sunglasses and drinking something brown from his glass, not saying a word. A little orange cat paws across the grass under the table.

"My niece is getting married!" the woman says again.

"What's that got to do with us?" the man finally asks.

"Buy your own son a pair of fucking trainers, then!" the woman says, standing and stomping off, carrying her bags with her and disappearing into the hotel. The man stands too, and for a second it seems like he'll follow her, but he doesn't. He slumps back into his chair and lights a cigarette.

Vincent and Loup smoke and talk, unable to focus too-too much on their conversation because the woman who bought the man's son trainers keeps returning to the garden to tell him so. The man replies with a "so what" over and over again. He sits and stands. Loup wonders aloud if the cat is coming back; Vincent wants to see it again too. At one point the woman leaves, only to return to share a cigarette with the man for a few minutes. The arguing starts up again. The orange cat reappears—*there she is!*—politely sauntering to the concrete and ducking under a bush. Vincent and Loup are sharing raspberry tea, and when they finish, Loup carries the empty teapot through the softness of the cool, dark air as they return to their room.

"Boys love birthday sex," Vincent says from underneath him. She is naked, he has his jeans on. "*Je ne te détruirai pas.*"

Loup is undoing his button, his zipper.

"*C'est toi qui décide,*" he says with his mouth against her ear.

"I'm yours."

"Are you?"

"Yes. Say it."

"Tu es à moi. Tu es tout à moi."

Vincent sticks her arm out, blindly fumbling around inside her bag for a condom. Their tongues are smoked with tisane. Loup makes a breathy sound of desperation as he presses his hand flat against the headboard.

4

Kensington. London. Sunday, April 15.

Tomorrow morning we leave London. We'll stay two nights in Leeds in a quaint little inn with a garden and chickens and take the shortish drive to Haworth on Tuesday, where the Brontë Parsonage Museum is. We'll probably spend our days wandering. Loup's been, but I haven't. Loup's been pretty much everywhere and he's also aware of the fact that he's led such a charmed life. That's something about him I really do love.

Also, it's hard for me to even think of one time he's talked shit about someone!

He's genuinely a kind, thoughtful person. I often find myself looking for the darkness in people and because of that, I'm more likely to see it when it's there. ? That's probably how it works, but I don't know. In a way, I guess I'm still waiting for the shadow of Loup's darkness to fall over me? I'm not saying he's PERFECT because he's not and no one is! He can be flat sometimes... and by that I mean the distinctly male trait of sometimes not knowing when I need EXTRA things from him. Almost like he's very minimalist when it comes to his emotions... like Theo. Loup has a tendency to state how he feels very plainly and just trusts that I understand the rest.

He doesn't really overcomplicate his emotions and seems like he can sort them out easily... or more easily than I can.

I don't like it when Loup says I'll destroy him, as if he knows something about us or me that I don't. And when it comes to him not overcomplicating his emotions I'd say it's maybe a dude thing... but Cillian is FULL of complicated emotions and Colm is too, so that's not it. And I'd say it's a cultural thing since Loup isn't American, but again... Cillian is an Irishman so that doesn't fly either.

Re: complicated feelings... I still don't know how I feel about Baptiste and Agathe. WHY DO I CARE??? It's not like they've betrayed me somehow. They don't owe me anything. Just feels weird not to have known. Loup and I haven't talked about it any more. I want to. I'm sure Agathe would tell me anything I wanted to know if I asked... Loup's right about that. I don't know why I won't do it.

We'll see when we get back.

Feels impossible to even make a decent dent in all I'd like to see and do here, but it's been lovely. Yesterday we did the Tower of London and Trafalgar Square. Friday, we spent the entire morning and some of the afternoon at Tate Britain.

Museums are so romantic and soothing but also they can be stressful for me. It's like I can't absorb everything fast enough... there's too much to take in.

I love watching Loup look at things... inspect things. It feels silly to talk about how sexy he is, because it's so OBVIOUS to me. But to watch him reading things and to watch him touching things... it can be overwhelming. He took his time reading the little cards and getting close to the paintings. We stood looking at the Whistler together for a while. Nocturne: Blue and Gold—Old Battersea Bridge.

And the Sargent. Carnation, Lily, Lily, Rose.

We could've stayed all day.

Sometimes when I walked up to stand next to him, he wouldn't say anything; he'd just reach back to take my hand. I don't know how he knows to do stuff like that. When I think he can read my mind, it makes me feel crazy. But! That's how good he is at anticipating tiny things like that. Not so much in words, because he can be slow to do that, but when it comes to touch.

He'll:

put his hand on the back of my neck

or hold my face when we kiss

or in bed, he'll take his time and linger on the curve of my hips or gently kiss the inside of my arm.

(Once he touched different parts of my body and said the French—le pied, le ventre, le sein, le cou.) These tiny things... patiently. Making me feel like he can't get enough of me, even though he's trying.

~~Cillian—~~

~~Cillian does a lot of these things too but...???~~

Oh and. Of course I know a HUGE reason why I don't feel as guilty as I could about this is because I feel like Cillian "deserves" it or whatever for not owning up to things.

The complicated part that won't fucking fit anywhere is that I do still really love Cillian.

Yes, I've been chipping away at it since the summer... trying my best to love him less to keep everything from hurting so much.

And yes, having a young, handsome lover helps. ← !

I don't know, I don't know.

How can I be looking forward to AND dreading seeing Cillian at Colm's wedding?

See! ~~A mess!~~ COMPLICATED FEELINGS!!!

Loup's gone out for food now. It's lunchtime and I'm outside in the hotel garden having tea. We had breakfast in this same spot this morning. Tried Marmite for the first time. SO SALTY! I'll have to try it again, not on toast but on something else. I had eggs and cheese, some slivers of roast beef. A raspberry teapot (again). Loup had hot chocolate and pancakes. So fucking cute. He brought his skateboard with him and wants to take it to some skate park over the Thames. We'll catch the Tube and I'll bring my book.

To: TullyHawke@gmail.com
From: VincentRaphaelaWilde@gmail.com
Subject: PURPLE.

Hi Tully!

How's your purple going? I'm taking a break from teaching this month, but if it's okay, I'll still give you colors. Tell me your purple memories! I snuck and read my mom's copy of *The Color Purple* when I was WAY too young to have done it. There's a light purple with a hint of gray that's my very favorite color. It's lavender, but the teeniest bit paler.

It's getting warm again. I can't believe it's spring already. Are you a flower person? I'm such a flower person! If you're ever feeling chatty about it, tell me about the flowers in Dublin or send me pics, even. I'd love that. Thanks in advance! ☺

Bummer you can't make it to Colm's wedding, but not without good reason! I love hearing that y'all are expanding the guitar shop! Congratulations on that! And I love that you and Colm are talking some and that he invited you. I know Olive wrote you as well. Just a warning that she can be slow emailing back. She's like a turtle in a shell when she's in school. It's the only thing she thinks about!

Told you that my dad would love all of your songs! I've said it before but I'm just so glad those connections helped and that the new major label contract worked out. (!!) Congrats again! I'm definitely ready to buy tickets for a Tully Hawke World Tour!

In the meantime, send me your purple anytime you'd like, and I hope you see lots.

Love,
V

They step out of the Tube station on their way to the skate park. An ambulance passes and Vincent crosses herself. Loup looks at her and does it too—one hand crossing, one hand holding his skateboard.

"Do you believe in God?" Vincent asks him.

"Maybe in the past I didn't, but I do now."

"What changed?"

"It's not complicated for me. The world is too amazing to not have a creator," Loup says. He takes his hand and spins one of the wheels on his skateboard. He's wearing a hoodie and he pulls the hood up over his head.

Who are you? Vincent wants to ask, but she thinks she already knows. If it takes her forever to feel like she knows-knows someone, why does she feel like she knows Loup already? What's different now, him or her?

"The world is really ugly too, though. I do believe, but it's not easy," she says, pulling on a *show me your darkness* thread. Loup puts his arm around her in a tender headlock. "What happens when or if it gets so ugly you can't believe anymore?"

"*Celui qui vit verra*," he says. *He who lives will see.*

The sky is a glorious blue, the kind that makes Vincent want to live forever. The Thames is immortal too, alive and glinting in the buttery sun. They walk over the bridge with Loup telling her he's never been to this skate park, but he's been to another not too far from it. Once they get to the graffiti and curves of concrete, Loup unzips his hoodie, and Vincent holds her hand out for it. He's wearing the palm fronds shirt she gave him. He goes over to the edge of the bowl and disappears into it, pops back up again. She watches him skate around once, then she sits at a little table by the water and holds his sweatshirt to her nose, wanting to make sure she'll have his sunny-afternoon-in-London smell memorized, even when their trip is over.

To: VincentRaphaelaWilde@gmail.com
From: TullyHawke@gmail.com
Subject: Re: PURPLE.

Hiya V. What's the craic? My purple is going well, actually. Someone handed me a purple pen today at work and I had a moment of *ah*, which I never would've had if we hadn't started talking colours. Thanks for sending me a colour although you're taking a break. Glad to hear it! I hope it's not too much for me to say you deserve a break, but you DEFINITELY deserve a break.

I talked to Cillian yesterday. He called me. I didn't tell him that you and I have been emailing. He talked about working on a new book... one that wouldn't "fuck up his life." I just listened. Then he asked me questions about my music and the guitar shop. He asked some more stuff about my life growing up. I think he maps it in his mind... what he was doing at a particular point of his life and what I was doing too. Like what he was doing the year I started school or the year I started playing football or guitar... like we were living parallel lives in entirely different dimensions.

Don't get me wrong... if Cillian had been older when my mam was pregnant with me, I'd be really angry with him. I've searched my heart for anger towards him now and come up empty. It was a perfect storm of mistakes he made and I'm not an angry person. Doesn't sound like you are either. My mam's definitely not. She's a bit of an angel, that one.

And again, I'm sorry I can't make it to Colm's wedding but if there's any other way we can all get together sometime later in the summer or even in the fall, let me know?

Eimear brought an aubergine back from the market last night... purple, almost black. I suspect she's got baba ghanoush on the mind. And the other day, the sky was so dark with rain, the clouds looked almost the same colour as the aubergine.

I'm working on the songs for the new album. I'm sure purple will find its way in there somehow. Your dad's the best and so are you.

I hope Paris is treating you lovely. Talk soon.

Le grá,

T

PS: I'm sending pics of daffodils and bluebells from my mam's garden. I believe everyone should be a flower person.

Vincent flicks through the flowers and glances up from her phone to see the back of Loup's head. He's standing on the lip of the concrete bowl talking to another guy holding a skateboard. There is a clump of young men jumping up and chunking their boards down on the ground. Vincent's spotted at least three young women too. She's glad Colm doesn't skateboard; the skate park doesn't trigger any maternal feelings in her.

Colm's fiancée, Nicole, has sent Vincent and Olive a photo of her wedding dress—tulle tiered skirt, moscato lace. So perfect it brings tears to Vincent's eyes. She writes them, saying exactly that, and stares at it on her screen. Her baby boy is getting married; Olive will be a bridesmaid in rose gold. It reminds her that she needs to check in with Colm about his wedding suit to see if he's going with the dark blue. She texts him and asks.

She looks for Loup and finds him doing a kickflip on the pavement. It's the one skateboarding trick she knows the name of, but she doesn't know how or when she learned it. Vincent watches him until her phone dings with Colm's reply.

Heyyy mama. Yep, got the dark blue one. My tie matches Nicole's dress exactly, I'm told. ;) Brown shoes like you suggested.

Only three months to go. Feels WEIRD
but I'm ready. Let's do this.

Love you.

Yay! Ok good. Love you so much.

She watches Loup some more when she can see him; sometimes he's too far away. She thinks about how no matter what he does over there on his skateboard, no matter who he talks to, no matter what he says, he'll be in her bed tonight—and she loves having Loup in her bed.

She hasn't tried to properly measure her Loup feelings yet, but they are strong. Stronger than she thought they'd be.

Quelle surprise, tout.

Sitting in the sunshine, going through her phone, Vincent sees a voice mail notification from Cillian from yesterday that she missed. She clicks to listen.

Vin, love. I texted you seeing if you wanted to video chat next week because I like having it to look forward to. I need it to look forward to. I started writing a new book and not that you want to hear about it, but that's what I've been doing. I even thought about getting a dog, for fuck's sake. It's lonely here. I don't want you feelin' sorry for me. That's not why I'm tellin' ya this. Peter's coming up this weekend. We'll go climbing probably. Please let me know if even a phone call is doable? Would kill to hear your voice. To see your face. I love ya. Okay? I love you.

Even if she wanted to video chat with Cillian next week, she can't. And she doesn't know if she wants to. She sends:

Next week won't work but will talk
soon, I promise.

And sorry I'm late about it, but
thank you for the forget-me-nots!

Out of the natural sweetness of her heart, Mrs. Laurent had asked Vincent if she'd like her to send photos of the Saturday flower deliveries she scoops up while Vincent's gone and Vincent said yes. Yesterday evening, Mrs. Laurent sent her a photo of the forget-me-nots in a round glass vase on their kitchen counter.

Vincent answers her brother's How's London? text with Lovely! Leeds tmrw!

She told Theo she's bringing "a friend" with her to Amsterdam and that's all. She puts her phone away and barely reads her book, stopping to look at the water, to people-watch and to Loup-watch.

When he's finished, he returns to her smiling and kind of sweaty. He puts his hand on the back of her neck and meets her mouth with a salty kiss, asking if she's hungry.

Leeds. Tuesday, April 17.

It's before sunrise. Loup is curled on his side sleeping next to me. This little inn we're staying in is so adorable. Last night when we got into town, we had tea in the garden with the chickens. The owners live downstairs... an adorable old couple. We have the entire upstairs apartment to ourselves. There's a huge kitchen and a washer/dryer. We did our laundry... sat on the floor and watched soccer while we folded our warm clothes. Loup put my panties on his head with the crotch over his face because boys absolutely cannot help themselves.

We had salad and sandwiches for dinner that we picked up at the grocery on the way in. Loup did all the driving. It was the first time I'd ever been in a car with him. We rented a little Mercedes. It's fast and gray. He's a good driver... I like watching his hands on the wheel. What is it with me and guys driving? I used to love watching Cillian drive... those forearms. What is it with me and forearms? ~~What is it with me not even worrying about sounding like a teenager in these travel journal entries??~~ I refuse to be embarrassed by my own feelings in this journal. What's the point?

~~"Obsession" is NOT "rational."~~

~~Feelings/thoughts don't always make sense.~~

→ LORD HAVE MERCY ON ME AND WHATEVER IT IS I'M DOING BECAUSE IT FEELS GOOD AND I LOVE IT. ←

Loup and I took a bath together last night, which is something I haven't done with someone else in a long time. Cillian's not a bath person, so we've only done it a few times. But when we first started dating, Cillian and I used to always take our showers together. If I was going to hop in the shower but he was on his way over, I'd just wait so we could take one at the same time.

Sometimes I overanalyze all of this and sometimes I resign myself to letting go even more, no matter what happens... even if this is all some sort of terrible decision I'll regret for the rest of my life, I don't care. Because I'll always have:

Loup kissing my soapy feet in the bathtub

and him asking me to turn around and lie against him so he could wash my hair

me, on my knees in front of him, dripping...

and the terry cloth knot at his hip afterwards

Brontë Parsonage after breakfast. I will cry and cry and cry.

Vincent has never been to the moors, where the ghosts of Catherine and Heathcliff roam. After the Parsonage Museum and St. Michael and All Angels' Church, they walk around under the gray skies of Haworth, looking out at the surge of green hills. Vincent has a cry-headache from being inside the Brontë home, where the women she so loves and admires worked, wrote, and lived. Emily died there and Charlotte and Emily are buried at the church. Vincent's *half-blown rose* tattoo may be hidden under her sweater, but in Haworth, her Brontë heart is on her sleeve.

She can't help but think that this is something she and Cillian could've done together. *Should've* done together. She feels every emotion, standing there considering it. The future she and Cillian could've had together, all the money and time to do what they wanted after raising their children. They could've traveled the world.

If Cillian had told her about Tully, she would've known and accepted him inside and out like he was her own. Colm and Olive would've too. She wouldn't have to get to know him over email thirty-one years too late.

Vincent has been trying to forgive Cillian for what he's done and she's nowhere close. Not angry, but mad again, a feeling she knows is fleeting. She likes the stretches when she can forget about all of it completely, let the distance swallow it up. Cillian's name means *little church* and Vincent imagines putting all of her Cillian feelings in a *little church* on the other side of the world. Crossing herself before walking out. Slamming the little door.

"Do you write about me in your travel journal?" Loup interrupts her roller coaster thoughts as they look out together. Vincent has taken a seat in the grass and he squats next to her.

"I do."

"I like thinking of you writing about me in there. Is that immature?"

Loup fully sits and leans back on his hands. The sky looks like it could open at any moment and Vincent stares up at it.

"*Pas de tout*. I don't think it's immature at all."

"I wrote about you in my journal... in your journaling class. I wrote about a lot of new memories I've made... and the ones we've made together," he says.

Vincent looks at him. "So you'll write about this too?"

"I'll probably paint it," he says, nodding toward the hills in front of them. "When I'm all the way over here and you've gone back home," he adds.

"You always put a timer on this. Why? I feel like we can't even have a proper conversation now without you bringing it up. On one hand you're laid-back and chill, but on the other, you're anxious? You think I'll up and disappear one day without warning?" she says, frustrated with him too quickly. She opens her mouth to apologize.

"Promise you won't. Promise you won't up and disappear one day and I'll believe you."

"Of course I promise. Loup, I wouldn't do that. How could I do that?"

"You'd do it if your life calls you back somehow. Are you planning on returning to Paris after Colm's wedding? Because that's the date I've set in my mind... the date that'll change everything, I know. Because Cillian will be there and I'm sorry I'm bringing this up here like this. I hadn't intended to. It's just a lot of little things... like how your apartment is always filled with flowers from him... it's not like I can forget. Vincent, I didn't feel this way at first, but I do now," Loup says, shaking his head apologetically.

"I'm coming back to Paris after the wedding. That was always the plan. Going back for the wedding and returning to Paris were the only two plans I had when I left, besides teaching at the museum. Everything else has just... happened."

He reaches out to touch her hand.

Now she's living in a Brontë book—these wild moors, these wild emotions. The wind, the sky, the trees. Like God has slowly turned up the dramatic irony effect without them realizing and now they have to let it play out, no matter what.

"Loup, honestly? I'd take you with me to Colm's wedding if it wouldn't cause a distraction. That's how confident I am that Cillian and I are over," Vincent says. It feels true enough to let out. She pictures the face Cillian would make if she showed up in New York with Loup. She imagines him asking, *How the fuck old is he, Vin?* in that Irglish accent with his cheeks on fire.

"No. I'm not asking that—"

"I don't think you are! But I wanted you to know. And well... I'm jealous of Dominique and her perfect ass."

"You're the one with the perfect ass. The reason you think you're jealous of Dominique is because she's the only girl I've told you about. That's no comparison to a husband of twenty-plus years."

"I'm jealous of Noémie too. Because you make music together. I don't even want to know if you've slept with her, honestly...don't tell me," she says.

Loup is quiet.

That's his answer and Vincent knew it already. She felt its shadow cooling on her the first time she saw Noémie walk onstage.

"It wasn't recently, was it?" she asks.

"You just said you didn't want me to tell you."

"How recently?"

"Like, three years ago. It was one time and we were both stoned. She dated Apollos after that. She dates Apollos most of the time now," Loup says. "There are zero complicated feelings from me, by the way. Just a night when we both smoked too much and did too much. Apollos doesn't even know because it doesn't matter. She's my friend, though...I care about her. But not like that. Never like this," Loup says, pointing to the air between them.

"Would Apollos lose his mind if he knew?"

"It would bother him, yeah, even though he had another girlfriend back then. It's just his personality. He's my best friend, my brother. I tell him everything else. Just not that."

"But you know Noémie thinks about it when the two of you hang out. She looks over at you and thinks...*I had sex with him.* I mean...that's what I do," Vincent says.

She loves doing that. She did it as they wandered through the museum and the church. She did it as she watched him reading the names on the tombstones and thought of how one day they'll both be dead too, but not yet, so it's time to keep living. And she thought of the night before, when they were both naked and half-asleep. He was holding her from behind. He reached up and touched her breast lightly, rubbed his thumb over her nipple, just because they were in bed together. Just because he knew she liked it. Just because he could.

"I actually do that about you, yes," Loup says, and laughs. "But I don't do that with her."

"It's not like you'd confess it to me, even if you did, though."

"Okay, maybe not, but I still don't."

He puts his hand on the side of Vincent's face. They're Catherine and Heathcliff. They're Jane and Rochester. They're Gilbert and Helen from *The Tenant of Wildfell Hall*. Vincent feels the ghosts of the Brontë sisters wisping around them on those moors. The elevated emotions rage like wildfire through her blood as Loup kisses her so slowly, so passionately, it's easy to forget where they are and who she is as they glow furious and white-hot in the green.

5

Loup knows a lot of the roads and sights through the Cotswolds, having grown up in England. He shows Vincent some cute spots his family frequented when he was little. The lavender farm in Snowshill his mom loves so much, romantic cobblestone roads that look right out of a period piece. They drive past the Parish Church of St. John the Baptist and stop for cream tea in Castle Combe.

They get into Bath with plenty of time for a walk across the Pulteney Bridge before dinner. It rained on their way down from Leeds, but the sun came out as they drove through Chippenham. Bath drowns in golden light.

Loup tells her how he and his friends would party here when he lived in England. How they'd hop on a bus and come over for the weekend. Bath is a hot spot for hen parties and gambling, much like it was back in the days when Jane Austen was sending everyone here in her books. They walk past one of the houses where Jane used to live and Vincent goes to the doorstep and puts her hand on the sign bragging about it.

They pass a place with fried chicken takeaway on the way back to their hotel and promise that tomorrow that's where they'll get dinner. There's also a gelato shop nearby that Vincent wants to try. And Sally Lunn's for the buns she's heard so much about. There's a comedy walking tour every night and Vincent thinks they absolutely *have* to go on it since she's never heard of a comedy walking tour and has no clue what it is.

At night their hotel resembles a paper lantern; the tempered window glass tricks and trembles the light. The light is different here and the light is different in Paris too. Vincent can't find light like this in the United States.

She wears a wrap dress with a slouchy cardigan and Birkenstocks; Loup wears his palm fronds shirt and black jeans, a pair of all-white Stan Smiths Vincent didn't know he had. Surely Baptiste's influence. She giggles inside, picturing Baptiste, the fashionista, helping Loup shop for clothes.

"Have you been talking to Baptiste?" Vincent asks him. Loup is across from her, looking over his menu. Vincent drinks her wine and there is already an order of rosemary flatbread, hummus, and Cerignola olives on the way to their table.

The restaurant is crowded with couples and some bigger groups of people at long tables in the back. Loup lets his eyes linger on them.

"The other day he texted me, asking if we were having a good time," he says when he looks at her.

"And you told him you were having an *awful* time, I'm sure. Terrible."

"Right. I said all of this was the absolute worst," Loup says, smiling. "Have you been talking to him?"

"He texted when we were in London and I wrote him back. Not since then, though."

"Do you feel like you need to keep up with everyone? It's like a maternal thing?" Loup asks as the waitress steps to the table to get their dinner orders. He motions that Vincent will go first.

"I'll have the chicken scaloppini. Thank you," Vincent says.

"The same, please," Loup says to the waitress. "Nothing else sounded better than that," he says to Vincent. The waitress takes their menus and lets them know their appetizer will be right out.

"A *maternal* thing? Did you think I was going to let that go just because the waitress interrupted us?" Vincent asks as soon as she's gone.

"Ah, V, I didn't mean it in a bad way. I meant it in a *good* way, actually. You're good at taking care of people."

V. Loup usually calls her Vincent or some jokey version. Rarely Vin. That's Cillian. Vincent likes Loup calling her V. She likes watching him drink his wine and glance around the restaurant. She likes how he moved his hand toward her when the waitress came to their table, like such a gentleman. How he pulled her chair out for her. How his eye contact can be so intense at times, she has to look away.

Is *obsession* the right word?

As she watches him—those fingers, those strong, beautiful hands—put his glass down on the table, she thinks *oui*.

"When it comes to my children, it's maternal, yes. I'm maternal. I'm a mother! I'm sure I made you aware of this back in October, right?" Vincent says. Making sure she's keeping in close touch with her children no matter where she is, starting up a correspondence with Tully, writing Siobhán... Okay yes, sometimes men leave it up to women to hold the world together. Absolutely, they do. And women are damn good at it.

"I only meant... are you worrying about everyone in Paris? Everyone at home? Is it distracting you from being in the moment and having a good time?" Loup leans forward and makes a little nest with his hands, wanting her to put hers there. She does. The waitress returns with their bread and olives on a wooden cutting board. They separate and lean back. Loup thanks her.

"No! I'm having a lovely time, really. I'd turn my phone off completely if I'd told my kids that I left Paris."

"Are you glad you didn't tell them?" he asks when he's finished chewing.

"I think I probably will... eventually. They're resilient," she says, half wishing she'd already told Loup about *Half-Blown Rose* so she could talk about how amazingly her kids had handled learning about Tully. That conversation with Loup is pinned in the future next to the one she'll have with Colm and Olive about him—if and when.

"Would you tell your parents about me?" Vincent asks.

"I've told them already."

"Told them what?"

"That I'm seeing someone. That you're American and forty-four and have two grown children," Loup says, nodding.

"Have you dated an older woman before? I can't believe I haven't asked you this, honestly," Vincent says. She'd assumed she was the first, but maybe she isn't? Had she forgotten to ask because she didn't want to know? Her brain, sneakily running defense behind the scenes?

Probably.

"I don't look at you as an 'older woman.' What does that mean?" Loup asks.

"Exactly what the words mean. Older than you are. Woman, as opposed to man."

"I've been with women older than me. And... I'm not attracted to men." Loup laughs and pops an olive into his mouth. He lets the tip of his thumb linger between his lips.

Yes, obsession *is the right word.*

"How much older?"

"Midthirties. Early last summer. In Spain."

Loup had told her about traveling to Spain with Apollos last June. When she was happily working art fairs a month before Cillian's book came out, Loup was in Barcelona romancing a woman in her thirties.

"Ah, *muy bien*. What happened with her?"

"It was just a quick thing... then it was time for me to leave."

Loup tells her the woman was from Valencia and that she'd been on vacation with her girlfriends, celebrating being cancer-free after a few rough years of treatment. "Her friends dared her to come up to me on the beach and tell me she loved me. And she did it. We ended up having drinks later and... well, it was fun," he says.

"What was her name?" Vincent asks, mildly jealous but also surprised at how much she loves thinking about Loup, sun-kissed in Spain, the Chosen One for this woman's *I survived* fantasy.

"She told me her name was Esperanza, but it wasn't. We decided to use fake names. I was Luc. So between this and Noémie and Dominique, you now officially know about all my slutty adventures," he says, blushing a little in the candlelight. It's endearing and Vincent wants to grab him and kiss him, but she doesn't. She eats some bread and watches their waitress deliver food to the table next to theirs.

"I never said you were slutty! I do love that you use that word for yourself, though. It's inspiring, actually."

"You're welcome."

"One story I have kind of like that is... I went to Italy for a few weeks with an art class when I was in college... took the train from Florence to Venice. This guy sat next to me after getting on in Bologna and after a little bit, he asked if I wanted to switch Walkmans... you've heard of those, right?"

Loup laughs and nods.

"So I said yes and we did. We sat there listening to each other's tapes. I'd traded him Stevie Nicks for Richie Havens and we chatted a little. He kept my tape and I kept his. His was the next stop in Padua, but I was staying on. We flirted a little. When the stop was about five minutes away, he looked at my mouth and asked if he could kiss me and I said yes. He said he and his friend had traded a list of dares and one of them was to kiss a stranger on a train. We kissed for like, the full five minutes, and when we stopped at the station, I got up and hugged him, then he was gone forever. I didn't even know his name. He may have been making the whole dare thing up anyway... I didn't care."

"What did he look like?"

"He was brown with curly dark hair and green eyes... wearing a scarab necklace," Vincent says, touching her collarbone. "Wow, I haven't thought about him in so long," she ends, letting herself remember all she can about that afternoon. How scared she was to take the train by herself; how empowering it was to do it anyway. How she made her way to Venice in a daze and couldn't get the boy on the train out of her mind for a while. How he told her he liked her earrings; she'd made them. How his mouth tasted like coffee and chocolate cigarettes.

"I love this story," Loup says.

"I love your story too. It's romantic. Do you ever think about her?"

"Occasionally. But what I really want is to be that lad on the train."

"Kiss me and never see me again?"

"Obviously not, but that lad's a legend in my eyes. I respect it."

"What if I told you that I also had a completely meaningless one-night stand the last night I was in Italy, but... I was thinking about the boy from the train the whole time?"

"See! Told you the lad's a *legend*."

"You have the same energy. I mean, obviously," she says. They eat. "So your parents know you're here with me now?" she asks.

"Not exactly here in Bath, but they know I'm traveling with you, yes. Lisette knows too. I was so excited, I told everyone," Loup says, wiping his fingers on the napkin in his lap. "Why would I hide it? I might be *your* secret, but you're not mine."

Vincent, quiet, watches Loup push one rebellious curl behind his ear.

Brighton. Sunday, April 22.

We're staying at the Grand Brighton. The IRA tried to blow up Margaret Thatcher here in the eighties, but their plan failed. They killed some other people instead.

The bomb was on a timer...

...I find myself thinking about timers a lot now.

How we're all on a timer...

...ALL of us and everything, from the moment we're conceived, right?

It's exhausting.

It's a moody day today... maybe that's why I'm in my head so much. I'm on the balcony looking out at the water. The ocean is fussy and gloomy, matching the skies above. Our room is huge and I could definitely stay here for a lot longer than the two days we've planned.

Tomorrow morning we'll leave and head toward Ashford, where the train station is. On the way, we'll stop at Seven Sisters, the chalk cliffs in East Sussex. Loup told me about them and they look amazing. The inn in Ashford has a garden and chickens too. I adore the little inns. I could live in one. So warm and cozy, like something from a children's book!

I didn't want to leave Bath. It's breathtaking in the golden hour.

The night we grabbed takeaway I saw one of the most beautiful men I've ever laid eyes on. Loup agreed with me! He looked Middle Eastern? Like a prince. He stepped out of a small, expensive car with another guy who was quite handsome too. They were ordering as we were leaving and once we were outside, Loup said, "Did you see that guy in there... how pretty he was?" And I love that Loup is the kind of man who can say another man is attractive. Maybe it's easier for him since he's so handsome himself? He's one of those types who doesn't seem to realize quite how handsome he is, though. Paris is FULL of beautiful people... it's probably normal to him.

Loup looks like un petit prince too, honestly. Sounds trite to say I love looking at him, but wow, I really do.

The comedy walking tour was fun. To our delight, it was exactly what it sounds like. The guy leading it was truly hilarious and our laughter echoed all around us, walking down those curious little streets. We talked to a couple from New York and another from Wales. I love meaningful instances of small talk (oxymoron?) when I can capture a real, delightful glimpse of someone's life. The French may not force themselves to perform small talk as much as Americans do, but it's fascinating how much some people are willing to share.

The couple from Wales told us they were considering divorce a year ago but decided to stay together.

The couple from New York had left their toddler back at the hotel with her grandmother and the mom kept checking her phone for texts.

I will always remember:

the beautiful princes in that glossy, extravagant white car

the Welsh woman's dark red hair, like Arkansas Black apples...

the New Yorker in his navy-blue Yankees cap

I'll especially remember these things because I'm aware that traveling isn't "real life."

I know it's magic.

It's liminal and the spaces within it are liminal too → Hotels. Elevators. Train stations. Rental cars. None of them are meant to go on.

Mrs. Laurent sent me a pic of the pink and red ranunculus Cillian had delivered yesterday. I texted him and said thank you and he wrote back checking in again about a phone call or video chat. I don't know what I want to do about it. It's not a big deal either way, but I'm thinking of giving him a date next month when I'm back in Paris and we can video chat then. I don't care if he wonders why I'm putting him off.

Olive is wildly busy prepping for finals, but she did send me a cute selfie and she got the Korean snack box I sent her. Colm is working with some new director he really loves for the film he wrote last year. I'm super excited for him!!! Both of them have been chatting with their dad like normal. There's no reason they wouldn't, but I do check in sometimes to make sure. Colm and Tully text each other regularly now, which is great.

Right now, I'm very content on this balcony with the ocean hushing in front of me, the cars whizzing by. Loup is somewhere down by the water, skateboarding. I stayed behind, took a bath and read Bonjour tristesse. When I got out, I sat here to write. I try to imagine the me a year from now (setting the timer!)... five years from now... reading these words. I wonder if it'll feel a lifetime away or if not much will have changed?

Where will Loup be then? I want to know him, I do.

~~But maybe that's too much to ask~~?

HALF-BLOWN ROSE

On their way to Seven Sisters, Vincent gets texts from Agathe.

> Salut, ma belle! Have no clue where you are right now but had to tell you: Zillah's stylist stopped in Citron Clair to visit Gigi and she loved your earrings!!!
>
> She took a lot home with her. Some necklaces too. More soon!
>
> And so glad you're giving the Gideon 7000 a break, eh? MDR.
>
> Happy Loup! Give him my love!

"Who's Zillah?" Vincent asks Loup.

He's behind the steering wheel on her right, which is still strange to her. There's a Band-Aid on his elbow—a fresh skateboarding injury. Last evening, he returned to the Grand Brighton with a bloody arm and Vincent made him sit on the toilet lid while she patched him up.

"*Zillah*?" Loup says.

They're driving along the water and Vincent looks out at the ocean. They pass a town sign. She loves how long, charming, and specific some of them are. Many of them are *upon* or *on*, giving exact details to where they're located. She remembers some from the map of Northern England: Newcastle upon Tyne, Stockton-on-Tees. Others are so cute, Vincent can hardly stand it: Puddletown and Flitwick and Humby. Picklescott! Honeybottom!

They've just passed Saltdean, heading to East Dean and Birling Gap.

Vincent reads part of Agathe's text aloud to Loup.

"That's brilliant. Yeah, that's amazing. Zillah's a huge rising pop star. Well, not even rising anymore, really. Just huge now. You've seen the Z posters up. They're everywhere," Loup says. He smiles over at her and nods. "Big news!"

Vincent maybe has a vague recollection of seeing a giant Z poster with a woman on it somewhere on one of her walks but can't remember anything specific about it.

"If she posts on social media about your earrings, your shop will blow up, trust me. You'll have to add on to your studio," Loup says.

"Oh! Well, I'm loving that," Vincent says. An exciting thing! She writes Agathe back about it with *wow*s and asks her to pass along her thanks to Gigi.

We're on the way to Seven Sisters!
Night in Ashford.

Nope, no need for the Gideon 7000.
The Loup 7000 is working just fine.
;)

Ending this ridiculous conversation
RIGHT NOW. Biz.

Ashford. Monday, April 23.

We're named the two garden chickens, Tikka and Masala! We couldn't stop laughing about it. It's so dumb! I really love a good, solid, dumb joke.

People seem to laugh more here than they do in the U.S. I noticed it in Paris too. And not only do people laugh more often, but it's louder. It seems like in general, people are happier here or at least feel more comfortable exhibiting that happiness . . . but I haven't overanalyzed it too much. (Yet.)

Am I happier over here? Before all this, I really was happy back home!

But am I HAPPIER here?

YES?

I don't know.

I've got major PMS so having tea in an English garden and laughing about the cute chickens was such a treat. There are benches on the edge of the property and we can see the trains smoothing across the green. We'll be on that train in the morning, heading back to Paris. We're only picking up the Citroën there, then driving to Lyon for the night.

Seven Sisters was SUBLIME. The white cliffs! The waves! I took a ton of pictures. It was half-crowded with lots of people down by the water but not as many making the steep trek up the hill for the best view. That's where we went. We picnicked at the top. We'd stopped for sandwiches on the way in—turkey and tomato. Split a spinach salad and a bottle of fizzy peach water. We've both gotten obsessed with this one particular kind of dark chocolate digestive biscuit. We buy them every time we stop!

This inn in Ashford is a lot like our place in Leeds. Huge apartment with a washer/dryer. We did our laundry again. Loup and I have cooked together often in the past few months but now we're in full domesticity mode → laundry, dinner dishes.

He's sleeping soundly next to me right now. We had sex and he fell asleep so fast afterwards... it was really cute. I can't help but be proud to wear him out. The only time we sleep in the same bed together and don't fool around is when I'm crampy and bleeding. (He wouldn't care about doing it then, he's told me that. But I would! Too messy and all I want to do is be left alone and sleep.)

I was never wanting for physical attention with Cillian either. He's very affectionate and unselfish in bed.

Last night when I was with Loup, I couldn't help but remember little things about Cillian.

Like:

exactly how he touches me and

exactly what he smells like in the middle of the night.

I haven't forgotten those things.

I haven't touched Cillian in nine months, but we talk so much it doesn't seem that long.

~~I do wonder if he and Hannah~~... I wonder if he and Hannah have ~~really~~ done anything. Not just sex, but if they've kissed or come close? Intense flirting? I don't know. I don't think she's really his type, but I don't know if a man has a type in a situation like Cillian's.

I'm not there and he's a normal man.

He gets downright tense and grumpy if he has to go for more than four days without sex. And in college... every day... it was like Our Thing. The way we were in college is the way Loup and I are now.

Last night Loup just kept saying, "You're so soft, you're so beautiful. How are you so soft? How are you so beautiful? Your body is perfect." Almost like he was in a trance. He just absolutely loves being close like that and worshipping every inch of me. He's touchy... in a sensual way... like he LOVES touching things and rubbing his hands all over things.

Cillian can be like that too, but I do try to avoid comparing them as much as I can because they live on two entirely different planets in my mind.

I'll be in NYC in 75 days.

I have no clue where this goes or how this ends with either one of them at this point...

... but right this second as I'm writing this... I don't have to...

"Let the Mystery Be" by Iris DeMent.

Vincent and Loup get to the train station early. The sun has just risen. They grab coffees and find good seats to wait in. A woman stands at the bottom of a spiral staircase, loudly asking for someone to help her with her boarding pass. She speaks mostly in a language Vincent doesn't recognize and that Loup thinks is Icelandic. Vincent knew it was Germanic; she would've guessed Swedish or Norwegian. The woman is getting loud and it's making Vincent uncomfortable, like something bad is going to happen. Back in the United States, she'd be bracing herself for someone to open fire, since Americans like to solve minor problems with guns.

Vincent tries her best to ignore the woman, and finally someone in a uniform comes down the staircase in an attempt to calm her. It takes a minute, but it works and they escort her to another area. Vincent thinks of how she'd feel so far from home, not knowing what train to get on or where to go. She says a silent prayer for the woman to get home safely. Remembering the staring, crying woman on the train to London, Vincent prays for her too. That whatever was making her cry is better now.

Vincent and Loup drink their coffee and talk quietly. She has *Bonjour tristesse* in her lap. Loup scrolls through his phone. And when it's time to board their train to Paris, he hops up and grabs the handles of their luggage and clicks his tongue at her.

"*On y va*. Our adventure awaits!" he says, rolling the suitcase wheels and smiling.

6

"Now that you know me, would you say I'm easy to get to know? Or hard? Cillian sometimes calls me an *emotional tease*," Vincent says.

Their hotel suite in Lyon has two tall glass doors that open to the balcony. Out there, a small table and two chairs. She and Loup sit with light cotton blankets wrapped around them and a pot of tea, sharing a cigarette. There is a soccer match on the television inside with the sound up just barely enough for Loup to hear it. Earlier they walked to dinner and, afterward, the Cathédrale Saint-Jean-Baptiste. Got sea salt caramel gelato and ate it watching the lights dance on the Saône River.

When she hands the cigarette to him, their fingertips kiss. Vincent thinks of how their movie would pause on that scene in the dim.

"You don't tell me a lot about Cillian," Loup says, and smokes. "In your defense, outside of basic information, I haven't really asked either," he adds with a plain face.

He didn't answer her question.

She stares out, listening to the street noise—car engines, chatter, the bright *bring* of a bicycle bell.

"I'll tell you more about him whenever you want," Vincent says.

She doesn't even know where she'd start.

He made me a mocha in the late nineties and I fell for him completely. Easily. He's handsome and brilliant. A charmer. His words rip me to shreds.

"I know you will."

She lets their sentences settle.

"Agathe and Baptiste like to brag about how well they know me. I did get close to them fairly quickly and it usually takes me longer," Vincent says.

There's an ambulance siren in the distance and she crosses herself. Loup crosses himself too and looks at her with a sad slight smile. It's precious, how he does it too, like it's a decision they've made together, although they haven't.

"I don't think you're easy to get to know, but I don't think you're an *emotional tease* either. I can't imagine Cillian would think he'd be getting on your good side with that line."

"Well, he only said it when we were fighting."

"Obviously I like how you are. I like that you're complicated. Same reason I prefer jazz or electronic music to...other kinds," he says.

Vincent motions for the cigarette, takes one last drag, and puts it out. She pours more tea into their cups and Loup lifts his to his lips.

"With Agathe and Baptiste, it's because they're both very charismatic and extroverted with big personalities...They absorb everyone else into their orbit, whether it's a shallow or deep connection. They probably feel like they get to know *everyone* quickly, not just you," Loup says.

"You know me better than both of them."

"C'est vrai?"

"Absolument."

"Is it because I'm the one who knows your *vagin* looks like a poppy?" Loup points at himself.

"That's exactly why," she says, swatting his hand.

They drink their tea together until the cheers from the television call Loup inside. He makes a funny show of opening his blanket like he's emerging from a cocoon; Vincent turns to watch the butterfly disappear between the long white curtains.

Saint-Tropez. Côte d'Azur. Thursday, April 26.

I've taken so many pictures of this little lime-colored Citroën. Ugh, I'm in love with it... I want to keep it. I feel more comfy driving in France (back to the American side of the road!), but most of the time, Loup drives and I'm the DJ... or I read to him from the only book he brought—Just Kids by Patti Smith. He's about halfway through and now, so am I.

I was sad to leave Lyon. I'm sad to leave everywhere.

Are there enough lifetimes for me to go to all the places I want to go and see all the things I want to see?

On our last day there, we wandered and ate. Loup wanted to skateboard and we went down to the skate park for a bit. I sat in the grass in my dress, having a coffee and some pain au chocolat.

I wrote Tully back. He sent me some more pics of flowers. I let him choose the color last time and he picked orange. I told him about the oranges I bought at the market and the orange skirt I love. He told me about chopping carrots and a tufted pillow Eimear brought home.

I also finished Bonjour tristesse sitting in the sun. Loved it... explosive and sad. Françoise Sagan wrote it when she was a teenager and it seems like I've heard of it my whole life, but have only now read it for the first time. Apropos, it takes place on the French Riviera.

The drive down from Lyon was lovely. The French countryside! Honestly, what's not to adore?

Agathe texted saying that Zillah's stylist sent her assistant to the art gallery again to buy up ALL that was left of my jewelry. Who knows what will come of it? ! Fun to think about, though. Loup and I watched some of Zillah's videos last night and she's out-of-this-world cute. Kind of reminds me of Jean Seberg. I dig her style a lot. She'd look really good in the big rainbow drop circles with her short hair. → There were a lot of those at the gallery. Hmm. ?

Loup went for a run. I'm here at the hotel, second day of my period. Feeling slightly better. First time I've been on my period on the French Riviera.

I've been trying to keep track of my firsts ever since I left Kentucky for Paris:

first pair of earrings I made from scratch in the apartment studio were stacked terra-cotta rectangles

first time I talked to Cillian on the phone from Paris I was standing on the balcony

first time I saw naked drumming guy was on the first Wednesday after I'd arrived...

I've been keeping track of my firsts with Loup too:

first time I tried to pee in front of him was in Mina and Baptiste's bathroom

first time he peed in front of me was at the apartment the next week

first time we slept in bed together was at his place after the first time we had sex

first time we had sex on a train was the one from Ashford to Paris (careful, quick, and quiet, around Le Touquet—women's bathroom, lights off).

Here on the Côte d'Azur is where Loup went cliff diving into the Mediterranean Sea. We stood in the water today. So cold! Sunday we'll drive to Nice, about forty-five minutes away, and hop on a train heading for Amsterdam. Can't wait to get on a train again. The one from Ashford to Paris was too short.

Talked to Monet yesterday. She said Theo told her I was bringing a friend with me. She wanted more but no, not yet. I promised to tell her later.

When we get to Amsterdam I'll let Theo know just enough about Loup or let him figure it out on his own. Theo and Cillian have always gotten along, but Theo's loyalty is obviously to me. When he heard about what Cillian had done he said → "What a TOTAL fucking ass." And it was EXACTLY what I needed to hear right then. Theo is usually really guarded with his emotions... they're always under control... he's extremely self-monitoring and has been ever since we were little. He's the complete opposite of Monet, who lets every emotion flash across her face and out of her mouth in real time with no filter. As the middle child, I guess it makes sense that I fall somewhere in the middle emotion-wise too.

Admittedly, I find it harder to hide my emotions when I'm in Paris or traveling. Everyone over here is getting a different version of me, but it's not on purpose... it's situational. I don't know how else to be right now.

That's what worries me about Loup...

~~REAL LIFE...~~

~~REAL LIFE?~~

where do we fit in my "real life"?

Do I even have a "real life" anymore? Isn't THIS it?

Do Loup and I exist outside of this romantic bubble?

I really do hope so, but I don't know. I can't imagine being able to squash these feelings easily. I can feel them growing roots... spreading.

It feels good.

I feel good around him.

We've created our own little world... our own universe...

More and more, I settle into his atmosphere...

let go in his gravity.

Down by the sea, Vincent looks at her phone to see the temperature: sixty-four degrees.

"Okay, I checked and it's too chilly for me to take my top off, sorry," she says to Loup. Truly a bummer they can't swim together because she really wants to see his face dripping with seawater, a perfect tear of it hanging from his earlobe, and through it, the world turned upside down. He's next to her in a roll-neck sweater and those peach shorts. His hair is still wet from the shower; so is hers. She trimmed his a bit in the bathroom mirror and when she was finished, he called her Delilah.

Loup's sweater is as blue as the water and has a complicated cable pattern on the front and back, like whoever designed it had to do fifty math problems to come up with it. Vincent said that to him and he told her that his grandmother knit it. She did it so no one else would ever have one like it. The sleeves hang a little past his wrists and the right one is fraying, but it looks like the kind of sweater meant to do that; the unraveling makes it *that* much more stylish.

Vincent has never seen Loup wearing the sweater and it's just a sweater! But on him, on the Côte d'Azur, as they look out at the Mediterranean Sea—how his clothes match and complement the water and sky, the buildings, the awnings snapping in the wind, the boats, how he is melting into all of it—this feels like a Deliberate, Precious Act of God.

"Well, that sucks. Okay... we'll just have to come back when it's warmer. We can jump off those together," Loup says, pointing at the cliffs.

"*Absolument pas. Tu rêves!* It's like how you were trying to get me to ride one of those electric scooters when we were in London. You'll never see me on one! And you'll never see me perched, ready to jump off a cliff, either. Regular life is plenty wild enough for me. Same way I know for a fact I'll never die in a hot air balloon accident—because I'm never getting in one." Vincent shakes her head and mouths the word *no* to make sure she's extra clear.

A white woman, a black man, and their twin brown toddlers walk past. Vincent smiles at the woman and she smiles back. Vincent had talked to her earlier in the hotel lobby. One of the toddlers had accidentally bumped into Vincent and the woman apologized twice. Vincent told her it wasn't a problem at all and that she sometimes missed when her now-grown children were that age. The woman is American, from

Rhode Island. She asked Vincent where she was from and they had a few minutes of friendly chitchat while the woman waited for her husband to finish speaking with the man behind the counter.

On the beach, Vincent watches the toddlers—in their sun hats and long sleeves—run down to the water with their buckets, their parents following them closely.

"Tell me more about your brother," Loup asks, watching them too.

"Theo's just barely a year older than me. Aurora always says we're *twins, the hard way*. He can be really quiet. He's like the *complete* opposite of Baptiste. He's cerebral and can be intense sometimes. He designs furniture and when he's working on figuring out a piece, he can be unreachable. I don't just mean by phone or email...even if I'm in his actual presence, he's like, in another dimension. It used to bother me when we were kids because I'd want him to do something with me, but he couldn't if he had anything else on his mind, because he can't do two things at once. He has to put all of his energy into doing *one* thing extremely well," Vincent says.

She tells him Theo has lived in Amsterdam for years, married to a Dutch woman named Yvonne. That she adores her nieces, Fenna and Florentina, but they won't be there. And how they usually try to get together for Christmas, but it's hard now since everyone is so spread out. Two Christmases ago, she and Cillian had hosted the whole family, and it's hard for her to imagine everyone all together like that again. She has to picture the scene without Cillian to make it fit reality. Feels impossible that they could somehow get back to that or even *near* it.

"I'm really excited to meet him. And your sister?"

Vincent touches Loup's sweater. Traces a line of the cable pattern from his wrist to his elbow. She watches one of the toddler twins get lifted up up up into the air by his daddy and swooped down again. Loup laces his fingers with hers and she puts her head on his shoulder. Tells him about Monet. That she's wild, hilarious, and nine years younger. That they're close, but can go for a while without talking and it's no big deal. Vincent tells him Monet went to college in California and has lived there ever since, in a cute little bungalow in Malibu, and co-owns a chic clothing boutique with her best friend.

"It's called Malibloom. They sell these there," Vincent says, touching the sunny yellow Go Wilde! earrings she's wearing.

"Okay, so literally *everyone* in your family is fucking cool?" Loup says, laughing gently—a breathy *eh eh eh* that always makes Vincent laugh too.

Her family *is* pretty fucking cool. Vincent doesn't have deep wounds from how she was raised and neither do her brother or sister. Rich kid clichés, but they went to expensive private schools and lived in a really nice neighborhood. Vincent had been to both London and Paris long before her sweet sixteen. But she was also raised knowing how privileged she is. Her parents hadn't been rich growing up. They were black people born in the American South in the fifties; there was no preciousness there regarding how hard life could be.

"Stop. Now tell me more about yours," Vincent asks, blushing.

He tells her about his family coming to Monaco once to watch his mother perform at the Opéra de Monte-Carlo. Loup talks about the Palais Garnier in Paris and the Royal Opera House in London. Vincent has never seen Loup's mother, but pictures a dark-haired woman resembling him, onstage in an elegant off-the-shoulder red dress. The audience showering her with roses.

"One day my mum went to an audition in London and my dad was the one playing piano for her. It's how they met," Loup says.

"That's *so* romantic. I love them."

"They'll love you. They really will. My mum's birthday is in July and I want to give her a pair of your earrings."

She imagines a foggy situation in the future when she's meeting Loup's parents. She will have to be officially divorced from Cillian; they will have to be so sure about this. What'll that take?

"Of course. Pick any of them," Vincent says.

"And I'll pay you."

"You will not."

"I will. And if you try to stop me, I'll wrestle it into your arms. I'm super strong. Feel that," Loup says, flexing. Vincent lifts her head and pokes at his biceps. Squeezes it.

"I'm wearing this sweater tomorrow," she says, poking at his arm again. She wishes she could text Ramona about his sweater. Like her, Ramona loves a good sweater.

"It's yours," he says.

Vincent focuses on the family in front of them—the toddlers with their butts planted in the sand now, kicking at the water.

In the evening, she and Loup walk to dinner—candlelight, wine, lobster linguine, tiramisu della casa—and return to their room spent.

Days of blue bliss fold into one another like origami and no matter where they find themselves, their bedroom is a James Salter novel. Sometimes when they're in bed together Loup speaks in French, not bothering to translate because she doesn't want him to. She just wants to hear that luring language she only half understands twisting and pouring from his mouth like the vines their bodies make when they're tangled and touching, kissing and kissing and kissing under billowy white sheets with the windows open.

Veedubs! Wow I miss you around here.
Amsterdam soon?

All this to say I'm very happy for you.
Du beau travail les gars! Keep it up!
;)

Vincent reads Baptiste's text aloud to Loup as they're en route to Nice. Loup is behind the wheel in his zipped-up track jacket with a cigarette tucked behind his ear; Vincent is in her jeans and his cable-knit sweater with the sleeves hanging past her wrists. It smells like him, but now he smells like her—soap, shampoo, perfume. This is what happens to lovers.

They woke before sunrise and their train leaves in two hours. Vincent has her window down enough to smell the salt water.

"*Qu'est-ce que c'est... 'les gars'?*" she asks him, pushing her windy hair back from her face. She knows *du beau travail* means *good work*.

"He's being cheeky... saying 'Good work, guys,'" Loup says, giving her a cheesy smile and a thumbs-up. He switches lanes, guns it around a slow car.

Vincent laughs. "He really is a little shit, isn't he?"

Tu es une petite merde. (And shut up. I miss you too.) Vincent types to Baptiste, adding the eye roll emoji. Baptiste likes it immediately, sending three little hearts in reply.

"How weird is it that Baptiste and I are friends but Mina kind of hates me?" she asks.

"She doesn't hate you. Why do you say that?"

"Well, she doesn't like me... and I don't blame her. If my husband had a lot of girl-slash-friends, I probably wouldn't like them either."

"You mean Cillian?" Loup looks over at her quickly.

"No... well, I meant... hypothetically."

"But Cillian *is* your husband. Do you have a problem with him having girl-slash-friends? The woman from work he's getting cozy with?"

She'd forgotten she mentioned that to Loup. Hannah's face flashes in Vincent's mind—her quirky glasses and sexy-librarian air. She wonders if they're somewhere in the dark together now as she motors across the A8 autoroute with Loup Michel Henry.

Vincent hasn't communicated with Cillian in days. Not since she wrote him back about waiting a couple more weeks to video chat, and he said okay and told her he loved her. She told him she loved him too. She was in the bathroom alone when she texted him; Loup was on the bed talking to Apollos about band stuff.

"Correct," Vincent says, eyeing Loup. His gaze remains on the road. "For now, he's still legally my husband. And he's friends with women. Most of them are fine."

"What am I?"

"What do you mean?"

"Cillian's your husband... what am I?"

Loup looks over at her quickly; his face is carefully plain.

"You're my lover. Do you not like that? Honestly, I get whiplash from you sometimes. I feel like you put on this facade, but you're secretly wanting to force more of a label on it. Men! You just can't help yourselves, can you? We talked about this on the moors... your anxiety creeping in. It went away after that... or so I thought. I promised you I won't up and disappear. I don't know what else to say," Vincent ends.

She looks out her window. The sea wind of the morning, a tiny storm in their car. The blue air glows cool.

"*Anxiety* isn't the right word. But admittedly, I can't always predict or anticipate my feelings, since I'm a real person and not a robot. You know I love being your lover," Loup says.

"It's done. You're here," Vincent says, looking at him, putting her hand on her heart.

"It's the same for me." He glances at her and looks away. Puts his free hand on his heart too. "You're in charge, I know that."

"I'm not *in charge*. I don't even know what that means."

"You know exactly what I mean by that."

"Not everyone thinks like you."

They're quiet. *A lover's spat*. Its anagram: *lover's pasta*. She and Loup eat a lot of pasta. She's hungry. She's had half a croissant and a cup of coffee this morning; she needs real food. *Faim de loup*.

"Not everyone thinks like you either," Loup says after about a minute of tapping his thumb on the steering wheel and staring at the road.

Vincent studies his profile—his blinking, brown-black lashes, his *très* Gallic, aquiline nose. After he'd called her nose *celestial*, she looked up the name of his because she's so obsessed with it and wants to sit on it.

It is the Only Nose in the World.

If his nose were a sound, she would want to record it like he did her orgasm and make a song out of it.

When they watched *The Dreamers* together she realized that the French actor in the movie, Louis Garrel, is practically Loup's nose twin. *Loup has a Louis*, she texted to Agathe, sending a photo of Louis upon the discovery. *Eureka!*

Loup doesn't look at her and she turns her attention away, depriving him of it.

As soon as her eyes leave him, he puts his hand on her thigh like she knew he would.

7

Vincent had been sad to turn over the keys to their green Citroën. They'd dubbed it *le petit citron vert* because she gets a kick out of the fact that one of the French words for *lime* is *citron vert*, which simply means *green lemon*. But she loves trains as much as three-year-olds do, so she's practically giddy as they settle into their cushy wine-red seats. The first leg is a bit over five hours, then they'll switch trains; the second leg is around three hours long.

One day she wants to take a train all the way across Europe to see everything.

She's been thinking of firsts but can't help thinking about lasts too. Her last lover's spat with Loup was over quickly. First train ride of this length with Loup. When they take the train from Amsterdam back to Paris in six days, will that be her last with him? He is her first lover. Will he be her last?

No matter what happens with Cillian, she can't imagine a world where she returns to Kentucky and is content staying there. Her wanderlust is stubborn, permanently revved.

The train is half-full. Loup is reading next to her, drinking his coffee. There is a package of prawn crisps and a glass bottle of water in front of her. Riding backward makes Loup a little queasy so they are facing forward. Vincent is by the window because she is a windowphile. A heliophile. Lucipetal.

After a while of watching the French countryside blur by, she puts her head on his shoulder.

"You always smell so fucking good. Always," he growls, with his nose in her hair.

"*Merci*. It's Huile Prodigieuse. I put it everywhere," Vincent says. She loves the French oil and the square glass it comes in. She sprays it all over her body when she gets out of the shower, *fitzes* it in her hair. When she wears it, she smells like France. "And Bal d'Afrique." Her new perfume—a mix of African marigolds, violets, and vetiver that smells like a heavenly smash of Paris and Africa.

Sharing her earbuds and listening to her train playlist, they both fall asleep with their heads touching and wake up to read and talk the rest of the way.

Vincent's Travel Playlist| Train | Nice to Paris

"Love Train" by the O'Jays
"Please Do Not Go" by the Violent Femmes
"True Affection" by Father John Misty
"Big God" by Florence + the Machine
"Cello Suite No. 1 in G Major Prelude" by Yo-Yo Ma
"Paris, Paris, Paris" by Joséphine Baker
"Mixed Feelings" by Keegan Fordyce
"More Than This" by Roxy Music
"NFWMB" by Hozier
"My Baby Just Cares for Me" by Nina Simone
"Dawn" by Jean-Yves Thibaudet
"Raconte toi" by Yves Simon
"Wild Horses" by the Sundays
"Quelqu'un' m'a dit" by Carla Bruni

"Message" by Jamie Woon
"Baby Can I Hold You" by Tracy Chapman
"Where Is My Mind?" by the Pixies
"Ease Your Feet into the Sea" by Belle & Sebastian
"La Parisienne" by Marie-Paule Belle
"To Build a Home" by the Cinematic Orchestra

While they're waiting in the Gare du Nord in Paris for the next train to come, they buy lunch. Two avocado and sprout sandwiches. Berries. A crunchy romaine salad, chocolate cookies.

They sit by their gate, people-watching.

A mother in a fuzzy red sweater with a long brown braid walks back and forth, patting and shushing a baby wrapped in a white blanket. An elderly couple sit across from them looking at a book of crossword puzzles together. The man has a pencil behind his ear; the woman points at the page and smiles at him. An announcement in French. An announcement in English. Three police officers stand in a clump, talking. One of them adjusts his belt buckle.

"Paris is a magnet. Look how we keep ending up here, even when we're not staying. You're sure you don't want to hop out and go home?" Vincent asks him.

"*Paris est un aimant*," he says, translating for her. "And you're not getting rid of me that easily. We had a little fight and you're ready to call it quits?" Loup *tsk*s and shakes his head. He puts his hand on her waist and pulls her close. Kisses her mouth. The bag of food crinkles between them.

"We're those annoying people who have absolutely no issue with public displays of affection," Vincent says, and kisses him again. She rubs her nose against his.

"I realize we'll tone it down around Theo. Do I have to pretend to be just your friend for six *whole* days? Think of the fucking handstands I'll be forced to do! I'm out of practice now," Loup says, leaning back and inspecting his fingers like they're disappearing in front of his eyes.

"You and I will be sharing a room. So make of that what you will. And honestly I miss the handstands. You won me over with those. I've been on my period long enough that you should've been doing *plenty* of them by now. This feels like a scam."

Loup looks around, bounces his legs.

"If only I had the room right here. It's how I feel, you know. I could eat you alive," he says, leaning close to her again. He puts his hand on one side of her face, his mouth on her ear. "I want you soft as powder, moaning underneath me, saying my name."

Loup kisses her neck and sits in his seat properly. He drinks his coffee and looks at the train schedule sign. Vincent, ablaze, lets her eyes refocus there too.

Vincent's Travel Playlist | Train | Paris to Amsterdam

"Wild World" by Yusuf/Cat Stevens
"Glory Box" by Portishead
"PS2" by Litany
"I Love Paris" by Ella Fitzgerald
"Amsterdam" by Gregory Alan Isakov
"Ripple" by the Grateful Dead
"Gone Girl" by Jasmine Cephas Jones
"Solsbury Hill" by Peter Gabriel
"Make You Feel My Love" by Adele
"Amsterdam" by Coldplay
"Honey and the Moon" by Joseph Arthur
"Amsterdam" by Peter Bjorn and John
"I Don't Know" by Lisa Hannigan
"It's All Over Now, Baby Blue" by Marianne Faithfull
"What a Diff'rence a Day Makes" by Dinah Washington

"Diamonds on the Inside" by Ben Harper
"I Need Love" by Sam Phillips
"I Hear a Symphony" by the Supremes
"Love Someone" by Jason Mraz
"Photograph" by Ed Sheeran

The train is delayed but once they're finally en route to Amsterdam, they eat the extra sandwiches they bought and listen to music, chatting and watching the rest of France go by. They sleep through some of Belgium, waking up near Antwerp. From Rotterdam past Bergschenhoek they share another salad and fruit, and they're properly worn out when they find a taxi outside Amsterdam Centraal Station and make their way to Theo's in Museumkwartier.

It's nearly gloaming. Their taxi driver is friendly and talkative, telling them Amsterdam's history in numbers: more than 800,000 bikes in the city, 165 canals. He is an older gentleman with a hoppy Dutch accent when he speaks to them in English, asking them where they're from and how long they're staying.

"We're on our honeymoon," Loup says, smiling at Vincent.

Vincent laughs and nods.

"Yes. He was in my art class and I knew he was the one the moment I laid eyes on him. Do you see this hair?" Vincent says, sticking her hand out from that sweater sleeve and touching Loup's head, tucking some of it behind his ear.

"*Gefeliciteerd!* Best wishes for a long, happy life together!" the taxi driver says brightly.

Vincent and Loup laugh and say "*Dank u.*"

She recognizes a few of the shops and the lights on the water. They are close to Theo's. The taxi driver has been married for thirty-four years and is telling them about how he and his wife honeymooned in Mykonos when he stops and says, "*Hier zijn we.*" *Here we are.*

"That's where we'll go next... Mykonos," Loup says to her.

"Okay. Let's do it," she says.

"I'm not kidding."

"Neither am I!"

Loup handles paying the man and tipping generously after he gets their bags out for them. They wave at him and he says *gefeliciteerd* again.

"Ah, he's a decent lad. I really liked him," Loup says, watching the taxi's taillights disappear.

"I really liked him too," Vincent says on the way up to Theo's front door. She knocks.

She texted her brother as soon as they got off the train, letting him know they'd be on his stoop soon.

But when the door snatches open, it's her dad standing there. It's her dad hugging her and pulling her inside, not her brother. Her mom pops up beside him; her sister, Monet, does too.

"Surprise!" Monet says, smiling wide and charging, throwing her arms around Vincent's neck.

Vincent's heart is dynamite.

"Hello there!" her dad's sugary gruff voice says to Loup behind her as the room goes fuzzy and hot.

8

Amsterdam. Monday, April 30.

We got here today when it was Sunday and technically it's after midnight on Monday as I'm writing this, but only barely. SURPRISE!!! MY ENTIRE FAMILY IS IN AMSTERDAM FOR FUCK'S SAKE. !!!?? I seriously thought I was going to pass out. I had to sit down. Yvonne made me a cup of tea and I sat there on their couch with my ENTIRE FAMILY AND LOUP surrounding me, making sure I was okay. I was fine... it's fine...

if ~~FEELING~~ CHAOTIC EMOTIONAL OVERLOAD is fine.

When I was alone with Mom and Monet, Mom held my shoulders and looked in my eyes and asked me if I was okay... if I'd been taking care of myself... if Loup was kind to me. It was very Aurora and made me cry, which might've made my yeses seem contradictory. At one point only the girls were in the kitchen and Yvonne made fluttery eyes when she leaned close and told me how cute she thinks Loup is. Monet was a little pissed I hadn't told her about him. I knew she would be! She's in the room next to us and she's probably dreaming about being mad at me. We'll see in the morning.

Theo had told our parents and Monet that I was coming to Amsterdam to visit and it was Monet's idea for everyone to come and surprise me. Theo was obviously mum about it because that's how he is. But... wow, the Loup-secret is out! ? Or it's at least... out to everyone in this apartment right now.

The parents are here until Wednesday, then returning to Rome for an art show. Monet is leaving Friday, heading to London to hang with some friends. Yvonne is going to Rotterdam to visit her sister on Thursday and won't be back before we leave on Saturday. Theo's apartment needs a revolving door this week with all the coming and going.

When Loup was in the bathroom, I gave them the quickest rundown possible:

I told them his name was spelled L-O-U-P, but pronounced Lou

I told them he was from Paris by way of London

I asked everyone to please not mention Cillian's book or Tully since I haven't talked to Loup about any of it yet and don't know when I'm going to.

Loup handled it all REALLY well in such to-be-expected Loup fashion. He shook Dad's hand, gave him a half hug. He started going on and on about Soloco and art and music. Seriously, they wouldn't shut up. It's not like I would've expected Dad to be rude to Loup, but it's a prettyyy weeeird thing to meet your daughter's lover in Amsterdam when her husband is back home in Kentucky, I'm sure.

Mom likes him a lot already, I can tell. She touched his hair.

When I met Theo alone in the hallway he hugged me so tight and just kept telling me he was sorry, so sorry and he hopes I'm not pissed. I'm not pissed... it's just WEIRD. I haven't seen Theo since he was in Paris in September, haven't seen Monet or my parents since last winter. I haven't seen Yvonne since I hosted Christmas two years ago.

Loup is sleeping soundly next to me. Monet crashed early and so did Aurora and Solomon. They'd only stayed up to surprise me. Loup fell asleep early too.

I was WIRED... kind of still am.

Theo and I shared a beer and a cigarette on his front stoop.

I love:

this apartment

Amsterdam

~~(I sat there thinking about how happy Cillian and I could've been somewhere together in Europe if all this hadn't happened.)~~

Theo asked if I was leaving Cillian for good. He said he'd understand it if I did. I told him I didn't know.

Cillian texted me earlier. He wrote "Good night, love." I didn't write him back, I just clicked the heart so he'd know I read it.

Last time I was here:

Cillian was with me

we slept upstairs in this same bed and Colm, Olive, Fenna, and Florentina stayed up late eating popcorn and candy downstairs, watching movies

I have the window open; it really is a lovely night. A wild! and weird! and lovely night!

I'm exhausted, physically and mentally.

I googled Loup's mother's name on my phone and clicked around. There aren't a lot of pictures of her, but I found one from the '90s where she's wearing a long amethyst dress poured over her like wine and I could see so much of Loup in her face. His eyes and that hair, her ribbons of red-brown curls. She's browner than I thought she'd be; she looks like a woman from a Bible story.

I clicked on an old video of her performing with another woman at the Palais Garnier in 2001. Sat under the window with my earbuds in, closed my eyes, and listened to them sing "Duo des fleurs" from Lakmé and → cried so hard my head throbbed and my period stopped. ?

I don't know.

I'm just tired.

Vincent must be the last to wake up in the morning. She hears Loup's light laughter downstairs and Theo's following it. She smells coffee and bread, something sweet, and makes a quick stop in the bathroom before going down the steps.

Loup is sitting at the kitchen table. Black coffee in a white mug. Theo and Yvonne's kitchen is white, white, white. At its heart, Theo's design aesthetic is minimalism. It's the opposite of Aurora's style, which is heavily based on aggressively shoving as much color and as many different fabrics and textures as possible at everything in sight.

Monet is a chatterbox, and she and Yvonne have been known to argue, interrupt, and yell over each other one minute, and the next, dissolve into a fit of giggles. They're together at the stove as Yvonne stirs the *appelstroop*. Theo, Solomon, and Aurora are at the table with Loup. Vincent makes eye contact with him and smiles. He raises his mug to her and says, "*Goedemorgen, zonneschijn.*" *Good morning, sunshine.*

He'd been overly attentive last night, wanting to make sure she was okay with staying in Amsterdam. When they were alone in the bedroom, he told her how excited he was to meet her people. How awesome it was that her parents and Monet had traveled to surprise her. But he wanted her to feel comfortable and she told him she did. She was shocked... but she was fine. It was all very kind and Vincent appreciated it, but it also made her want to be alone, just to process everything without everyone eyeing her as she did it.

Vincent doesn't always have to have coffee first thing in the morning, but if she sees someone else with it, she wants it. Loup's coffee looks delicious. She goes to him and motions for his mug and he hands it to her. She takes a big sip even though she doesn't like it black.

"My baby girl!" Vincent's dad turns and says to her, putting both arms in the air, barely missing her elbow.

If Loup feels like a bottle rocket at times, Solomon has a fifteen-firecrackers personality—the kind that could blow someone's face off.

He's very physical in the same way Loup is, always buzzing and moving around. Vincent can't even count the number of times her dad has unintentionally knocked something over or accidentally swatted someone while telling a story.

Solomon's face is framed by his gray hair and an almost-white beard. He's a big fan of wacky eyewear, and this morning he's wearing a pair of round yellow glasses that make him look a bit like a turtle. Suddenly awash with love for her daddy, she touches the top of his head.

"Are you up for museums today? It's okay if you're not. Your spirit could be drained, honey. You have to feed it, or you'll stay emotionally starved," Aurora says, stepping over and putting her hand on Vincent's cheek. Her bracelets jingle. "You feel warm. Do you have a fever? Maybe you should go back to bed?"

"I'm up for museums. I'm only warm because I just woke up! And... I'm working on feeding my spirit, Mama," Vincent says, sitting next to Loup.

Her sister-in-law sets a mug of coffee already done up with cream and sugar on the table in front of her; Monet follows with a plate of warm biscuits and the bowl of *appelstroop* for everyone. Theo grabs a biscuit and butters it.

"We can go to the Van Gogh Museum after breakfast and do the Rijksmuseum or the Stedelijk tomorrow? It's supposed to be chilly today and it may rain," Theo says.

Monet launches into a story about how the last time she was in Amsterdam it rained for an entire week, but she loved it and got a new pair of red Wellies, then splashed around in puddles on her walks with Fenna and Florentina.

"Maybe Vincent and Loup want to spend some time together without us breathing down their necks?" Yvonne says. Her hair is as white as Noémie's and she matches the décor perfectly. She sits next to Theo at the table—a large white marble tulip with six chairs that Theo designed years ago. Monet, left standing, sits after Solomon offers his chair. He stands behind her, massaging her shoulders.

"Y'all...I know this is weird...but please don't *act* weird," Vincent says. She drinks some of her coffee, puts a spoonful of *appelstroop* on her biscuit, and takes a bite while everyone watches her. When was the last time she ate? She takes another bite and tells Yvonne and Monet how good it is. "But seriously...I'm fine to do the art museum today. Loup and I are fine hanging out with everyone. And when it's time, I'll tell Cillian about Loup," Vincent ends, drinking more coffee. Delicious. Coffee and breakfast in a real apartment, made by someone else? God-is-real amazing.

"I'm happy to be here," Loup says, putting his arm around the back of Vincent's chair. "Thanks again for letting me crash. This place is awesome."

"Thank you. Of course, of course," Theo says.

"You see how excited we all are," Monet says to Loup.

"Absolutely. We enjoy smothering our Vinnie with love," Solomon says, moving over to start massaging Vincent's shoulders now.

"Whew. Got that out of the way. Monet, tell me what's going down in London. Mama, tell me about Rome," Vincent says, looking at them. Loup puts his hand on her leg under the table, squeezes twice.

—

It'd been easier than expected, getting seven people out of the apartment at the same time, even though halfway to the museum Solomon had to go back to grab his diabetes medication and Theo took his time searching for *drie paraplu's. Three umbrellas.*

Vincent and Loup wander the Van Gogh Museum, letting their hands touch when her family is out of sight. She is wearing Loup's sweater. It is her new favorite thing and she wishes she could keep it forever. They stand together, holding one pair of headphones to both of their ears so they can hear someone read one of Van Gogh's letters to his brother.

* * *

While Loup is across the room talking with her dad and Theo, her mother steps next to her and puts her arm around her waist.

"Well, he's adorable. And *very* young," Aurora says softly.

"I'm aware. He's only six months older than Colm," Vincent says, looking straight ahead at *Almond Blossom*—the blue behind the white, matching the sea and the sky and Loup's sweater.

Aurora moves her hand to Vincent's back.

"You know I think being over here is good for you. Colm and Olive are grown now and you're able to re-find yourself. I'm proud of how you've handled this. I've never had to worry about you too much . . . a lot of mothers would've had to worry more," Aurora says.

Vincent's bottom lip trembles. She turns to see Loup next to Theo through the small crowd of people. Monet steps over to them and starts talking to their dad. Yvonne is on the bench by the wall, scrolling through her phone.

"Proud of you," her mom says again, touching Vincent's chin so she'll look at her. Aurora's eyes—green as lake water. They have the same mouth; Vincent's grandmother had it too.

Aurora stopped dyeing her hair years ago and now she has natural gray curls stopping at her shoulders, held to the side with two black bobby pins. She's wearing one of her favorite dresses, a bonanza of flowers printed on stretchy cotton stopping at her knees, and a pair of sandals she'd spray-painted gold after getting tired of the silver. And Aurora always jingles. Her earrings, her bracelets. Her little tinkling bells rub Vincent's back.

"Got it. Thank you, Mama," Vincent says. She wipes her eyes and sniffs, hugging Aurora tight.

Vincent is overwhelmed with love for her namesake—the glowy *Sunflowers* exhibit and his tools laid out in a neat row under glass. In the gift shop, there is a little pocket notebook with one of Van Gogh's quotes on the cover. Her mother is standing next to her when Vincent picks it up and reads the words aloud.

"I try more and more to be myself, caring relatively little whether people approve or disapprove."

Aurora reads another. *"The best way to know life is to love many things."*

"You're good at both of these. Remember that. You were always going to be Vincent, boy or girl. I just knew it," her mother says, putting her hand on her stomach. It is something Aurora has told her many times. Whenever Vincent visits Van Gogh's *Self-Portrait* at the Musée d'Orsay, she hears her mother's voice. But it holds a holy meaning as they're standing in that museum together.

Aurora takes the notebooks to the counter to buy them and afterward gives them both to Vincent.

On the way out, Vincent sees a postcard with more of Van Gogh's words on it.

"*I am not an adventurer by choice but by fate*," Loup reads it aloud.

Those words are underlined in her paperback copy of his letters, the one she keeps on her nightstand. She takes the postcard back to the cash register to buy it.

"I knew you would like that one," Loup says.

Everything is warm and yellow. Even the air is honey.

They make a quick stop in the grocery store right by the park for apples, strawberries, and cheese in order to have a proper picnic. Theo swears that the truck by the Van Gogh Museum has *the* best hot dogs in the world. Vincent has never cared about what the best hot dog in the world tastes like, but she gets one anyway. Like Theo instructs her, she slathers it with curry, relish, and mustard. It really is the best hot dog she's ever had and she knows how smug Theo will get upon hearing it, but she tells him anyway.

The rain has stopped and thin slips of sunlight pour through the clouds. Vincent's parents sit next to each other on the bench and the rest of the family sit in a little half-moon around them, everyone eating and sharing food. It's pleasantly disorienting trying to keep up with the different conversations. And even more disorienting that Vincent is in Amsterdam with her family and Loup, *without* her husband and children. The feeling wraps her lungs in something loose and gauzy that she can't forget is there, but she can breathe through it.

When they're finished eating, they'll walk back to Theo's, dodging the bikes and the trams. They'll probably take naps and read and listen to music. When they're hungry again, they'll move to the kitchen to clatter in the cupboards.

Vincent and Monet go for a walk alone in the drizzle after dinner. Theo has an extensive vinyl collection, so the boys hang back to drink whiskey and listen to records; Vincent thought Loup was going to do a handstand in the middle of the living room, he was so stoked. Aurora and Yvonne are having wine, chocolate, and chats in the kitchen.

"Yvonne drives me fucking nuts sometimes," Monet says as they head toward the canals. They're both terrible at navigation and their big brother knows this. He'd wrapped his arms around them and given simple directions they could remember: *Walk out and turn left... at the end of the street, turn right and keep walking until you see a canal. The city is full of them, so you'll be fine. And when you want to come back here, look at your phone.*

As soon as they get to the end of the street they have to remind and reassure themselves Theo had said turn right. They turn that way, continuing down the sidewalk.

"You two fight like sisters. You definitely argue with her more than you do with me... your *actual* sister," Vincent says.

She's holding the umbrella over them. The pattering rain is comforting and makes Vincent feel cozy and sleepy, the same way she feels when she brews a fresh pot of tea and it rains against the windows of the apartment in Paris. Monet's hair smells like oranges and her curls are pulled back in a sloppy bun. She may run a trendy Malibu boutique, but she doesn't do fancy, and she's one of those women who can make casualness seem chic. She's forever wearing sneakers with her dresses and once she grew out her dreadlocks simply because it's windy living by the ocean and she got tired of brushing her hair. The plain terra-cotta studs Vincent sells in her shop are named after her sister—Monet extra-large to Monet extra-small, in all colors, both bright and subdued.

"I think she's jealous of us when it comes to Theo. I know it sounds crazy, but she's the type. Haven't you noticed how territorial she is about him? I don't even think he pays attention. He lives on another planet," Monet says.

"They've been together so long, it probably doesn't matter," Vincent says. "But you're right, Theo does live on another planet... and I don't blame him. Earth is majorly overrated."

She admires Theo's ability to shut out the world when he needs to. Her brother has always been focused and driven. Keeps his head down and minds his business. It's why Vincent hadn't been worried about showing up on his doorstep with Loup in the first place.

"Half the time I love her and the other half, I could choke her. Earlier, she was trying to tell me Theo hated tuna, but Theo loves tuna! It's so dumb because I feel like she tries to act like she knows him better than I do, and I realize she's his wife... she knows him in ways I never will, thank God, because I'm not a *total* freak... but he's my brother, not some rando! I'm just glad Fen and Flor take after our side of the family," Monet says. And it's true. Their nieces look and act more like Aurora than they do Theo or Yvonne.

Vincent and Monet wait at the crosswalk for the bikes and the tram to pass before walking to the other side, continuing their hunt for canals. It's right after sunset and the streets are busy with people walking, riding, and going out to dinner. Vincent could easily live in Amsterdam. She loves the people, the flowers, the peacefulness. When she's there, she feels sheltered from the chaos of the rest of the world.

"So...when were you going to tell me about Loup?" Monet asks Vincent.

"When I knew what to say."

"How old is he?"

"Have you been just *dying* to ask me that?"

"Yes!" Monet says, laughing with her mouth wide open. Her laugh always makes Vincent laugh; they're both such physical laughers around each other. Monet nudges her arm hard and Vincent pushes her back. Monet has to step out from underneath the umbrella and she says *damn*, which makes them both laugh harder.

"He just turned twenty-five and he's a god in bed and no, I don't know where any of this is going. Cillian's probably sleeping with some woman at work, so...I'll keep you posted from here on out regarding any new developments," Vincent says, still laughing a little. She's tired and needs a long, luxurious bath. She's also happy. She's bubbled a million different emotions since the summer, but she really is incandescently happy to be walking around Amsterdam with her little sister. *Une femme libre.*

"You know for sure Cillian is seeing someone else?"

"No. I just think it."

"Tell me why," Monet pushes.

"Because I'm here...and he's there...and they day-drink together now, apparently. I heard her with him once. I don't know! It's not like I trust him anymore. It's not like I'll believe a word he says about it anyway."

"I'm so sorry, Vinnie. But let me tell you what I'm not sorry about: Honestly, I don't know if I can be civil to him after all this. Have the cops on call at Colm's wedding, please, because I may go off on him."

"Please don't. Girl! If you get arrested at the reception on Saturday you're going to have to wait until Monday for me to come bail you out," Vincent says, and they laugh again. "It's sixty-eight days from today...when I'll be in NYC. Feels like tomorrow and a hundred million years from now."

"But what happened to Cillian, though? I used to love him so much! He was so great!"

"Don't look at me, Monet! I don't have any answers."

They cross another street and, upon seeing a canal in the distance, Vincent points. "I actually recognized this spot on the way to Theo's and was very proud of myself," she says.

"So... getting back to this 'god in bed' thing..." Monet says.

"He's very *enthusiastic* and focused. Like if I'm not fully satisfied by him, it's over for humanity. No woman will ever sleep with a man again!" Vincent says. "When he kisses me, he holds my face, like it's our last kiss. It's almost too intense. Like he'll die if he can't kiss me again. And the dirty talk... it's, uh, truly *filthy*... I... yeah, I'm gonna stop now."

Monet looks at her with wide eyes. "In French or in English?!"

"Girl, both."

"Um, wow."

"Yep... let's leave it there at *wow*."

"Okay, okay. This all makes sense, though! It's all hyped up because of Cillian and because you and Loup are both at your sexual peaks. I don't care what anyone says about that because I know it's true. And men date women like a full *sixty* years younger than they are, but women get shit for dating a man even if he's only a little bit younger! There's a word for *cougar* but not a word for men who do the same thing? Bullshit. I mean... I'm sorry Cillian did this... but good for you, V. Loup is so pretty. You know Mama and I were talking about it. And you know I think Cillian is handsome, because he is! But Loup is like... *pretty*. That nose! He looks like a sculpture, but he's not perfect. It's a whole... thing he's got going on. The way he *looks* at you is like... Good for you, is what I'm saying."

"Girl, please! You aren't telling me anything I don't already know! I've been obsessed with him from the moment I laid eyes on him. I *haaated* having to be around him, because I knew. And I tried... I really did. The sexual tension was truly murderous," Vincent says.

They're at the canal now and the drizzle is slowing. Vincent puts the umbrella down and tells her sister about how Loup keeps taking her classes over and over again. About the handstands and Anchois and "Une tigresse." How she heard it for the first time at the show in London.

Monet gives a big squeal at the overload of new information. "Vinnie! Please stop! I can't hear any more!" she says. They're both laughing so hard at this point, Vincent has gotten a little dizzy. They watch the lights on the water. Slowly, a glass-topped boat slides underneath the bridge and disappears.

Once they've composed themselves, Vincent demands an update on Monet's work life and love life too and they wander over more canals in the milky streetlamp light, talking and listening to each other. When they're ready to go back to Theo's, Monet pulls out her phone and puts in his address. They can at least head in the right direction. And when it starts to rain again, Monet says it's her turn and opens the umbrella, holding it over them.

Vincent indulges in a long, hot bubbly bath and gets ready for bed. Loup pulls the covers back and sits with his hands behind his head.

"I like watching you do your nighttime ritual. You do it the same way every time, even when you're tired. Even if you've had wine. It's admirable," he says, nodding.

"*Merci*. I should probably start charging you for the peep show, though," she says. She rubs the rest of her hand cream in and turns off the light. Gets under the covers.

"Turn the light back on, please."

Vincent clicks the lamp and Loup kisses her. He kisses her mouth, her neck. He pulls her shirt down and puts his lips on her shoulder. She makes a small sound of submission and presses herself against him.

"I want to watch your face," he says. It's something he likes to say.

Sometimes when they're in bed together, lying on their sides spooning, he asks her to turn around.

"Physiognomy gets you hot? Admittedly, I kind of dig the *phrenology* thing. Charlotte Brontë was into it. You do have a really great head," Vincent says, putting both hands on Loup's head and gently massaging like she's giving him a good shampoo.

"You're outpacing me here, but don't stop...it's turning me on."

"Just in case you've forgotten, my parents are on one side. Monet is on the other," she whispers.

"So you'll have to be a good girl and be very quiet," he whispers into her ear. He kisses her again and slides his hand inside her underwear.

When she comes, he is watching her face in the lamplight. She's a little louder than she intends, and being a gentleman, he holds his hand over her mouth to make extra-sure no one can hear. And when it's his turn, she takes pleasure in kissing him to keep him quiet.

9

Amsterdam. Wednesday, May 2.

The parents fly back to Rome this evening, but it's early now, barely after sunrise. I don't think anyone is up yet. Am still in bed.

Yesterday we did the Rijksmuseum and Yvonne and I made stamppot with rookworst.

I sat at the table and chopped:

potatoes

onions

carrots

It's usually eaten in the winter, but comfort food sounded so good to all of us and the day—wonderfully gray and capricious—called for it.

It's around midnight in Kentucky and Cillian texted right before I woke up. He said he was going to sleep soon and that the bed is too big and lonely without me. He said he was counting the days until we were both in NYC together and that he promises he's going to make this all up to me somehow. I don't know what to say back to him. I don't know how to tell him that I don't think I even want to live in the United States anymore/anytime soon. There really is more to consider here than just our marriage and how to make that work.

It's not the only thing about my life. It's not all I think about anymore.

I love being in Amsterdam. I'm just as happy here as I was when Loup and I were traveling all over England and France together.

We've been gone for about three weeks. I'm not ready to go back to Kentucky or the United States, really...not even close. I'm looking forward to seeing our son get married, but when it comes to staying stateside...to leaving all this behind...I'm nowhere near ready and not sure if or when I will be.

~~*I haven't responded to Cillian.*~~

I talked to both Colm and Olive on the phone yesterday, made them send me pictures of their faces. I like to video chat with them more than they do with me anyway, but I haven't been pushing it these last few weeks, obviously. They're both so busy! And I'm definitely working on getting over worrying about how all this is affecting them. I mean, obviously they're affected by Cillian and me individually and by our marriage, but:

They are living their own lives and I want them to!

I don't want them worrying about me or Cillian at ALL.

It took having kids myself for me to realize that my parents' marriage is a whole separate thing from me, Theo, and Monet.

We have our own lives and they have theirs.

Honestly, Olive really is the type of daughter/woman/person who would understand what I'm doing with Loup, but I'd never put that on her. I do imagine what it would be like if Olive weren't my daughter...and were my friend instead...and I could tell her things a woman can tell her best friend.

It feels so crooked and wrong not to be sharing all of this with Ramona too. One day I'll tell her EVERYTHIIIING. We texted yesterday, just not about this. She cut her hair and sent me a pic. I love it. Also, she got a new silkie chicken for their farm and she sent me a pic of her too, so fluffy and white! She named her Dolly Parton. It's always a soothing spot in my mind, thinking of Ramona back home, making her yard sculptures and weeding her birdy garden, all cottagecore and happy.

Tully uploaded a new acoustic cover video yesterday and I wrote him about it. New week = new color too. Pink! He responded and sent me some more pics from Siobhán's garden. He and Dad have been emailing a lot and his new video got a ton of views fast, which is awesome for him.

I don't know if Siobhán is aware he's taking pics of her garden and sending them to me. If he says to her, "Yeah, hey Mam, I'm taking pics of your petunias to send to Vincent Wilde because we talk at least once a week about music and colors."?

I sent him a picture of a pale pink frame hung on the wall downstairs... babies Fenna and Florentina, wrapped in pink blankets.

Loup just rolled over. The gentleman stirs!

And I think I hear Mama downstairs.

Loup walks to the skate park alone to check it out. Vincent loves the subtlety and courtesy he displays in finding something to entertain himself in order to give her some time alone with her family. She would've been okay with him staying! This is their trip together! But Loup is flexible and easygoing in almost all things and finds new ways to impress her every day.

Yvonne works as a wedding planner and has left the apartment already. She'll be gone until late. She's already said her goodbyes to Solomon and Aurora, since she won't be back before they leave for the airport.

Everyone in the living room is related to Vincent and it's a little loud. There is blippy, bassy music playing from Solomon's phone and the television is on—a Dutch word game show. She is in between her mother and sister on the couch. Her dad and Theo are standing and her dad is holding his phone close to Theo's ear.

Solomon starts telling them a story he loves repeating. About how he and Aurora came to Rotterdam in 1975 when Aurora was pregnant with Theo and they went to see Led Zeppelin at the Ahoy. And how afterward, he and Aurora hitched to Amsterdam and loved it so much, they thought of trying to find a way to stay, but Vincent's grandfather had gotten sick and was dying and Aurora wanted to come back home. And after her father passed away, she couldn't bear the thought of leaving her mother in Kentucky alone. It wasn't until Vincent's grandmother died that Aurora and Solomon decided to spend as much time as they possibly could outside of the United States, popping in only when necessary.

The story always makes Vincent wistful about her parents' lives before she and her siblings came along and thankful for the wide-eyed hope and adventure they've instilled in them. Vincent, Theo, and Monet grew up traveling all over and staying up way past their nonexistent bedtimes in swanky art galleries and ultracool music studios. When she was a little girl, anytime Vincent learned about a new country or culture and got excited about it, her dad would open up the Rand McNally or find the globe, and they'd look at it together and dream out loud of going to those places and soaking it all in. Growing up, her parents always made her and her siblings feel like their emotions and dreams were valid—and that it was just as okay to be clueless or confused about their feelings too. Vincent tried her best to raise Colm and Olive the same way.

No matter what happens with her and Cillian, she'll always be proud of how they raised their children.

She is staring at the TV, far away in her brain, thinking of Colm and Olive as babies, those long days when Cillian was teaching in the afternoons and evenings and Vincent was home alone with both of them, making jewelry in the living room and kid snacks in the kitchen all day.

Her dad sits beside her and it's only then that Vincent realizes Monet has gotten up. She hears the water rushing into the kitchen sink.

"I talked to Tully yesterday," Solomon says.

"Good. He adores you," Vincent says.

"I told him the new album was *cracker*. And I told him I love saying things are *cracker*."

"That's a fairly decent Irish accent, Daddy. You've been practicing?" Vincent laughs a little.

"I have, thanks!" Solomon says. "And Loup...well, he fits right in too...Will we be seeing more of him?" he asks. He puts his arm around Vincent and squeezes her shoulder. Physical affection is her dad's strongest love language. He reaches over farther and playfully taps Aurora. Vincent feels like a kid again, in between her parents like that.

Theo is watching the TV screen and correctly guesses the answer to the word puzzle. He says *sweet* to himself in satisfaction and leaves the room; he's so tall, there's only a smidge of space between his head and the top of the doorway.

"I don't know, Daddy. I'll see Cillian at the wedding and...*to be continued*," Vincent says, putting her head on his shoulder.

"What about counseling?" he asks. Her daddy smells the same as always—like coffee and soap.

Vincent's parents are honest about counseling and how positively it's affected their relationship. Occasionally one of them will bring up something they learned in therapy and how it helped them to defuse arguments and communicate more openly. Therapy was the first thing her mother had mentioned to her after she read Cillian's book.

"I don't want to do that right now. I want to be here...and I want him to stay over there. I want to *see* everything and *feel* everything on my own. Sometimes with Loup, but in here on my own," Vincent says, putting her hand on her heart.

Maybe she feels like crying? Maybe she feels like screaming? Maybe she wants to get drunk on wine and howl at the moon? Her stomach whirls like a washing machine at the thought of Loup's ears blushing at the skate park. His hair, like a flag in the wind.

"You're our little girl and that's all we care about. You'll let us know what you need, won't you?" Aurora says, turning the TV off.

"Of course I will. I appreciate y'all. You know that," Vincent says.

Her brother and sister laugh in the kitchen and the electric kettle clicks off. Solomon stands and says he needs to finish packing his bag. Theo is taking them to the airport after dinner.

When Loup returns, he takes a quick shower and they all sit down together and eat from the vegetarian charcuterie board Vincent and Monet put together while their dad and brother sat out back, smoking cigars and talking. Aurora joined them out there, drinking a glass of rosé, after her daughters demanded she relax.

Vincent tears up when her parents leave because she hadn't realized how much she'd missed them, and she thinks of her own children across the ocean—no matter how old and grown up they are—missing her.

In bed in the dark, Loup says he has a surprise for her when they leave Amsterdam: They'll take the train to one more place before returning to Paris. When they were planning their trip, he told Vincent he'd take care of getting their tickets home.

"I added a surprise stop. Sorry I got so excited and told you about it," he says.

"Really? And we'll get back on, what, Sunday?" Vincent asks. She's not a huge fan of surprises, but with Loup, everything is different. She's too tired to even imagine where he could be taking her and lets her eyes close.

"*Ouais.*" He snuggles against her and nuzzles her neck.

"Well, thank you. I want to see everything you want to show me," she says, yawning.

He jerks a little. There is a mumble, something in French.

"Let's do it. Let's do everything," he says through sleep.

Yvonne hugs everyone goodbye and leaves for Rotterdam. Vincent, Loup, Theo, and Monet walk to a Thai restaurant for lunch and go to the Stedelijk Museum afterward. There is a big theater-like room inside where people can sit in the dark and watch quotidian images projected on the white wall in front of them. Wind through green trees, a man catching a fish, an overturned headstone in a cemetery. A mama and her baby ducks taking big leaps into water.

There is one of a butterfly landing on a flower and when Loup sees it, he touches Vincent's arm like he wants to make sure she hasn't flown off.

Back at Theo's, the rain is light. It's Monet's idea for them to smoke a joint and listen to records. Theo doesn't need convincing. He reaches into the drawer behind him and produces a little box filled with plump green buds. In Loup's sweater again, Vincent looks over and asks Loup if he wants to. She hasn't smoked weed since the time she and Theo and Cillian smoked together in Amsterdam when Colm and Olive were little. Yvonne and her sister had taken all four kids and a few of their cousins to the children's museums for the day, and they slept over at her sister's in Amstelveen.

Vincent never thinks about smoking weed and doesn't care about smoking weed, but she's in Amsterdam again and Loup's nose is right there and she touches it.

"Only if you do, I will," he says, looking at her with those deep root-beer eyes. *Lover.*

"*C'est bon bon bon*," she says.

Like usual, at first she doesn't feel anything, then it happens all at once.

Loup's eyes are red and he's laughing in reverse slow-motion at something Theo just said. Vincent and Monet missed it, but that doesn't matter because now they're laughing too. Monet puts on D'Angelo—

a frothy cloud of pulsing black-blue music floating and handclapping across the room.

Vincent thinks she can see it.

Monet lights a row of squat white candles and puts them in the fireplace. Everyone looks ethereal in the candlelight.

"I'm so glad you're here," her sister says. Vincent thinks she's talking to her, but she's not, she's talking to Loup. "You're perfect for my sister, you're like... Vinnie, look at his hair. Loup, your hair is hella soft. This is the softest hair I've ever touched and I've touched a *lot* of hair. Cillian's hair is *not* this soft. Your decision is made."

Loup is sitting on the floor in front of Monet with his eyes closed, letting her pet him. He leans forward to make it easier for her.

"Maybe they'll be together forever," Loup says.

"Who? Vinnie and Cillian?" Monet asks. One of her hands is touching Loup's hair and the other is loudly crunching around in a big bag of paprika crisps.

Loup nods and Vincent gives a soft gasp.

"Please stop talking about this! It's ridiculous," Vincent says.

"Pshh, I don't even know if Yvonne and I will be together forever," Theo says, plopping onto the couch on his stomach, letting his hand hang.

Vincent gives the same soft gasp again and stifles a laugh. Monet notices her trying not to giggle, which makes it worse because instead of not laughing, she opens her mouth and lets loose. Theo is cracking up now too.

"I just mean there are surprises everywhere and who knows what can happen in this life, right? We've been married for a *looong* time," Theo says, turning on his back and looking up at the ceiling. He has a pleasing, calm face, like their dad. Easy to look at for a long time and comforting in a way Vincent can't fully explain. All she can compare it to is the face of the peaceful, sleepy bear in a children's book she used to read to Colm and Olive when they were little. In the book, the bears had fake fur for the kids to touch. Vincent strokes the rug on the floor, remembering that little book. It feels so good that she keeps doing it.

"I'm just convinced Yvonne thinks I want to fuck you," Monet says to Theo. She's stopped petting Loup's hair and is standing with her hands in the air, moving to the music.

"Wait, *quoi*?" Loup stutters out. His eyes are wide because surprise talk of incest will do that. Monet giggles at his French and repeats it, winking at him.

Theo laughs a little and rubs his face. "Although it certainly doesn't go *that* far, she's always been jealous of you two...my two little sisters."

"Can you inform her that just because it's been like six months since I've gotten laid, I'm not trying to have *sex* with my brother? I mean...it would take at *least* a full year for me to feel that way about you," Monet says, throwing her head back and cackling.

"Right?!" Theo says.

Monet gets on the couch next to Theo, pushes him so she can lie on her side in his lap; he reaches over to smack her bottom once, then lets his hand rest on her head. The three of them smack and pinch one another's asses all the time and kiss on the mouth and walk around in their underwear in front of one another. They've always been like this. Not every family is as touchy, or loves and gets along with their siblings this much, but Vincent's grateful hers does. And she's grateful Colm and Olive get along too. She thinks of Tully and how he's missed out on their family. She really wants them to get to know one another. Cillian broke that, but they can fix it, they can.

"No worries. I'll let Yvonne know how you feel, Naynay," Theo says, calling Monet by the nickname he's always had for her. His *Vinnie and Naynay*. To them, he's *Theodora* when they're feeling extra silly.

"I was also going to say, maybe you and I will be together forever too...but you told me to stop talking, so I thought I'd be a good boy and listen," Loup says to Vincent when she sits next to him.

"You look like a sculpture," Vincent says to him for the first time, like talking about it with her sister and being slightly high finally gave her permission to confess it aloud.

"*Comment?*" Loup says, and Vincent can see it move across the air between them—each individual letter, like animation from a children's show.

"Your hair really is hella soft," she whispers. She touches where it falls against his neck. Thinks about how it feels when a wild strand of it tickles her nose when he's on top of her.

She would like him on top of her right now and tells him that too.

"*Oui. Maintenant, s'il te plaît,*" he says with his breath in her ear. Theo and Monet are on the other side of the room. Vincent watches them laugh and opens her mouth again.

"*And* you have a beautiful cock."

"V, I will soon lose the ability to function properly." Loup's face is pressed against hers.

"It's a very pretty color too. All fawn and rosy. I've decided that this is the most perfect exact time for me to tell you that. Can't you feel it in the atmosphere? I can. In the glimmers," she says, floating. Wiggling her fingers at him because it feels good. "I want to eat you up like you're a cake."

"I want to eat *you* up like a cake. You're a cupcake . . . with sweet cherries. Your mouth is a cherry. *Ma cerise,*" he says slowly, kissing her. He laughs as he kisses her forehead. "Can we discuss this further, in more detail? Can we go upstairs now? Can we disappear?" he asks.

"*Oui. On y va.*"

Amsterdam. Friday, May 4.

Monet left today and we leave tomorrow. Her flight to London wasn't until this evening, so we got up as early as our still-kinda-stoned brains would allow and walked to the grocery for bread, fruit, and coffee, then to Vondelpark to have our breakfast on a blanket in the grass. We wandered up to Amsterdam-Centrum after that. I love it there. And the Anne Frank House, Grachtengordel, all the canals. There was a man on the street singing "Luka" by Suzanne Vega...insta-nostalgia for late '80s / early '90s music...

...Loup wasn't even ALIVE then...

...yeah.

When we got back, I texted Cillian saying we can video chat on Monday. He responded and said "So glad to hear it, love" and told me how much he misses me. I told him I miss him too. ~~I tell him that because I don't know what else to say.~~

Monet and I always cry when one of us leaves and this time was no different. I'm glad I'll see her and Theo again soon at the wedding. My parents too. It would've been harder to say goodbye if not for that.

I'm not sure what Theo meant by saying he doesn't know if he and Yvonne will be together forever. He's never been a skirt-chaser. I could see Yvonne stepping out, though. I've always liked her, but she can definitely be cold. And since Theo is as reserved and minimalist with his feelings as he is with his furniture design, they probably freeze each other out completely when something's going on and just wait until it melts.

Last night was so fun, though:

getting stoned and stupid...

just listening to records...

laughing and eating all of Theo's crisps...

Monet almost peed herself, she was laughing so hard about some starfish tattoo the last guy she dated had. It was on his leg and she hated it so much she broke up with him the day she saw it. Theo sat at the table and tried to draw the tattoo exactly how Monet was describing it in real time. It was hilarious. I couldn't stop laughing. Loup was on the floor!!

Stoned Loup is a joy. When he's not laughing, he just gets kind of quiet and hungry and horny, so not all that different from Regular Loup. We had actual sex last night (twice...once when we went upstairs while

Monet and Theo were in the kitchen making brownies and again... (later) for the first time since we've been in Amsterdam. The second time it was very sleepy, quiet sex, which is sometimes my favorite kind.

Vincent and Theo are the only ones awake. She'd risen in *l'heure bleue* and now they sit out back drinking dark coffee from white cups as the sunrise stretches across the horizon. Vincent watches a magpie with blue wings land in the grass in front of them.

"I'm really sorry if this turned into a stressful thing. I know you didn't intend on introducing Loup to the whole family like this," Theo says with his voice sleepy-deep like it always is in the morning.

"Stop apologizing. It's not your fault! I said I was bringing a friend... I should've told you who Loup was. Eh, it turned out okay, considering," Vincent says, and shrugs.

Another magpie joins the first; they caw and fluff. She tells her brother one of the birds is him and the other is her.

"Cillian called me two days ago, just saying hey," Theo says.

"While I was here?" Vincent's heart beats a little faster at the thought of Theo and Cillian talking on the phone while she was in the apartment. It's around midnight in Kentucky and Cillian probably hasn't even gone to bed yet, while she's just woken up on the other side of the world.

"Yep." Theo nods and looks at her. "I didn't talk to him for long. You were upstairs. I didn't want it to bother you, so I waited to say something."

"Thanks for that. But... he's been your brother-in-law for a long time. I mean, it's good you're friends too."

"I know he's hurting, but he just has to deal with it. Handle his own shit like a man, that's all," Theo says.

"Yeah, that's pretty much what I tell him every time we talk."

Theo goes to his quiet place and Vincent watches the birds.

"Yvonne and I spend a lot of time apart now that the girls are gone.

Either I have work or she has work...and it's not a bad thing for us. Or maybe it is, I don't know anymore. But we've always needed our own space," Theo says. He drinks his coffee. Vincent drinks hers.

"But you're still in love with her, right? That's what I'm trying to figure out about me and Cillian. I mean, *obviously* I still love him. I always will. But maybe I can love him and want something different too. Or something more," Vincent says quietly, and nods toward the bedroom window where Loup is sleeping.

"I'll always love Yvonne. She'll always love me. We'll find a way to do that well, no matter what ends up happening. I believe the same thing for you and Cillian. He's crazy over you. That's the whole reason he fucked up so bad...not wanting to lose you and then keeping it a secret for so long and getting it twisted up with his writing career and showing his ass like that...I don't know," Theo says.

He asks about Tully and how often they talk now.

"At least once a week. We all wish he could make it to the wedding. I'm trying to figure out another way we can get together soon. I think it's important," Vincent says.

Theo reaches over and pats Vincent's leg; she puts her hand on his.

"Look at that bird!" Vincent says later, pointing to a nearby bush. "It's so cute. It's blue. What is it?"

Theo is a total bird nerd and he's Vincent's go-to when she comes across one she hasn't noticed before. Whenever she's walking around Paris and sees a new bird, she tries her best to take a picture of it for Theo.

"That's my bluethroat buddy. He'll probably poke back out, then disappear again. They're skittish. When I first got into birding, I learned how important it is to notice what they do. The behavior means as much as their song and what they look like," he says, sounding like he's narrating a nature documentary.

"Okay, absolutely...early-morning bird ASMR is exactly what I need. Keep going," Vincent says, leaning her head back and closing her eyes.

At the train station, Theo steps out of the car so he can give Vincent a proper hug. She's crying because she'll miss him and she's crying because he'll be returning to his apartment alone, after it was full of so many people. It's what his introverted heart loves, but it still makes her sad.

"Yvonne is coming home tomorrow. I have a table to finish," he says, without Vincent having to say a word of what she's feeling aloud. He knows.

"Wow, thanks for everything, Theo. This was awesome," Loup says. He shakes Theo's hand and Theo tells him it's no worries. His pleasure.

"I'll text you later," Vincent says to her brother, sniffing and waving.

As they watch Theo drive away, Loup puts his hand on the small of her back and calls her *un pétale*.

10

Loup waits until they're inside the train station to tell her what the surprise is. They're going to Auvers-sur-Oise, where Van Gogh died and is buried. It's only about an hour's train ride from Paris but he's made reservations for them to stay in a house with a large garden.

"Really?" Vincent says. She's still crying and can tell it's one of those days when she will probably be on the verge of tears until it's time for bed. It's all the traveling and she woke up so early and Loup is right: she's a petal.

She already knows of spots in Auvers-sur-Oise that are on her list for Someday. Van Gogh's doctor's house, the Maison van Gogh, Garden Daubigny, the cemetery where he and his brother are buried, the medieval church, the town hall. She's overwhelmed by everything. Because of how emotional she will be. Because of how emotional she is already. It sounds so lovely and she doesn't want their trip to be over yet.

"That's okay? I was worried you'd just want to get back to Paris or you've been there before... but you're sure it's okay?"

Vincent nods and takes a drink of water.

They're sitting, people-watching again. A young couple walks by holding hands. A grandmother pushes a stroller as the child inside gleefully says *Oma!* The child is holding a spinning red pinwheel. A man at a small table tosses his necktie over his shoulder to keep it from dipping into his salad. Vincent sees an American couple in college T-shirts, shuffling through the crowd. She doesn't need to hear their accents to know they're American. Many Americans are incredibly easy to spot. Freebies, like a middle square on a bingo card.

"It's perfect. I'm so excited. I'm just tired, that's all. Thank you," Vincent says, reaching for him.

Vincent's Travel Playlist | Train | Amsterdam to Auvers-sur-Oise

"Here Comes the Sun" by Richie Havens
"Van Gogh Part I" by Armand Amar
"Train Song" by Vashti Bunyan
"Blue Moon" by Billie Holiday
"Wanderlust" by Joep Beving
"We Have a Map of the Piano" by múm
"Everything I Am Is Yours" by Villagers
"Ambre" by Nils Frahm
"Ágætis byrjun" by Sigur Rós
"The Winner Takes It All" by ABBA
"How Big, How Blue, How Beautiful" by Florence + the Machine
"Claire de Lune, L. 32" by Claude Debussy
"A Case of You" by Joni Mitchell
"Petite suite pour piano (Quatre mains), L. 65:1. En bateau" by Claude Debussy
"Monument" by Efterklang
"Five Sunflowers in a Vase" by Clint Mansell
"Your Best American Girl" by Mitski
"Just Like a Woman" by Nina Simone
"The Night Café" by Clint Mansell
"Starry Starry Night" by Lianne La Havas

Vincent sleeps for two hours on the train and they have a couple more to go. Loup shares an earbud with her for a bit, then he puts his own in and fiddles around with a music-making app on his phone. They share a big salad and pretzels, a strawberry pop. Vincent wants to cry thinking that this is her second-to-last train ride before they get back to Paris, but she doesn't. She just can't get enough of the trains—all achingly romantic and intimate. Sitting so close and quiet with Loup. The other passengers, some alone, some together, talking, laughing, sleeping. The flashing windows swapping the gentle Dutch morning light for the yellow-yellow of the French afternoon.

Loup has his hair pulled back in a little knot, but one rogue curl has escaped, boinging down by his ear. It's unreal. It makes her miss him and their adventures already. If she reaches out for him, will her hand go right through?

The room Loup has rented for the night is on the top floor of an old white house. Vincent pushes open the windows as soon as she can get her hands on them and looks out. The garden below drips in yellow, orange, and red. Buzzes with bees, birds, and butterflies. She texts Theo and lets him know they made it and tells him she'll text again when she's in Paris. She talks to Colm and Olive on the phone and sets up a video chat with both of them for Tuesday.

She and Loup walk to Van Gogh's doctor's house first and after that, the hotel where Van Gogh stayed and died. In the garden, it feels like they're in one of his wheat field paintings—the sky is stubbornly blue with skinny, almost translucent clouds and there's just enough coolness swirling in with the wind.

* * *

It's when they get to the cemetery that Vincent finally loses it and cries into her hands.

"Hey, you're all right? Can I do anything?" Loup asks, rubbing her back. She shakes her head and tries to catch her breath. Maybe sitting will make it better. She gets down on one knee, then plants herself on the ground.

"He was always asking his brother for money... money for paint... money to pay models to pose for him... he was trying so hard and I just wish he could know how much we love him," she says through her tears. Her head is aching and Loup is sitting next to her now. When she can look over at him, she sees his lip wobbling because he's crying too.

"I think he knows, I really do... and I can't even remember the last time I cried," he says, laughing a little. "Probably my *pépé* and *mémé*'s funeral a few years ago... my mum's parents. They were married for sixty-three years and died a few days apart, so we had their funerals together at this little church in Normandy. It's the only time I've ever seen Baptiste cry... he was there with Mina. I didn't know Baptiste *could* cry." Loup sniffs and laughs again. He leans forward and touches Van Gogh's headstone. Loup loves touching things.

"Oh God, that's one of the sweetest things I've ever heard. I'm sorry I can't stop crying. I don't mean to bring up all these feelings! *Je suis désolée*," Vincent says. Now Loup is soaking up her spilled emotions and when did he start doing that? It's happened as gradually as a sunset and she didn't notice until now.

"Please don't be! This is great! It sounds trite, but it's so good to *feel*. We're made to feel and we're feeling. It's the magic of Van Gogh and any good art, right? We don't want to fight that. We have to lean into it," Loup says, wiping his eyes.

Vincent has never cried this hard in front of him and she's not a pretty crier. Her throat hurts, her cheeks are hot. She brushes her hair from her face, letting the wind touch every part of it. A man and a woman walk by, speaking quietly.

"Okay," Vincent says, committed to letting herself cry for as long as she wants. For Van Gogh, for her marriage, for whatever is to come with Loup. For her children, for Siobhán and Tully, for eternity past and eternity future, amen.

"Let's just stay here for a little while," Loup says. He wipes his eyes again, lets his hands sit still in his lap.

Auvers-sur-Oise. Sunday, May 6.

Early. We are leaving for the train station in an hour and a half. I'm up before Loup.

Yesterday after visiting the graves we stopped at the church and the town hall. Then we came back here and had fresh vegetable soup we picked up at the grocery store with crusty bread and Beurre de Bresse. Dessert was a shared cigarette and a teapot of chocolate rooibos outside with the flowers. (Bunnies in the violets!) I had on Loup's sweater and took a blanket too. Loup was wearing mauve nylon shorts and his gray sweatshirt with the hood pulled up. I love his clothes. He's really precious with the hood pulled up like that...just nose and hair.

(Also note: I'm not a pretty crier, but Loup is. He says I'm wrong about this and it's the other way around.)

We were kind of quiet on the rest of the walk back to the house. We were both so tired. There's no way I could've traveled for this long with someone who wasn't easy to be quiet with.

I'm ~~nervous to talk~~ talking to Cillian tomorrow evening.

I don't start teaching at the museum again until next week and this week will just be jewelry-making and reopening the shop. I'll be busy...Loup will be busy too. He has two bartending gigs and Anchois has a show at the end of the week. Maybe Agathe will come with me?

I miss Paris, but I will also miss traveling like this.

This morning, with Loup sleeping next to me, I officially don't know anything. He's naked and the sheet is only half covering his little twenty-five-year-old peach of an ass.

→ Mercy, please!! ← (One French word for mercy is pitié... the same word for pity...)

REMINDER: Tell Agathe I really did bite it.

We were just fooling around, being silly in bed because we were both spent from crying at the cemetery and he was already naked because he loves to be naked. I had my head down there so I nibbled on his butt. And he said, "Did you just bite my butt?" And I said yes. And he said, "Can I bite yours?" I said yes. He turned me around and pulled my panties aside and gently bit my bottom. The window was open a little and the air was cool. We got under the white sheets together.

Afterward we opened the window all the way and shared a cigarette and I told him how much I love his armpit hair and I was petting it because it's so soft. He told me I reminded him of Marpessa Dawn, which is one of the best compliments he's ever given me because I adore her and her angelic beauty. (We don't look alike but I've stopped by her tomb in Père Lachaise.) Then he told me I reminded him of a Jane Birkin photo too, where she's smoking topless. I don't look like her either, but! I asked him if he was just trying to get laid AGAIN, by comparing me to iconic women who love/d Paris...

Being with Loup in a bedroom always reminds me of À bout de souffle when Michel and Patricia just talk and talk and talk in her apartment. Just the two of them, away from the world. It's one of my favorite scenes in any movie... the stripes and cigarettes... the art... the open windows. À bout de souffle means breathless and that's how I feel sometimes → breathless.

And at times → like I've just come up from the depths for HUGE gulps of air.

In Amsterdam, Loup had asked my dad if it was okay to record them talking about art and music and Dad got a kick out of it. Loup played me some parts of their conversations for the first time.

He recorded the two of us on his phone last night "just because," he said.

We laughed a lot discussing our trip and our mutual insatiability. He told me to say anything as long as it was completely honest, no filter, and I said, "This is Vincent and it's a little after two a.m. in Auvers-sur-Oise on Sunday, May 6. My Loup-orgasms remain hellacious and exquisite."

When it was his turn he said a chunk in French I didn't understand and ended with "This is Loup and I take the pleasure of contributing to your theater of orgasms very seriously. But even with that glorious perfection aside, there's nowhere else I'd rather be... no-fucking-where."

Vincent's Travel Playlist | Train | Auvers-sur-Oise to Paris

"This Must Be the Place (Naive Melody)" by Talking Heads
"Kiss" by Mélanie Laurent
"Voulez-Vous" by ABBA
"Dans ma rue" by Zaz
"Fine Line" by Harry Styles
"Mon amie la rose" by Françoise Hardy
"J'aime plus Paris" by Thomas Dutronc
"Lilac Wine" by Jeff Buckley
"Echo" by Mina Tindle
"L'anamour" by Serge Gainsbourg
"For Once in My Life" by Stevie Wonder
"Fleur de Seine" by Yves Montand
"Something's Gotta Give" by Sammy Davis Jr.
"Darling" by Carla Bruni
"Garden Song" by Phoebe Bridgers
"Papi Pacify" by FKA twigs
"Make Me Cry" by Pip Millett
"Take On Me (MTV Unplugged)" by a-ha
"69 année érotique" by Serge Gainsbourg
"Cheek to Cheek" by Ella Fitzgerald and Louis Armstrong

Part Three

A WOMAN CALLED VINCENT

1

INT. VINCENT'S APARTMENT – EVENING

Vincent is on her bed.

Narrator (V.O.)

She hasn't unpacked yet and it'll probably be a month until she does. Unpacking is so sad! It means the trip is over. Putting off unpacking makes her feel like traveling is still a possibility. She likes to leave her full suitcase unzipped on the floor until she's tired of looking at it.

She kept her hair loose and did her quick face of makeup, adding a little extra red lipstick on accident, or maybe it was on purpose. She snaked her silky peony robe out and put it on, got her laptop and propped herself up against the pillows.

When they got to Paris yesterday, Loup had taken the Métro from the train station and gone to his apartment; Vincent had taxied home. She'd been so tired she slept for most of the afternoon after stopping downstairs to say hello and thank you to the Laurents for keeping an eye on the apartment and plants, for picking up her flower deliveries and her mail. The yellow tulips that Cillian had sent on Saturday were on their kitchen counter and Vincent insisted that Mrs. Laurent keep them.

The Laurents asked about her travels and Mr. Laurent asked about Cillian and her kids. He reminded her that staying married was hard, but worth it, but Mrs. Laurent interrupted him to say that strong women have more options than they did back when she and Mr. Laurent got married. She said that everything was different now and sometimes divorce is the best answer. Mr. Laurent jokingly asked if Mrs. Laurent had anything she wanted to say to him and they laughed and Vincent laughed too.

Vincent always likes listening to them, even when she and Mr. Laurent don't agree. Mrs. Laurent made her a cup of tea but Vincent only drank half of it. Mr. Laurent invited her to stay for dinner just in case she didn't feel like cooking. Vincent told them she had a can of soup and some crackers she'd been saving for just such an occasion and would be fine.

She restocked at the Franprix this morning, and tomorrow afternoon she has plans to let Baptiste welcome her back to Paris by getting coffee and her favorite *pain au chocolat* with him at the café.

When Cillian bloops up on her laptop screen, he's smiling. He's had a recent haircut and his glasses are new. Vincent imagines him going to the barber alone, picking out his glasses alone. She's teary already and it's been half a second. Where would they be and what would they be doing right now if he hadn't fucked everything up?

She'd returned to two wax-sealed letters from him but hasn't opened them yet.

She smiles at him without saying anything. They'll talk about the kids, catch up a bit. Half an hour, tops. It's fine.

"You look beautiful," Cillian says.

"*Merci*. You got your hair cut like, what, yesterday?"

"Yeah," he says, touching his head, all boyish and blushing like this is a first date.

"It looks good. And your glasses." Vincent points at her camera.

"Your lips are very pretty and red. And your necklace...it's new, I love it," Cillian says, pointing back.

"Oh. Thank you," Vincent says, fingering the cool pendant.

A small gold tiger head that lies flat on her skin—Loup had gifted it to her on the last train ride back to Paris. He slipped it on his own short chain necklace and put it in her hand, telling her that he'd secretly bought the pendant on his walk back from the skate park in Amsterdam and wanted to wait until they were almost home to give it to her. He told her he'd had one of the best times of his life traveling with her and that he hoped it was the first of many trips they'd take together. Vincent told him how much she loved traveling with him too and that she adored the necklace. She cried because she was tired and their trip was over and because everything lately was making her cry. She put the necklace on immediately and hasn't taken it off since.

"It's been too long since I've seen ya, everything seems new," Cillian says. He adds that there are sixty-one days until he sees her in the flesh.

"I know."

"Not like I'm keeping track or anything, right?"

"Aren't writers supposed to steer clear of clichés?"

"Forgive me. How's Paris?"

He likes to ask *how's Paris?* casually, as if she's an acquaintance he's making small talk with.

"Paris is lovely. Paris is always lovely, even when it isn't. I could live here forever. It rained yesterday. I love Paris in the rain," she says.

A short downpour had welcomed her and Loup home as they exited the train station. It was *très* Paris, *très romantique*. Like a proper ending to a French film, they'd kissed in the rain, saying *goodbye* with wet heads. How silly to miss him this much when they've barely been apart for twenty-four hours!

Loup had texted not long before she started chatting with Cillian, just saying hi, and he sent her a pic that he'd snapped at night when they were in Bath. She hadn't known he'd taken it. She's turned away and looking up, in front of a tree wrapped in white twinkle lights.

Vincent isn't planning on seeing Loup again until she and Agathe go to the Anchois show on Friday night.

It's Monday.

"What's the twenty-fifth wedding anniversary gift, again? Can you believe ours is so soon?

"Silver. And no... not really. I don't understand time anymore."

"Would you like me to send you something silver?"

"No. Please don't. I'm serious! But thank you."

Cillian takes a deep breath. "Vin, my love, honestly... what can I do to get you to come back to me?" he asks. She hears Cillian's secret son singing "Come Back to Me" in his mellow Dublin accent.

"Hmm. Okay. It's not silver but... y'know... I was watching *Stealing Beauty* yesterday and I was thinking... I need a villa. I need a villa in Tuscany. I watch all these TV shows and movies and everyone's romping around in these villas and eating dinner under trellises and the full Italian moon... riding bikes to get gelato... and that's what I need. I need a villa in Tuscany, Cillian. Buy me a villa in Tuscany and I'll come back to you, is that a deal? It doesn't have to be exactly like the one in *Stealing Beauty*. One from a Luca Guadagnino film will work too. The one in *Call Me by Your Name* or *A Bigger Splash*... I'm not picky on specifics. Just make sure it has some antique tiles on the walls in the kitchen and some sort of studio. A swimming pool in the grass, surrounded by statues. And flowers... lots and *lots* of flowers."

After listening to some snippets of conversations and sounds Loup had recorded on their trip—skateboard chunks and chatter in London, Vincent singing "I Love Paris" in the shower in Bath, the church bells in Lyon, birdsong in Amsterdam, Monet's starfish story the night they got stoned—they'd half watched *Stealing Beauty* on her iPad on the train. She's seen it a million times. The train ride was short, but they'd left it playing while they napped.

"It's yours," Cillian says, with his eyes on hers.

"Ha ha."

"I'm serious. If that's what it will take, I'll start looking for villas as soon as this conversation is over."

"Then, yay, I guess we're moving to Tuscany. Uh-huh," Vincent says, laughing lightly. She's had a little wine. The rest of it is sitting in the glass on her nightstand; Cillian watches her finish it.

She asks if he's been talking to their children and how things are at work. The same questions she always asks. He asks her some of those same questions back. She acts as if she hasn't left Paris. Like she's only been busy making jewelry and teaching at the art museum.

He's leaned closer to his camera without Vincent noticing when and her body whooshes like maybe his screen is an enchanted portal to Paris. Like he'll be able to step right through. She leans a little closer too, right as Cillian picks up his laptop, telling her he wants to show her how her plants are doing. She sees her shoes by the door, her spare set of keys hanging on a hook in the kitchen. Cillian is giving her a tour of her own house and she feels tender and evanescent, like Ezra Pound's *petals on a wet, black bough*.

They've been chatting for an hour now. She's gone to the kitchen to pour another glass of wine and Cillian is on his third short glass of whiskey. She took the laptop in there with her and gave him a quick tour of the apartment, showing him things too. How tall the fiddle-leaf fig tree has gotten; her favorite spot on the couch. She tells him about the naked drumming man and turns the computer toward the window up at his apartment, through the night.

She's in her robe on the bed, lying on her side.

"If you're attempting to seduce me, it's workin'," Cillian says.

"What?!"

"Your sash . . . it's open. You're basically flashing me and I miss your body so much, I'm broken."

"Oh please," Vincent says, rewrapping her robe. Maybe she's a little buzzed?

"If you were here...would we make love, you think?"

"*Make love*?" She laughs. "What? Cillian, you don't talk like that."

He laughs too. A hearty laugh she hasn't heard from him since she left. Maybe he's a little buzzed?

"I'm trying to be a gentleman! What do you want me to say...if you were here, would you let me fuck ya?" he asks, making his accent extra thick. Sweet, sweet frosting on his fluffy word cake. He leans away and she misses the closeness already. He's in his pajamas—a threadbare college T-shirt he's had forever and black shorts. She feels a reluctant, stabby attraction toward him, hearing him say the word *fuck* about her like that. She touches her tiger necklace and thinks of Loup. Her blood purrs.

"I'd be tempted...maybe," she says, letting the wine tell the truth.

Cillian pushes his laptop a little, and now she can see more of his body. Sure, he looks good. Sure, she misses him. *Uh-huh*. That doesn't mean they're having video chat sex. He puts his thumb just barely into the waistband of his shorts.

"You'd let me make you come?" he asks, moving his shirt up and softly rubbing his belly.

"Maybe," she says. She's mad at him and she misses his touches. The way he'll grab behind her knee and hold her leg up when he's inside her. His nighttime voice, his dark musk.

She looks at his left hand and sees his wedding ring. He's in their living room, on their couch; the laptop is on the coffee table.

"Do you touch yourself and think of me?" he asks.

"Maybe...sometimes."

Sometimes it's Loup. Sometimes it's both of you.

Sometimes it's Stormzy in Banksy's stab-proof vest or Gong Yoo in an expensive turtleneck sweater. Sometimes, Idris Elba.

Vincent's told him a little about Agathe, but not about the vibrator. He's the kind of man who hates them, afraid they'll put him out of work.

"You want to do that for me now?" he asks, making his voice all deep and rough and he knows she likes that.

"That's annoying."

"What is?"

"You... doing your voice like that."

"Doing my voice like what?" Cillian says, doing it again. Vincent laughs and it's a real laugh. A two-glasses-of-wine-in-Paris-while-video-chatting-with-her-estranged-husband-who's-desperately-attempting-to-make-her-horny laugh. "I can't talk about how much I miss being with you?" Cillian asks. He adds *woman of my heart* and *beautiful girl* in Irish. His voice is even worse now. Vincent is close to moaning over it.

"Stop it," she says, sitting up. Okay, maybe they *will* have video chat sex?

No.

Even though he's speaking Irish and she loves when he speaks Irish, it's really not going to happen like this. She thinks of Loup. She thinks of Cillian finding out about Loup. She touches the tiger on her neck and thinks of "Une tigresse." She thinks of *Half-Blown Rose* and Cillian day-drinking and laughing with Hannah.

"Open your robe," Cillian says.

Vincent unties the sash. Why is she untying the sash?

"I'm begging you to let me in," Cillian says, leaning toward the screen. His face, his eyes, his voice. So many of the things she's loved about him since she was eighteen years old—they've always been there and also, they're all coming back to her now. She hears the chorus of that super-dramatic Celine Dion song in her head.

"You want me to open my robe like this?" Vincent asks, letting one side slip to reveal the bare honeydrop of her breast.

"Exactly like that," Cillian says, moving his hand down the front of his shorts.

Vincent watches as he moves. Slowly, slowly.

But before it can go where it needs to be, he pulls his hand out and looks away, toward the door.

"Shit. Stay right there. Don't move. Promise you won't move?" he asks.

"Yep."

She's a little thankful for the interruption and pulls her robe closed just in case there's someone else at the house who can walk past the laptop. But he's alone, right? Obviously. Would someone else be there? Who else would be there?

With Cillian gone, Vincent looks at her phone. There's a new text from a number not in her contacts.

Vincent. I'd like to talk to you about Loup . . . when you're free.

Admittedly, I may be overstepping some boundaries, but he IS my family. -Mina

Why in the world would Mina think it was okay to text her about Loup? And *fucking* Baptiste! Giving her number to anyone who asks! If the wine weren't in her system, she wouldn't be as calm. She looks at her laptop screen and sees the pink velvet couch in their house. Vacant. No sign of Cillian.

Hi Mina. What about Loup?

Obviously I know he's your cousin and BTW, I think it's great you two are so close.

Mina begins texting quickly and Cillian hasn't returned.

About your "relationship" . . . if that's what it is? B told me you're still married?

I thought you were divorced.

Does Loup know you're married?

Mina, I like you. But I don't see how this is your business, really.

Loup is a grown man. But I will tell you that YES he knows I'm married. ?

And he knows it because I told him.

Sure, he's a grown man, but he's 25 and you're 44... you don't think that's a little odd?

I'm just looking out for my cousin.

Mean-a.

Whoops. The wine has stopped working. Vincent's face is hot. Again, she stares at her couch in their house on the screen. She doesn't see Cillian. She doesn't hear Cillian. What is he doing? Her texting thumbs are flying.

That's nice of you... looking out for your cousin.

But maybe you shouldn't worry about us and you should worry about your own business.

Wow, is that a dig at my marriage?

Is this because you're friends with Agathe?

Do you think I don't know about B and Agathe??

You've lived here for what... not even a year and you think you know more about my marriage than I do just because you work with my husband?

It's probably best to end this conversation.

Agreed.

With Vincent attempting to process what has just happened, Cillian sits down on the couch, looking flustered.

"What were you *doing*?" Vincent asks.

"Someone was at the door... They're gone now."

"Who was it?"

"It doesn't matter."

"But who was it?

"If I tell you, you'll think it means somethin' it doesn't."

Vincent's body floods with adrenaline, compelling her to stand; sitting down with her heart kicking that hard is too unsettling. It was Hannah. She's sure it was Hannah. Maybe she's sitting next to him, just out of view.

"Was it Hannah?" Vincent asks, feeling so stupid she wants to rip her own fucking face off.

She has Loup and Cillian has Hannah. That's how this is working. That's how they're getting through this.

Cillian puts both hands up. "Yes, it was Hannah, but she's on her own thing right now... it doesn't have very much to do with me... She gets these obsessions and they change with the wind. In a flash it'll be someone else."

"What? What does that mean?"

"She says she's in love with me, but she knows I'm married to you...that I'm in love with you. Sometimes she just gets these ideas in her head and they lead her to my door. She's usually crying or wants to talk...I don't know what it is. Vin, I swear to you, I don't know."

"Ah, Cillian. It's quite cute of you to think I believe *anything* that comes out of your mouth anymore."

"Vin, I'm swearing on our children...it's not like you think."

"Don't you dare. Well, unless you want to swear on Tully too. I mean, he's not *our* child, but he is yours," Vincent says. She's pacing now and turns the laptop so he can still see her.

"She kissed me once. I'm telling you that! I was going to tell you that anyway. One drunken kiss and that was it and then afterwards, she got like this...coming to the house and saying she loves me. It's a fuckin' *mess*," Cillian says, putting his head in his hands.

Vincent won't say a word about Loup. She won't tell Cillian a thing. He did this. He needs to feel this.

"Where is she now?"

"She's gone. She left."

"Really shitty timing for you that she'd show up while we're talking. Wow. You know what? It doesn't matter. It really...it probably doesn't matter anyway," she says. She's laughing but she doesn't remember when it started. Maybe she's losing it. She's probably losing it.

"What do you mean? Why are you laughing?"

"Cillian, I'm going to bed. Good night."

Vincent closes her laptop and puts it on the dresser. She turns her phone off. She turns the light off. She takes her robe off. She lies down on the bed. Her laughter melts into the pillow as she lets the room spin.

2

The next afternoon, Vincent waits and waits for Baptiste to text her and cancel their café date because of Mina, but he doesn't. She puts on her linen overalls and goes to meet him.

Cillian has called her seven times and texted her ten. After the tenth, she finally texted him back.

> Cillian, leave me alone right now.
>
> I'll talk to you when I want to talk to you.
>
> Why do you act like you don't remember who I am??

Both of his letters remain unopened on the kitchen counter.

Loup sent her a good-morning message. She told him about Mina's texts and he apologized like he was the one who'd done something wrong. He said he'd talk to his cousin and tell her to drop it. He told Vincent he was going to play soccer in the park and had a bartending gig later. He didn't say anything about hanging out or coming over and she didn't say anything either. She misses him and feels guilty for the almost video chat sex with Cillian, which is somewhat crooked and unhinged because Cillian is her husband and it's not like he hasn't seen her breasts.

None of her feelings are going in the right slots. It's like those blocks her kids had when they were little—the circle should go in the circle hole and the square one in the square. That's the way it works! But Vincent's feelings are all mixed up and not where they're supposed to be. The triangle teeters.

When she spots Baptiste sitting outside the café, she finds herself more upset wondering if Loup misses her than she is about some woman in Kentucky kissing and obsessing over her husband.

Baptiste's white T-shirt glows against his dark brown skin. He is smoking, sitting with his legs crossed, talking to a man standing next to him. When he sees Vincent, he smiles at her and says *au revoir* to the man, who leaves. Vincent sits.

"Ah, we have quite a lot to discuss, *non*?" he asks, smiling widely.

Baptiste has already ordered a café au lait and the *pain au chocolat* on the table for her. She sips her drink and lights the cigarette he's offered from his pack.

"I'll start by saying I missed you," he says.

Vincent blows smoke.

"Look... Loup let it slip to me that you're technically still married and I shouldn't have told Mina. He didn't even know Mina knew about it until she texted you. I didn't give her your number. She got it out of my phone. She goes overboard. You've seen how *intense* she can get," he says.

"Loup said you were a vault when it comes to keeping secrets. And I guess you *can* be, right? Like how you didn't tell me about you and Agathe," Vincent says, since it's truth-telling time.

"How did you know about that?"

"I saw you two kissing at the Anchois show before Christmas. You hadn't found me yet."

"Did you ask Agathe about this?"

"No! I'm asking you. You like to talk, so talk," she says. It's a perfect May day in Paris and the city is enrapt with life, sparkling with sunlight. A large group of teenage schoolgirls laugh and wiggle past them.

"I don't know why. Just thought everything would be easier if you didn't know. Then we wouldn't have to talk about it at all," Baptiste says, shrugging. He puts his cigarette out and picks up his little white cup.

"You and Mina have an open marriage? I promise you I wouldn't usually make someone else's marriage my business, but she texts me out of nowhere going off on me because of Loup and I don't even know what's going on."

"Our marriage is how it is... there's no real label. We love each other. I sometimes sleep with Agathe. Mina has a friend too. His name is Tom. He was her sweetheart from school," Baptiste says, as if he's talking to Vincent about the plot of a movie, not the private inner workings of his marriage.

"That's why Mina hates me! It's not because of Loup, it's because I'm friends with Agathe."

"Yeah... maybe. The Loup thing is out of line, though. Loup is a grown man. He knows exactly what he's doing."

"So, you do admit she hates me?"

"Only a little," Baptiste says, holding up his fingers with the tiniest space between them. He laughs and Vincent laughs too. Everything is absolutely ridiculous.

"This is a lot... but before you and Loup happened, Agathe wondered if you'd want to join us, actually... I'm talking in bed. She really did ask me, but I told her you weren't into that sort of thing. I was right... right?" Baptiste asks. He leans back and it's sexy. Vincent has always found Baptiste handsome. He's sleek and smart and virile. But!

She's never considered him as anything more than a friend. Thinking of him and Agathe discussing a threesome with her is wildly out of range for what her brain would have done on its own.

Quickly and just for fun, she imagines it. The three of them in her bed in the apartment. Her in between them. Both Agathe and Vincent on their knees in front of him. Kissing Baptiste, touching Baptiste, letting Baptiste touch her. Kissing Agathe, touching Agathe, letting Agathe touch her.

Vincent's quiet, staring off and thinking, smoking her cigarette. She watches an old man and his little dog pitter-patter up the street and dodge a man on an electric scooter.

"Right," she says after probably too long. Baptiste shakes his finger at her with an expression on his face she's never seen before—a mix of mischief and sexual satisfaction. She does feel a slick of desire for him, seeing that new face, but it's a snail sliming slowly and she's always one step ahead of it. "However, I do appreciate the consideration. *Merci,*" she says, smirking at him.

"*De rien*. And see...I was correct," he says. "Ask Agathe. We had several conversations about it."

He lights another cigarette and slips easily into a topic change, asking her how her trip with Loup was, letting her know he's talked to him about some of it already. Baptiste congratulates her on Zillah's stylist buying up all her earrings from the gallery. He tells her about the friend dinner parties she missed and asks who's hosting the next one because he's forgotten. He asks how things are going with Loup, although Vincent already knows how much he and Loup talk about her.

"Seems like you have enough to worry about without obsessing over me and Loup, right?" Vincent asks. The couple next to them are holding hands across the table. Vincent glances over again but looks away as the man leans in to kiss the woman's mouth.

"It's wrong for me to be interested in two people I love so dearly?" Baptiste asks, and finishes his coffee. "You tried your best to fight Loup off, you did! I watched it happen! I saw that steamy train coming from a mile away. Loup...he's *intensely* and fully into you. No other woman exists to him right now. Let that be a comfort or a warning to you. Whichever you'd prefer," Baptiste says.

Both. She prefers both. His words spin her brain and heart and make her feel like the world has tilted under her.

"I...I don't know what to say. He's—"

"I know you're leaving in July."

"But I'm coming back! I'll only be gone for a week!"

"Sure, but it's a big leave, right? Seeing the ex and all?"

Vincent nods.

"That's some rough shit for my man. I mean, you understand that," Baptiste says.

They chat some more and smoke another cigarette. Vincent brings the conversation back around. "When it comes to Loup, I guess you would know all about complicated relationships, wouldn't you, Baptiste? Do you want to give me your tips?"

"Oh *merde*, look at the time. I've got to run." His class starts in fifteen minutes. He winks at her and reaches over to touch her hand. "I'm sorry about Mina. She'll be fine, really, she will. She shouldn't have said anything to you about it."

"Did you tell her you were meeting me today?"

"No."

"Can we not openly have coffee together anymore? You have to keep me a secret?" Vincent's feelings—a garden of tromped-on flowers. This is all so weird and unnecessary.

"Obviously I can do what I want, right?" he says, stepping over to kiss her cheeks. "Anchois show on Friday and I'll text you later, *ça te dit*?"

With the Go Wilde! shop open again, Vincent is busy-busy baking clay, making earrings, updating the website, and getting packages ready to send out. She sets aside a new pair especially for Loup's mother's birthday: big dangly teardrops the same blue as Loup's cable-knit sweater she loves so much. She stole that sweater from him with his permission. It's on her bed with her blankets and smells like him. She sleeps with it.

Tuesday night she calls Monet and tells her about Mina's text, and they fuss and laugh about it. Monet is the best person to call when someone pisses Vincent off because no matter what, Monet is always on her side and, in sisterly solidarity, instantly hates the person who has bothered her. Vincent tells Monet about Cillian and Hannah kissing and Hannah stopping by her house too. She calls Theo and tells him the same things because they are secrets she is already tired of keeping.

She video chats with her children and later with Ramona and doesn't tell them any of it. When she connects with her parents, she keeps it light. Tully emails about the gold-colored things he's seen—an electric guitar at the shop and a spray-painted planter in front of a pub. He tells her he's decided to name his first album with the major label *Golden*. Vincent tells him how much she loves it and writes him about her gold tiger necklace without revealing who gave it to her. She mentions the gold lid on her little jar of capers.

Vincent and Loup text and also talk on the phone, something they've never done often. She calls him and gives him a live play-by-play of the naked drumming guy the first time she spots him since being back. She wants Loup to come over, but she doesn't want to have to ask him. He's busy and she'll see him soon. On Wednesday, he jokes he's close to handstands again. On Thursday, he sends her a video of himself doing one in his bedroom.

Also on Thursday, even though she has another bouquet of flowers coming on Saturday, Cillian has an extra delivery of sunflowers sent to her door with a card that reads *For Vincent Raphaela, my love and light. I'm so sorry for everything.*

The wax-sealed, handwritten letters were classic Cillian—romantic and thoughtful. Desperately apologetic and tender. She's really not trying to continuously punish him, and she's never questioned whether he's truly sorry.

She just can't decide if it matters anymore.

On Friday, Agathe shows up at the apartment in ruffles and heels, bearing three kinds of homemade cookies—lemon shortbread, coconut chocolate chip, and butter. After setting them on the counter, she and Vincent have wine on the couch.

In about an hour they'll walk to the club for the Anchois show. Vincent hasn't seen Agathe since returning to Paris and they haven't talked about Baptiste or Mina. Vincent had been anxiously anticipating a text from Agathe all week about everything, but it never came and Vincent didn't want to bring it up.

"Okay. I'm so excited but I had to wait to tell you in person!" Agathe says, curling her feet underneath her.

"What?" Vincent takes a sip of wine.

"At midnight, Zillah's new video premieres and she's wearing like seven different pairs of your earrings. The song is called 'Les couleurs de mon cœur.' She's going to link your shop and give all the details. It'll be *huge*. Have you seen her last video? It has like twenty million views and only came out a few months ago. Her stylist told me all this and played the song for me. It's so good. But I promise I haven't seen the video yet. Her stylist wanted to talk to you about everything, but I kind of lied and told her you'd given me permission to move forward with everything and I told her you were on a romantic adventure with your young lover and the details would be an amazing surprise when you returned! Isn't it an amazing surprise? I talked you up so much and told her she'd be crazy not to go with your jewelry since it's so amazing. Basically I'm the *very* best friend you've ever had and it's okay to admit it."

Agathe leans back with a cute, smug look on her face.

"Uh... wow. All I can say is wow. All I can *think* is wow!" Vincent says. She's smiling so hard it's starting to make her face hurt. Seeing Zillah in her earrings will be such a fun and also anxious out-of-body thing, Vincent wishes she had a time-turner to get it over with already. Agathe talks and talks and it's endearing how excited she is. Vincent asks questions about everything and Agathe is all too happy to spill.

Vincent waits until some of the excitement calms down to tell Agathe she knows about her and Baptiste, only because she can't put it off any longer. She tells her that she and Baptiste have talked about it and what Baptiste said about a threesome with her.

"I knew you knew about us... Baptiste told me. I wasn't going to say anything until you did. You don't have a thing for Baptiste, do you? The Baptiste 7000?" Agathe says, smiling when she's finished.

"I don't have a thing for Baptiste, no. I mean, clearly he's attractive... but, no. And... when we were at the Anchois show in December and you said 'he could get it regularly, no questions—'"

"I was feeling you out, but you didn't say anything!" Agathe says, laughing. "And well, the threesome thing... it's only because I had a crush on you over the summer and I told Baptiste about it. I did the next best thing and gave you a vibrator for your birthday."

She drinks her wine and looks into Vincent's eyes without glancing away. Agathe reminds her of an old Hollywood actress—those long legs kicked out like a Swiss Army knife; the elegant fashion choices; her short, almost flapper-girl hairstyle with the slick *Amélie*-esque swoop right under her cheekbone. If Vincent were bisexual or a lesbian, she'd want to date a woman like Agathe, but outside of one drunken *just to see* kiss with Ramona in college, Vincent hasn't ever done anything sapphic.

But she can imagine herself enjoying being in bed with Agathe since she's already so affectionate and attentive anyway. Maybe that's because it's Agathe or maybe it's Paris.

Everyone who says Paris is a woman is right.

Paris is *la vie en rose*. Paris is sexy. Paris is splendor. Paris is full of light. Paris is full of life. Paris is a new beginning. Paris, *mon amour*. Paris is the only city in the world.

Paris is Vincent. Paris is Loup. Paris is Vincent et Loup.

Paris feels like home now.

"I'm very flattered and I adore you. A threesome would be too much... too weird... too complicated and overstimulating for me, but I appreciate the sentiment. I'm floored by it, actually. And I didn't think you had a crush-crush on me, I just thought it was how you were with everyone," Vincent says, drinking her wine faster. She would like to be more buzzed for this conversation. She knows she's blushing. She touches her cheek and Agathe leans forward and touches it too.

"Well, I adore *you*. I'm glad all this is out there. It feels better now, doesn't it?"

"I think so," Vincent says. She tells her about Mina's texts too.

Agathe says a peck of French. "Look. Mina is just a bitch," she translates. "One minute she is fine with it and the other, she's the angry, jealous wife. She can't have it both ways! Do you know she sleeps with another man too? A big bearded Englishman named Tom who whisks her away to the sea, where she lets him do anything he wants to her. And also, Loup is twenty-five! He isn't some sort of virgin schoolboy," Agathe says. She huffs and leans back again, circling the rim of her wineglass with her finger.

Vincent is laughing and shaking her head.

"*C'est vrai!*" Agathe is laughing too. "Eh, it's not crazy you came here and fell in love without meaning to. There wasn't much you could do about it. *C'est Paris*," she says.

3

Anchois begins playing "Une tigresse." Loup had called earlier in the day and asked if it was okay. Vincent loves having that secret with him and she's floaty, hearing the song wrap around her in the crowd. She'd almost squealed seeing him for the first time since they got off the train from Auvers-sur-Oise. She didn't get to talk to him because she and Agathe were running late, but they'd pushed to the front to wave to him. He spotted her and waved back before their set started.

Agathe looks over with wide eyes. "This is you," she guesses, nodding and drinking from the little black straw shooting out of her cocktail. Her short fingernails are a matte mushroom brown; her height in that purple dress makes her look like an iris. "This is Vincent's orgasm you're listening to right now," Agathe says to Baptiste after he turns and cocks his head at them. They've drifted toward the back, where it's much easier to hold a conversation.

Vincent doesn't say a word. She just smiles and drinks her gin and tonic.

"It's my new favorite song," Agathe says.

Baptiste smiles, throws his arm around Vincent.

"Damn. Well, now it's mine, too," he says.

At the back door after the show, Loup walks out with Noémie at his side. They are talking and laughing. Vincent imagines his stoned sex with Noémie as she leans against the building next to Agathe and Baptiste, who are only sometimes flirty with each other. Vincent has not seen them kiss again since that first time. Occasionally Baptiste will touch Agathe's waist or Agathe will take his hand, but it's very subtle and if Vincent weren't looking for it, she would miss it entirely.

After loading his things into the van, Loup rushes at Vincent and hugs her. He pulls away to look at her and kisses her mouth softly, then harder.

"How long has it been, a year? Two years?" he asks, kissing her again.

"One hundred years," Vincent says. She rubs her nose against his. That absurd *wonder* of a nose.

Noémie and the rest of the guys say *salut* to everyone and everyone says *salut* back. In French, Noémie asks if Loup is coming home tonight and Loup shakes his head. Hugs and kisses and goodbyes to Agathe and Baptiste, with Agathe congratulating Vincent again and reminding her that the Zillah video goes live in an hour.

Loup asks what she means and Vincent says she'll tell him on their walk. She's been so busy she hasn't taken a proper long walk around Paris since they returned.

Like always—drunk on stars—they set off toward the Seine.

By the time they sit, Vincent has relayed all the Zillah info and Loup has made a fist and shaken it more than once in excitement.

"Congratulations again, Saint Vincent! This is brilliant," he says, gently squeezing her thigh. She puts her hand on his and thanks him.

The banks are crowded with large and small groups of people walking by. A trumpet softly quacks in the distance.

"Why did Noémie ask if you were coming home?" Vincent had forgotten, then remembered.

"Yeah, I meant to tell you she's staying with us for a bit. Well, with Apollos...she's staying with Apollos until she finds another place," Loup says.

"Gotcha" is all Vincent says.

"Does that make you feel a way you don't want to feel? Do you think I'm interested in Noémie? Because I'm not and I never have been...not in any real way," Loup says. He slips the cigarette from behind his ear and lights it, looking out at the water.

"I believe you. It makes me jealous, but I believe you. Baptiste said Noémie is *interesting*...what's so *interesting* about her?"

Loup tells her that Noémie's dad is from Sweden and Baptiste likes to joke that she comes from a long line of Nordic warrior princesses just because she reminds him of an actress on a Viking drama he used to watch. Loup says Baptiste and Noémie have a little inside joke about it, that in past lives he was an African king and she was a Viking queen. The night they'd talked about it, Noémie had told Baptiste he was *interesting* and he'd said it back to her.

"Have you talked to Cillian?" Loup asks, spinning the topic.

"Where is this coming from?" Vincent asks. She looks at her phone and sees it's two minutes until the Zillah video. Her body feels funny; her limbs are light.

"You said you were jealous of Noémie and I'm jealous of Cillian, so I asked about him. Do you see how much more power you have here?" he asks, looking at her. "If you're allowed a husband, I'm allowed a friend."

"Power? Why are you obsessed with our relationship being unequal? Can't you imagine just for one second that we have the same amount of responsibility? The same amount of investment? Of course you're *allowed* a friend...whatever that means. Of course you are. Wow, this conversation is stupid!"

Loup shrugs.

"I've talked to Cillian and he told me the woman he works with kissed him. And you know what? I felt half of something...but I'm actually more jealous of you living with Noémie than I am of Cillian and Hannah kissing, so make that make sense for me," Vincent spits out.

"Well, did you tell him about us to get him back? You know I don't care, right? That I'm not scared of him?" Loup smokes. He's a little edgy and she can feel it coming off him in invisible zigzags.

"No, I didn't tell him about us. I told you I'm not doing this for revenge. We've had this conversation, Loup."

He pulls out his phone and says it's time to watch the video. He taps the app and types in Zillah's name, finding her new upload. It feels like there's a lit sparkler inside of Vincent when he pushes *Play.*

The video is an explosion of colors and every time there's a new one, Zillah's wearing another pair of Vincent's earrings. Her hair changes color too. The song is sweeping, the chorus is big and loud, and when Zillah opens her red mouth wide, the camera goes inside, where there's another Zillah in a new color and a new pair of earrings, singing harmony with herself. It's flashy and overwhelming and by the end, not surprisingly, Vincent is in tears. Loup scrolls down to the video information and finds her name and the link to the Go Wilde! website. Her phone is vibrating already and she looks down to see it blipping with messages.

Agathe sends screencaps and Don't you just love it? IT'S GORGEOUS. CONGRATULATIONS. Biz!

Baptiste texts Félicitations Veedubs! You are a STAR.

She texts them both a load of heart and star emojis, thanking them. She reminds Agathe to thank Gigi, Zillah, and her stylist for everything.

"Can we still hang out now that you're famous?" Loup asks, smiling at her when she's finished. That quick, his edginess is gone. Had she imagined it?

"Shut up. I'm going to be really busy tomorrow and may need your help. Do you have plans?"

"Football in the park, but that's in the afternoon and I can skip it."

"No, don't do that. Just help me in the morning and maybe if you want to come back in the evening? I have a good stock of everything, but obviously not fully prepared for this. Also, I've got classes to teach. Agathe only told me about this tonight!" Vincent says.

"I'll happily be your little helper."

"Thank you."

"I missed you so much this week. Kind of felt like I was going crazy," he says.

"Do we need to finish our fight? I don't want either of us to be in a bad mood. Look at the moon! It's spring and it's Paris! Who cares about anything else?" She puts her mouth on his.

"Yeah, I definitely don't care about anything else—" Loup says in between kisses. "But, um, don't look now, but your best mate, your *real* best mate, is walking behind you."

Vincent ignores his command and looks behind her to see a man in a T-shirt and jeans whom she doesn't recognize.

"What? Who?" Vincent looks around for someone else.

"It's your naked drummer. It's him. I'd know that hair anywhere," Loup says.

Vincent tries not to be obvious but she looks at the man again and Loup is right. It *is* him. She waits until he's walked past to cover her face with her hands and laugh.

"You were wildly rude. I can't believe you didn't say hi to him," Loup says, laughing.

She kisses him again. "We're *equal*. I'm not trying to get revenge on Cillian. You've said it more than once and it's just not true, *pas du tout*."

"Okay. I won't say it again. And I believe you."

Loup has his hands all over her on their walk to the apartment. He ties his hair in a little flipped twist, he pops up on the ledges and jumps down with both feet at once. He tugs her arm to pull her toward rue du Cloître Saint-Merri just because she loves the little street's lights and prettiness, made even prettier under crescent moonlight.

When they get to la Fontaine Stravinsky they sit on a bench and listen to the ragtag band across the water playing cymbals, buckets, and guitars fashioned out of different-sized cardboard boxes and colored rubber bands.

Her bedroom is suffused with tenuous amber light. The windows are open and she is rocking on top of Loup as he closes his eyes and holds her hips. She says his name at the same time he says hers and, in the warmth and shimmer, those syllables coalesce.

4

Go Wilde! jewelry orders don't slow down in June. They've more than quadrupled from her normal level and on the mornings she isn't teaching, she's baking clay and making earrings, packing up orders and stopping by the post office on her way to the art museum. After the classes, it's back home again to bake more clay and cut out more designs. Glazing, assembling, packing up the rest of her orders. A French women's online magazine wants to do a feature on her and her jewelry, so they come to the apartment and take lots of pictures of Vincent and her earrings and the studio. When it goes live, the Go Wilde! orders shoot through an even higher roof.

Some days she eats her lunch standing up so she still has time in her schedule to walk to l'Église Saint-Eustache to light a candle and sit in the quiet of the church and talk to Jesus. Most often she can feel Him listening, but she imagines Him shaking His head at her too. She prays for her children, she prays for Cillian, she prays for Loup, she prays for everyone else in her family. She asks God for His forgiveness and mercy, even when she cannot *truthfully* say she knows not what she does.

She knows what she is doing.

Mina hasn't contacted her again, but Vincent can tell Baptiste is treating her differently. They haven't been going to the café as much after classes because she's been so busy, but he doesn't text back as quickly either. And at the last dinner party at the end of May, he only stopped by for a bit and left without telling her goodbye. Maybe it was an honest mistake and maybe Baptiste has been busy too, but Vincent feels Mina's disapproval fogging up her friendship with him.

Vincent's been talking about Colm's wedding and how she hasn't picked out her mother-of-the-groom dress yet. Agathe tells her to come over and raid her closet. She says she has a handful of designer dresses she got for free when she dated that German model Vincent vaguely remembers her mentioning.

Vincent goes to Agathe's opulent apartment in the 11th arrondissement for tea and sweets and afterward, Agathe watches the fashion show from the chic egg chair in her bedroom. Agathe pulls one cigarette from a blue box of Gitanes, lights it, and opens the window. A warm breeze prowls through the room; the sun spills in from the veranda. Vincent loves Agathe's closet—a Babylonian treasure of lace, cashmere, velvet, dark solids, and stripes. On the wall, in between baskets of scarves and handbags—a full-length mirror dripping in necklaces.

Vincent slips through dress after dress after dress and finds The One. An airy, pale gold with three layers of tulle falling at her ankles, tender as petals. Agathe raises both hands in agreement and tells her how beautiful she looks.

Vincent takes the dress off, stands there in her bra and underwear. Agathe gets up and steps close to her, touches her hair.

"Agathe—"

"Vincent! There's something in your hair. Just because I admitted I had a crush on you last summer doesn't mean I'm trying to seduce you right now, God!" Agathe says, holding up the piece of fuzz she'd plucked from Vincent's head.

"Right. Thank you," Vincent says, mortified. She steps into her jeans.

Agathe's laugh is a quick brush-off, as if Vincent were so kooky, but how else could she respond?

"I...I do love the dress. Thank you," Vincent says when she has her clothes on again.

"It's yours to keep," Agathe says, sitting back in the chair and slipping another cigarette from the box. She offers Vincent one but she says no and kisses Agathe's cheeks before leaving, taking the dress with her.

She hasn't spoken to Agathe since. Vincent has been the busiest she's ever been since Colm and Olive were little, and things are awkward and weirdish with her two best friends aside from Loup. When she leaves the museum after her classes, she comes home exhausted and just wants to sleep, but there are earrings to make.

Often, she says no to Loup when he asks to stay over because she needs to get things done and when Loup stays over that doesn't happen. He's good at following directions and is helpful filling orders but eventually, they end up in her bed, and afterward it's hard to get back up and work. When he asks her if she really wants him to leave, she tells him yes and to look on the bright side: Think about how strong his arms will be from all the handstands.

Her work visa will expire in July and although she's told Loup and her friends she's coming back after Colm's wedding, the truth is, she doesn't know what's going to happen after that. Yes, technically she's returning, but for how long? If she wants to stay, she'll have to apply for another visa she doesn't fully understand yet, and she's been meaning to ask Mr. Laurent about it, but she's been so busy.

She's been ignoring Cillian, only responding about once a week. She sets her alarm to remember to email Tully and she makes a point of texting her children every day to tell them good night, even if they haven't talked any other time. Ramona knows how busy she is and isn't high maintenance. Her parents, Theo, and Monet understand too. Vincent sees the people at the post office, her students at the art museum, the Laurents in the apartment building, and occasionally Loup. For as social as she'd been when she first came to Paris, by the beginning of the summer Vincent has made herself *une petite* island.

Toward the end of June, when it's Vincent's turn to host the friends dinner party again, she wants to do something special. The rotation won't put her on the hosting schedule again until autumn and she doesn't know where she'll be when autumn returns.

She suggests that everyone dress like their favorite French New Wave film character.

She and Loup will be Anna Karina and Jean-Paul Belmondo from Godard's *Pierrot le fou*. Vincent will wear winged eyeliner and a red collared dress; Loup will pull his hair back and paint his face blue.

Sunday and Monday, she ignores Loup's texts in order to get her work done.

Tuesday evening, she texts him to let him know he needs to come back to the apartment with her after class on Wednesday, to get dressed in their costumes and help prep.

Vincent thinks back to the first time he came to her place to help with dinner. When he'd walked around her living room touching things and wearing her scarf and their heartstrings were already tied together although neither of them knew it yet.

Loup doesn't reply and she doesn't hear from him by Wednesday morning either.

By the time she's walking to the post office, she's nervous. She shouldn't have ignored him earlier in the week. Why hasn't he responded? Where is he? What is he doing?

When he doesn't walk into the classroom, the worry peels to panic.

Today we'll be discussing misremembering. We'll take some time to get down the memories we know we misremember. If there's a memory you have... that you feel like you either underplay or overplay emotionally now looking back on it, write it down. If it's something you can't put into words, draw or paint it. Try to put on paper as much as you can and in a bit, those who want to share their thoughts will be able to.

While everyone is quietly writing and sketching, Vincent excuses herself and steps out into the hallway to call Loup.

"Saint Vincent," he says with an extra-thick French accent. She'd told him once that she liked when he said *Vincent* slowly, the same way Yves Montand says it in "Rue Saint-Vincent," so he's started saying it like that sometimes just to make her smile.

She loves hearing him say her name. It's magic in his mouth—a blinding flash, a puff of smoke, Nina Simone singing "I Put a Spell on You."

"Loup, I was worried about you. Where are you?"

He picked up.

He's fine.

She overreacted.

Her period was last week and her emotions are spilled out and rolling wildly around her body like marbles.

"I'll skip and give you some room to breathe since I was hanging around too much. And in class, you're probably tired of seeing me stare at you the whole time. You've heard enough of my memories and me talking about colors."

"You weren't hanging around too much... that's not what I meant. You misunderstood me. I'm not tired of you being here," Vincent says.

"I thought you wanted to see less of me."

"That's not what I meant at all."

"Well, it's my fault I can't make it tonight. I forgot I told Apollos I'd fill in for him at this bartending gig so he can go to his cousin's wedding. I'm so sorry I won't be able to dress up as Belmondo for the dinner party. I really wanted to do that. I made fake dynamite and everything! All afternoon I've been trying to find someone else to cover for me and I was going to call you because I've been trying to think of something special to do to make it up to you... I thought you were mad at me. And the signals... your signals... you could unmix them," Loup says.

Vincent can hear electronic music in the background—low, rhythmic beeping and high swoops of sound, like she's found him on Neptune.

"What does that mean?" she asks as quietly as possible. She thinks of Cillian telling her she gives off mixed signals. They both know her so differently, it must be true.

A woman who works at the museum walks past pushing a small cart of vintage books. Vincent fake-smiles at her and the woman gives a real smile, which makes Vincent feel awful.

"It means I can tell when you're pushing me away," Loup says. Was that a sigh? Did she make that sound? Or maybe it was him.

"Loup, I'm not—"

"But look. This something special I want us to do... I've figured it out and it's perfect, but it falls on the night before you leave for New York. Is that okay?"

"Yes. Of course that's okay."

"*Parfait*. This is a relief. Can you hear the relief in my voice?" She thinks she can. "Will you talk to me later? I may not be able to get my phone while I'm working but I will call or text you back," he says.

Vincent tries to pay as much attention as she can to those who are sharing their memories. An older gentleman in the class with his wife talks about misremembering their wedding day. He always thinks it rained that morning, but she swears it didn't. That it hadn't rained in a week. It was fifty years ago but they find themselves discussing it from time to time. Their last name is Bisset and they were both born and raised in Paris. A young man talks about how his boyfriend says their first kiss was in the stairwell of his apartment, but he remembers it being outside of their favorite café. His name is Antoine and his nails are painted black. He was born in Lyon.

I have a memory of telling my lover I needed him to leave so I could finish my work and he's a distraction to me because all we do is kiss and touch each other and it's so much harder to get anything done when he's there looking at me and he has that hair and that nose and that fucking nose and his hands and his voice and when he speaks French and his tongue and he's twenty-five years old and I have a husband and soon I will see my husband and soon I will see my children and I want to see them but I don't want to leave Paris I want to stay in Paris and my lover thought I meant what I said in a way that I did not and now I can't stop obsessing over it, over not seeing him in my apartment tonight, over when I will see him again and obsessing over the other women he's touched and if he wants to touch them again and obsessing over what has happened with us and what is happening with us and what will happen with us.

Vincent takes a deep breath and shares a memory of her children. One of them missed their bus on the first day of first grade and she never knows which one. It's a pinch of guilt she has. She remembers she'd gotten up early to bake clay and lost track of time. She had to drive one of them to school and they were late. She remembers Colm, relaxed and buckled in the back seat as she drove. But she also remembers Olive back there, crying about how she was nervous she'd get in trouble. Both memories can't be true. When Colm was in first grade, Olive hadn't started school yet. When Olive was in first grade, Colm was in third. How could he have made it onto the bus if Olive hadn't? Neither Colm nor Olive can remember what really happened and Cillian can't either.

Her memory sparks another woman's memory. Her name is Lena and she talks about how her parents accidentally left her at church one

Sunday afternoon. They'd shown up an hour later, frantic. She remembers being alone and crying in a pew by herself. Her parents told her she was never alone, that her cousin was there with her the whole time.

Vincent lets the class go five minutes early so she can get to the apartment and start the lemon and tomato linguine.

Vincent's visual playlist: Jean-Luc Godard movies on a loop with the sound down.

The June evening weather is nice enough to have dinner in the park, but since it's Vincent's last time hosting, at least for a while, she has it at the apartment with the windows open. She's invited the Laurents and they show up with wildflowers to celebrate her feature in the women's magazine. Agathe comes over with Gigi and the same guy she brought to Baptiste and Mina's. She is dressed like Catherine, and Gigi and the guy are dressed like *Jules et Jim*, respectively, from the scene where the three of them run across the bridge. Agathe kisses Vincent hello and says nothing about the awkwardness of their last encounter. Baptiste appears in a tweed coat and sunglasses, as Belmondo from *À bout de souffle*, bearing a bottle of red, a pack of tea light candles, and an old copy of the *New York Herald Tribune*. When Vincent asks him where he got it, he laughs and says it's a long story.

She'd seen Baptiste as they both left the museum. They hugged and he told her he was going home first, that he'd be at her place later *sans* Mina. When he shows up, he doesn't ask where Loup is, so Vincent knows they've talked already.

Everyone talks and laughs and drinks and eats, but the weight of Loup's absence is heavy enough to zap Vincent's appetite. She has two glasses of wine and when one couple leaves early, she starts on another.

Baptiste says he's heading out and will see her tomorrow. Agathe, Gigi, and the guy are leaving too and Agathe tells her to let her know if she wants to meet at the café one day over the weekend, only if she's not too busy.

The woman from the art museum who likes to switch from French to English in the middle of her conversations tells her a story about the new Asian-art curator. How he used to live in China and how his Russian grandfather was killed in a swordfight. Mr. Laurent regales everyone with a similar story about an artist he used to know who died in a duel over another man's wife.

Vincent stands by the balcony doors drinking wine and smoking cigarettes, imagining these people she doesn't know and world history and violence and bloodshed, how it all just becomes stories for humans to share at dinner parties years and years later.

On their way out, the Laurents invite her to a political rally on Sunday.

When everyone is gone, Vincent sets the rest of the dishes in the sink, smudges on more red lipstick with her finger, and leaves the apartment. She puts in her earbuds and turns on the playlist of sexy songs that she and Loup made together.

A little drunk, she heads to his place.

Down rue Rambuteau as Anna Karina and walking walking walking and listening and pulling one earbud out so it's not so disorienting then turning right and left and right and turning back again because she went the wrong way then right and left and oops wrong way again where is it where is it where is it it's right here somewhere oh there it is: rue des Arquebusiers.

She sees his apartment building and steps up, pushes the button.

"It's Saint Vincent," she says in a French accent. He buzzes her in and the tiny elevator's going up up up it really is just so tiny American elevators are huge and she's tapping on his door.

When he opens it, she's crying, but she doesn't know when it started.

He's holding her and shushing her and asking her what's wrong.

She's saying nothing's wrong, nothing's wrong. She doesn't know what's wrong. *Loupmania?* She was so worried about him earlier and she doesn't know what's going to happen with anything. Her relationships with Baptiste and Agathe. She's been too busy making jewelry and she feels guilty for being this far away from her children and the wedding is next week and she'll be staying in a fancy hotel alone when her daughter isn't there and maybe Loup should come with her. Really, maybe that's the answer. She tells him that.

They're on his bed and her head is on his chest. He's petting her hair and, quietly, he says a big chunk of something in French that Vincent can't understand and she doesn't care what it is. It sounds pretty and it makes her feel better.

"I don't think I should come. I think you need to talk to Cillian alone first," Loup says.

"Okay. I'm sorry if you feel like I'm giving you mixed signals or pressuring you—"

"You're not pressuring me." His little laugh blows hot, tingling her scalp.

"It'll be fine. I just didn't eat enough and I drank too much wine. I got lost on the walk over," Vincent says, laughing through her tears. Loup teases her about it and makes her laugh more. He kisses her.

She's feeling puny and a little too vulnerable for her liking. Realizing this, she sits up and wipes her eyes. Looks at him. He motions to the corner of the room and she sees the fake *Pierrot le fou* dynamite—red and yellow sticks of it hugged with twine.

"I want to stay here tonight. Can I?"

"V, why are you like this? Why do you even ask?" he says, shaking his head.

Loup's *something special* is the opera. *Lakmé* at the Palais Garnier. He spills the secret to Vincent the day before, but only so she can dress appropriately. She puts on the gold dress Agathe gave her and waits for him. In the morning, she'll fold the dress into her suitcase.

Loup is at her door in a tuxedo with his hair slicked into a knot, holding white peonies. She gasps and tells him how handsome he looks. She imagines him walking the streets of Paris in that tux, getting in a cab in that tux, taking the steps down to the Métro in that tux. How did he get to her apartment? What magic? The tux is a time warp that's snatched her out of reality.

He gushes over her dress and Vincent puts the flowers in water. Loup tells her that his mom paid for him to get a tux made last year because she said every man should have a tuxedo even if he thinks he doesn't need it. He tells her his mom used her opera connections to get them the best seats in the house and it reminds Vincent that she's packed and wrapped the pair of earrings for her birthday. She puts the glittery box on the coffee table and tells him not to forget it when he leaves in the morning. She's given him a key to the apartment. While she's in New York, he will come by and water the plants.

Vincent wants to walk; her strappy heels aren't that high. She and Loup hold hands and whish through the golden light, nearing night. Her dress is made for summer evenings like this, the breeze pushing and pulling the tulle against her legs. She grabs some of it as they cross the intersections, careful not to trip.

The overwhelming Napoleon III style of the building. The leviathan chandelier and all that red—a knob of diamond in a thumping heart. She cries through the "Flower Duet" in act 1. Loup puts his hand on her leg and she looks at him. Even in the dark, his face glows with splendor. By the end, her head hurts. She's been to the opera, but never like this. Never in Paris. Never with her lover.

Never with LOUPLOUPLOUPLOUPLOUPLOUPLOUPLOUP.

When they return to the apartment, she knows sleep is out of the question. Loup has his jacket off and his bow tie undone. He's at the electric kettle asking if she wants tea.

She doesn't.

She wants him.

She tells him that.

They devour each other like it's the last time they'll be able to. Like they both know that when she comes back from New York, everything will be different.

"Are these mixed signals?" she asks, letting her tongue taste every part of him.

Loup, reduced to primitive sounds, grunts and quickly shakes his head no.

"Do you love me?" she asks. She knows how unfair it is to ask him now, like this.

"I do. I love you," he says, with his palm on the back of her head, her hair slipping between his fingers. His hand, eversoslowly making a fist.

Afterward, in bed, Vincent apologizes for asking him if he loves her. She didn't mean to do it. She's in his arms with a smoky, smudgy wine mouth, wearing nothing but her tiger necklace.

"I would've told you a long time ago if I didn't think it would scare you off."

"It doesn't scare me. *Je n'ai pas peur*."

"It's my turn to ask."

"Then ask me," she says. Her eyes are closing. "Ask me."

It's so quiet and his breath is deep and hot on her neck, like he's already sleeping.

"Do you love me, Vincent?"

"Je t'aime, Loup. Ne sois pas stupide," she says soft and sharp as a velvet pin. She's slipping under.

Don't be stupid.

Waiting at the airport, Vincent texts him.

I'm obsessed with you.

He writes her back.

I'm obsessed with you.

She responds:

I'm obsessed with you.

He texts.

I'm obsessed with you.

They text.

I'm obsessed with you.

I'm obsessed with you.
I'm obsessed with you.
I'm obsessed with you.

I'm obsessed with you.

I'm obsessed with you.

I'm obsessed with you.
I'm obsessed with you.

I'm obsessed with you.

I'm obsessed with you.
I'm obsessed with you.
I'm obsessed with you.
I'm obsessed with you.
I'm obsessed with you.
I'm obsessed with you.
I'm obsessed with you.

I'm obsessed with you.

I'm obsessed with you.
I'm obsessed with you.
I'm obsessed with you.

Until she boards the plane and has to turn her phone off.

Vincent's Travel Playlist | Airplane | Paris to NYC

"Ne me quitte pas" by Jacques Brel
"NYC" by Interpol
"The Promise" by Sturgill Simpson
"Hardest to Love" by The Weeknd
"New York State of Mind" by Billy Joel
"Iowa (Traveling, Pt. 3)" by Dar Williams
"Fetch the Bolt Cutters" by Fiona Apple
"Crowded Places" by Banks
"Manhattan" by Ella Fitzgerald

"La Lune" by Billie Marten
"New York" by St. Vincent
"Betray My Heart" by D'Angelo
"Master of None" by Beach House
"Babylon" by David Gray
"No Sleep Till Brooklyn" by the Beastie Boys
"The Emperor's New Clothes" by Sinead O'Connor
"Flash Light" by Parliament
"Gentleman Who Fell" by Milla Jovovich
"Ode to My Family" by the Cranberries
"The Only Living Boy in New York" by Simon & Garfunkel

5

It is knee-deep summer in New York City. Vincent's in her pajamas, just finishing up her bedtime ritual. She gently presses the moisturizer onto her cheeks and wipes her hands on the towel.

She knows Cillian by his knock.

She's waiting on the other side of the hotel door and attempts to brace herself for whatever feeling will gallop through her body upon seeing his face. Will it be cool or warm? Tingle or swoop?

She makes him knock again before she opens it.

"Hiya," he says, holding a bouquet of white cosmos in brown paper, smiling at her like she's an angel delivering the Good News.

She takes the flowers and puts them on the dresser. When she turns back to him, she's smashed into his arms with the door closed. A febrile feeling swoops warm from her ears. Through her stomach. To the backs of her knees. Coolness tingles her nose and arms. Is that a siren? No, just Cillian. She resists the urge to cross herself anyway. Her husband is holding her face, kissing it, kissing her mouth, telling her how much he loves her. How much he missed her. She missed him too. She missed his mouth and how he smells. This is how it could've always been, but it's not. She imagines confessing this to Loup, this willingness to let Cillian have her like this again so easily and how her heart is a ticking bomb.

Why? Because it's Cillian.

Olive flies in tomorrow afternoon, and tomorrow night the four of them will all have dinner together for the first time in a year.

"You're fucking beautiful. I can't believe I'm lookin' at ya," Cillian says. "I'm just so happy."

He has on a navy T-shirt and dark jeans; she picked them both out for him. She's been picking out his clothes for twenty-five years.

He's wearing his wedding ring.

The tiger necklace is in her suitcase and so is Loup's blue sweater. She'd texted Loup as soon as she got to the hotel and he sent her hearts and a *je t'aime*, telling her to talk anytime.

Cillian sits on the bed and Vincent sits next to him. The hands of her body clock are ticking backward slowly. It's around six in the morning in Paris. She yawns. She can't help it.

"I'm right next door," he says, thumbing to the wall behind them.

"Did you bring Hannah as your date?" she asks, making silly, wide eyes at him.

"Vin."

Cillian rubs his face with both hands. He looks good, but she doesn't tell him that. Maybe the muscles in his arms are even more defined than they were a year ago? Probably from rock climbing. Just the other day Ramona told her that Peter had driven up to Kentucky to go to the climbing gym with Cillian. Vincent has probably (and happily) gained five or ten pounds from life and all the *pain au chocolat*. She likes how her body carries the new weight—her ass is just a little softer and rounder. She surely would've gained more if she didn't walk at least five miles a day around the city.

```
INT. NYC HOTEL ROOM — NIGHT

Vincent and Cillian are relaxed and cozy on the
bed. There is an uncomfortably tight close-up on
their faces.
```

NARRATOR (V.O.)

Vincent and Cillian are exactly the same as they were a year ago. Vincent and Cillian are so different than they were a year ago.

"I'm kidding, Cillian. This is awkward and I'm tired. I'm only kidding," she says, patting his leg. They'd never finished their conversation about Hannah after being interrupted, and Vincent doesn't want to know any more anyway. If Cillian only knew the things she'd done with Loup . . . the things she'd let Loup do to her. Sitting next to her husband and looking at him, Vincent realizes there isn't a blip of her that's worried about Hannah at all. Cillian is hers if she wants him.

He tells her Hannah moved to Seattle to take another job.

"Okay, well . . . sorry you've lost your new girlfriend," Vincent says. Cillian just looks at her and shakes his head.

"And what about you . . . did you meet someone? We haven't touched on that, have we? I'm scared to ask," he says. He scratches at his scruff. Broaching the topic clearly makes him uncomfortable, enough so that he stands and leans against the dresser in front of her—a position of power, Vincent thinks.

"There is nothing I need to tell you, if that's what you're asking," Vincent says. It's what she's been planning to say to him for months.

"No one has asked you out? You haven't been interested in *anyone*? I'm sure you're around a lot of men. I know men have come on to you," Cillian says, crossing his arms.

"When I said that about Hannah, I really wasn't meaning to get into this tonight. I'm exhausted. I just flew over the ocean." Vincent lies back on the bed and lets out her breath.

"You're right. I'm sorry," he says.

They are staying in a newly remodeled modern luxury hotel in Times Square and Vincent loves that it's only a five-minute walk to Bryant Park. That's what she's planning on doing tomorrow. Colm and his fiancée live in Brooklyn and that's where they'll be. Olive will be staying in Vincent's room when she arrives and Vincent is looking forward to staying up late with her and watching *Leap Year*. It's Their Movie.

Theo and his family, Monet, her parents: They'll all be in New York by tomorrow evening, staying on the same floor of the hotel. Vincent knew this was coming and she is excited about it, but all of it is still making her very sleepy.

Later, Vincent is staring up at the ceiling, and Cillian steps to the side of the bed to look down at her. She can write Tully about the gray-blue of his father's eyes. They're back to discussing blue this week. She can go on about blue forever. In their last email exchange, she talked to him about *Bluets* by Maggie Nelson and *The Bluest Eye* by Toni Morrison. Cillian's eyes are *très très bleus*.

"I still can't believe I'm lookin' at ya," he says again.

Cillian doesn't move around as much as Loup. Loup would've been bouncing off the walls by now. She imagines him flicking off the lamp and turning it on again. Squishing his hands into the pillows.

"You're not sleeping here tonight. I get this whole big bed to myself. Olive will be in it tomorrow," Vincent says, sitting up so she can pull back the covers and crawl inside.

"Can I sleep on the floor, then?"

"Really, Cillian?" she asks him. "In your clothes?"

He reaches over her slowly and plucks one of the spare pillows off the bed.

"This spot looks comfy," Cillian says, pointing to the floor next to her.

"Wow. All right. Good night, Cillian" she says. She turns off the light.

Vincent and Cillian share room service breakfast and, after asking if she minds, he goes out for a run. Colm shows up while he's gone. Now Vincent is in her robe, sitting by the window having another cup of tea, wondering why American hotels haven't caught on to electric kettles. Colm is on the bed, scrolling through his phone. He's browner from the summer and can grow a full beard now. She resists the urge to smush his face and kiss his mouth, her baby boy.

"I haven't seen my son since last September and I still can't keep his attention," she says, faking her annoyance.

She knows how busy he's been with the wedding and the new film he's working on. Both she and Cillian have always been proud of how independent their children are. She would've been a terrible mother to needy children. There are some mothers who could never run off to Paris for a year. There are some mothers who wouldn't have been able to devote nearly as much time as she did to building a business when their children were little.

"I'm sorry! I'm sorry," Colm says, tossing his phone aside. "Nicole is freaking out about... well, everything. Her parents just got here and they're already driving her crazy. Thanks for not driving me crazy, by the way."

"I can *definitely* try harder," Vincent says.

"Please don't."

"Show me the trailer you've been working on," she says, motioning for him to pick up his phone again and sit at the table with her.

After they watch it together, Vincent puts her mug down so she can clap properly. It's a film loosely based on the friendship between Langston Hughes and Zora Neale Hurston, set in Harlem in the future. A year ago he'd described the idea to her as an Afrofuturistic pop-up book. His friend in L.A. is still tweaking the script.

She tells him about the French movies she's been watching on repeat in Paris. She and Colm can talk movies for hours, dissecting them, comparing them, watching them, and pausing to discuss things. She tells him she dressed up as Anna Karina at the last dinner party and who her guests dressed up as, leaving out her missing Belmondo date.

Colm asks her if she thinks she and Cillian will stay together and Vincent tells him it's not what he needs to be focusing on right now. She makes more tea and convinces Colm he should drink some chamomile and lavender although he's not normally much of a tea drinker. She tells him it'll be good for his nerves since tomorrow and Saturday will be a speedy blur. On Sunday, he and Nicole leave for Pantelleria.

Colm drinks and asks her to tell him more about Paris. She does, leaving out not only Loup but her friend drama too. But she does tell him about Zillah and pulls up the video to show him. She doesn't mention too much about her monthlong travels in the spring. She wishes she could tell him about visiting Van Gogh's grave. Instead, she focuses on Amsterdam and tells him how she felt when her parents and Monet surprised her at Theo's.

When Cillian knocks on the door, Vincent opens it to find him freshly showered. He hugs her, then wraps his arms around Colm. Olive texts the group chat letting them know she's landed at JFK.

It's late in Paris and Loup is probably sleeping, but Vincent goes for a walk to Bryant Park alone while her kids are busy with other things and stops to send texts so he can wake up to them.

Dinner with the family tonight and tomorrow is full of wedding things.

Saturday is the big day.

I may be slow getting back to you but you are in mon cœur.

At dinner, Cillian proposes a toast. He doesn't stand, saving them the embarrassment of being stared at, but he taps his glass and raises it. Vincent had been sure to let Nicole know she was invited to dinner too, but she's hanging with her own family in Chelsea.

The rest of Vincent's family is back at the hotel, and Cillian's mother, Aileen, is still in Boston visiting friends before she takes the train into the city in the morning. Vincent isn't looking forward to seeing her mother-in-law. She hasn't seen her in years and hasn't talked to her since Cillian's book came out, although Aileen did call and leave her a voice mail last summer, apologizing for playing her part in keeping everything about Siobhán and Tully a secret. Vincent stood on her apartment balcony in Paris, smoking. Listened to it twice and deleted it.

She isn't mad or angry at Aileen. Neither is worth her energy.

"It's been a hell of a year and that's on me. I own it. I destroyed a lot of what your mother and I had built...this family..." Cillian says, his voice cracking at the end. Olive looks around to see if anyone is watching; Colm is steady, keeping his eyes on his dad. "Thank you for forgiving me. For loving me. For welcoming Tully. You are all the most important and precious things in my life."

Cillian's Irishness is known most fully when he's emotional and Vincent doesn't hate it. She loves having an Irish husband. His accent gets thicker, he blushes more, even his eyes get bluer. That part of his DNA is apparent in their daughter because Vincent is convinced Olive's eyes get browner when she's upset too. Olive and Colm are sitting quietly at the table and Vincent feels like she has to say something.

"I'm glad we get to be here together. And Colm, your dad and I wish you and Nicole all the happiness we've had, we really do. The past year aside, your dad and I were happy...our little family was happy...and cheers to more of it in the future," Vincent says, holding up her glass.

Cillian broke them, yes. But here they are together again. Her little family has made it through to the other side. She never wants to forget the hope she's feeling now. She could drown in it. Looking at his face and their children's faces in the candlelight is a slowly healing bruise.

"Cheers," Colm and Olive say at the same time, and clink.

Both Cillian and Vincent wipe their eyes as the waiter—who Vincent only now realizes has been standing there for the last part of the toast—gently asks if he can interest them in the dessert menu.

Olive is in the bathroom getting ready for bed and Cillian and Vincent are in the hallway. After dinner, she stopped in her family's rooms to say hi, Ramona's too. Everyone's tired and they'll all catch up tomorrow afternoon. Right now, Vincent wants to be in bed with her daughter watching *Leap Year*, but she can't yet because Cillian wants to talk.

"So, you're not actively seeking a divorce?" Cillian asks, leaning against the wall with his arms crossed.

All of their conversations are like this now—starting in medias res and ending just as quickly as they begin. Only one other time has Cillian asked her if she was considering divorce and that was right after his book came out.

Vincent's aunt walks down the hallway toward them in her pajamas, carrying a bucket of ice. Vincent steps forward to hug her and tell her how good it is to see her. Her aunt says hi to Cillian too and walks away, disappearing into her room.

"I'm not actively seeking a divorce, no," Vincent says once she's gone.

"I just don't want to walk around like a fool, thinkin' there's a chance here if there isn't."

"Does this mean you're not still hunting for villas?"

The thought of him buying her a villa is ridiculous, but she doesn't hate thinking about how dramatic and romantic it would be for him to do it for recompense and she doesn't hate thinking of going to Italy soon. Of extra-frothy cappuccinos and *crespelle*. Night swimming under Tuscan starlight.

"I'm definitely still doing that."

"Right. Sure you are. You can buy it with the big bucks from the *Half-Blown Rose* movie, right?" Vincent says.

"Do you know I can't even *imagine* loving another woman as much as I love you? That I wouldn't even know how to muster it up?"

Cillian folds his hands atop his head and looks at her, waiting for a response. She loves when he stands like that.

"Good" is all she says.

"Who's Wolf?" Olive asks when Vincent sits on the bed.

"What?"

"Your phone buzzed. Someone called Wolf texted you. There was a big red *X* next to the name. Don't worry! I didn't read it," Olive says, as if reading her mother's texts is the dumbest thing she's ever heard. She's loading up *Leap Year* on her iPad; her face is dewy and bonny, like a flower in the rain.

"Oh. It's... just a student. From the museum," Vincent says. Her heart is skipping rope, but she resists the urge to grab her phone off the nightstand. Instead, she curls up next to her daughter as she presses *Play.*

They share a glass of wine and a pack of lemon cookies and pause to talk anytime something in the movie reminds them of something else. One day when Olive was home sick from high school, Vincent had rented the movie and they watched it together and fell in love with it. It was the first film they'd declared *theirs*. The boys didn't understand it and the girls liked it better that way; it belonged to them and them only. Now they watch it every time they're together, even if they only turn it on to leave it playing while they do other things. The fact that so much of the movie takes place in Ireland is just a happy accident.

Olive is wearing a pair of ladybug pajama shorts and Vincent asks her if she knows that a group of ladybugs is called a *loveliness*. They talk about how that's the cutest and best thing they've ever heard. Vincent can't remember how she stumbled upon the fact, but she thinks of Loup calling them *ladybirds* instead of ladybugs and how precious it is when his bits of Britishness poke through.

Her daughter goes on and on in a good way about her funny roommate and how they still have a secret cat since pets aren't allowed in their apartment complex. Her roommate is a delightful, crazy cat lady and even wanted them to adopt a ferret until Olive put her foot down. And as far as dating goes, Olive is too picky and busy to care right now. But she does tell her mom about a cute guy in the lab who wears great sweaters and is a little smarter than she is, which admittedly *does* turn her on a little.

Vincent talks about Zillah and shows Olive the video too. She loves it and wants to watch it again.

When the movie's over, Olive asks Vincent if she can ask her a hard question.

"Okay," she says, almost slipping into *d'accord* instead. She misses Paris more than she misses Kentucky. She aches for Paris. She's convinced her bones actually hurt.

"Tell the truth. Do you still love Daddy? Even after all this?"

Olive is sleepy-eyed sitting against the headboard, braiding her long hair over her shoulder. She looks so much like she did when she was little, Vincent's sweet baby girl. The baby girl she labored with for thirty-six hours, who did things in her own time then and whose personality hasn't changed since. Vincent is filled with wonder yet again over how she and Cillian *made* Colm and Olive—two whole new, wonderful people in this wide, wild world.

"Yes, I do," Vincent says.

What a relief to be able to tell the truth, even if it's only now and then. Even if it's only a half-truth.

Fuuuuck. Tu me manques.

I've been sleeping in your bed. It
smells like you.

My arms are going to be beyond
ripped by the time you return.

Loup had written and sent another handstand video; this time he is in her bedroom in the apartment with his bare feet against the wall.

And never fear! Your plants are sun-
happy and watered. They love me!

6

On the morning of Colm's wedding, the sun is shining. It's shining through the curtains and across Cillian's bare torso as he lies on the floor next to the bed where Vincent and Olive are sleeping. He tied one on with Colm and his friends after the rehearsal dinner the night before and is snoring softly on his back. Olive is sleeping too, but Vincent is awake because her body thinks it's noon even though the sun's only been up for an hour or so.

In Paris, Loup had asked her if there was any chance she'd sleep with Cillian while she was in New York. She told him no and meant it. She'd made that decision before she and Loup had kissed. All throughout their marriage, if Vincent was even the slightest bit miffed at Cillian, she couldn't open herself to him physically like that. It drove him crazy and it wasn't something she was particularly proud of, how she could be so cold toward him in bed if he'd only mildly displeased her. She could kiss him, yes, but she couldn't easily disconnect her brain and heart from actual sex. Maybe *he* could, but she couldn't.

She looks at Cillian sleeping on the floor of her hotel room.

His willingness to make himself vulnerable. How he doesn't try to hide the desperation in his eyes, his voice. How cute he'd been last night, drunk and silly, tapping on her door after knowing Olive was asleep. How he kissed her with a beery mouth and told her he loved her. How he took off his shirt and folded it over the back of the chair.

She missed his body even when she didn't want to.

He is a *man* in his forties. So different from Loup's violent youth. Cillian's body is brutish. Solid and sinewy, like it was made to chop down a tree with an ax.

They're a *family*.

They did this.

This is *their family*.

She *does* feel a different sort of tenderness toward her husband in his presence. A strong, passionate, nostalgic energy that she had to travel all the way across the ocean to experience and remember. The weekly flower deliveries hadn't done it, nor had the wax-sealed letters. The video chats hadn't done it, nor had the texts or the phone calls. What's doing it is him breathing deep in sleep on the floor and her on the bed, watching him, with their daughter sleeping beside her.

Vincent offers up her room for the girls to get ready, as many of them as can fit in front of the mirror. Nicole and her mother are in there and all five bridesmaids, including Olive. Aurora and Monet, Yvonne, Fenna, and Florentina. Ramona too. Cillian's mother isn't there but at the church during the rehearsal, Vincent did go to her and say hello. Aileen stood and hugged her and it felt like hugging a cactus, but Vincent hugged her back.

It's when everyone turns to see Nicole walking down the aisle that Vincent's brimming eyes overflow with tears of both sadness and happiness. Her son, her little boy, this young man. Colm, so handsome in his dark blue suit, stands at the altar with his hands clasped in front of him;

his bottom lip quivers at the sight of his bride. Cillian reaches for her hand and she lets him take it.

Vincent has a skinny glass of Veuve Clicquot with her chicken, potatoes, and mushrooms. After eating and speeches, she's on the dance floor with Aurora, Monet, Olive, Ramona, and her nieces, shaking it to "ABC" by the Jackson 5. The reception is in the same hotel they're staying in and the capacious room is filled with flashing lights and tables flickering with white candles in glass.

She can feel Cillian's eyes on her. There's a short glass of whiskey in front of him. He is sitting next to Solomon, who is turned around talking to Vincent's cousin. When the song ends, Vincent walks over to them.

"Vinnie! Hey, Vinnie!" her cousin says, holding his hand in the air as if she can't see him. He's her dad's first cousin who drove down from Cleveland and he's a funny drunk. She's seen him like this at other weddings and every family reunion. "I was just asking your husband what the *hell* he was thinking, but he didn't have a good answer for me. Has he had a good answer for you yet?" he says a little too loudly, holding her shoulder and leaning into her ear. The DJ moves on to Marvin Gaye, and Monet's dance-floor scream is right on time. The song is decidedly her jam.

"Your guess is as good as mine!" Vincent says into his ear.

"Men can be dumbasses and we depend on your feminine grace and charm to allow us that . . . to not kill us in our sleep," her cousin says. He misses the cocktail straw on the first try, takes another drink.

"Oh, trust me, I know! Bless your dumbass hearts," she says. He laughs and she laughs too. Cillian is watching them, fully aware the conversation is about him. He looks down, sheepish and blushing.

"Into the Mystic" is Vincent and Cillian's song and after dancing to James Taylor with Colm while Nicole danced with her daddy, Vincent accepts Cillian's hand. They move through the crowd when it comes on.

They danced to "Into the Mystic" at their own wedding, when she was pregnant with Colm. They played it every wedding anniversary on their way out to dinner. Cillian had been the one who'd told her Van Morrison was Northern Irish; she'd never wondered.

Cillian has his arms around her tightly, his hand warm and pressed against the dip in the fabric on the back of her dress. Agathe would be proud of how irresistible Vincent feels in it—elegant and glowy. She made the bridesmaids' earrings—big dangling blue circles to complement their rose-gold dresses and to match the boys' blues. She made herself and Nicole's mom a pair of rose-gold ones.

"You look fuckin' *gor*geous," Cillian says.

"Thank you. You look good too. You really do. You totally could've let yourself go while I was gone," she says. He's wearing a suit almost the exact same shade as Colm's blue. His hair is short and he's grown out his beard the way she likes it best—lush but a little trimmed. The bastard.

"What'd you do with your wedding ring?" Cillian asks.

"It's in my bag. I leave it there."

"You didn't toss it in the Seine?"

Vincent shakes her head no.

"You gonna get down on the floor with me after this and do 'Rock the Boat'?" he asks, singing the words *rock the boat* instead of saying them.

"Maybe," Vincent says, laughing a little at the surprising, soft cacophony.

Cillian puts his cheek against hers and she closes her eyes. While they're dancing, everyone else disappears.

She thinks of all the reasons she should forgive him.

He was young; it was partly his father's fault. And his mother's, too.

Vincent *can* be unapproachable and cold when she wants to be; maybe that was why he didn't feel like he could tell her.

He's been *such* a good father to their children.

He's been a good husband too.

He's admitted how wrong he was and begged her for forgiveness.

His body in that suit.

His arms around her.

And those *eyes*.

Cillian is her husband; Loup is sleeping in her apartment three thousand miles away. The love between her and Loup is different from this and she doesn't need to be loved by anyone else the way Cillian loves her. The spot's been filled.

The Loup-love is so quick, couldn't it snap quick too?

This Cillian-love is elastic, stretching out over more than half her life.

Those loves aren't the same.

How could they be?

Alone, they kiss in her room. Olive is staying up late in the other room with all the girls. These are real kisses, the way they used to. The way she and Loup kiss. She's not ready to tell Cillian about that but she wants to tell him something she's been keeping from him, to release a little of the pressure.

Vincent tells him about Tully. How they email so often. How she listens to his music and connected him with her dad to score a major record deal. How he sends her pictures from Siobhán's garden.

Cillian's tie is undone and his mouth is smeared with her red lipstick.

"Wow, really? Well...I mean, I think it's odd you'd keep all this from me, but it's great Solomon helped him...and that you two are talking," he says after letting it all sink in. "Wow."

"You're not in any position to be angry with me for not telling you something."

Vincent has caught her breath now and sits on the love seat in the hotel room with her dress petaling at her feet. Cillian pats his thigh twice, instructing her to put her legs on him. She does.

"That's fair, Vin. I can't be punished forever for this, but it's fair. And I accept it."

Her bag is on the floor. She leans over and gets her wedding ring out of the little zipped pocket inside of it, holds it up to prove to him that she still has it. He takes it, clasps his hand around it, and lets her have it back again. With anyone else, this much intense eye contact would wear Vincent out and she'd have to break it, but this is her husband and she's prepared for it.

Cillian pushes her dress up to her knees, touches her skin.

"Do you really expect me to believe you haven't had sex... in a *year*?" she asks.

"My right hand as my witness," Cillian says, raising it. "I mean that because of all the jerking off."

Vincent laughs and he laughs too.

"Yeah... I got that. Didn't need that explained, but thanks."

"Do you really expect me to believe *you* haven't had sex in a year?" he asks her. "The Vincent I know would be... in a world of hurt right now."

"Cillian, there is nothing I need to tell you, although my friend Agathe did get me a vibrator for my birthday."

She thinks of it back in her drawer in the apartment. She imagines Loup finding it. She thinks of Loup inside of her and Loup's mouth and the two of them, touching and kissing and breathing and sleeping and and and.

Cillian, there is nothing I need to tell you. At least, not yet.

"A vibrator. That's interesting," he says.

"I know, right?"

"I'd like to hear more about that, actually," Cillian says, leaning over and kissing her mouth.

"You can sleep in the bed, but I'm not having sex with you. Not tonight. We'll have to work up to that. Only kissing. Deal? You can go jerk off in the bathroom while I'm sleeping or whatever," she says, laughing again.

"Absolutely. Deal," he says, taking her face in his hands.

It's nine in the morning in Paris when Vincent sits on the bathroom sink and texts Loup because kissing Cillian doesn't mean she doesn't miss Loup. It doesn't mean she doesn't love Loup either. She doesn't know what it means.

It's the middle of the night here.

I get obsessed with the time difference because it's the only way I can keep up with it.

New York is fine, it really is! But nowhere is Paris. xo

She texts him more, tells him the wedding went well and sends him a photo Monet took of her, Olive, and Colm outside the church. She sits there afterward swiping between two pictures on her phone: one of Loup in bokeh candlelight on the Côte d'Azur and another of the two of them on the train back to Paris after leaving Auvers-sur-Oise. In it, Vincent is looking into the camera; Loup is looking at her.

Ah, si belle! Paris isn't the same without you.

I am heading off to have breakfast with Lisette and Emiliano. They're a thing now. I'll fill you in. Maybe if you get a chance later in the week, call me?

Would love to hear your voice, Saint Vincent. x

And later she sends him a photo of her breasts in the low bathroom light, crops her face out of it.

VIN. CENT.

I will never delete this.

KILLING. ME.

R.I.P. ME.

You're perfect. Promise you're still real?

Je promets.

Sunday morning is a big breakfast in the hotel restaurant to send off Colm and Nicole, leaving on a jet plane. The room is packed with Vincent's family, Nicole's family, Colm and Nicole's friends. Vincent sits at a table with Ramona and Peter because in all the bustle, she hasn't had much time to talk to her best friend and with everything she's keeping from her, it doesn't feel like it's only been since Christmas that she's seen her—it feels like years.

Cillian is at the big table with them. He's on his second cup of coffee, and he and Peter are talking about the Yankees-Mets Subway Series. Ramona asks Vincent if she's okay.

"Yeah, sure. I mean...I have no clue who or where I am, but I'm fine," Vincent says, smiling. She finishes her toast and Ramona gives her a look.

"When it's time, you'll spill the beans? Because I know you well enough to know that everything isn't *completely* okay. Come on, Vinnie. It would be insulting for you to think I can't tell. It would actually hurt my feelings," Ramona says softly. Her back is turned to her husband; he and Cillian get so loud around each other, Vincent and Ramona could morph into aliens and blast off and it would probably take their husbands at least a few minutes to notice.

"I'm sorry. And yes, yes. Of course I'll tell you everything! You know I will. For now, just know we slept in the same bed last night. So, progress...sort of?" Vincent says. She doesn't know exactly why she's saying these things, but it's too much to get into. It doesn't matter right now! She'll figure the rest out in Paris. The smooth rock of her secrets is a comfort, even in the chaos.

"And?" Ramona asks.

Vincent hears Monet laughing behind her and she turns to see her and Theo cracking up with their dad. Olive and Nicole are at a nearby table, talking. Colm is sitting with them too, looking at his phone.

"I did feel something shift," she says.

"What's that mean?" Ramona makes her big brown eyes even bigger.

"I'm not exactly sure," Vincent says.

"Are you happy?"

"Are you?"

"I am. And I want you to be," Ramona says with a sad look on her face.

She's Vincent's most tenderhearted friend. The kind of woman who carries extra snacks and gift cards around in her car so she can give them to homeless people who stand at the intersections. The kind of woman who tends and weeds the community gardens of senior citizens when they're unable to. It stresses her out when the people around her aren't happy. It stresses her out when her *chickens* aren't happy. There have been times when they've been chatting and Ramona has launched into a story about how she thought one of her chickens or llamas was depressed, or how her rabbits needed extra attention, so she'd moved them out of the barn and into the house.

Ramona had cried with Vincent when Cillian's secret had come to light. She cried over how hurt Vincent was and that the hurt was sending her best friend away and she cried because it meant their foursome had a crack in it. Ramona was rooting for Vincent and Cillian to stick it out and stay together. Peter was too. Vincent looks at Peter and he must feel it because he turns to her and their eyes meet. He lights them up for her and smiles.

"It's good to be looking at you, Vincent Wilde. How many times have I told you that this weekend?" Peter says with a mouth full of Tennessee. Peter is another one of the men in Vincent's life she feels a brotherly affection for. He and Ramona have been together forever, and he's been nothing but great. Plus, he's a ginger. Vincent has always had an affinity for gingers.

"Well, I don't get tired of hearing it!" Vincent says, smiling back.

Cillian is drinking his coffee and watching her. She remembers their kisses last night. They've been kissing for practically half their lives. She remembers their mutual desire, idling.

Her parents crash their table. Her dad rests his hand on her shoulder and Vincent puts her hand on his. Her mom is talking to Ramona and Theo steps over to them, starts talking to Cillian and Peter. Colm interrupts to hug Theo and the restaurant is loud and busy with everything happening all at once.

This is her family.

She may be a different woman in Paris and the woman she is in Paris may even be who she *really* is, but in New York like this, surrounded by her entire clan, she is swept away by how much they love one another. How much they've forgiven one another.

She's not willing to give it all up yet, not even after what Cillian did.

And she's definitely not unhappy, but.

She'd be happier if she could split herself in two.

Before Colm and Nicole leave for the airport, Colm comes to Vincent's room, where she, Olive, and Cillian are hanging out, half watching whatever Olive switches the channel to. It was *The Fast and the Furious* for a bit, then a home renovation show. Now it's a travel show with the young host heading to Vietnam to find the spiciest noodles they have to offer.

"You'll be back in Kentucky for Thanksgiving? Christmas?" Colm asks Vincent. They are sitting at the table by the window.

Olive has her head in her daddy's lap and Cillian is gently petting her hair. Vincent is overwhelmed with emotion, watching them. How did they get to this level of goodness already? The air is charmed and it's almost like nothing bad has happened to their family, but how? Was it as simple as her leaving? As simple as them spending some time apart? How much of their happiness is depending on her? If she says yes to Loup and no to Cillian, is she saying no forever to all this too?

"I'd like to find a time before then for us to get together somewhere... with Tully too," Vincent says.

Olive shoots up. "Really? I mean, you've said it, but do you think it'll actually happen? Do *you* want this to happen?" She directs the last part to Cillian.

"Yes. Absolutely. Of course I do," he says, nodding.

"Maybe we should just do it at Christmas?" Colm says. "Here or there, it doesn't matter to me."

"It doesn't matter where to me, either," Vincent says. They could meet in Dublin. Tully could come to Kentucky. New York in December is lovely.

But no, not Paris. It can't happen in Paris. Paris is hers.

"I'll talk to him and figure it out," Cillian says.

"I've really missed being together like this. My babies—" Vincent says, fully crying now.

"Mama, please!" Olive says, shaking her head. She sticks her bottom lip out to fake-pout and it makes Vincent laugh.

"We'll make a real plan soon. It'll be nice to have all of this to look forward to," Colm says. He looks at his phone and tells them he has to leave in ten minutes. Vincent says she knows, of course, she's fine, she'll be okay.

Colm and Nicole fly away in the afternoon. Ramona and Peter are gone by evening. Monet and Olive will share a cab to JFK in the morning to head back to California and Tennessee. Theo's family will be in New York City for the rest of the week; her parents will be too. Cillian says goodbye to his mom, who's jetting to San Francisco on a late flight.

Vincent, Cillian, and Olive have dinner with her siblings and parents at a fancy steakhouse in the Village. Her dad makes a joke when he asks Cillian if it's okay for him to cover the bill, reminding him that in *Half-Blown Rose*, Cian trashed Pica's parents for doing the same thing. Her dad had sweetly touched her face and smiled when Vincent told him that part. They'd laughed about it together because it was all so stupid.

"I know I've apologized to you all directly, but I'd like to do it again. I'm a different person now. And I know that was only a year ago, but trust me, I've more than evolved in a year. I almost lost my family and I would never do anything to jeopardize that again," Cillian says.

Solomon reaches out his hand for Cillian's and he takes it, shakes.

"There's no doubt in my mind that you wouldn't do something like that again, Mr. Wilde. Not to my daughter or my grandchildren. Don't worry about me. I didn't read the damn thing anyway," Solomon says without laughing. Vincent's blood rushes harder at the memory of her dad and Loup drinking whiskey, listening to records together in Amsterdam. She is grateful to her family of secret keepers for not letting a peep of it escape their mouths.

"I told Vinnie to keep the cops on standby up here, in case you pissed me off," Monet says loudly from across the table.

"And that's why I adore you, Monet," Cillian says.

Theo is quiet and smirking when Vincent clears her throat. "I think it's okay to change the subject now," she says.

"Honestly, this is the most dramatic family on earth and when I get home, I'm going to sleep for a fucking *week*," Olive says. She covers her mouth and apologizes to her grandparents for cursing. Cillian, smiling at her, puts his arm around the back of her chair.

—

Vincent cries again saying goodbye to Monet and Olive and has lost track of the number of times she's spilled out tears over the weekend.

She and Theo go for a long walk alone afterward and he tells her that he and Yvonne are most likely heading for separation. He says that Yvonne's sister came with them to New York and is staying in a different hotel where Yvonne is now; their daughters are with her. Theo's leaving the hotel in the morning too, to go spend the rest of the week with a friend in Harlem. Vincent tells him she's sorry about Yvonne, but he doesn't seem upset. He seems relieved.

"You *are* different when you're with Loup, though. I noticed," he says as they wander past the Flatiron Building on their way to Washington Square Park. It's hot, but the wind is a blessing. Cillian has gone for a run and Vincent imagines bumping into him, earbudded and sweating in his shorts.

"Is this your way of saying I should divorce Cillian and me, you, Loup, and the next woman you hook up with could disappear to Europe together? Leave our kids to fend for themselves?" she asks, taking his arm.

"Wow. Now that you put it like that..."

"Different how?" she asks as they cross Twenty-First Street.

"I don't know. Just more...open and *untied*...it may be just because I've never seen you with anyone besides Cillian, really. Anyway, it's less about them...more about you. You know you'll be fine, no matter what happens."

"So will you."

"Right." Theo nods. "Is there something wrong with us? Are we freaks?"

"Definitely," she says. They make faces at each other and laugh. "Wow, I miss Paris," she pouts after they cross Fifteenth. "New York is fine but I'm tired of Americans. The fucking politics and flag-waving patriotic bullshit make me want to die. I want another country's problems, not these. I mean, everyone wants to *go* to Paris, right? But I want to *die* in Paris. I want to die an old woman smoking with the windows open, flowers in my hair...a mango dripping in my lap."

"Ah, that's the desperate curse of it all, ain't it? No matter where you are, you will always miss Paris. Your words are poetry...so pretty," Theo says, giving her the most emotion she's seen from him in a long time. Maybe she's imagining the tears in his eyes, but she knows hers are real. Her big brother wraps his arm around her.

To: TullyHawke@gmail.com

From: VincentRaphaelaWilde@gmail.com

Subject: Live from New York

Hi Tully! I've attached some pics from the wedding! One of the lovely couple and another of all of us, including my sister, brother and his daughters, and our parents. You were missed! Cillian's going to talk back soon about making a real plan for all of us to meet up before the end of the year. Maybe he already has? We don't care where. Either here or we can come to Dublin. What do you think? There's nothing weird with how your mom may feel about it? I really want this to be the easiest it can be on everyone.

I told Cillian that you and I have been emailing and everything else, so feel free to talk or not talk to him about it as much as you'd like.

I know it wasn't so long ago that we did purple, but it's my favorite color...forgive me! I saw purple hydrangeas on my walk through the Conservatory Garden in Central Park. And I saw the most precious pair of twin toddlers in purple dresses on my way out.

Hope your show went well last night!

Am leaving here in a few days. I miss Paris so much it hurts.

Talk soon!

Love,

V

PS: You pick the color for next week?

To: VincentRaphaelaWilde@gmail.com
From: TullyHawke@gmail.com
Subject: Re: Live from New York

Vincent,

I love this pic of all of you. And it's magical because your mam's dress is purple too. ☺ No apology necessary for us doing purple again. I love it. Eimear bought a new pair of scissors with purple handles the other day and excitedly showed them to me because she knows about the little game you and I play. She picked them on purpose...I mean how cute is that?

The show last night was grand. Thank you for remembering. It was definitely the biggest show I've played so far. I'll be riding that high for a good long while. ☺ I plan on emailing your dad as soon as I finish this one.

I haven't talked to Cillian about it yet but meeting up anywhere sounds good to me. (!!) I'll admit to you that I'm nervous! I'm ready, but I'm also scared to be together with everyone...I know I'm the odd man out, trust me. But also, we're all adults.

Soloco is on my list of people I have to meet now, too!

And no worries about my mam. I've already talked to her about this. Told you she was aces.

Safe travels!

Le grá,

Tully

PS: Let's do yellow again.

To: TullyHawke@gmail.com

From: VincentRaphaelaWilde@gmail.com

Subject: Re: Live from New York

Dear Tully,

Yay for yellow!

And my dad would love to meet you! He never stays in one place for too long. He'll definitely let you know next time he's near Dublin.

Also! You're not the odd man out. You're our family. We love you.

To: VincentRaphaelaWilde@gmail.com

From: TullyHawke@gmail.com

Subject: Re: Live from New York

Thank you, Vincent. I love you all too.

The rest of Vincent's New York week is filled with walks in Central Park with Cillian and breakfasts, lunches, and dinners with Cillian. One solo shopping trek waiting for him to finish at the rock-climbing gym. He asks her if it's okay for him to go, to leave her alone, and she tells him yes. She gets a falafel and sits in the sunny grass FaceTiming Loup for the first time since she left. He is in her apartment, keyed up. He can't stop telling her that he misses her. And because she's so far away and her feelings are twisted, for a split second the intensity is a little cloying—a flick of hot caramel stuck in her tooth.

She hates herself for thinking it.

But! She loves seeing his face and knowing Paris is still there and Loup is still in it. She loves seeing her bed and blankets beneath him, his dark hair spilling across her pillow like ink from a jar. He tells her he loves her as they're saying goodbye and she says it back.

When she sees Cillian emerge from the gym, sweaty and flushed, she lets him kiss her and kiss her and kiss her because maybe she loves him in a way she can never love anyone else and maybe he knows it too. Maybe Loup loves the Paris Vincent and Cillian loves the Vincent she is in New York and Kentucky. Maybe all of those things are true.

"When you left for Paris, I thought there was no way we could ever work this out. I deserved it, I know. But I just figured you were giving up," Cillian says in the dark of her hotel room.

They kissed until their lips were numb and his thumb grazed her breast. She'd gently pushed him away. She's lying down, half-asleep now, but Cillian is sitting up, all sexually frustrated and chatty.

"I *was* giving up," she mumbles.

"But what about now?"

He pulls the strap of her tank top to the side and touches her tattoo.

"I don't know. Buy the villa and we'll talk about it."

"I'll give you anything you want, love." He kisses her shoulder, her neck. "Do you have to go back to Paris? Can't I come with you?" He reminds her that he's on sabbatical now and he can do it. He's free.

"Cillian, no. Yes, I do. And no, you can't. Paris is mine."

"I can't live without you," he says.

Or maybe he says, "I can't *leave* without you."
Vincent doesn't ask.

Vincent's Travel Playlist | Airplane | NYC to Paris

"Les Champs-Elysées" by Joe Dassin
"C'est si bon" by Yves Montand
"La mer" by Charles Trenet
"Paris" by Édith Piaf
"Je veux" by Zaz
"I Love Paris" by Frank Sinatra
"Tous les garçons et les filles" by Françoise Hardy
"Ne me quitte pas" by Nina Simone
"Le moulin" by Yann Tiersen
"Un jour comme un autre" by Anna Karina
"La bohème" by Charles Aznavour
"Le temps est bon" by Isabelle Pierre
"Une belle histoire" by Michel Fugain et le Big Bazar
"Les amoureux des bancs publics" by Georges Brassens
"Le temps de l'amour" by Françoise Hardy
"Il est cinq heures, Paris s'éveille" by Jacques Dutronc
"Je t'aime tant" by Julie Delpy
"Je cherche un homme" by Eartha Kitt
"April in Paris" by Billie Holiday
"J'ai deux amours" by Madeleine Peyroux

7

Loup is doing a handstand in her bedroom.

"Be careful! Loup, my books!" Vincent says, pointing. Moments ago, he was on the bed with her and they were cross-legged in their underwear, playing a game of hand slap. "Plus, we just had sex so you shouldn't need to do a handstand anyway!"

She got in last night and told Loup not to wait up. She found him naked, sleeping in her bed, and she took off her clothes, climbed in with him. They had sex twice with Loup touching her like she'd been resurrected.

She thought of Cillian while Loup was inside of her and wished she could force herself to see far enough into the future to know what she truly wanted.

Paris and Loup were stuck together and she couldn't unglue them. Her love for the city and her love for him had mixed months ago and they'd stained each other, making a lovely pattern on her heart. *Decalcomania.* She feels so grossly two-faced when she talks to herself about Cillian. His handsomeness, his natural charm . . . they'd worked on her when she was in New York the same way they worked on her when she was eighteen, pulling her into the mystic. Vincent keeps compartmentalizing what he's done and making excuses for him because he's Cillian, *her* Cillian, and she'll love him forever.

*   *   *

"Oh, I was just showing off with this one," Loup says, putting his feet down carefully. "And I felt like being ridiculous."

"I'm reopening my shop today and that doesn't mean you have to leave, but I have a *lot* of work to do."

"What's today?"

"*Vendredi*," Vincent says. Friday is her favorite day to translate.

"Anchois has a gig tonight. I'm sorry I forgot to tell you."

"Okay...um, I can maybe do that." She's jet-lagged but wouldn't mind going out if she gets everything ready for the post office in the morning.

"Don't worry about it. Just text me later?" he says, getting his shorts off the bed and stepping in. She leans forward to meet his mouth.

Le Marais. Agathe is standing outside the club in stripes and black flats.

"*Bonsoir!* Look at how French you are!" Vincent says. Before Agathe can respond, Vincent apologizes for what happened in her closet when she was trying on the dresses.

"Pshh! Don't! I love you exactly how you are. Oh, it's so cute and American for you to apologize though you've done nothing wrong. I would never do that," Agathe says, patting her face.

"I really didn't want things to be awkward between us."

"It's not *me* you need to worry about," Agathe says into her ear. She squeezes Vincent's shoulder and Vincent turns to see Baptiste and Mina walking toward them.

Baptiste smiles and Mina's face does something that Mina may think is a smile but really it looks more like she's holding in a rancid burp. Vincent has seen her real smile and this is not it.

"Hi, Vincent. Can we talk? Quick-quick?" Mina says when she's in front of her. Vincent doesn't say anything, just follows Mina as she steps away. Baptiste and Agathe stand on the other side of the entrance, talking. Vincent is already worn to a frazzle from travel and work, but thinking of Mina being more concerned with Vincent and Loup's relationship than she is with her own husband standing ten feet away with his lover is a-whole-nother level of fuckery that makes Vincent want to lie down on the sidewalk and scream, then sleep.

Mina is boldly wearing the pair of Go Wilde! earrings that Baptiste bought her for Christmas—plum and terra-cotta rectangles swinging underneath her flippy hair.

"Look. I'm probably always going to be a wee bit bitchy about you and my little cousin because he's... well... he's my *little* cousin. But B says you think I hate you and that's daft! We're adults, not schoolmates," Mina says.

Vincent doesn't know if she'd feel more like arguing with Mina if she weren't so tired. Coming out was probably a mistake, but she's here now and Mina is looking at her on pause, waiting for a response.

"Mina, for fuck's sake, leave it. If you want to hate someone, hate me. But you refuse... so here we are," Agathe says, stepping next to Vincent.

"Agathe, actually, this is about Loup—" Mina starts.

Baptiste is beside them on the sidewalk now, looking calm as a cloud. He winks at Vincent when she meets his eyes.

"It's not about Loup, it's about me and it's because Vincent is my dear friend. Just leave it, honestly," Agathe says. She holds Vincent's hand.

"I don't feel like I need to say anything, really," is Vincent's reply.

A group of young men squeeze past them, making their way to the entrance. One of them is wearing the same Anchois T-shirt Vincent has.

"I think we should go in and enjoy the show, *non*?" Baptiste asks, like a father attempting to defuse a fight between his children.

"This is not about Loup," Agathe says softly to Vincent, not letting go of her hand.

Mina's face softens in defeat. Agathe nudges Vincent and they go inside, leaving Baptiste and Mina on the sidewalk alone.

When the show is over Vincent checks her phone to see a good-night text from Cillian saying he can't wait to see her soon. He sends more.

> You're thinking August? When you get everything in Paris all wrapped up?

> Maybe we can go on a trip if you're not too tired of traveling? Italy?

> I love you.

She writes him.

> August...probably, yes.

> You know I think Italy always sounds lovely.

They'll talk about it later. Once she commits to *something*, she's convinced the other pieces of her life will fall together in a way that makes sense.

Loup loads up his things and says his goodbyes to his bandmates, then he joins Vincent under the streetlight. Mina and Agathe are chatting amicably now and Vincent will never be able to figure them out and won't even bother trying. There's too much she doesn't know and doesn't *want* to know. As long as they leave her out of it, it's fine!

"Want to walk?" Loup asks her after he talks to Baptiste and Agathe and quickly speaks to his cousin. They usually kiss cheeks and hug goodbye, but tonight Loup only waves to Mina. And while Vincent doesn't entirely relish feeling this way, she is a little pleased that he's not back to normal with Mina yet. "Oh, wait. Meet Lisette. Meet my sister," Loup says. Vincent watches him touch the arm of a young woman talking to Emiliano.

"Oh. Hi. Hi, Lisette, I'm Vincent," she says, holding out her hand.

Lisette ignores it and kisses Vincent's cheeks instead.

"You are the woman who has stolen my big brother's heart," Lisette says, shaking her finger at her and smiling.

Loup's sister looks exactly like the photos of her that are in Loup's apartment. Vincent probably would've recognized her on her own if she weren't so tired. Or sick. Maybe she's both. She's starting to feel like garbage, but she smiles at Lisette anyway and tells her how much she adores Loup.

"But you're leaving Paris soon? What's happening?" Lisette asks. Loup is looking at her and Vincent feels like *all* of her friends are waiting for an answer to that question, but she doesn't know it. Not yet. She doesn't!

"Did you apply for a residence permit?" Mina asks.

"No, not yet," Vincent says, starting to sweat.

"When does your work visa expire?" Mina asks. She's talking to Vincent in a professional tone now, like she's the impatient person behind the embassy counter and Vincent is a dumb, confused American.

"Um, soon. Before the end of the month."

She never talked to Mr. Laurent about it, and she tried to look up the guidelines online, but it'd all been so confusing she'd stopped.

"Then it's too late to apply for a residence permit. I mean, you should definitely go and make sure because I'm not positive... but you probably waited too late," Mina says.

"There might be some loopholes since your parents own the apartment. Let me help if I can?" Baptiste chimes in. Agathe echoes the same sentiment.

"Wherever you go, you have to take my brother with you because he'll be a mess!" Lisette says dramatically, smiling at him. Loup is smiling too, but Vincent knows he's upset.

* * *

They say goodbye and peel off from the crowd. Loup is quiet.

"I forgot to talk to Mr. Laurent about my visa. I'll figure it out," she says, touching his arm.

"Or... you'll leave and I'll never see you again," Loup says, snaking around a bike and two short poles on the sidewalk.

"No. Loup, no. It's taken me a while, but I actually *feel* like a Parisienne now. I don't feel guilty anymore about not knowing enough French, because I know a *lot* of French now! When I got here last year, I was nervous whenever I went to the *pharmacie* and when I went in there a bit ago I talked to the same guy in French the whole time. I meant to tell you that! I just needed a door to open in my mind... and the door is wide open now. Do you really think I want to leave this place?" Vincent gestures at everything around them. *Everything*. She's been in Paris for almost a year and they are on rue des Archives, which has been there since the thirteenth century. Paris is a living, breathing creature with its tentacles wrapped around her.

She's too tired to wander tonight and tells him that.

"Then I'll walk you home," he says, stopping. He holds out his arm for her to take.

By the time they get inside her apartment, she's feeling downright shitty. She goes to the bathroom to brush her teeth and wash her face. When she's finished, she finds Loup on her bed in his underwear, flipping through a book of poetry by Phillis Wheatley.

"It's quite romantic to emerge from the bathroom to find you reading poetry in bed. Thank you," Vincent says. She puts on her hand lotion and climbs under the covers. He sets the book on her nightstand and slips under with her.

"Are we in a fight? I don't think we are, but it feels like it."

"I'm sorry it feels like it. I don't think we are. I'm just tired and I don't feel good," she says, turning off the light.

He's the big spoon and they sleep.

In the morning, Loup makes her toast and tea and asks if she's sure she'll be okay if he goes to play soccer at the park because he won't leave her if she's not. She tells him she'll be fine. It's probably everything combined. She almost always gets sick when she flies, plus jet lag and PMS and the aftershock of being with her entire family in New York. It's all caught up to her and is making her feel terrible.

Loup tells her he'll bring food by later and can help if she needs to get some work done.

And when he's gone, she's thankful for the quiet.

She sleeps some more. She FaceTimes with Olive, who is on the fence about chopping her hair off like Zillah and Jean Seberg or just getting bangs instead.

8

But Vincent knows she's pregnant the first day she's late. She *knows*. Her period is never late and it's too early for menopause; she's asked her doctor about the symptoms of perimenopause at least five times in the past, and she doesn't have any of them.

She's been pregnant twice. She *knows*.

And she knows which night it was too. Fucking opera night. The gold dress, Loup's tux. They'd started in the kitchen and barely made it to the bed.

There were no condoms in her drawer.

Cillian had a vasectomy. She hasn't had to think about condoms in twenty years! It was the only time she and Loup hadn't been super-super careful and Vincent thought: What are the odds?

What are the odds that a forty-four-year-old woman would get pregnant this one time she does something completely reckless in Paris?

As if Paris alone were protection enough.

She gets a test from the pharmacy just to be extra sure and sits on the bathroom floor after taking it, holding the positive pee stick in her hands and snottily crying with her mouth open.

When she goes to her bed and looks at her phone, there's a text from

Cillian saying hi and he's excited about August and their being reunited again soon.

Cillian. YOU HAVE GOT TO LET ME HAVE THE REST OF JULY FIRST.

I don't know exactly what I feel yet!!

She can't hold anything back from him anymore. Hormones! These pregnancy hormones specifically! They make her feel completely out of control and maybe if she tells him this... if she tells him she's pregnant with her lover's baby this can all be over.

She tosses the phone on the floor and cries some more. She wants to tell Monet, but she's so far away. Ramona doesn't know about Loup. Mrs. Laurent is too close with Aurora. The only woman in Paris she can tell is Agathe.

And she's a day behind on the Go Wilde! orders that continue to pour in from the Zillah video and the magazine feature. Her phone keeps vibrating. She lifts her head and crawls over to pick it up.

A missed call from Cillian and four new texts.

The villa. YOUR villa. Our villa. I tried to get you on the phone so you could hear my voice but this is OURS.

Meet me in Tuscany in August? I promise not to pressure you about anything, I just want you to see it.

I snuck there in June and I was hanging on to see how NYC went for us and for the right time to tell you.

I'll be going back in August, waiting for you.

He's sent a link to a villa in Serravalle Pistoiese, Pistoia, Tuscany.

He's sent multiple photos of it.

He's sent a photo of himself in a white linen shirt and brown pants, standing in the doorway.

She tries to let it sink in that while she'd been keeping her trip with Loup a secret, Cillian had been keeping his Italy trip a secret too.

She taps through apps on her phone in a daze, waiting a full hour to respond.

What??? Cillian, it's a dream. I don't know what to say. I can't believe any of this.

What are we supposed to do with this??

Live there! Stay whenever we want! Rent it out when we're away!

Whatever you want to do with it, it's yours.

You said you didn't want anything silver for our 25th and this isn't silver.

This is the GOOD that came out of all this bullshit of mine, Vin, it really is.

Can you call me soon, please?

I will. I will call you soon.

But first, she calls Agathe and asks her to come over. Agathe says she'll be there in twenty. Vincent asks her to please bring a bag of *pain au chocolat* because she can't imagine stomaching anything but bread and peppermint tea.

"I can't believe you told me. You don't like telling people things," Agathe says, hugging her so tight, Vincent can barely breathe. She's gently petting her hair.

"You were so good at keeping everything with you and Baptiste a secret, I really do trust you with this," Vincent says. She tears off a piece of bread and nibbles at it. They are on her bed with the windows open. Vincent hears a siren and crosses herself, which makes her cry again.

"Here's the other bombshell if you didn't know it already... I was pregnant a couple years ago too. Baptiste's. I lost the baby. Well, it wasn't a baby yet... a blighted ovum. Part of me considered keeping it before I lost it. Baptiste wanted it too. I was surprisingly wrecked by it and so was he. It was really hard for us to get over. And Mina's vehemently against anyone having children. Have you met her? She's a little absurd," Agathe says, laughing through her tears.

After Vincent tells her how sorry she is, she laughs through hers too—a surprise, considering how she feels and the surreality of what's happening.

"Dear God, I'm too old for this. I already did this! My babies are grown!" Vincent says later, putting both hands on her stomach.

"What do you think Loup will want?"

Vincent gives herself half a minute to think about it.

"I have no idea, I really don't," she says. It's all she can come up with. "I'm going to tell him tonight because he'll know something's up anyway. He picks up on everything."

"Understood. He's ultra-sensitive. It comes with Loup 7000 territory," Agathe says, making Vincent laugh again while the rational part of her brain plays catch-up.

With Agathe gone, Vincent takes a shower and waits another hour to call Cillian. Her excitement about the Tuscan villa is real and she's glad she doesn't have to fake it.

It happens again: Hearing Cillian's voice zaps her back to reality and their life together. How can she not meet her husband in Tuscany at the villa he's bought for her? She'd be out of her mind not to, regardless of the state of her uterus.

She thanks him for the villa for the first time and tells him of course she'll be there. She'll take the train and meet him. The whole time they're talking, she's clicking through the pictures over and over again—the flowers, the pool, the statues in the garden—imagining being there and making it hers. Making it *theirs*. She suggests that they also invite their children and Tully and Siobhán too. She tells him to let everyone know about it and send pics and make sure August lines up with their schedules, especially Olive's because she won't want to miss any classes. Cillian says good yes okay and asks if she's sure about Tully and Siobhán and she definitely is. She's sure.

When Loup arrives, he asks Vincent how she's feeling and she says okay. They go to her bedroom and she begins to tell him about Cillian's book, Tully, and the real reasons she ran off to Paris.

Loup, sweaty from soccer, confesses that he was at the bookstore a few weeks ago with Apollos and Noémie and saw *Half-Blown Rose* there. A stack of them. He saw Cillian's name and the title and put it all together. He bought a copy and read the whole thing, wondering if she was ever going to say anything to him about it.

Vincent is crying on her bed. Lately, Vincent is always crying on her bed. She'd planned on spilling everything about Cillian's book first, then telling Loup about the pregnancy. But now they're stuck in a conversation circle about Tully and how her husband could do something like that.

"I don't know, Loup. I don't! Everyone likes to come to me for an answer to this, but I don't have it!"

"I just don't see how you can forgive him and go back to him after this," Loup says. His hands are folded atop his head the same way Cillian stood in the hallway of their hotel. She loves it on Loup too, but it doesn't matter. He's pacing the rug on the floor in front of her bed.

"I *have* to forgive him because he's the father of my children," Vincent says. The tears come harder, thinking not only of Cillian being the father of her children, but Loup being the father of the tiny almost-baby in her uterus too. "And who says I'm going back to him?"

She's barely able to keep her own stories straight now.

What had she told Loup she was doing in August? No way is she not going to the villa, but will her heart stay in Paris? What good is a body without the heart?

"You're going back to him, I can tell... You didn't even renew your visa," Loup says, raising his voice a little. He stops walking. She explains again that the visa thing was an honest mistake. Yes, she has to leave in a week or so, but that doesn't mean she can't return.

She apologizes for not telling him about the book and the rest spills out—her correspondence with Tully and how he's become friends with her dad. The villa. She shows him pictures of it and taps the YouTube app on her phone to show him Tully's page too.

Loup is sitting on the edge of her bed now, looking at her.

"Also... and this is a shitty time to tell you with everything else we're talking about... and I already told Agathe because I needed to talk to a woman first...but Loup, I'm pregnant. And before you say anything to piss me off, it's yours. I didn't sleep with Cillian when I was in New York and that's not how pregnancy works anyway. I haven't slept with Cillian for over a year. It was opera night when there were no condoms in my drawer. That's the night it was...my dress and your...tuxedo. If it wasn't that, it'd be the stripes or your hair...your fucking *thighs*, my *God*," Vincent says, flicking her hand at him.

Who's Wolf? her daughter had asked her.

Who's afraid of this gentle wolf sitting on her bed?

Loup's dark eyes warm quick and the side of his mouth turns up. He reaches out for her, hugs her.

"*Tu es sérieuse?*" he whispers against her ear.

"Yes! Loup! I'm serious! Don't you think I have enough going on right now? Do you think I need to make something like this up just for my own amusement?" She fusses, pushing her hair off her face.

"And you want to have this baby?" Loup asks carefully. "I'll say up front that I want you to keep it...if you want to."

"*C'est moi qui décide*," she says.

They're quiet and quiet, but the church bells are ringing.

"You're...insouciant," Loup says. "You won't say anything else about it?"

"Insouciant? I am not! Just because I stopped crying for a millisecond, I'm insouciant? You're judging my feelings so closely and I don't even know what I feel yet! And who says that? *Insouciant?*"

"I'm sorry. Please...I just can't read you anymore," he says. "But if you run off to Italy with the baby there's nothing I can do about it. You could disappear and I'd never see you...*either* of you again." He puts his head in his hands.

"Loup...why do you think I...why would I do that? *How* could I do that?" she asks.

She's so tired. She feels hungry and full at the same time; she's dizzy. Her head hurts. She remembers these feelings from when she was pregnant with Colm and Olive. With Colm, they had lasted a full fifteen weeks. With Olive it had been easier, or she'd been more used to it, she didn't know which was the truth.

"And if I do keep it... you're young... it would be my choice and I wouldn't expect anything from you. I don't need your money and you wouldn't have to *do*... anything. I just wish you were older! I can't help but feel like I'm stealing time from you. I'm sorry, but it's true. This is a mess," Vincent says.

Her tongue feels numb. It's like she's talking about someone else's life. She said the words, but it doesn't sound or feel like a real thing she needs to process and figure out yet. She's detached herself from the baby already, at least for now, just to practice and see how it feels.

"It doesn't have to be a mess. We don't have to look at it like that. I can't change how old I am, and I don't know how to respond when you're actively pushing me away," Loup says. His face is sad. So sad, it makes her cry.

"Do you remember when we were on the train to London and I told you this would be like one of those tragedies... one of those old books written by a man where the woman takes a lover and has sex for pleasure and has to die in the end? It's the only way the universe can sort out women like me. Some sort of punishment. Pregnant at forty-four... forty-*five* when the baby is born. And doing all of that over again. I can't believe this is happening, really. I... *we* messed up. That's all there is to it," she says. She wipes her nose with the crumpled tissue by her foot, dabs at her eyes.

Loup lies down on the bed and looks up at her ceiling. She asks him what he's thinking.

"I don't know."

"Loup, I do love you. That's getting lost here, but it's true. I do."

"Maybe it's not punishment. Maybe we didn't mess up. I want you to keep it. I could buy you a villa. Tuscany is full of them," he says. He's crying too, pressing the heels of his hands against his eyes.

Vincent's glance lands on the shelf.

Mon cœur mis à nu. Bonjour tristesse. Vivre sa vie.

She gets up from the bed and goes over to the stack of books by the dresser.

Pulls out *Two Trains Running* by August Wilson and, remaining silent, holds it up until Loup eyes it.

"*Quoi?*" he says.

Vincent taps the title and touches her mouth with her finger.

Once he realizes what she's doing, he pulls out *Roots* and flashes it at her. She gives him *Brave New World* and he's already picking up *Tender Is the Night* by F. Scott Fitzgerald. Hers is *Remembrance of Things Past* by Proust. His, *The Volcano Lover* by Susan Sontag. She takes her time and follows with *Their Eyes Were Watching God*. And when he holds up *Kindred* by Octavia Butler, she starts crying all over again.

He holds her and they cry together because everything is changing and sometimes when everything is changing the only thing left to do is cry.

They eat a little. They sleep.

In the morning, Vincent gets up early and tries to get some work done. Loup helps her bake clay and put packages together. She'll go to the post office before her jewelry-making class. It's almost the end of July, almost the end of her time at the museum; on her way out of the apartment building, Mr. Laurent gives her a sad smile when he reminds her of it.

9

Our memories make up who we are. And I don't say that lightly. Our hippocampus helps us to store and recollect them. Our brains contain a vast wealth of memories in their storehouses. Imagine our minds, our hearts, without our memories. I believe that you'd find yourself wanting to hold on to even all of the bad ones if met with the idea of losing every memory in one swoop.

What is something you've learned from this journaling class that you'll take forward with you? Something you'll revisit via memory? Do you have a favorite memory of this class? Not only within these walls, but on your walks to the museum or as you entered or left the building? There is nothing too small to consider and nothing too big to attempt to process.

A young man who's also in Vincent's jewelry-making class talks about the day they shared their negative memories and how hearing everyone talk made him realize he wasn't the only one in the room with bad memories that haunted him. It made him feel more connected to everyone, not just in the class but in the world. That feeling of being connected makes him want to be kinder to people. The young man's name is Guillaume and he's from Bordeaux.

An older woman shares a story about how halfway between her flat and the museum, she'd gotten hot and stopped to get her water bottle from her backpack. She sat by a fountain and noticed a small gray cat cleaning itself next to her. They sat there together, two little creatures in need of a break. It'd helped her to realize it's okay to slow down, and that she's an animal too.

Vincent shares a memory from the first day of class. How she'd dropped a cup of colored pencils outside the door and everyone stopped to help her pick them up. How it'd been a great icebreaker and something she should probably do on purpose from now on. She also shares a happy memory of going to the opera with a friend. How they walked to the Palais Garnier and how breathless the sky was on their walk back to her apartment.

Loup has returned for the last class and his eyes are on her intently as he's listening to everyone and chewing on the end of his pen. He sits directly across from her in the circle in his *Sunflowers* shirt with his ankle resting on his opposite knee. When a woman shares the memory of the day she found out she was pregnant, Vincent puts her hand on her own stomach. She looks up to see Loup still watching her. She's astonished that the museum doesn't shake and sink under the weight of everything left unsaid.

One night I walked to her window and watched her, moving around in the light. She didn't know I was there.

One night I walked to his window and watched him, moving around in the light. He didn't know I was there.

10

Vincent's Travel Playlist | Train | Paris to Tuscany

"Une tigresse" by Anchois

"Come Back to Me" by Tully Hawke

"The Girl from Ipanema" by Stan Getz and João Gilberto

"America" by Simon & Garfunkel

"Clay Pigeons" by John Prine

"Mambo Italiano" by Dean Martin

"Ain't No Mountain High Enough" by Marvin Gaye and Tammi Terrell

"(What a) Wonderful World" by Sam Cooke

"Buona Sera" by Louis Prima

"Harvest Moon" by Neil Young

"Come Thou Fount of Every Blessing" by Sufjan Stevens

"Postcards from Italy" by Beirut

"Forever Young" by Rhiannon Giddens and Iron & Wine

"iMi" by Bon Iver

"Both Sides Now" by Joni Mitchell

"Gypsy" by Fleetwood Mac

"The Weakness in Me" by Joan Armatrading

LEESA CROSS-SMITH

"All I Want" by Toad the Wet Sprocket
"Butterfly" by BTS
"Delicate" by Damien Rice

It's the longest train ride Vincent has ever taken alone. Paris to Lyon. Lyon to Torino. Torino to Milan. Milan to Bologna. Bologna to Tuscany. She's seated next to a nice, older Italian woman who reminds her of her grandmother. Vincent sleeps a little and gets up at regular intervals to pee. Sometimes, puke. She eats crackers, drinks fizzy water.

She got the blood test at the doctor's office and he told her she was almost six weeks pregnant, and asked if they wanted to hear the heartbeat via transvaginal ultrasound. *Yes*. Loup was there with her, smiling and holding her hand even though she told him she was fine. She didn't want to keep reminding him that she wasn't some clueless girl who hadn't done this before, so she let him touch her shoulder and ask if she was okay. Loup had gotten tears in his eyes when he heard the hummingbird beat of their baby's heart; Vincent stared out the window in a sort of sweet, disenchanted wonder.

Agathe is still the only other person she's told. Vincent let Loup know that she didn't want to keep him from sharing the news with his friends, she just didn't think they should talk about it until they knew what they were doing. But she didn't want him walking around with that heavy secret either, so she told him it was okay to tell Apollos and Baptiste, knowing that once Baptiste found out, Mina would know too.

When Vincent left Paris she promised to let Loup know as soon as she got to Tuscany, but he was still texting her anyway, saying he missed her, telling her again that he was so excited about the baby and nothing had changed just because she was leaving for a bit.

He sent her a song he made for their baby. He named it "La lentille" because the doctor told them their baby is now the size of a lentil. Loup had recorded their entire appointment and hooked his phone up to the heartbeat monitor to get the sound as clearly as possible.

Their baby's *thumpthumpthumpthump* whooshes in the background of the song like a drum machine. Vincent cries listening to the soothing, hypnotic beeps on repeat for so long with the Italian countryside blurring by, she can't tell whether her world is ending or beginning.

Loup texts her again. A baby! Made in Paris.

Made in Paris. She cries some more and thinks tenderly of the staring, crying woman she and Loup saw on the train to London.

The woman next to her touches her arm and asks if she's okay and Vincent nods and says yes, thank you. She's okay. She tells the woman she's pregnant and the woman says she could tell just by looking at Vincent's face. That it's a gift she has and she's never been wrong about it, not once in seventy-three years. She tells Vincent her baby will have lots of hair and probably be a boy, but she's only been right about that a little more than half the time.

Safe in Tuscany! Breathtaking, really. Don't worry, though! I do miss you.

Glad to hear it. Talk to me soon, Saint Vincent. Please?

Outside the train station, Cillian is standing by a little pencil-yellow Fiat holding wildflowers. When he sees Vincent he opens his arms wide and she falls into them. He tells her how glad he is to see her and how lovesome she looks in that white dress. Cillian has a thing for her in white dresses and she considered *not* wearing it for that reason, but it's her favorite too—breezy dotted Swiss.

"Your cheeks are flushed. Was it hot on the train?" he asks, touching her hair.

"No, it was nice. I'm fine." He hands her the flowers. "Thank you, Cillian."

He puts her bags in the car, and they're off.

They have to drive a half hour north to get to the villa and when they arrive, Vincent covers her mouth in disbelief. It's more beautiful than the pictures or what she imagined—blond and brown stone, pretty and hot against the blue, gold, and green—straight out of one of her favorite movies. She wants to linger outside, but Cillian takes her hand and leads her inside, where he's brought some of her things from home to make her feel comfortable.

Her gray cable-knit blanket from their bed, the pillow she left behind. Her teapot and teacup, her little white cappuccino mugs. A cardigan she doesn't wear often anymore, but she used to. It is folded on the couch and she picks it up and smells it.

It smells like their house. It smells like home.

Because of Olive's schedule, they're flying her and Colm out in two days. They're flying in Tully and Siobhán too. Vincent has told them to bring their significant others. She asked, but Tully's younger sister couldn't make it. There are four bedrooms in the villa; they have plenty of room.

Their first night in the villa together, she lets Cillian kiss her in bed, knowing where it's headed. And she's missed him, she has. He's the same and he's different.

He's inside of her and so is Loup's baby.

They sit there afterward with the windows open, sharing a peach.

"Your necklace is flickering... like a little fire," Cillian says across the candlelight, leaning over to touch the tiger.

Her mouth is sweet and sticky and she's the one with the big secret now.

"You don't want wine?" he asks.

"No."

"Why not?"

"Just because."

"Do you think you'll ever put your wedding ring back on?" he asks.

"Maybe," she lies through the dark.

They spend the next two days lounging under bougainvillea, swimming in turquoise glow. Cooking and eating. Spilling some stories they've been saving. Vincent shares hers like an embroiderer following a difficult pattern. Sometimes stitching and sometimes skipping over, revealing only what she wants him to see.

They are together three times and all three times, Vincent pretends she's with Before Cillian.

All three times she thinks of Loup and wants Loup and misses Loup.

Windows open. White jasmine in water glasses on both bedside tables, more in a milk bottle on the dresser. Cillian snores softly next to her. In the blue light, she texts je t'aime to the young man in Paris and he texts je t'aime in return.

It's not enough, so she leaves the bedroom and calls him. Confesses everything in careful whispers.

Je suis désolée. Je suis si désolée.

Vincent gets back in bed and sleeps in her woodsy French perfume and oversize Anchois T-shirt, nothing else.

She dreams of Loup.

Tully Hawke is just as charming a person in real life as he is over email and Vincent cries upon seeing him. He's taller than she thought he'd be, his body a bit fuller. He is bearded and mellow, wowing at their new place and hugging her, lifting her off her feet a little. He's brought his girlfriend, Eimear, with him. She's quiet, summer-brown, and bright-eyed in a long striped dress and white sneakers. Vincent is fully in tears seeing Tully meet and hug Colm and Olive for the first time. He hugs Cillian too.

Siobhán looks like her pictures, but she's shorter and smaller than Vincent imagined her to be and even prettier. She feels an absurd retroactive jealousy thinking of her and Cillian together in Dublin. Siobhán approaches him slowly. It's the first time they've seen each other since they were teenagers. She is crying when she hugs him, which makes Vincent cry more. Siobhán's husband and Cillian smile timidly at each other and shake hands.

Olive has cut her hair short and Vincent is behind her, touching it in the kitchen.

"I love it. Paris is my inspiration," Olive says in her best French accent. She is sitting down, chopping yellow peppers for the pasta sauce. Colm and Tully are at the table with her, talking. Nicole and Eimear stand at the counter putting together the salad and shaking the dressing.

There is music playing from Colm's phone—a song his grandfather Solomon wrote.

Vincent steps outside into the early August air. Siobhán is sitting next to her husband, and Cillian is across from them, looking at her. Vincent imagines the two of them as teenagers back in Dublin and how they could've had no idea where their roads would lead them, how parallel and perpendicular to each other they would end up one day.

Vincent thinks of the new baby inside of her, the kind of life it could have.

When Cillian looks over Siobhán's shoulder, smiling at Vincent, Siobhán turns around to look at her too.

"Can you *believe* this place?" Siobhán asks all of them. Her voice is filled with awe and it's light and pleasant; her Irish accent is much stronger than Cillian's and so is Tully's.

"No. I can't," Vincent says, shaking her head.

"This is Vin's dream. She said she wanted a villa. She gets what she wants," Cillian says, beaming at her.

"I can't thank you enough for having us," Siobhán says.

"It's the only thing that makes sense" is Vincent's reply as she joins them at the table. She and Siobhán reach out at the same time to touch hands.

Tully hasn't brought his guitar but there's an old, poorly tuned one that Cillian says was at the villa when he arrived. After dinner, Tully tunes it the best he can and plays some songs for them. It's surreal for Vincent, hearing these songs in person and having their family together like this, in this place. Siobhán knows every word of Tully's lyrics and Vincent watches his mom close her eyes, mouthing them and holding her hand to her heart.

"We do have a little announcement," Colm says to the table. They are under a trellis of olive green in the sunset light—Tuscany is all orange golden hour and twinkles.

Vincent knew her daughter-in-law was pregnant as soon as Nicole stepped out of the car. The thought had crossed her mind at the wedding but now Vincent could just *tell*. And Nicole hadn't touched her dinner.

Vincent watched her push her salad around her plate and nibble her bread the same way Vincent had.

"Baby Wilde is due in March," Colm says, reaching over to touch Nicole's stomach. Nicole smiles and looks down.

"Colm!" Olive says, clapping her hands together. "Congratulations, you two!"

"Holy shit, a grandchild!" Cillian says brightly.

"I'm overwhelmed with love for *all* of you. Congratulations," Vincent says, getting up from her seat to go over to Nicole and hug her and Colm. To touch their faces.

Vincent's grandchild will be around the same age as her baby, and her spirit, her soul, her heart is imbued with love and light. Everyone is standing and hugging and congratulating. Vincent and Cillian find each other and hold on tight.

"Do you feel really old? Because I feel really fuckin' old," he says into her ear.

She doesn't say anything. Just cries and nods.

11

When she knows everyone is sleeping, Vincent goes outside in her white nightgown and Loup's blue sweater.

Earlier, he'd sent her "I'll Stand by You" by the Pretenders.

She calls him from under the moon.

"I know you may think it's wild, but I really do want to do this with you. None of it scares me," Loup says.

"If you ask me to marry you, I'll scream. Don't you dare."

Loup laughs and Vincent laughs too.

"*You* don't scare me either," he says.

"Good. The past year in Paris was a liminal space for me. Like trains... trains are liminal spaces. Maybe that's why I love them so much. Pregnancy is too. We're in a liminal space...that's what we'll do for now, okay? I'll stay here for a little bit and we'll wait."

She is looking up at the sky. Loup is quiet.

"There is so much we need to do...like Mykonos. We can take the baby to Mykonos," he says.

"And we still have to run through the Louvre like *Bande à part* and *The Dreamers*."

"Take the train to Vienna like *Before Sunrise*. I'll watch you while you listen to 'Come Here' by Kath Bloom."

"We'll kiss on the Riesenrad."

"You can make a fake phone call in Café Sperl. And when we're back in Paris, we can take those tango lessons on the Seine. Or salsa. They teach salsa too, I checked."

LOUPLOUPLOUPLOUPLOUPLOUPLOUPLOUPLOUPLOUP.

"Loup, it's you. Please. Just come to Tuscany. Everyone is here. You should be here too. It's the only thing that makes sense. *I am not an adventurer by choice but by fate*," she says.

"Quoi?"

"You heard me. Get on the train and come to Tuscany. I'll send you all the info you need."

Loup listens to her breathe.

"*Tu es sérieuse?*" he says with stars on his tongue.

"Yes! I'm serious! I'll tell Cillian everything. Just come here and we'll figure it out. I don't know what else to say, but this is what I want to happen. This is how it *has* to happen," Vincent says, putting her hand on her stomach—their *lentille*, their *sacre coeur*, their *souvenir*, their *half-blown rose*, their little French baby made in Paris.

"I'll do it, V . . . you know I will. *Je t'aime*."

"*Je t'aime*," she says.

Nous avons décidé. Nous décidons. Nous déciderons, she thinks, closing her eyes.

We have decided. We decide. We will decide.

A WOMAN CALLED VINCENT

Un film

EXT. TUSCAN VILLA – NIGHT

Vincent opens her eyes and looks up at the moon.

NARRATOR (V.O.)

Vincent knows exactly what she'll say. She'll pull Cillian out of bed and they'll stand under the moon and stars and their children and everyone else will be inside the villa sleeping and Loup will be in Paris tapping around to find a train ticket for the morning and it'll be six hours back in Kentucky but that won't matter anymore because they're all in Tuscany now and maybe Loup and this baby are answers to the wishes she hasn't wished yet, because although she doesn't know what she's going to do . . . how can *anyone* know what they're going to do when everything is so wildly unpredictable? One last breath and we're gone, one last heartbeat and that's it. So yes! Vincent will look at her husband, this man she does love so much, although she loves Loup too and she loves herself and her art and Paris too and she loves her children too and her unborn grandchild just as much and maybe, just maybe, she loves this baby just as much too. She does . . . she knows she does. And she sees herself alone with this baby – *their* baby, *her* baby. Alone – no Cillian, no Loup. She sees herself with each of them, with both of them. She pictures her children, her brother and sister and parents and what they will say when they find out she's pregnant. She doesn't know anything yet so she has to wait, because if she waits a little longer she'll know for sure. She will! She'll think these things and know these things and look at her handsome, sleepy-eyed husband in the moonlight. She will tell him that Loup hasn't hurt her like he has . . . not yet and maybe not ever. She will tell Cillian she loves him!

He's right there.

She loves him!

But that is not all.

LOUPLOUPLOUPLOUPLOUPLOUPLOUPLOUPLOUPLOUPLOU.

VINCENT

Cillian, there is . . . there is something I need to tell you.

VINCENT breaks the fourth wall and looks at the camera. She winks and her chin trembles as a single tear sparkles and smooths down her cheek. We see the red rose of her heart turning over and over again in bloom, hear it beating quickquick-quick like the baby's.

The sky colors and swirls into the deep blue and canary of Van Gogh's *The Starry Night*.

The card reads FIN.

But! Vincent's mouth is moving again. Her nightgown glows, drenched in lemony moonlight. Cillian pushes her hair back and like a lover, he touches her face.

ACKNOWLEDGMENTS

As always, a big thanks full of love to my literary agent, Kerry D'Agostino, for everylittlebit you do. And to my editor, Elizabeth Kulhanek, thank you for being such a gem. I appreciate you both so much.

Huge thanks to my GCP team: Andy Dodds, Amanda Pritzker, Alli Rosenthal, and Alana Spendley for everything, everything.

There is a special place in my heart for copyeditors. Many thanks to Tareth Mitch and Laura Cherkas for being so lovely.

Special thanks to everyone at Curtis Brown, Ltd.

Special thanks to Linda Duggins. xo

Special thanks to Erica House and our Zoom French class that brought me such joy and light in the dark. *Merci*, Erica, for your bright, sweet spirit. *Merci bien.*

Special thanks to Alayna Giovannitti for wow...a lot. Thank you so much, beauty. You are a forever fave and I'm so glad we found each other.

Thank you for virtually screaming and crying with me about...every teeny tiny thing, really...every day. Truly.

I wrote this book at my kitchen table or in my bed or on my couch... locked away from the rest of the world during a global pandemic. I can't imagine that darkness and weirdness and any of 2020 or the rest of my life without the light of Kim Namjoon, Kim Seokjin, Min Yoongi, Jung Hoseok, Park Jimin, Kim Taehyung, Jeon Jungkook, BTS, and ARMY. They truly mean so much to me and I love them so much and I treasure that now and forever-ever. *Borahae.*

As always, thank you to Vincent van Gogh: an inspiration and a brilliant artist and writer so dear to me, he feels like a real friend. Sweet Vincent, my heart.

Thank you, Paris.

Thank you, dear reader.

Thank you to my family, always. I love you.

Thank you to R & A for being everything you are. I love you and I love being your mom.

And to my husband, Loran, who yet again has kept me fed and watered as I work, thank you for taking such good care of me and for loving me so fully, like Jesus does. I love you. I'm yours. Always.

ABOUT THE AUTHOR

Leesa Cross-Smith is a homemaker and the author of *Every Kiss a War*, *Whiskey & Ribbons*, *So We Can Glow*, and *This Close to Okay*. She lives in Kentucky with her husband and their two teenagers. Find more at LeesaCrossSmith.com.

Facebook: LCrossSmith
Twitter: @LeesaCrossSmith
Instagram: @LeesaCrossSmith